The Forged Path

The Mirrored Consequences of Our Choices

Antonio Fleming

Iqra Publishing Inc

Distributed by:
Iqra Publishing Inc.
157 Sunset Avenue
Atlanta, GA 30314
http://iqrapublishing.com
Edited by: Iqra Publishing Inc.

Dedication

All praise and gratitude belong to Allah Ta'ala, the Most Generous, the Source of all inspiration, who has blessed me with the ability to bring stories to life through words. It is by His will alone that I have been able to craft The Forged Path, a story born from creativity, reflection, and the depths of human experience.

Ya Allah, You have given me the gift of expression—the ability to shape thoughts into narratives that resonate, entertain, and provoke reflection. Though this story is not entirely rooted in Islamic teachings, it carries the essence of the values You have instilled—truth, justice, struggle, and redemption. Without Your guidance, none of this would be possible.

If there is any benefit in these pages, it is by Your mercy. If there are flaws, they are mine alone. May this work serve its purpose, may it reach the hearts it is meant to, and may it be a stepping stone in the journey of creativity You have allowed me to walk.

Ya Allah, accept this effort from me, purify my intentions, and continue to guide my pen toward what is meaningful and good. Ameen.

IN THE NAME
ALLAH
COMPASSIONATE,
ALL MERCIFUL

A ll praise and gratitude belong to Allah Ta'ala alone, the Sovereign, the Sustainer, and the Creator of all existence. He is the One who grants life and ordains destiny, the Most Merciful, the Most Wise. May the choicest blessings and perfect peace be upon the Seal of the Prophets, Muhammad (peace and blessings be upon him), upon his noble family, his righteous Companions, and all those who sincerely follow his path until the final hour.

Allah commands in His noble revelation:

"Say: I am but a man like you. It has been revealed to me that your God is One. So whoever hopes to meet their Lord, let them strive in righteous deeds—purifying their soul—and let them not associate anything in worship with Him." (Surah Al-Kahf 18:110)

And let this be a warning and a reminder, for Allah has said:

"And whoever opposes the Messenger after guidance has become clear to him and follows a path other than that of the believers—We will turn him to what he has chosen and burn him in Hell, and what an evil destination." (Surah An-Nisa 4:115)

May Allah guide us to the straight path and keep our hearts firm upon His truth. Ameen.

Contents

Chapter 1

"Checkmate"

"**C**heck!" Onyx's opponent, World, exclaimed, his voice brimming with a mix of excitement and disbelief. The malice in his eyes tainted the purity of his focus; this wasn't just a game of chess—this was a battle of wits, pride, and dominance. He sat across the steel table, his every muscle tense, his mind whirring like a finely tuned machine. For years, Onyx had been the undefeated champion of the compound—a legend on and off the board. But now, World was only a few moves away from accomplishing the unthinkable.

The gathering crowd murmured with anticipation. The air in the dayroom was so oppressive that it felt as though everyone was holding their breath. Onyx, seated with unnerving calm, leaned back on the stool, his fingers resting lightly on the table's edge as if the stakes were nothing more than a routine sparring match.

World leaned forward, a devilish smirk spreading across his face as he moved his piece, convinced he had Onyx cornered. The sound of hip-hop blasting from a bystander's phone caused his head to bob involuntarily, but his concentration remained unshaken. "Make your next move, shawty," Onyx said evenly, his tone measured but hard-edged, like a well-placed strike. He briefly glanced at his watch, then at the growing crowd. But his composure, like his reputation, was unshakable.

The compound had been on lockdown for fifty-five days after a bloody gang war left nine men critically injured, forcing emergency airlifts to the hospital. Violence had rippled through several dorms like a firestorm, burning away what little normalcy they clung to. Recreation, visitation, and television privileges were stripped away. The tension simmered beneath the surface, visible in the hardened eyes of the men who now watched the game unfold. Despite the weight of vengeance looming over the room, the warden's threats of harsher punishments ensured an uneasy truce.

"I said, *Check!*" World barked again, his voice louder this time, breaking through the murmurs of the crowd. He made his move with his rook, driving Onyx's king further into a corner. The crowd reacted with gasps and whispers of disbelief.

Onyx's face was unreadable as he studied the board. To the untrained eye, he looked trapped, his pieces shrinking under World's relentless attack. But Onyx's mind was already three steps ahead, his trap closing in like a noose. The crowd marveled at World's audacity. For years, Onyx had embarrassed every man who challenged him—his victories were as clinical as they were ruthless. But now, here was World—a fearless upstart, daring to push the lion into a corner.

World's pride swelled, but he knew better than to lose focus. One wrong move, one distraction, and the opportunity of a lifetime would slip through his fingers. Then it happened. Onyx's lips curved into the faintest of smirks. He kissed his fingertips, a gesture that sent ripples of unease through the crowd. With a deliberate motion, he moved his knight. "Double check."

World froze.

"What the hell!" he blurted, staring at the board in disbelief. How had he missed it? He had been so sure, so careful. The crowd leaned in closer, the energy in the room shifting as they sensed the tide turning. Onyx didn't gloat. He didn't need to—his silence commanded respect. He glanced briefly at a Muslim inmate reciting a Surah under his breath as he passed the table, the soft cadence momentarily piercing the tension. The brief distraction shattered World's focus just as effectively as Onyx's move had dismantled his strategy.

"Check," Onyx said again, his tone final. His pieces moved with calculated precision, forcing World into a corner with no protection. When the final blow came, it was swift and merciless. "Checkmate," Onyx said, rising from his stool with quiet triumph. The crowd erupted, some cheering, others shaking their heads in disbelief.

World leaned back on the stool, his eyes narrowed as he sensed the weight behind Onyx's words. He hesitated for a split second, defeat written across his face.

"Good game, fool," Onyx said, extending his hand. As their palms met, Onyx leaned in close, his voice low enough for only World to hear. "You're the big dog now. J-5 is solid—you can trust him like I trust you. But everybody else? Handle them without expectations. Keep the grip tight, and the business tighter."

World nodded, his disappointment tempered by the weight of the words. For the first time, he saw something in Onyx's eyes—a glimmer of respect. "*Ushirika*," World muttered, the Swahili word for brotherhood.

"*Ushirika*," Onyx replied, his tone resolute.

As the crowd began to disperse, the loud buzz of the front door cut through the noise. "Tadarius Thompson!" The voice on the intercom called, signaling the moment Onyx had waited for. The room fell silent, the significance of the call sinking in.

Onyx didn't linger. He headed to his cell, his movements deliberate. The Columbian Diego met him on the way, slipping a piece of paper into his hand. "This is my father's number," Diego said, his voice steady. "You saved my life in here—twice. If you ever need anything, call. No games, though. Only if you're serious."

Onyx stared at the paper, the weight of the gesture sinking in. He knew what Diego's family represented. Their name carried power, influence, and a reputation that could open doors most men would never even see, let alone walk through. This was no small offer. It was a lifeline, one forged in the fires of survival and loyalty. Diego's voice, calm and sincere, hung in the air.

"I appreciate it," Onyx said, his voice low but firm. He folded the paper carefully, slipping it into the small pocket of his prison stripes.

There was no time to dwell. He tossed his meager belongings into the rattling metal cart and pushed it across the dorm. The atmosphere felt suffocating, so Onyx did what came naturally—he started freestyling. His words were crisp, rhythmic, and filled with the grit of the life he was leaving behind.

The inmates in the dorm buzzed with energy, heads nodding in time with his flow. Even the guards slowed their steps, caught up in the electricity he created. Onyx's freestyle wasn't just a release—it was a statement, a reminder that he was leaving on his terms, carrying the same fire that had kept him alive all these years.

When he reached the door and exited the building, the heavy buzz of the electronic door echoed behind him, and for the first time, he felt a weight lift from his shoulders. The air outside was colder than he remembered, crisper. Following the officer along the worn concrete sidewalk, his eyes swept over the facility's looming fences and barbed wire, the watchtowers that had loomed over his every move. Each step felt lighter, yet the memories clung to him like shadows. He told himself, *I'd rather die as a coward in the streets than ever return to this torment.*

"What's happening, fool?" Onyx's voice broke the silence as he stepped into the intake department. There, he spotted J-Man, a Mac-Town shooter scheduled for release with him.

"Shiddd, n***a," J-Man said, grinning wide. "'Bout to go cut this bitch that's been holding me down before linking up wit' my baby mama."

Onyx smirked at the man's excitement but said nothing. The air in the intake room was thick with anticipation, the walls closing in one last time before freedom.

Grabbing the box with his name scrawled across it as instructed, Onyx ripped it open. The clothes inside were stiff and smelled faintly of bleach, but he didn't care. He threw them on quickly, his mind focused solely on freedom. He glanced at the clock on the wall, given he left his watch with World. The seconds crawled by, each one feeling like an eternity.

"Why haven't they called my name yet?" he muttered, pacing the narrow cell. He could feel the pressure building in his chest, the anticipation tightening like a knot.

When his name finally rang out, the door buzzed open, and Onyx stepped into the next phase of his release. He went through the motions: reciting his name, birthdate, inmate number, and the last four digits of his social security number. Each repetition felt surreal, like pieces of a puzzle finally clicking into place.

Finally, he reached the front entrance. The elderly female officer sat behind the desk, her glasses perched on the edge of her nose. She slid a stack of papers toward him. "Sign these," she said, her voice gruff but not unkind.

Onyx complied, signing his name without hesitation, though the weight of his past felt heavier with each stroke of the pen. When he was done, she stood and walked to the main door, her keys jangling softly. "You're a free man now, Mr. Thompson," she said, holding the door open and stepping aside. "You've got the gift and charisma to be someone in life. Don't let the streets pull you back down."

Onyx met her eyes, her words sinking in. He let a small smile form. "Nah, I ain't coming back," he asserted, stepping into the sun like he owned it. The sunlight hit him immediately, warm and blinding.

"Yeah, that's what they all say," the officer muttered under her breath as the door clanged shut behind him.

Onyx didn't look back. He inhaled deeply, the air tasting different—free. His steps were confident, purposeful, but his mind was already racing. He didn't know what the future held, but one thing was certain: he wasn't the same man who had walked into Edgefield all those years ago.

As he reached the edge of the sidewalk, he stopped and retrieved the paper Diego had given him from his pocket. He unfolded it, staring at the number scrawled on it in neat handwriting. The weight of the gesture hit him again, but this time it felt lighter, like an opportunity rather than a burden.

"Time to move different," he whispered to himself, tucking the paper back into his pocket.

With one final look at the prison gates behind him, Onyx turned away, feeling the possibility of something more. Freedom wasn't just about walking out—it was about never looking back.

And Onyx was ready.

Chapter 2

"Freedom's First Steps"

Walking along the sidewalk like a tourist, Onyx basked in the sun, feeling its warmth soak into his dark skin. He savored the sensation, a simple pleasure he hadn't known in years. The barbed wire fences and concrete structures loomed behind him, a haunting reminder of what he'd just left. But with every step, he focused on the freedom he'd reclaimed—the texture of the pavement under his feet, the rhythm of his breathing, and even the sight of a bird soaring overhead with wings outstretched. "I'm never going back in that bitch," he muttered under his breath, the words a vow as much as a release. Inhaling deeply, he let the fresh air flood his lungs, each breath affirming his liberation.

As he reached the parking lot, anticipation twisted his gut. His eyes darted around, scanning for a familiar face, but the space was silent. No crowd shouting his name. No glimpse of his mother or sister— confusion crept in. Amani wouldn't leave him hanging—he was sure of that. Swaying his head left and right, he searched for any sign of her, but all he saw was the perimeter car creeping behind him like a shadow.

"You can't be standing round too long sir," the officer called out when she circled back minutes later.

Onyx's hesitation reflected the deep struggle inside him—his mind pulled in two directions. On one hand, he couldn't shake the responsibility to check on her, to know if she was safe. On the other, the weight of that gate, the suffocating familiarity of the prison, was a cage in itself—one he refused to re-enter. He couldn't let that fear, that old confinement, claim him again. As he moved toward the street, his thoughts were a blur of anxiety and resolve. Whatever had happened, he wasn't going back—not even to make a call.

Just as doubt began to creep deeper, a red BMW M5 with dark tinted windows turned into the lot. Onyx stopped in his tracks, his eyes locking with Amani's through the windshield. Relief and joy flooded him as she pulled up, jumped out, and screamed, "I love ya… I love ya… I LOVE YA!" Her voice carried across the lot, raw and loud, as if she needed the whole world to know.

Onyx couldn't help but smile as she ran to him, her arms flying open. "What's up, baby girl?" he said, his voice cracking as she wrapped him in a bear hug. The warmth of her embrace felt like spring after a brutal winter, melting the ice that had encased his heart for years. Her scent—coconut oil and a faint trace of vanilla—was familiar and grounding. For a moment, he forgot about the years that had separated them. "I love you too, lil sis," he murmured, his voice draped with emotion. "Damn, you done got big on a n***a."

Her laughter bubbled up, light and unrestrained. "Ooooh, you like? I been eatin' good while you was in there!" She stepped back, giving him a once-over, and her face twisted in mock disgust. "But you? Tight-ass prison clothes and them ugly-ass shoes? Bro, you look like a damn fool!" They couldn't help but laugh at his appearance before hugging once more.

The BMW M5 gleamed under the sunlight, a bold statement of power and luxury that seemed to pull Onyx toward it. Its sleek, crimson exterior was polished to perfection, the dark-tinted windows concealing the world within like a well-kept secret. As they walked toward it, the scent of freshly cut grass from the nearby field mixed with the faint tang of exhaust lingering in the air. Amani popped the locks with a casual click, the lights flashing briefly in acknowledgment.

"Damn, sis," Onyx muttered, running his hand along the smooth curve of the hood. "You really out here stuntin' on folks now."

Amani grinned, flipping her hair over her shoulder. "You already know. Time for you to step your game up, big bro."

Opening the door, the faint aroma of fresh leather and a hint of vanilla from the air freshener hit him immediately. Inside, the cabin was immaculate, the seats a deep black with red stitching, their buttery leather cool under his touch. The dashboard looked like it belonged in a spaceship—sleek lines, glowing dials, and a crystal-clear touchscreen that resonated with sophistication. Onyx slid into the passenger seat, the fabric molding to his body like it was made for him. The scent of the interior—new car with a subtle undertone of Amani's fragrance—wrapped around him; luxurious yet familiar. Amani climbed in, starting the engine with a low, throaty growl that made the car vibrate ever so slightly. "You might wanna call on the lord, bro," she said, smirking as he adjusted her seat.

Onyx leaned back, running his hand over the armrest as the bass thumped from the speakers. "Whatever," he said, his voice soft with admiration. "You really leveled up in my absence, lil sis."

Amani flashed him a quick grin before throwing the car into gear. "Always, baby boy. Always."

The ride away from the prison was surreal. The landscape shifted from barbwire fences to open land dotted with cows and cotton fields. With each mile, Onyx felt the weight of confinement lifting, replaced by a mix of hope and uncertainty. "So… how's the fam?" he asked as they pulled away from a country restaurant drive-thru, a bag of fried chicken and waffle fries between them.

Amani took a bite of her sandwich, steering the car with her knees like a pro. "Everybody good. Mama's busy workin' at the church—I had her house renovated, so she livin' nice. She wanted to come, but I wasn't 'bout to drive all this way listenin' to gospel tracks on blast." She paused, smirking. "Still don't know why she play music when she deaf as hell. Like, what she hearin', bro?"

Onyx chuckled, shaking his head. "That's Mama for you."

"The twins? Bad as hell, but what's new? They out in the ville trappin' and robbin' for pocket change. Auntie Tamika? Still gettin' money like always. Everybody else straight, but I ain't gon' lie, bro—your name been buzzin' in the streets since word got out you was comin' home."

Onyx leaned back, her words sinking in. The streets still remembered him, but it wasn't a comfort. It was a reminder of what he'd left behind—and what he couldn't go back to. The city skyline came into view, towering and gleaming in the distance. Amani reached over and squeezed his hand, her voice softening. "You home now, lil bro. I know you gon' spread your wings and stack that paper. But take your time, you feel me? Your absence broke me and Mama in ways you'll never know. But I gotcha now. No worries. I mean that."

Her words hit him harder than he expected. He'd thought about the streets, about the years lost, but he'd never truly considered the pain he'd caused the people who loved him most. Guilt mixed with determination in his chest. As Amani raced down the highway, her BMW pulled alongside a green Camry, where a group of girls were dancing to the bass-heavy rhythm blasting from their speakers. Onyx's eyes lingered a second too long.

'Yo,' Amani said, cutting her eyes at him. "You tryna be a boss or a clown? Make your decision now."

Onyx smirked but didn't look away. "When you've been locked in a cage for ten years, even a fly look good with lashes. But don't get it twisted—I'm a boss. Been one since I left Mama's womb."

Amani rolled her eyes, a grin tugging at her lips. "A'ight, Boss Man," she teased.

After exiting the SR 166 at Lakewood Avenue, Amani drove through the familiar streets of Atlanta, the city's rhythm pulsing around them. She finally pulled into the driveway of a white bungalow-style house, the tires rolling against the concrete as she came to a stop. With a sly smile, she tapped the horn impatiently. "Get out," she ordered, her gaze locking onto Onyx.

He stepped out, his eyes scanning the house and the quiet street. He was home—free. But more than that, he had a chance to rebuild. A chance to be better. And for the first time in a long time, he believed in it. Everything seemed perfect, but with Amani not getting out of the car, confusion sat in. He knew it wasn't their mom's house, and Amani had told him she was living in a condo downtown. So where were they? And why had she made him get out of the car alone, he wondered.

Chapter 3

"The Gift of Pleasure"

A woman emerged from the house, her kohl-black hair cascading over her shoulders, her lips soft and saccharine, tinged with a lilac hue against the saffron glow of her skin. Her velvety eyelashes fluttered as she moved in her grungy clothes, which failed to conceal the curves of her waist. Onyx glanced at his sister, who sat behind the wheel, smiling quietly, before stepping forward without a word.

He watched her every breath and every step she took toward him. His khaki pants began to feel tighter, the pull of her presence undeniable, and he realized with clarity that he was drawn to her in a way he hadn't anticipated. When she reached him, she stopped in front of the car, her gaze steady, and for a brief, disorienting moment, Onyx froze. She walked straight up to him and squeezed his elevating erection and whispered the soothing words in his ear. "I can't wait to put that dick in my throat."

Her touch was electric, nearly overwhelming, as her breath brushed against his ear, sending shivers down his spine. It lingered, warm and tantalizing, brushing against his neck, igniting a fire that left him trembling. With her fingers aggressively massaging the fabric of his khakis, subconscious emotions swirled and twisted through his body. A quiet storm of longing and desire surged with increasing intensity. Onyx sank into a suspended state, both mentally and physically, as he leaned against the hood of the car. Time slowed, his body awakening in ways it hadn't in years. He reveled in every second of it, the engine's heat soaking into his skin, intensifying the moment as his senses came alive.

"Mhmmmmm.. mhmmmmmm!" He moaned with unyielding pleasure, as she unfastened the bottom on his tight khakis with her free hand and inserted her other hand into his boxers to stroke his hardness. The softness of her hand made his eyes flutter as drool formed at the corner of his mouth.

"I know it's been a while, shawty, but just relax. I can suck this phat ass dick rite here if you want to truly feel that sexual rush or you can come in the house." She advised, exposing his manhood to the air and allowing spit to fall off her bottom lip onto his head to lubricate it a little.

"What the f**k you lookin' back at me for?" Amani yelled sarcastically, phone against her ear, as he looked over his shoulder without answering. He didn't want to come across as arrogant or disrespectful, sitting on her hood for all to see, and letting her suck his dick like a vampire, Onyx inserted himself back in his boxers and followed her into the house with anticipation rising with each breath.

Following her instructions, he removed his shoes at the door and stepped into the kitchen, where vibrant flowers and fresh fruit filled the space with life. The scent of bergamot lingered in the air, a warm, comforting fragrance that seemed to settle in his chest, easing even more of the nervous energy he was carrying. As she bent down in front of him to light a candle, the soft flicker of the flame bathed the room in a gentle glow, adding a quiet sense of intimacy. She then led him over to a sleek, star-lined road storage ottoman, her touch guiding him as the atmosphere wrapped around them both.

Lowering to her knees as she eased his hardness back out of the rough fabric boxers, she allowed the tip of his head to barrel roll across her howling mouth before swirling it with her tongue and engulfing all of him.

"Ummmmmmmmmmm…"

Instantly starting to grip and tug at the fabric as her neck moved like a seesaw and her hands caressed his thighs, Onyx exposed all of his vulnerability when the effects of her tongue caused him to start gulping for air. Spreading his legs wider as the pleasure overwhelmed him, making him yearn to whisper. "This your f**kin' dick," when she briefly removed it from her mouth to spit on, then massaged the saliva into his head before inserting it back in her throat. Shifting his hips back and forth with her desire to force him deeper, Onyx began to gasp for air, as he erupted in the hollowness of her throat.

"Ummmmmmmmmm…ummmmmmmm…ummmmmmmm…"

As gentle and unique as a baby's whimper, her closed mouth moans seemed to turn him on even more as she swallowed all of him before easing his dick out of her mouth and kissing the tip three times. "I'm surprised you lasted that long Suga, given that you just got out." She stated wiping her mouth as she stood back up. "I woulda given you a taste of this slow death pussy, but the cycles of womanhood saved cha'."

The intensity of their connection left him trembling, consumed by a longing that burned through him. He sat there, utterly undone, desperate for them to be locked in an endless cycle, trapped in time's grasp, where the world outside ceased to exist and their pleasure could stretch on forever. His combined experiences—even with Vaseline—couldn't compare to the intense orgasm he just endured. Taking a moment to steady himself, Onyx rose to his feet, his gaze fixed on her every movement, his mind racing with curiosity about how her body might look and feel beneath those clothes. He wanted to slide his dick in some pussy so bad, yet after having it sucked the way she just did was momentarily satisfying.

He muttered to himself, "I'd love to fall asleep with this dick in your mouth," as he walked across the room to slip his shoes back on. The years away from the privilege and pleasure of affection had him yearning to feel her skin against his, to taste the softness of her nipples, but the warmth spreading through his chest and the flood of emotions left his tongue momentarily paralyzed. He couldn't do anything but stand there, staring at her—her beauty radiating from the kitchen as she casually tapped away at her phone, unaware of the effect she was having on him.

Onyx felt like a new man, as if something deep within him had shifted in a way he hadn't anticipated. The world outside seemed to fade as he reached for the doorknob, his thoughts drifting toward leaving. But just as his fingers brushed the cold metal, he felt a presence at his side. He turned, stunned to see her breathing beside him, slow and purposeful. Without a word, she sank to her knees in front of him again, her gaze locking with his in a silent challenge. Her fingers brushed the doorknob he'd just touched, pushing it shut—a silent gesture that changed everything.

He froze, heart skipping a beat. The moment felt charged, electric, as if every unspoken word between them hung in the air, waiting for its release. Her gaze lifted slowly, meeting his, allowing everything outside their little bubble to cease to exist.

"Are you sure of that?" she whispered, her voice low, carrying a weight of unspoken desires. She wasn't just asking—her ears, sharp as a cat's, caught every subtle sound. It was as if her heightened senses allowed her to hear even the words he whispered to the wind, the ones meant only for himself, and she understood their depth before he even spoke them aloud.

Pushing him against the wall and aggressively pulling his pants back down to his thighs, she lifted the limp muscle with her tongue, then bounced the tip of it on her bottom lip until it grew to her satisfaction. Without granting him the pleasure of re-entering the depths of her throat, she gently stroked it while laying his entire dick on her face to measure its length. "Damn n***a, your sh*t exceeds my face," she voiced, brushing her lips against his ball sac, which caused Onyx to sign with unyielding waves of passion.

Easing him slowly into her mouth, while sliding her tongue against the bottom of it and massaging his balls at the same time, she started sucking his dick with a sense of passion she wasn't before. The rapid movement of her neck had Onyx curling his toes in the prison shoes and moaning uncontrollably as he struggled to grip the wall for support. The more she pushed him deeper into her throat, the more pleasure swirled inside of him. With his butt muscles tensing as he squeezed them together, Onyx released for the second time in her throat.

"Ummmmmmmmmmmmm…"

With his naked butt pressed against the sheetrock, he stood there for a moment, watching her, as indescribable emotions surged through his body. It took all of his strength to bend down and pull up his pants. Cee-Cee had given him something his body had been yearning for. As they exchanged small talk, she couldn't help but admire Onyx's physique and the way he was still bulging in his pants. A part of her hated the timeframe of her cycle, because she wanted to climax with him inside of her.

After fetching Onyx a bottle of cranberry juice from the refrigerator, she gently walked him back to the car, her nails grazing the back of his neck with a soft, almost teasing touch. He could feel the shift in his own body, the change in his gait—his knees now shaky, betraying the swagger and confident strut he had when he first arrived. He moved now as if something far heavier than his body was pressing down on him, each step burdened by an invisible weight.

Cee-Cee approached the car's window as Onyx slid into the passenger seat. She exchanged a few words with Amani, her tone calm but laced with something unspoken, then gave a nod of reassurance. *Her brother had been served.*

"You don't have to take my word for it," Cee-Cee said, her voice light but laced with that sharp, knowing edge. Her eyes shifted to Onyx, sitting silent in the passenger seat, her playful and triumphant smile daring him to deny it. "Just look at him."

Amani didn't miss a beat. "Bitch, I heard him hollering like a damn howler monkey while in there wit 'chu," she blurted, laughing. "I already know you did your thing."

"So, y'all comedians now?" he asked, shaking his head with a half-smile.

She shot her brother a sly glance, her soft giggle bubbling up despite herself. It wasn't every day her girl left someone speechless—unfortunately, this time, the victim was her brother.

"You can drop him off anytime," Cee-Cee said, her grin widening. "And trust me, it's definitely on me."

Amani shook her head, laughing at her boldness. "Imma hit your nasty ass up later bitch," she said, her voice still tinged with amusement as she pressed the start button and shifted the car into gear. The engine's low hum filled the space, but the air between Onyx and Cee-Cee was light, charged with the easy camaraderie of a real, unspoken understanding, and still carrying the quiet joy of their shared presence."

"Bruh, I brought you here first, before goin' straight to Mom's, because I wanted you to really feel what freedom tastes like again," she said, her voice steady but serious. "You've been carrying so much weight for years, and I didn't want you freezing up later if the opportunity arise—because you too chained up in your emotions of missing Mom so much." She let out a teasing laugh, nudging him as he shot her an intense look, his pride flashing in his expression.

"Sis, I'm a stallion. I'll never be anything less," Onyx shot back, his voice firm.

"But for real," she said, her tone softening, "Mom's never seen you in prison clothes, and I'll be damned if that's how she sees you after you've fought so hard to reclaim your freedom. So we're stopping by the condo first. You're gonna clean up, get your swagger back, and throw on something with real drip. And don't half-step—'cause I've got a surprise for you later."

Onyx turned his head to look at his sister, his face a mixture of confusion and amusement. As the memory of what had just transpired coursed through him, he couldn't help but smile, his expression frozen. "That's love, sis. I'm good, for sure," he said calmly, refocusing his gaze out the window. Inside, however, he was struggling to hide the lingering sensation Amani's friend had stirred in him—a throbbing need for more affection and emotions he had never experienced before.

Chapter 4

"Streets of Change"

Knowing Onyx was eager to change clothes and visit family, Amani decided to hit the side streets instead of jumping back on the expressway. The afternoon sun touched the city in a different way, bouncing off the high-rise windows and dipping into alleys where old buildings still held their ground. Onyx rested comfortably in the passenger seat, scanning the streets. "Damn, Amani. When they do all this? City lookin' crazy."

Amani smirked, tapping the screen of her cellphone. "Told you sh*t been changin'. They been buildin' up for a minute now. Gentrification hittin' hard, though. Some spots ain't even ours no mo'."

Onyx shook his head, his eyes sweeping the streets. "Man, it's wild. Ain't the same city no more. Feels like I stepped outta one life and into a whole different world."

Amani glanced at him. "Yeah, but some folks still out here grindin', just wrapped up in something new."

Onyx's eyes caught on a mural—a Black man in a fresh suit holding a kid's hand, both gazing at a rising skyline. Above them, bold letters read: ***"Build, Protect, Thrive."***

"Yo, that's fire," he said, leaning forward. "Lemme use your phone real quick."

Amani side-eyed him. "For what? You finna call somebody?"

"Nah, just wanna snap that image. For the boys on lockdown."

Amani sighed, unlocked her phone, and handed it over. "Here. Don't go scrollin' through my sh*t."

Onyx chuckled. "Girl, I ain't worried 'bout your lame-ass DMs. Chill."

He snapped the shot and stared at it for a second, nodding to himself. "Man, they gotta see this. Might light somethin' under their ass. Show 'em what stayin' focused looks like."

Amani smiled faintly, her tone softer. "Yeah, they need to see it's more than just the hood out there now." As they rolled up to a corner in Summer Hill, Onyx's eyes locked on a locally owned convenience store with a saggin' yellow awning and a crooked hand-painted sign that read "OPEN 24 HOURS." It looked like it'd been fightin' time and losing, but it was still standing.

"Yo, pull over right here," he said, nodding toward the store.

Amani frowned. "For what? You tryna grab snacks?"

"Nah, I just... I gotta see somethin' real quick."

She sighed but swung the car into the lot, parking by the door. "Don't take all day. We got stuff to do."

Onyx hopped out, the warm air wrapping around, thick with nostalgia. The bell over the door jingled as he stepped inside, and everything hit at once—the shelves packed with snacks, the faint smell of Pine-Sol, and the whir of a dusty fan in the corner. Behind the counter, Mr. Lee stood the same way he always did—only now, his hair was all gray, and he looked smaller. The old man squinted, then froze, his face breaking into shock.

"Trigga?" His voice cracked. "Is it really you?"

Onyx felt his throat tighten. "Yeah, it's me, Mr. Lee. I'm back."

The old man didn't say a word, just came around the counter and pulled him into a hug so strong it almost knocked the air outta him.

"Ah, my boy," Mr. Lee said, his voice strained. "I prayed for this day. You look good. Different, but good."

Onyx tensed, then hugged him back with an awkward pat on the shoulder. "I missed you too, Mr. Lee. It's been a minute."

Pulling back, the old man studied him with watery eyes. "Too long, son. We missed you. My wife... she always asked about you. Always said, 'That boy got a good heart. He just needs time to find it.'"

Onyx's chest got heavy. He swallowed hard. "How she doin'? She still here?"

Mr. Lee's face fell, and he shook his head. "She's gone. Passed last year. Cancer."

"Damn," Onyx muttered, looking at the floor. "I'm sorry. I didn't know."

The old man waved his hand, his smile returning but sadder now. "It's life, son. She always believed in you, though. Told me you'd come back stronger. She'd be proud to see you now."

Onyx nodded, his throat too tight to speak.

"Trigga, promise me one thing," Mr. Lee said, gripping his shoulder. "Don't waste this second chance. You got it now—don't let it slip away."

"I won't," Onyx said quietly, meaning it.

Amani honked outside, her impatience cutting through the moment. Mr. Lee gave him one last hug before letting him go. As Onyx walked out of the store, the weight of his final conversation with Mrs. Lee hung heavily on him. Her voice, filled with quiet sorrow, echoed in his mind, causing a pang in his chest. He tried to shake it off but couldn't. Her death instantly made him realize how precious life was and how important the time God grants us to share with one another.

Back in the car, Onyx slumped into the seat, lost in thought. His mind replayed her words, and it was hard to forget the way she treated him—always so kind, so encouraging. She had seen something in him, something he had trouble seeing in himself. She believed in his ability to rise above his surroundings, to be better than the struggles that had weighed him down for so long. Her unwavering faith in him was a gift he couldn't easily shake off.

"You good bruh?" Amani asked, glancing over at him.

"Yeah," he said after a long pause. "Just... a lot to think about."

Amani smirked, her tone lightening up. "Boy, don't overthink sh*t. You got me, you got Mama, and you definitely got Mama church members. You know they'll throw a bucket of holy water on you to keep your head right."

Onyx cracked up, shaking his head. "You so damn stupid."

Amani laughed with him, her grin wide. As the city rolled past, old and new clashing in every corner, Onyx felt something he hadn't in years—a raw, unshakable sense of being seen. Like the weight of all the days he'd spent feeling lost, like a ghost walking through his own life, was finally starting to lift. Maybe—just maybe—he could still belong here, not just passing through.

Chapter 5

"Rebirth of A Boss"

The streets of Atlanta had a way of molding people, sharpening them like blades against the grindstone of survival. Onyx inhaled deeply as Amani turned her BMW M5 into the driveway of her gated condo. The rumble of passing cars and the murmur of a bustling city blended with the humid evening air, but more than the city's sounds, it was the pulse of opportunity that hit him. Ten years in prison had made every detail sharper, every moment louder.

"So, why Onyx now? What happened to Trigga?" Amani asked, her voice light, teasing, but her eyes scanning him with curiosity. "Is that your new rap name, or just the latest persona you tryna push?"

"Nah, sis, it's just me now," he replied, watching a pearl-white '70 Chevelle Supercharged LS7 roar past them. The old-school muscle car's engine growled like it was flexing. An elderly white man was behind the wheel, and Onyx's eyes lit up with admiration. "Damn, that bitch clean as fuck. Old head needs to let me take that for a spin."

Amani chuckled, pulling up to the security gate. She keyed in her code, and the gate creaked open with a mechanical groan. "Onyx, huh? It's kinda cute. But look, I hope you're serious about handling your business this time. Don't be out here tryin' to please people who ain't got a damn thang to offer. And I damn sure ain't tryna be bouncing around in your cheap-ass music videos, looking like Puff Daddy's sidekick either."

Onyx laughed, shaking his head. "I've always been about my business, lil' sis. Whether it's cash moves or gunplay, I execute with precision. You know how I roll." A grin tugged at his lips as he enjoyed how the name "Onyx" sounded coming from her.

Amani smirked, but her voice turned more serious as she parked. "A'right, Onyx. Just promise me you'll stay focused. No broke bitches.

No dusty dudes. And help out when you can. Don't make me regret this."

They both laughed at her dramatic tone, but Onyx could feel the weight behind her words. Amani wasn't playing. She never had been. She stepped out of the car with her usual confidence, and Onyx followed, taking in the scene. The condo complex was alive with activity. Women of every shade and size strolled about, laughing, chatting, or scrolling on their phones. It was like a summer cookout without the grills. "Damn, sis, the peaches out today," Onyx said, grinning.

"Yeah, but keep your mouth shut," Amani shot back with a playful elbow. "You're acting like you're from the 1 or the 6 instead of Zone 3. Remember, you're a boss now. Start acting like it before they figure out you're just a fresh-out rookie trying to play in the big leagues."

"Fresh-out rookie, huh?" Onyx retorted, tugging at the tight clothes that clung to him like the material had something to prove. "I've been in a cell for a decade, Amani. My standards low right now, but I'm still a boss regardless."

"Boss or not, don't get too comfortable out here," Amani shot back, chuckling as she led the way toward the main entrance of her condo building. The sharp staccato of her heels striking the pavement exuded the power and allure of someone who had been running the game for years.

She chose to enter through the main entrance to demonstrate how to use her code. She led the way while Onyx's street instincts kept him alert, scanning the surroundings with every step. Despite being out of prison and in an upscale area now, his awareness remained vigilant. His gaze landed on a sleek Ocean Blue Infiniti QLS parked across the street, its gold-rimmed wheels gleaming under the radiance of the sunlight. Behind the wheel sat a bald-headed, dark-skinned man with a heavy frame, his eyes locked on them. Onyx's senses went on high alert.

"Hold up," he said, tapping Amani on the shoulder, his voice low. "You know who that is?"

Amani rolled her eyes, not even breaking stride. "Oh, that's Major and his little sidekick, Vot," she said dismissively, pulling her phone from her purse, dialing a number, and making sure he understood the security process. She flipped her hair over her shoulder with practiced ease, the gesture was much a statement as her words.

"He look like he makin' noise out here," Onyx muttered, catching the passenger, Vot, sizing him up. The man's gaze lingered on Onyx's fresh-out clothes and prison-issue sneakers, a smirk tugging at the corners of his mouth.

Before Amani could respond, the call connected. Major's booming voice greeted her before she could speak. "Amani! Amani!"

Though Amani carried herself with an effortless elegance, there was no mistaking the fire that burned beneath her polished exterior. Her honeyed complexion and striking, sculpted features exuded a quiet power, while her midnight-black hair fell over her shoulders in soft waves. But it was her smile—those oyster-white teeth flashing like lightning—that hinted at the ferocity of a woman who didn't play when it came to her money or her respect.

Onyx, watching her handle herself, felt a pang of realization. He'd underestimated her. Amani wasn't just surviving out here—she was thriving, running her own tight operation. Her network of girls, skilled in cashing checks and running stolen credit cards, operated with precision, state to state.

"Yeah, why your fat ass sitting outside my building for, n***a?" Amani snapped into the phone, her tone dripping with attitude as she approached and pressed the elevator button.

Onyx's brow furrowed at her sharpness. He hadn't seen this side of his sister, but it suited her.

Major chuckled on the other end, unfazed. "Shawty, chill. We just finished handling some business and Vot saw your gorgeous ass walking in. You know I love seeing you, baby." His voice oozed a blend of charm and arrogance that grated on Onyx's nerves.

"Well, you saw me. What's up?" Amani shot back, stepping into the elevator with Onyx close behind. She shook her head in irritation, clearly unimpressed by Major's attempts to flirt.

Major ignored her tone, his voice picking up. "My people got a batch of new names and numbers we 'bout to grab. Can we link up in an hour or two to process some cards and IDs?"

Onyx watched as Amani sighed, her lips pressing into a thin line. She was torn between annoyance and the practicality of keeping Major in her network.

"Sh*t, Major, you always pick the worst times to execute," Amani said as they stepped off the elevator and walked towards her door. "I've been running around all day gettin' my brother straight. Just hit my line later or somethin'—and don't be sending me no more of them nasty-ass pictures of your fat ass."

Major's laughter echoed through the phone, but Amani ended the call without waiting for a response. She unlocked the door, stepped inside, and keyed in the alarm code with the efficiency of someone used to juggling a million moving pieces. Onyx followed her inside, still processing the exchange. "Damn, sis," he said, kicking off his shoes by the door. "You really out here running things, huh?"

Amani smirked, dropping onto the plush leather couch that seemed to swallow her in its rich, buttery softness. "I told you, big bruh. I'm a boss in my own lane. And now, so are you. Welcome back to the game."

Onyx grinned, but his expression faltered for a moment as doubt crept in. "This is literally all you, though? Like, legit legit?"

Amani glanced at him, her eyes steady and unreadable. "Yeah, bruh. This all me. But don't worry about all that right now. I'll put you on game later. Just relax and enjoy it."

Onyx couldn't help but take her advice. The condo was a masterpiece, dripping in understated elegance that still managed to flex wealth. The open floor plan stretched wide, with polished wood floors that gleamed under the recessed lighting. A floor-to-ceiling window framed a breathtaking skyline view, the city lights twinkling like scattered diamonds. The living room was anchored by a massive entertainment system, complete with a curved OLED TV and custom-built speakers. A glass coffee table with a gold base sat in front of her couch, holding a single crystal vase of fresh orchids.

Even the air smelled luxurious, scented faintly with amber and jasmine from the flickering candles scattered strategically around the room. Amani's touch was everywhere—from the abstract art on the walls to the strategically placed decorative books on success and power resting on the side table. It wasn't until Onyx opened the door to the guest room that the full weight of her efforts hit him. The room was immaculate, painted in sleek shades of charcoal gray and white, with a king-size bed dressed in black-on-black linens that looked plush enough to drown in. A framed portrait of Harlem's legendary gangster, Bumpy Johnson, dominated the wall above the bed, a silent testament to ambition and grit.

On the dresser sat a neatly wrapped white box with his name scribbled on a tag. Onyx opened it, his breath catching as he stared at the contents. Ten thousand dollars in cash lay inside, stacked and banded with precision. His chest tightened as he ran his fingers over the bills. "Damn, Amani. Ya really went all out." He stepped back, his eyes scanning the room like he was trying to take in every detail at once.

Walking over to the closet, the doors stood slightly ajar, revealing a wardrobe that could rival a high-end boutique. Designer labels, ready to wear designer outfits, and multiple pairs of gleaming red-soled sneakers lined the shelves and hangers. For a moment, Onyx wondered if the clothes belonged to one of her boyfriends, but he quickly dismissed the thought. Amani wouldn't play him like that. He stepped back into the living room, the question burning in his chest. "Say, sis," he called out.

Amani, still lounging on her couch with her tablet in hand, didn't look up. "Yeah, big bruh?"

"Why you do all this? I don't want you stressin' yourself for me."

Amani finally set the tablet down, her expression softening as she looked at him. "Because you're my brother, stupid. And because I know what it's like to come back from nothing and have the whole world expect you to stay there. You're not just any n***a out here, Onyx. You're a boss. My f**kin' brother. And bosses gotta look the part."

"Bosses gotta look the part, huh?" Onyx repeated, his lips twitching into a half-smile. He reached over and grabbed her hand, pressing it against his chest. "I love you for this sh*t, shawty. Plus, I'ma return the love the first chance I get. *Ahadi yangu.*"

Amani smiled, pulling her hand away. "Naw, I'm good. Just stay focused out 'chu and get money without losin' your damn identity."

Onyx nodded, but curiosity got the better of him. "How you know to put that particular portrait up? Outta all the ones you coulda picked?"

"Boy, you my brother," Amani said, rising to her feet. "We from the same cloth. A fabric that's untaintable, unbreakable, and impossible to replicate. I know what your ugly ass like, plus all that Mob sh*t you be talkin'. I had it put there to keep you reminded of your task at hand— and to inspire you to be more than just another n***a out 'chu in these streets." She threw him a sarcastic grin, rising off the sofa and leaving the room, her words lingering like a challenge.

Onyx stayed still, feeling the weight of her words sink in. Amani was always playful, but she never missed a chance to remind him of what he could be. She had a way of making everything feel like both a joke and a reality check at the same time. Her footsteps faded as she left, but her words stayed with him, biting at his mind like an unfinished thought.

the weight of prison life had melted away. He moved from the shower, steam still lingering in the air, and walked over to the closet. Inside, designer clothes awaited him. As he dressed, he felt like a new man—fresh, sharp, and ready to take on whatever came next.

"I'ma crush 'em," he muttered to himself, admiring his reflection in the mirror. The fabric felt like freedom against his skin, nothing like the stiff, unforgiving prison uniforms. Walking back into the living room, he stopped in his tracks. Amani stood in the kitchen, pouring herself a glass of wine. She wore a red knit net sleeve midi dress that clung to her frame like it was made for her, paired with matching red-bottom heels. Her hair was pulled back into a sleek bun, exposing the sharp line of her jaw and the curve of her neck.

"Damn, sis, you killin' that sh*t," Onyx admitted, shaking his head in admiration.

Amani smirked, handing him his new cellphone and a card. "Tell me somethin' I don't know. I stay shuttin' these hoes down. And you look sharp too, bruh." She tapped the phone. "I programmed my number and Ma's in here. Now let's roll. Time to show the world what a boss really looks like. And I'm talking about me, not you," she teased, her voice dripping with raw confidence as she strode toward the door, a sultry giggle escaping her lips.

Chapter 6

"Her Silence Spoke Volumes"

Amani's condo was a sanctuary of independence, a reflection of her triumphs. Sleek lines and minimalist décor reflected that she had built a life on her own terms. It was spotless, uncluttered, and infused with faint hints of amber and jasmine from candles throughout the condo. To Onyx, though, the silence inside her home pressed against him like the walls of his former cell. Yet this silence was different—not oppressive, but unfamiliar. Even therapeutic. It whispered of safety, of starting over.

It wasn't where he wanted to be—not yet, anyway. But it was his sister's place, not a prison cell, and that alone made it bearable. He reminded himself that in time, he'd have his own space again. A house with high ceilings and floor-to-ceiling windows that let in the sunlight, a sleek kitchen where he could cook meals that felt like more than just survival, and a living room with leather furniture and a view of the city skyline. A place that was truly his, where every corner reflected his hard work and determination. That was the life he was working toward, the life that would finally feel like home.

The sight of Amani and Onyx walking side by side drew curious stares as they strolled through the sleek hallways of her condo building and out toward her car. Their bond was undeniable, a quiet harmony that radiated strength. Strangers might mistake them for a couple—the way they moved together, a blend of ease and unspoken understanding—but theirs wasn't a romantic connection. They were siblings, and the depth of their connection came from a lifetime of shared struggle and unshakable loyalty.

Once they reached the car, Amani unlocked it with a click of the key fob, and they both slid inside, the doors closing with a soft thud. The engine purred to life as she pulled out of the condo complex, the familiar streets of the city unfolding in front of them. The hum of the tires on the road set a steady rhythm, and before long, they were stopping by one family member's house after the next, just so Onyx could say hello.

"Yo, don't get all soft up in there, bruh," Amani teased as they cruised down Columbia Drive after leaving their aunt's house. Her hand shot out to punch him lightly on the arm. "I know you been waitin' ten years to see Ma, but I ain't tryin' to hear you bawlin' like a lil girl while she got gospel music blastin' in the background."

Onyx smirked, brushing off her jab. "Shawty, fall back. You just mad 'cause you ain't got that connection. Firstborn stuff—you wouldn't understand, hater."

But her words had hit closer than he'd admit. Pressure built in his chest as Amani turned onto their mother's street and neared the one-story house in Decatur. The memories were already surging, weighing him down with each breath.

He stepped out of the car, the cool evening air doing little to calm the storm inside him. The house looked the same, other than the new paint—modest but full of life. It wasn't just a house to Onyx; it was *home*. The place where birthdays were celebrated with off-key singing and dollar store balloons. A place where he'd endured countless whippings with switches he was forced to retrieve himself. Where holiday gatherings turned into late-night card games, and where he last heard their mother say, "I love you," before the accident stole her hearing.

Each step toward the door felt heavier than the last. He could almost hear her calling his full name, just like she did whenever he got into trouble. When the door opened, the smell hit him first. A mix of fried chicken, collard greens, and jasmine oil—comfort and love in the form of aromas. Gospel music hummed softly from the speaker she kept on the counter, its vibrations something she could feel even if she couldn't hear. The walls, lined with family photos and scripture-stitched tapestries, seemed to breathe with her presence.

Feeling the faint shift of air, she turned from the stove. Her eyes found him, and her face lit up with a joy so radiant it made his chest ache. She took a step forward, her hands trembling, signing as her expression shifted between disbelief and overwhelming love. The weight of the last ten years crushed him. His knees buckled, and he sank to the floor.

In an instant, she was at his side, her hands flying as she signed furiously, her movements frantic and tender all at once. She touched his shoulders, his face, his hands, as if she couldn't believe he was really there. Her prayers flowed silently through her fingers, her touch full of urgency and relief.

For years, her letters had been his lifeline. Every word, written in her careful script, carried pieces of her soul. They told him to hold on, to believe in a future outside those walls. She had written about her days, her faith, and the aching void his absence left. She believed that God would bring him back home, whole. And He did.

His tears spilled freely as he rose to his feet, his hands trembling as he signed back to her. Each motion was slow, deliberate, but filled with more emotion than he could put into words. "Thank you, Ma. For never givin' up on me. I love you." The weight of the years and the love between them overwhelming him all at once. The bond they shared, forged in years of separation, now felt unbreakable. The rawness of the moment hung in the air, a promise, a confession, and a lifetime of gratitude all wrapped in those simple words.

Her smile was radiant through her tears, and when their eyes met, Onyx felt the flood of emotion he'd kept buried for so long. It had been ten years since he had last seen his mother, and the sight of her—still his anchor—was overwhelming. She kissed his forehead gently, as if time had never passed, before pulling him into another tight embrace. He held her close, feeling the warmth of her love seep through him like a balm to his soul. The years apart, the pain, the uncertainty—they all seemed to dissolve in that moment.

They pulled away slowly, savoring the quiet intimacy, the peace that came from being together again. Then, without a word, she gestured for them to sit down and served him his favorite meal: fried chicken, collard greens, and mac and cheese. He devoured it, every bite a reminder of the home he'd been starved of for so long. The familiar flavors grounded him, filling him in a way that wasn't just physical. It was the comfort of love, of belonging.

After the meal, they sat together on the porch, the evening air cool against their skin. Her hand rested on his, and in the soft light of the fading day, she signed how proud she was that he'd returned. Her hands moved with precision, each gesture deliberate, each word unspoken but filled with weight. She made him promise, with a look that left no room for doubt, that he would never go back to the streets. In that moment, Onyx understood that her love was both his refuge and his responsibility, a bond that would always pull him toward something better.

Being in his mother's presence made him forget entirely about the surprise Amani had mentioned. Deep down, he no longer cared what it was—nothing mattered more than bringing comfort to his mother and seeing her smile grow brighter, filling his heart with unyielding love and purpose.

Each time she felt the Holy Spirit guiding her, urging her to do something, she made him enter the house and insisted on cleansing him with holy water she had purchased from her church. Three times, she washed his face, her hands moving with purpose and reverence. Each time, she commanded him to bow his head in silent prayer, her movements precise and confident. Her faith filled the room, a quiet yet powerful force that demanded reverence. Onyx stood still, letting her work, though he couldn't hide the small smile tugging at his lips. The moment was heavy with meaning, yet there was something soothing in the ritual.

In the background, Amani's voice cut through the air, loud and playful, mocking their mother's gestures with sarcastic humor. "Watch out for evil spirits! I see them dancin' on that big ass head of yours." Her words were sharp, confident, and full of mischief, contrasting with the sacredness of the moment. Onyx shook his head, the warmth of the familiarity spreading through him as he stood between the two—one rooted in faith, the other in love and humor.

An hour later when Amani texted him from the bathroom, saying she'd had enough gospel music and was ready to go, Onyx couldn't help but laugh. She always found a way to use him as an excuse. So when she returned to the living room, Onyx grinned mischievously. "Ma, how 'bout Amani texted me sayin' she ready to go because she's tired of listening to your damn music. Like she don't appreciate bein' here with you."

Amani froze, her eyes narrowing. "You serious right now?"

Their mother looked between them, her brow furrowed in confusion but a smile tugging at her lips. She leaned in slightly, trying to read their lips, and signed, "What's funny?"

Amani's face softened as she laughed, shaking her head, remembering her mother was deaf. "You got jokes, huh? A'ight. Bet."

When it was finally time for them to leave, Onyx lingered on the porch steps, his heart heavy. He looked back at his mother, standing in the soft glow of the porch light in the doorway. Part of him didn't want to go. He felt torn—like leaving her again might shatter the fragile bond they'd just rebuilt. She stepped forward, placing a hand on his cheek, her eyes filled with love and a silent plea. He kissed her hand, then leaned forward to kiss her cheek. "I love you, Ma," he signed.

Her hands replied with a final "I love you" and "Be safe."

As he walked away and slid into the car, he couldn't tear his eyes away from her. The sight of her standing on the porch, her arms wrapped around herself, filled him with both comfort and guilt. The weight of unspoken words hung heavy in the air between them. His heart was screaming, though his lips remained closed. As the house grew smaller in the rearview mirror, he whispered to himself, "I love you so much."

He had promised her, and this time, he wouldn't let her down.

Chapter 7

"The Return"

The city lights blurred into a kaleidoscope of colors as Amani's BMW M5 glided through Atlanta's late-night traffic on I-20. The hum of the engine filled the silence between her and Onyx, who sat quietly in the passenger seat, his head tilted as his eyes stared out the window. Freedom still felt unreal. Just last night, he'd been staring at the cracked ceiling of his prison cell, listening to the distant shuffle of guards and the muffled snores of his bunkmate. Now, the city skyline stretched before him like a bright, unattainable promise.

Amani's crisp voice invaded his thoughts as she handled business on the phone. Her tone was commanding, dripping with the confidence of someone who knew her worth and wasn't afraid to demand it. Onyx watched her out of the corner of his eye, a faint smirk tugging at his lips. She'd become a boss in every sense of the word. Her car, her clothes, her attitude—it all spoke of someone who had clawed her way to the top and wasn't coming down for anyone.

Still, Onyx couldn't shake the unease bubbling beneath his calm exterior. Amani had been talking about a "surprise" all day, and while he appreciated her efforts to make his first night out special, his instincts told him to stay on guard. Years in prison had honed his awareness, and trust didn't come easy anymore—not even with his own blood.

His eyes wandered back to the city outside as she eased up the exit ramp and merged into traffic. Neon lights shimmered in the night, casting a colorful glow over Atlanta's bustling downtown streets. The lively chaos stirred memories of the world he thought he'd left behind. Fast money, danger, and power pulled at him like a siren's call, tempting him to dive back in. But Amani's laughter cut through the noise in his head, snapping him out of it. He turned just in time to see her roll her eyes, a playful smirk on her lips.

"You gon' sit there lookin' and actin' like one of them zone 6 n***as all night, or you ready to turn up?" she teased, her voice lighter now as she ended her call.

"Two times," he replied, the corner of his mouth quirking up. He didn't know what she had planned, but being with her after ten years apart was already lifting his mood. After a quick detour through downtown to show Onyx the city's newest developments and hot spots, Amani pulled into the VIP section of **Paradise Station**. She handed a crisp hundred to the valet but opted to park on her own when she didn't spot any of her girls' cars in the section.

The parking lot was buzzing with anticipation. Car speakers thumped with the same heavy bass that spilled from the club's doors, vibrating the air with energy. Groups of sharply dressed men and women mingled, laughing and posing for photos beneath the glow of the club's sign. The atmosphere was electric, a preview of the wild night unfolding just beyond the entrance.

Onyx stepped out, taking in the scene. The bass thumped in his chest, and the air was saturated with the scent of perfume, cologne, and faint traces of weed. It had been a decade since he'd been in an atmosphere like this, and the raw, electric energy made him feel alive in a way he hadn't in years. Amani's phone buzzed, and she answered with her usual sass. "Bitch, I know y'all triflin' ass hoes ain't parked behind sum building suckin' dick for entrance fee." Amani joked.

On the other end, her friend Yoshe giggled before responding. "Hoe, I ain't Stacy, so don't try me. But you know damn well it's your contaminated-ass throat n***as line up at the spot for," Yoshe snapped back.

"F**k you! All y'all trailer park broke hoes can suck my pussy blindfolded," Amani ranted, while giggling at the way Onyx was looking at her through the window.

"Seriously where you at, gurl? We pulling into the parking lot now," Yoshe said, phone pressed to her ear as she scanned the VIP section.

"I'm parked next to this exquisite white Mercedes 600 in VIP," Amani said, checking her makeup and fluffing her hair in the mirror as she spoke.

"We pulling up now. But you better not have any of those dusty-ass, broke n***as waiting for us like last time. I should've given his ugly ass your number for playing hoe," Yoshe said, her tone playful yet serious.

Amani laughed, shaking her head as the memory flashed in her mind. "Bitch, you knew better," she shot back playfully. Then, stepping out of the car, she threw a smug glance at her brother before flashing a knowing smirk.

"Wait 'til y'all see who I got with me tonight," she teased, nodding toward Onyx. "Y'all gonna wish y'all had something this fine on your arm."

After parking side by side in VIP, Yoshe, Stacy, and Jasmine stepped out of their cars and into the night, their presence commanding the streetlights to dim in comparison to the radiance they exuded. They didn't need a spotlight to shine—they were the spotlight.

First was Yoshe, whose striking green eyes caught every flicker of light as her golden hair cascaded past her shoulders, glowing like sunrise itself. Her four open-faced gold teeth, each with a diamond gleam, added to her aura of royalty. She was respected on both the East and West sides of Atlanta, considered hood royalty just like Amani. Next was Jasmine, her curves wrapped in a skin-tight black dress that clung to her body like liquid velvet, every move she made shimmering with an irresistible sensuality that drew every gaze. And last, but far from least, was Stacy—her long chestnut brown locs framed a face that was pure temptation. Her slender figure moved with a magnetic confidence, turning heads in every direction. Her playful smirk told Onyx everything he needed to know: she was used to being admired.

"Damn, Amani, you wasn't lying," Yoshe said, eyeing Onyx appreciatively as they approached. "You brought us a whole snack to nibble on throughout the night."

Amani laughed, throwing an arm around her brother's shoulders. "Chill, this my big bro. Fresh out. Y'all behave."

With each woman eyeing Onyx attentively as they all stood at the rear of Amani's M5, Stacy, bold as ever, stepped forward and grabbed Onyx, sizing him up to see if he was working with anything. "Seriously though, bitch, you got'em out here lookin' the part. But, if his sexy ass got sum sauce, imma get me a dose of this fresh prison dick tonight," Stacy asserted, staring into Onyx eyes as Jasmine and Yoshe started giggling. "I know this fresh tender dick can't stand up in this tight pussy n***a, but you deserve to be f**ked by a Boss Bitch your first night out shawty..."

"Girl, you crazy as hell, and my brother don't want no dry, loose booty his first night out. He'd probably get more pleasure if you just stroked it with Vaseline." Amani interjected, busting into a hard laugh as they all started walking across the pavement joking and admiring one another's fashion attire.

Onyx smirked but said nothing, before letting Amani steer the group toward the entrance. The heels of their stilettos clicked against the pavement, a rhythm that matched the pounding bass spilling from the club. Inside, the energy of **Paradise Station** hit like a storm, electrifying the air around them. Strobe lights flashed across the dance floor, painting the crowd in shifting hues, while the bass rattled the walls. The air was thick with the scent of Hennessy and hookah, and bodies swayed, lost in the rhythm of the DJ's beats. Security guided them toward a private VIP section, where a banner hung, proudly declaring: **The Boss Onyx Has Returned.**

Onyx tried to keep his excitement in check, but the thrill pulsing through his veins was impossible to hide. He hadn't felt this alive in years—surrounded by beauty, admiration, and a sense of power that he hadn't tasted since before his incarceration. After a decade behind bars, it felt like he was finally stepping back into a world where he could reclaim his presence, his purpose, and his name.

He was so absorbed in the glamour of the night, the intoxicating allure of the women around him, and Stacy's flirtatious moves that he didn't even notice the banner above the VIP section until Amani snapped him out of his trance.

"Bruh wipe your damn mouth and stop standin' there lookin' like one of those zone 6 sprung n***as. Stacy my girl and I love her, but she's a bonafide hoe bruh—not a trophy you build a foundation around. F**k her if you wish, but know she fight 'bout dick she consider hers and will cut your black ass." Amani leaned in close, her voice low in his ear as the champagne girls sat three tubs on the table, each holding three bottles chilling on ice.

The music pulsed through him, the lights flashing, the energy swirling around him. As a waitress popped a bottle and poured him a glass, Onyx barely had time to process it all before the DJ's voice boomed through the speakers.

"Yoooooo, Paradise Station! I need everybody to throw three fingers in the air for a legend from Zone 3 in the building tonight!" the DJ's voice boomed through the speakers, commanding the crowd's attention. "Onyx! The boss is back in the city!"

The crowd erupted, and Onyx froze, overwhelmed by the noise and attention. Amani nudged him, her expression softening. "Relax, bruh. This your moment. Enjoy it."

"Sis, you did all this?" Onyx asked, turning to his sister.

"Damn right I did," Amani replied, a wide grin spreading across her face. "You home now. We celebrating proper. Like the sign says, the boss is back."

Onyx pulled his sister into a tight hug as she tried to raise her three fingers. "I love you, and I'll die proving that," he said, his voice low and sincere in her ear. Then, releasing her, he lifted his own three fingers high, matching the energy of the crowd around them.

Not wanting to lose control by celebrating too hard, Onyx sipped his champagne slowly, letting the buzz settle without letting it take over. He was determined not to embarrass himself—or his sister—by getting drunk and losing his composure.

The night was a whirlwind of handshakes, photo flashes, and champagne bottles popping in their section. Amani kept nudging him, urging him to go grab the mic. He resisted, continuously shaking his head with a quiet laugh, but she wasn't one to take no for an answer. With a sly grin, she texted the DJ, giving him a nudge to put her brother on blast, which he did moments later.

The DJ's voice ripped through the pulsating bass and buzzing chatter like a thunderclap. "YOOOO! Paradise Station! I need y'all to turn all the way up for this one! Word is, Zone 3's own Onyx got bars for days! So you already know—he *has* to hit the stage and bless us with that heat!"

Onyx was completely caught off guard as the crowd erupted into cheers, their energy surging like a tidal wave toward the VIP section. His sister, grinning ear to ear, nudged him hard. "C'mon, O! Don't play shy now," Amani teased, her eyes sparkling with mischief.

"Really, Amani?" he muttered, shaking his head with a smirk, but he couldn't deny the adrenaline now coursing through him.

The room was electric, the crowd chanting his name as the DJ hyped him up even more. "C'mon, Onyx! Zone 3's been waiting! Let's see what you got!"

With no escape, Onyx stood, adjusting his shirt as the crowd roared louder. The energy was magnetic, pulling him toward the stage like gravity. As he walked through the crowd, hands reached out to dap him up, the vibrations from the music matching the pounding in his chest.

"Your sister says you're fire," the DJ said with a grin as Onyx reached the booth. "It's up to you not to embarrass yourself, shawty. Let's light this place up." The DJ switched the track, the beat dropping heavy and raw, shaking the entire room. Onyx gripped the mic, took a deep breath, and let his eyes sweep over the crowd.

"Y'all with me? Throw them threes up!" he commanded, his voice cutting through the air with a confidence that silenced the room. Arms shot up, fingers raised high, the crowd now fully locked into him.

Then he began. His flow was magnetic, each bar sharp and deliberate, riding the beat with effortless precision. The crowd erupted, their cheers amplifying with every line he spit. Onyx moved with the rhythm, his words shredding through the noise and igniting the room.

By the time he finished, the club was in a frenzy, the chants of his name echoing in waves. Onyx handed the mic back to the DJ after two songs, his chest heaving as he soaked in the energy of the moment.

"Zone 3 in the building!" the DJ shouted, slapping Onyx's shoulder. "That's how you rock the spot, fam!"

Onyx turned, meeting Amani's proud grin, her eyes glowing with satisfaction. Standing there, he felt invincible—alive in a way he couldn't put into words and fully free. The crowd continued to roar, their cheers vibrating through the room, the stomp of their feet echoing like thunder.

As Onyx made his way back to the VIP section, the club erupted with a roaring chant: *Zone 3... Zone 3... Zone 3...* The energy was electric, the crowd's excitement palpable. Amani wrapped him in a tight hug, her eyes shining with pride. "I told you, O. You're back," she whispered, her voice thick with emotion. "You absolutely killed it. I'm so proud of you."

Onyx grabbed the glass Amani had been holding for him and, with a firm grip on her hand, turned toward the crowd. He lifted the glass high, his gaze sweeping over the room before he spoke with conviction, "I'm back."

The words hit him like a surge of electricity, charged with more than just the weight of his freedom. He wasn't merely declaring his return—he was claiming his future. He literally saw a path that didn't lead back to the streets. He had always known music was his true calling, but the streets had a hold on him—money came fast and easy there, and the world didn't care if you were unsigned or unknown. But now, with the weight of the past finally lifted off his shoulders, he stood in that moment, raw and unrestrained. He felt it deep within him—this was his shot. And he promised himself right then and there, he would give the future everything he had.

Feeling the beat pulse through her, Jasmine was drawn to Onyx's irresistible energy. With a bold move, she walked over and began twerking in front of him, her body moving to the rhythm. Onyx couldn't help but laugh as Stacy's voice rang out from behind him, filled with playful jealousy. "Bitch your ass moving like it's been injected with bacteria. He don't want that sh*t!"

"Y'all muthaf**kers crazy!" Onyx laughed, clinking his glass with his sister's in a toast. **"***Tunang'aa bila kuruhusu mwanga wowote kuzimika. Uaminifu na upendo kabla ya aibu.***"**

Chapter 8

"The Night Unfolds"

Even though the club closed at 3 a.m., they didn't slow down. They hopped from one after-hours spot to the next, as if time had no hold on them. Amani thrived in the energy of the night, using the excitement as a tool to push her brother forward. She wanted him to see the potential she had worked hard to build and, more importantly, to inspire him to reach for something greater than street dreams. The years of scamming had her well-established, but now, it was time for Onyx to step into a new chapter.

As the group lingered in the parking lot of Club Exotic, tipsy and undecided on their next move, Stacy pulled Onyx toward Amani's car. With a playful grin, she slid into the backseat beside him, setting the tone for whatever mischief the night had left.

"Bitch, I know damn well you not 'bout to contaminate her leather with that toxic ass pussy," Jasmine said, giggling as she knocked on the back window.

"Bitch, please!" Stacy shot back, cracking the door open so she could be heard clearly. "You just mad cause I'm about to cum all over this fresh release dick and you not hoe. We can turn his ass out together if your undercover freaky ass 'bout that life though."

"Mad! Hoe, if he knew what we knew, he'd ask Amani to drop your fungal vaginitis-carrying ass off at a quarantine center on the way home." Jasmine said, rolling her eyes while walking back over to Amani and Yoshe who were standing beside her SUV laughing.

Amani glanced at her watch, noting the time—7:23 a.m.—and realized no one had a clear destination in mind. With a sigh, she hugged Jasmine and Yoshe goodbye before making her way to her car.

As she passed by the group of guys in the Audi A8 trying to catch her attention, Amani couldn't help but sway her hips harder, the confidence in her movement undeniable. She slid into her car, shut the door behind her, and quickly pressed the start button. The engine roared as she presses the accelerator, and turned up the music, eager to drown out the sounds of their selfish passion in her backseat.

Stacy was her girl, but Amani couldn't shake the nagging feeling that her brother should've focused his attention elsewhere. It wasn't a secret that Stacy laid with almost every man that crossed her path, her promiscuity as notorious as her charm. There was no telling what kind of diseases might be lying dormant in her cells, just waiting to spring to life. The thought of it made Amani's stomach churn. As she pulled out of the parking lot, she found herself wrestling with the decision. Maybe it would be better to drop the two of them off at a hotel—keep them far away from the comfort of her home. Stacy's wild energy had a way of violating the sanctity of everything she touched, and Amani wasn't sure she could stomach the thought of it spreading within her walls.

"Big bruh, did you enjoy yourself?" she asked, accelerating through the light, the weight of her thoughts lingering in the back of her mind.

With Stacy stroking his hardness with her hand and flicking her tongue against his head, Onyx struggled to answer without releasing a sigh of passion. "Hell yeah shawty! You…umm…you made tonight memorable and I love you for that."

"Bitch, you know he did with something like this in his presence all night. Who wouldn't?" Stacy lifted her head to chime in, before shifting her eyes to look at him as she returned to sucking his head with unrelenting rhythm.

"Hoe, stop dreaming! You'd f**k your mom's Maltese just to get off if he was here instead of my brother." Amani snapped, causing everyone in the car to laugh.

"And his lil crazy ass would love it too," she shot back as she continued to watch Onyx's reaction to her movements.

"Ummm… ummm…" he softly groaned, trying his best not to let Amani hear him.

Once Amani navigated through the early morning traffic, she hit the gas, speeding down the expressway without a care for the law. The sounds her brother was making from the backseat had her giggling and she couldn't help but shake her head when their eyes briefly met in the rearview mirror. *"So, he wasn't joking when he said his standards were low. The whole city has her on speed dial,"* Amani thought, shaking her head in disbelief.

She turned into her building's driveway, punched in the gate code, and parked, still hearing the banter in the backseat as the value of her leather was being called into question. Stepping out, she breathed a sigh of relief, glad to finally be home.

Once they were out of the car, she couldn't help but shake her head, the annoyance simmering inside her. Stacy's wild energy always left a trail of chaos, and Amani wasn't sure how much more of it she could take. "Bitch! You and my brother gon' have the inside of my car fumigated later today," she scolded, while hitting the lock button on the fob and rolling her eyes as she walked away.

Removing her stilettos once inside the building, Amani felt a sharp chill as the cold tile kissed her bare feet, sending a shiver up her spine. She moved through the condo with a confident, seductive sway in her step, her body speaking a language only she understood—physically drained, tipsy, and fighting off the haze of lingering desire. Her mind craved more than sleep; she needed sexual release. With no man to satisfy her, she settled for the thought of a quick shower, the soothing water washing over her, and the image of her rose rhythmic vibrations promising the exact release her body was aching for.

Once the three of them were inside the condo, Amani locked the door, activated the alarm, and made her way to the kitchen, grabbing a cold bottle of water. The faint, seductive aroma of amber and jasmine lingered in the air, caressing her senses like a lover's whisper. She closed her eyes for a moment, inhaling deeply, letting the intoxicating scent fill her lungs, the fragrance seeping into her skin, grounding her and awakening something deep within—stirring something she couldn't ignore.

Chapter 9

"The Forbidden Dance"

The soft click of her bedroom door closing was all the confirmation Stacy needed. It was her cue, her moment to command the night with unbridled confidence. She turned to Onyx, her eyes dark with intent, a slow, knowing smile spreading across her lips. Stacy wasn't one to hold back, and now that the stage was hers, she planned to perform in a way that left no room for doubt—this was her domain, and she was about to do what she did best.

Grabbing Onyx's hand with a boldness that left no room for hesitation, Stacy led him down the hallway to the guest room, her every movement deliberate. The air between them was charged, the tension palpable. She pushed him onto the bed with a confidence that bordered on audacity, caring little that the door remained wide open.

She wanted his sister to hear, to catch the faint echoes of his surrender beneath her touch, to wonder just what Stacy was capable of. Maybe she'd even walk by and see for herself. Stacy had never been one to shy away from risks. She thrived on it—on the thrill of the forbidden and the allure of pushing boundaries. Exploring deeper depths wasn't just a pastime for her; it was a challenge she took with relish, a test of how far she could go and what limits she could shatter.

Her hands moved with practiced ease, her lips curling into a playful smirk. "Don't hold back," she whispered, her voice low, a promise and a dare all at once.

Onyx's breath hitched, his resolve faltering under the weight of her confidence. She leaned in closer, her intentions clear, ready to take him to places he hadn't dared imagine. Stacy wasn't just unafraid—she was unstoppable. Grabbing at his pants with an impatient ferocity, Stacy's hands fumbled at the stubborn belt buckle. Her annoyance bubbled just below the surface. Each second felt like an eternity as the anticipation between them thickened, charged with an almost palpable intensity.

With a hard tug, the buckle finally gave way, and the metallic clink broke through the silence of the room. She wasted no time unzipping his pants and yanking them down in one swift motion, her movements devoid of the tender preludes of foreplay. This wasn't about taking it slow or savoring the moment—this was about raw, unfiltered desire, a hunger too demanding to wait.

Her eyes lifted up to his, a mixture of challenge and dominance sparkling in her gaze. "No games," she murmured, her voice clear and commanding, matching her actions.

There was no hesitation, no second-guessing. Stacy was always in control, and this morning was no exception. With his dick completely exposed and her mouth yearning to feel him expand in her throat, she spread his legs and leaned forward, taking him without shifting her eyes. Gently caressing his balls while sucking his softness like a pacifier, Onyx grew in her mouth and couldn't believe she was far better than Cee-Cee hands down.

"F**k!" Onyx's voice broke through the air, a raw, guttural sound of surrender as waves of passion coursed through his body. Stacy's tongue moved with deliberate precision, igniting every nerve ending and leaving him teetering on the edge of euphoria.

His hands clenched the comforter with such force that his palms turned red, the blood pooling beneath his skin as it struggled to circulate properly. The pressure in his grip mirrored the tension building within him, an almost unbearable heat coiling tighter and tighter with her movement.

Each passing second felt like an eternity, the pleasure so overwhelming it bordered on pain. And then, with a deep, shuddering breath, Onyx surrendered completely. His body convulsed as the release overtook him, leaving him gasping and utterly spent, while Stacy's satisfied smirk promised she wasn't done testing his limits.

With every drop of his cum sliding down her throat, Stacy moved with an almost otherworldly determination, as though she were possessed by a force greater than herself. Her focus was singular, her movements deliberate and unrelenting, driven by a primal need to conquer him.

Easing him out of her mouth, she slid her tongue along the side while massaging his head as she sucked his balls. Stacy wanted to feel that dick throb inside of her pussy and she knew she had to keep the blood flowing. Her every movement precise and intentional. She couldn't let it falter; if the circulation wavered for even a moment, it would go limp, and she wasn't about to let that happen. Her focus heightened, her determination unwavering as she worked with a fervor born of both skill and desire, ensuring every pulse and throb remained steady under her command.

The fire in her eyes blazed brighter as she inserted him back into her mouth without using her hands. The graceful sway of her neck, moving back and forth with an almost hypnotic rhythm, sent waves of indescribable pleasure coursing through his body. As Stacy began to remove her clothes, each motion seemed more seductive, her fluency painting a picture of raw confidence and allure. The subtle arch of her back, the curve of her shoulders—every detail amplified the intensity. Satisfaction was a challenge she intended to master.

"Damn tender dick! You 'bout to nut again already?" She whispered, sliding his erection out of her mouth to tease the head with her tongue.

Being the expert she was known to be, she noticed the shift in his body, the way his muscles tensed and his breathing quickened, a clear sign of his unraveling. But she stopped suddenly, her own desire now impossible to ignore. Her wetness was already cascading down her thighs, an undeniable reminder of her own yearning, and she was determined to reach her climax too.

Massaging him gently, Stacy whispered for him to scoot back on the bed with her voice low and commanding. As he complied, she climbed onto the bed with feline grace, positioning herself above him. Slowly, she eased him inside her, the sensation sending a shiver through her body. The way he stretched her pussy, filling her completely, awakened a deep, primal need within her—a hunger that demanded to be satisfied. Every nerve in her body ignited, her breath hitching as pleasure overtook her senses.

It had been years since he felt something this electrifying. The Vaseline, his long-time escape, had never come close to matching the overwhelming flood of affection he felt now. She was guiding him with a rhythm that consumed him completely, her body swaying and pressing closer, as if to pull him deeper into her. The sensation was so intense that Onyx couldn't help but let out a breathless moan, uncaring of how far his voice traveled.

"Yesss…oooh f**k!" Onyx allowed it to escape from his lips. A low, guttural growl that was thick with raw, unfiltered intensity, as if every fiber of his being had wound itself tighter and tighter, straining against the inevitable release. It was a sound born of pure, primal desire, the kind that came from the deepest recesses of his soul, trembling with the weight of his longing before it finally broke free, unleashing everything he had been holding back.

Her hands gripped the fabric of his chest, her fingers digging in as if she needed him closer, tighter. He tried to match her intensity, his own desire building with every movement, but it was almost too much to contain. The pressure inside him grew unbearable, each second pushing him closer to the edge, as if the very world around them had disappeared, leaving only the raw, undeniable connection between them.

The look on her face confirmed without words that she was just getting started. Easing off of him so he didn't explode, she started sliding her pussy against his hardness in a way that kept them both stimulated. Stacy understood his body still carried the scars of his time in prison. She knew she had to be patient with him, but that didn't stop the fire inside her from burning brighter. She could feel the heat of him, the raw strength that still pulsed beneath his skin, and she couldn't help but crave it, need it. She wanted to make him ache for her—body and soul—until every part of him was left yearning for the connection they shared, even after it was all over.

Lowering to kiss on his neck and suck on his chest, she liked the way he squeezed her breast and slapped her on her butt. The slap sent a sharp, electrifying shock through her, a sensation that swept through her like fire and ice all at once. It ignited her skin with fierce heat, then chilled her to the bone, leaving her trembling, every nerve alive and craving more.

Turning around to get into the cowgirl position, she exclaimed, "Aww! F**k! Damnnnnn!," as she slid him back inside of her. The way his dick stretched the muscles in her pussy sent a shockwave through her, a searing wave of heat that spread through her body, igniting every inch of her skin.

"F**k this pussy Daddy! F**k me!" she purred seductively as Onyx's hardness went deeper and deeper inside of her. Stacy cared not who heard her as pleasure erupted within her, a surge of raw sensation crashing through her body. Every part of her seemed to pulse with the intensity of it, her breath coming in quick, desperate gasps, her entire being consumed by the storm of desire. She moaned freely, lost in the moment, her body betraying her with every tremor as she surrendered to the fire that ignited her from the inside out.

Climaxing on his dick felt like a kiss—hungry, wild, and untamed— an unspoken promise that sent shivers through her. Her body trembled as her juices slicked him, a warmth that echoed the lonely nights he spent in secrecy, Vaseline his only companion in the cold confines of his prison cell.

"Ooooh sh*t baby I knew this dick was going to be good," she cried between the waves of pleasure flowing throughout her body. "Don't stop throwing that dick..." The raw, desperate connection between them burned through her, consuming her in a way that kept her breathless and wanting more.

Not wanting Stacy to have all the control, he flipped her over and began f**king her from behind. "Oh sh*t!" She screamed with more animation and excitement, while biting into the comforter. She was feeling him pressing against her organs, each movement sending an intense, almost painful pressure against her, yet somehow, it only heightened the pleasure.

He, too, was overwhelmed, consumed by the connection that surged between them. Every stroke, every inch of contact, left him gasping, his body trembling with the force of the connection. The sensation was like a slow burn, igniting every part of him, making it impossible to distinguish where the pleasure ended and the ache began. He was lost in her, unable to escape the raw intensity of what they shared.

"F**k this pussy n***a! Oooh sh*t I'm 'bout to squirt on that dick," she seductively whispered, while starting to rotate her hips with more passion to intensify her climax. Gripping into the comforter as Onyx's dick pushed her walls aside and her juices splashed onto his body with every stroke, Stacy couldn't believe this free out of prison dick had her body feeling as though she was riding a rollercoaster.

Seeing the way she reacted to his movements made Onyx smile. He thought nothing of cumming in her, especially given how good it felt. "This dick got that pussy feeling some type of way I see shawty," he uttered with arrogance as she pushed him backwards to ease his dick out of her and turned around so she could suck her sweet nectar off of it. The way she had his dick throbbing and standing at attention had him truly feeling like a Boss.

"Shut up, n***a," she said, slightly gagging as she massaged her clitoris, preparing him for another round. Locking eyes with him, she eased him back into her mouth, determined to make that dick hers. She knew she could hypnotize any man with her skills, but keeping one? That was a whole different challenge."

Leaning back, she spread her legs wide, her body arching like a falcon's wings in flight. He tapped her clitoris a few times gently with his hardness, each touch a brief, teasing connection before sliding his head between her lips, allowing the pull of desire to guide him as he eased it inside her.

As the morning unfolded, they lost themselves in one another, their bodies speaking a language of passion. Each touch, each movement, was a slow exploration, a dance of pleasure that defined their connection. Together, they discovered the art of passion, surrendering to the rhythm of their bodies until the morning was nothing but the echo of their shared ecstasy.

Chapter 10

"Roots and Reckoning "

As the cab rolled to a stop, Onyx retrieved his phone, glanced at the screen, and shook his head. Stacy again. He slipped it back into his pocket without answering—he wasn't in the mood for clingy questions or drama. After three weeks of reconnecting with family, re-establishing his relationship with his mother, and unwinding with Amani and friends, he was ready to grind again.

Those first moments with his mother had been overwhelming, her tears speaking louder than any words could. She had looked at him—hands trembling as they traced his face, shoulders shaking with the weight of ten years. Onyx's own hands had moved clumsily, signing the words he hadn't used in so long: "I'm sorry, Mama. I'm here now."

Her expression softened, the smallest smile breaking through as she signed back, "You're my son. I love you, no matter how long it's been."

The silence that followed wasn't uncomfortable—it was a kind of healing. A shared understanding. He spent hours at her side that first week, watching her hands move as she told stories about family he hadn't seen and friends he barely remembered. She forgave him, he could see that, but what he couldn't escape was her hope—that he would finally become the man she always believed he could be. Now, as he stepped out of the cab, her last message to him lingered in his mind: "Don't let the streets take you again, Onyx. You have a gift. Use it."

Coming home after a decade away felt surreal—familiar faces on the same streets he used to run, yet everything seemed smaller, both changed and unchanged. Still, Onyx knew one thing for sure: dreams didn't come true for people who sat still. And if there was one lesson those quiet moments with his sister had taught him, it was this—his time to level up was now. The hunger to get back in the studio, to electrify the crowd like he'd done on release night, drove him forward as he closed the door behind him.

Georgia Avenue greeted him like an old friend: the cracked sidewalks, the faded paint on buildings, crackheads scattered along the sidewalks, the unmistakable pulse of the streets—alive, raw, and restless. "Damn, I was gone too long," he muttered, half-smiling as he walked toward Gram's old studio. But as much as the hood had changed, it never forgot its own.

"Trigga, I know that ain't you. What's up, fool?"

The voice shot across the street, pulling Onyx's attention. Lil Dee, blunt in hand, sauntered over with a crooked grin. Lil Dee was still the same—shorter than Onyx remembered, wiry, his eyes darting like a man always plotting his next move. Known to the streets as an opportunist, Lil Dee was dangerous not because of strength, but because of desperation. Years ago, Onyx had heard he'd robbed and killed a cousin on his dad's side. Trust wasn't a word you threw around with him.

"What's good, Lil Dee?" Onyx replied, his voice steady but cautious as he gave him a quick embrace.

Shiddd, lil n***a, I ain't seen your ass since we lit them Miami boys up," Lil Dee said, bursting into laughter, tapping Onyx's waist inconspicuously as they hugged—checking whether he was strapped.

Onyx didn't miss the move. "Yeah, fool, I got knocked not long after that. Just got back," he said evenly, stepping a little closer, close enough to strike if Lil Dee tried something.

Lil Dee paused, pulling hard on his blunt. "Damn, bruh. How long?"

Onyx shifted, eyes moving over the street—always aware, always reading the environment. "Whole decade."

Dee's eyes widened, and for a split second, Onyx could see the man's mind ticking over. A decade was a lifetime in these streets—too long for anyone to keep their sanity. If it had been him, Dee thought, he would've found a way to cut that time short. Man, I woulda had to snitch on somebody, he mused silently, pulling again on his blunt to cover the thought. His gaze lingered on Onyx's designer gear, suspicion sparkling in his eyes. "Damn, bruh. Fresh out, huh? So what's up, Trigga? I know you lookin' for a come-up."

"Shawty, my name's Onyx now. Don't call me Trigga," he said firmly, his voice carving through the moment.

Lil Dee squinted at him. "Why Onyx? You Muslim now?"

"Nah. It's about growth, shawty. Ain't no future in standing still. Back then, I was reckless—young, wild, taking lives without thinking. I'm past that now. I'm Onyx. Don't forget it."

Lil Dee nodded slowly, not quite buying it, but not willing to press the issue. "A'ight, a'ight. Well, I got gas, zanies, drink—whatever you need to get right, bruh."

"I'm good," Onyx said, throwing up a quick deuces as he turned toward Heywood, making his way to Gram's spot.

The walk was a mix of nostalgia and disbelief. He waved at familiar faces, some thrilled to see him back, others barely looking up from their hustle. The old neighborhood was frozen in time—men still serving nickels and dimes, still talking about plans they'd never follow through on.

A sudden commotion ahead snapped his attention. Two women were brawling in front of a sagging trap house, yelling and clawing like gladiators. One of them—a woman with a ripped jean jacket and slick braids—snatched the other's wig clean off, tossing it into the street. Hood whips with candy paint and oversized rims sat parked in the driveway behind them, untouched, gleaming under the sunlight as if the chaos unfolding was just part of the scenery.

Onyx barely slowed his pace. He knew better than to get involved in someone else's mess. Police sirens wailed faintly in the distance. He picked up his stride, mumbling to himself, "I got to level up. Can't get stuck in this broke sh*t forever."

The sight of Gram's studio, still standing on the corner like an anchor, filled him with a burst of energy. As he approached the gate and reached for the latch, a voice boomed from across the street:

"Trigga! Trigga!"

Onyx turned, startled—but the sight of a tall, dark-skinned man with wavy hair jogging toward him brought a wide smile to his face. "44, my dawg!"

"Blessed love, mi bredda!" 44 called as they embraced, his deep voice carrying the lilt of his Rastafarian roots. "Mi cyaan believe mi eyes. You a sight mi neva expect fi see!"

Onyx grinned, still holding 44's firm grip. "Man, I can't believe you still out here holding it down."

44 shook his head, the diamonds around his neck glinting in the sunlight. "Nah, Trigga. Mi nuh hold down nuttin but mi family. Streets nah change, yuh know? Same cut-throat vibes as always."

"Yeah," Onyx muttered, glancing at the studio. "I'm tryin' to get back in there. Drop somethin' crazy on Gram's tracks."

44's expression shifted. "Bredda, yuh to late. Gram gone—moved too Memphis last year. Shut this place down."

The words hit like a punch to the chest. For a moment, Onyx stared at the empty studio windows, his plans unraveling. The weight of disappointment settled heavy on his shoulders, but he forced himself to stay calm.

Gram's voice echoed in his head, clear as if the old man were standing.

Chapter 11

"Crossroads and Second Chances"

After an hour of chilling and catching up on life, the sharp blast of a horn outside and the vibration of his phone on the coffee table made 44 rise from the sofa. He reached down between the cushions, retrieving a Glock 23, then tucked it into the back of his waistband, the steel disappearing beneath the hem of his shirt.

"Time fi we move," he muttered, his deep voice laced with a low Rastafarian drawl.

Onyx followed 44 to the door, watching as he turned off the lights and made sure everything was secure. The sound of a child's voice carried through the humid air as he opened the front door. "Daddy! Daddy!"

A little boy ran up the steps and jumped straight into 44's open arms. The smile that broke across 44's face softened his otherwise steely demeanor. "Dis mi son, Polo," he said, holding the boy close. Fatherhood had molded him, but not softened his edges—if anything, it had pushed him deeper into the grind.

"Shiddd, I need me one too—I gotta secure my legacy," Onyx said wistfully as Polo gave him a fist bump before they all headed toward a sleek midnight black Range Rover parked by the curb.

44 chuckled, tossing Polo into the air, his voice dripping with teasing confidence. "Be easy, mi dawg. One of dem gyals gon' grab yuh fresh-out tail soon enough. Give yuh more than a baby—maybe some headache, too."

"Nah, n***a. I'm tryna get a bankroll first," Onyx shot back as he slipped into the backseat beside Polo.

"Onyx, mi bredren, link up wid Amelia," 44 said, giving a subtle nod as he slid into the front passenger seat and fastened his seatbelt. "Dis mi empress right here—she hold mi firm, y'know. She's got mi back like nobody else." He glanced over at Amelia, a look of quiet pride

55

in his eyes, before settling into the seat, the bond between them palpable in the air.

Amelia was a mocha-skinned beauty, her presence undeniable. A smirk tugged at the corner of her lips, one that could disarm a man with a single glance. Her eyes resembled two pools of liquid fire—sparkled with an intoxicating blend of confidence and curiosity, as if they could read the very soul of anyone who dared meet them. As she turned with a grace that seemed almost otherworldly, she extended her hand, her voice soft yet commanding, carrying a weight of unspoken power. Every movement she made exuded an effortless allure, the kind that drew people in without a word.

"Onyx, right? Nice to meet you." Her words carried a subtle warmth that matched her radiance, making Onyx's gaze linger for a second longer than intended.

Onyx shook her hand, noting the way 44 pulled her close afterwards for a quick kiss before they took off. His mind drifted to Stacy and her games, but this—this was different. 44 held his women down, and they knew their place in his world.

The rest of the day was a haze of adrenaline and nostalgia. They hit a soul food spot where Polo made a mess with mac and cheese, then raced go-karts like they were still kids. Onyx felt the genuine love— street love—that 44 was showing him, a reminder that real friendships didn't fray with time. But when they rolled up to the mall and 44 bought him some new kicks and three fresh outfits, the weight of it all had Onyx wondering.

Outside, as they walked toward the Rover with bags in hand, Onyx stopped short. "Shiddd, what you sellin', Shawty?"

44's laugh was low and knowing, his eyes sweeping the parking lot where young dudes posed in front of someone else's Ferrari. "Remember when dat was us?" he asked. "Mi dawg, everyting sell. But dat's not why yuh here. Back in da day, we risked our lives fi nuttin' but scraps. Mi nah leave yuh hangin' now. Mi wasn't dere when yuh needed me because I lost contact with your mom and sister after I got knocked.

Mi fault myself for dat. But mi here now. Bredren from two wombs, ya undastand?"

As they walked to the rear of the Rover and inserted their bags, Onyx heard the weight of truth in 44's words. A moment of silence lingered, the hum of distant engines and laughter from the lot filling the air.

"For a minute, I thought you was tryna bait me into robbin' a bank or sumthin'," Onyx said, cracking a faint smile to ease the heaviness.

"Hell no, mi dawg. Yuh too wild—yuh shoot everyone in de place just to make sure no witnesses leff!" 44 joked, his Rastafarian lilt deepening as he burst into laughter, the sound rich and unguarded. "Mi keep it clean now. Dummy bricks an' green fi di hustlers. Keeps mi outta de limelight."

Onyx smirked, shaking his head, but he couldn't ignore the admiration he felt. 44 had grown into something bigger, more purposeful—something Onyx wasn't sure he could reach. Yet, here 44 was, extending a bridge.

Leaving the mall and speeding through traffic, Amelia cruised off the expressway at Camp Creek and made a left. Onyx stared absently out the window. The sight of a small bakery stirred memories of his sister, and his chest constricted with emotions. He hadn't heard from her since they flew to Nevada early this morning and he was starting to worry. He knew the risk she and her girls were taking, flying to another state to cash checks. Now, the paranoia was creeping in. Maybe that's why Stacy was calling, he thought.

Pulling out his phone, he fired off a quick text to both of them as the SUV rolled to a stop at the light. Each silent second gnawed at him. The hustle always came with a gamble, but his sister was his rock—his balance. The thought of losing her again wasn't something he could stomach.

The soft whisper of the suburban streets came alive as they turned into a pristine subdivision. Amelia pulled into the driveway of an impressive two-story brick home. The neighborhood had a peace Onyx wasn't used to—birds chirping, soft breezes rustling trees, kids laughing in the distance. For a moment, he soaked it in, wondering if this kind of serenity would ever be his.

"Polo's excited screams broke the calm. 'Mommy! Mommy!' he yelled, kicking at the straps of his car seat."

Onyx turned to see a plus-sized, warm brown-skinned woman with half-moon cheekbones stepping through the front door. Her smile was wide and warm as she approached, calling out, "There go my Sunshine!"

Onyx unfastened Polo's seatbelt, watching as the boy leapt out of the vehicle and into her arms. The tenderness of the moment hit him in a way he wasn't prepared for. He wanted this—kids, a family, something real to hold onto—but right now, those dreams felt like smoke in the wind. The thought of Stacy carrying his child made him scoff to himself. That wasn't the life he wanted.

"Come on, bredren," 44 said, motioning for Onyx to follow as Polo's mother and Amelia exchanged a few words in the driveway.

Onyx lingered after stepping out of the SUV, watching 44. The way he playfully mushed Polo's face before passionately kissing his baby mama's spoke volumes. There was no tension, no jealousy—just acceptance. Amelia stood to the side, still on her phone, completely unbothered. It was a dynamic Onyx hadn't seen before, a balance that seemed damn near impossible, yet 44 managed it like a man who knew his purpose.

Moments later, as the women disappeared into the house with Polo in tow, Onyx followed 44 over to the garage. The faint sound of a woman's voice caught his ear. Turning slightly, he spotted a neighbor walking to her mailbox. Her coils framed her mocha brown skin like a crown, and the sundress she wore clung in all the right ways. Each step she took had a grace that made Onyx pause, his curiosity sparking.

"Who is that?" he asked, unable to keep his eyes off her.

44, fumbling in his pocket for the lock key, snorted without even glancing her way. "Dat a stuck-up gyal, bredren. She'll mek you regret everyting quick-quick. She sent her man to prison for findin' another woman hair in har bathroom. Man say it was his sista's, same ole story, but she nah believe him. Now him a sit behind bars."

Onyx smirked, tempted to ignore the warning. "She bad, though," he mumbled, his eyes lingering as the woman turned and disappeared back inside. A vibration in his pocket snapped him back. Pulling out his phone, he saw Amani's name flash across the screen with a simple message: *$$$* 🖤.

Onyx exhaled, his nerves easing as he thumbed a quick reply: "*Nakupenda.*"

"Yo, help mi out wit dis," 44 called, drawing Onyx's attention back to reality.

Onyx walked over as 44 knelt beside a storage bubble, grinning as he tugged the cover free. Slowly, the Grabber Blue convertible 1970 Oldsmobile 442 W-30 emerged like a treasure brought back to life.

"Damn," Onyx whispered, stepping closer. The Olds gleamed under the soft light flooding in from the open garage. Its paint, a deep oceanic blue, looked almost wet, the chrome trim catching every glint of sunlight. White racing stripes ran clean down the hood, leading to the W-30 badging at the front fender. The black vinyl interior was pristine, a mix of custom touches and classic charm. The car sat on polished five-spoke wheels, aggressive and low—like it was ready to pounce.

"This what the f**k I need," Onyx said, running his hand along the glossy finish, his voice full of awe. "That's that bitch, shawty!"

44 chuckled, shaking his head as he leaned against the garage wall. "Mi bredren, patience is key. Ya nah ready fe dis life yet. All ya see is da shine, but ya nah see de storm behind it. Trust mi, youth, ya need fe spread ya wings properly before ya jump ten toes back inna da streets."

Onyx turned to him, the admiration still clear in his eyes. "Shawty, I hear you, but I can't keep bein' a burden to my sister. We bred to get money, feel me? I gotta move; I gotta get in the studio before these streets swallow me whole again."

44 studied him for a moment, his expression serious. "Seen. But hear mi now, bredren—music can save you, mi know it. But da streets? Dey nah care 'bout ya dreams. You haffi choose carefully. Da man who chase two rabbit catch none."

Onyx nodded slowly, stepping back to take in the full view of the car. It was a masterpiece—powerful, dangerous, and undeniably beautiful. "Magnificent," he muttered.

As if sensing the shift, 44 popped the hood, revealing the heart of the beast: a roaring 455 V8 engine, perfectly restored and gleaming like a jewel. "Mi put blood, sweat, an' tears into dis one," 44 said, pride thick in his voice.

Minutes later, as 44 disappeared into the house, Onyx remained standing still, admiring the craftsmanship of the whole setup. The house, the car, the life—it all seemed so meticulously put together, yet there was something raw and unfinished about it, much like him. A few minutes later, 44 returned, holding a stack of cash in one hand and a half-eaten peach in the other. He looked at Onyx, sitting inside taking selfies, and shook his head with a knowing grin.

"I see yuh still flossin' like dem yutes at di mall, mi dawg," 44 laughed, walking over to him. "But seriously now, here's a likkle sumthin' fi yuh pocket." He extended the money to Onyx, his tone becoming more serious. "If music a yuh way fi escape di streets, then pursue it full force, don't just dream. But if yuh can't open a new door without confrontin' di fire inside yuh, den prove to yourself yuh a boss, not just a product of di streets. Mi got yuh back regardless, yuh know dat."

Onyx took the two racks of cash, feeling the weight of 44's words. As 44 walked to the trunk, Onyx felt the gravity of his message. He wanted to establish his own lane, to earn the respect of the streets again, but he knew he couldn't do it while stuck at a crossroads. He hated the feeling that his path was already forged, as if fate had written his story before he even had a chance to turn the first page. The weight of inevitability pressed down on him, stifling his desire for freedom and choice. It felt as though every step he took was already mapped out, leaving him no room to carve his own way.

"To be honest, shawty," Onyx said, his voice steady, "I feel like I need to explore both lanes to truly find the path that's forged for me."

44 paused, shaking his head as though he disapproved as he pulled two duffle bags from the trunk. His silence spoke louder than words, and Onyx could tell 44 wasn't fully on board with his decision. Transfixed by the elegance of the Oldsmobile, Onyx felt an urge to capture the moment. He pulled his phone back out, went live, and began rapping his song, ***"Being Broke Ain't No Option."*** The lyrics came from deep within him, not just as a performance, but as a statement of intent. In this moment, he was chasing something bigger than himself, hoping someone would see the fire burning inside. The comments started rolling in fast, hyping him up as he flashed the cash 44 had handed him moments earlier.

"Let's bounce," 44 said, startling Onyx as he reappeared, wiping his hands on a rag. "Grab ya things outta da Range."

Onyx jumped out, scooping up his bags before tossing them into the Oldsmobile's trunk. As he climbed back into the passenger seat, he caught one last glance of the neighbor's house, shaking his head with a grin.

44 chuckled as he turned the ignition, the Oldsmobile rumbling to life beneath them like a sleeping giant. "Mi tell ya dis once—f**k da streets, Onyx. If ya chase music, chase it. But if ya ready to mek some moves, mi got six bricks ready fe wrap up, no street risk. Ya haffi decide, bredren."

"Shawty, what's the move?" he asked, already anticipating the hustle ahead.

"Mi nah rush it, mi dawg. Just hold a vibes, we'll reason 'bout it later." 44 voiced in a patient tone.

Onyx leaned back, silent, as the Olds rolled out of the driveway. The engine purred beneath them, steady and menacing, as they hit the open road. Choices lay ahead, but tonight, all that mattered was the ride.

44 and Onyx cruised through the city, the low rumble of the Oldsmobile filling the air as they chopped it up, the conversation flowing like the rhythm of the streets. The night felt alive, the glow of the city lights reflecting off the chrome of the car as they passed by familiar blocks, the faint buzz of the city's heartbeat in the distance. 44's

deep voice broke the silence, "Yuh know, mi dawg, life always a balance, seen? Yuh cya't just run down one road without knowin' where it lead."

Onyx nodded, his eyes scanning the streets as they turned onto Cleveland Ave. The liquor and corner stores blurred by, the air heavy with the energy of the night. "Yeah, I feel that," Onyx replied, his tone thoughtful but edged with that street-wise confidence. "But sometimes you just gotta take a risk, right?"

44 chuckled, the sound rich and knowing. "Mi no know 'bout risks, mi know 'bout reward. But dat's what yuh need fi figure out, mi dawg."

As they pulled up to the club, the neon lights flickered, casting a glow over the entrance. The place was like a magnet, pulling them in with its promise of escape and indulgence. The sound of bass-heavy music leaked out as they parked and walked inside, the air thick with perfume and the scent of alcohol.

They found a booth on the side of the stage, the low light casting shadows across the plush seating. The women on stage moved like liquid, their bodies swaying to the rhythm of the music, their skin glowing under the spotlight. One woman, her curves resembled smooth waves, bent low to the stage, a teasing smile playing at the corners of her lips. Her eyes locked with Onyx's as she straightened, sending a wink his way, then a slow, purposeful twirl that made the crowd around them holler in appreciation.

"Yuh see dat, mi dawg?" 44 said with a knowing grin, his Rastafarian accent thick. "Dem gyal ready fi di spotlight, but dey keep it humble. Yuh betta know how fi play di game, mi dawg, cause yuh been gone ten years an' tings way more dangerous out here now. Dat's why mi keep mi self inna mi lane an' stay far from di madness."

Onyx smirked, leaning back against the chair cushion as the women around them danced, their bodies moving with hypnotic precision. The music was loud, but the energy in the air was louder, and Onyx felt the rush of it all. He couldn't take his eyes off one dancer in particular. She had the kind of beauty that made time slow down. Her skin was like melted caramel, glowing under the lights, her hair cascading down her back in thick, glossy waves. Her eyes? Deep and mysterious, with a hint of something wild and untamed beneath them.

She walked off the stage, her hips swaying with a mesmerizing, bowlegged strut that made every eye in the room follow her. As she neared their booth, Onyx's heart picked up pace. The way she moved was seductive, her every step dripping with confidence. She didn't just walk—she *owned* the room, like she was made for this.

Her lips curled into a smile as she slid into the chair next to Onyx, her presence enveloping him. "What's good, baby?" she said in a voice that was smooth like velvet, each word dripping with seduction. "I'm Chardonnay. I see you lookin'. You ready to take this to the next level?"

Onyx couldn't help but grin. He had a feeling tonight was about to get a whole lot more interesting. "Yeah, let's make it happen," he said, his voice low and steady.

Chardonnay's smile widened as she stood, offering him her hand. "Follow me, baby. VIP's where all the real fun happens."

As they walked toward the back, Onyx couldn't help but admire the way she moved. Her bowlegged walk was effortless, the sway of her hips drawing every eye in the club. There was something about her— dangerous and alluring—that had him hooked, like she could break him and still have him begging for more.

She led him past the velvet ropes and into the VIP area, the music growing louder, the lights flashing in time with the beat. The night had just begun, and Onyx had a feeling it was one he wouldn't soon forget.

Chapter 12

"Crossroads "

With voices echoing from the other room and light streaming through the window, Onyx pushed himself out of bed, his body aching in protest. The strip club haze still clung to him—half-formed memories of the smoke-filled VIP room, the bass pounding through his chest, and fleeting affections that felt real enough in the moment. The gummies hadn't worn off either; his limbs felt heavy, every movement like pushing through wet cement. An hour of sleep—just one miserable hour—hadn't come close to quieting the exhaustion that gnawed at him.

He stood under the scalding water, eyes closed, wishing he could peel his spirit from his body and let it float somewhere quiet and free. But a promise was a promise, and Amani had been too good to him for him to let her down with a selfish excuse. After toweling off, he stepped out of the stall and quickly pulled on his linen drawstring pants, letting them hang low on his hips. The damp air hit his skin as he walked out of the room, the coolness of his bare chest easing the lingering heat from the shower. The living room was already alive. "Morning," he muttered, voice flat, eyes heavy.

"Morning," Amani and Stacy said in unison, neither glancing up from what they were doing. Stacy stood by the large sugar glider cage stationed near the window, sunlight filtering through the sheer curtains, her tablet in hand. Her outfit hugged every curve like temptation itself. Onyx's gaze didn't linger long. He wasn't in the mood.

"How was y'all's flight?" he asked out of habit more than anything. The words dragged from his mouth, heavy with disinterest.

Stacy looked up, her stare lingering a second too long, as if searching for something deeper. He ignored her and shuffled into the kitchen. The blender whirred to life, breaking the silence as he tossed in spinach, blueberries, grapes, and fish oil. If he couldn't get sleep, maybe nutrients would hold him together.

"Bring me one of them muffins in the box on the counter," Amani said, her tone casual but leaving no room for argument.

Onyx didn't reply. After pouring his smoothie into a glass, he grabbed a muffin and walked out of the kitchen. He handed it to her, then, without waiting for a response, settled beside her on the couch, invading her space. Conversation wasn't on his agenda, but Amani was already deep in her hustle, stacks of paperwork spread across the coffee table—numbers bold enough to make him pause.

"Sis, y'all just hit for $127,739 yesterday. Why are you already back at it today? And you're sure about these numbers you want me to print on the checks?" Onyx asked, eyeing the list she handed him.

"Yeah, bruh." Amani didn't even look up. "They goin' in business accounts I been brewing for a minute. We good. This sh*t don't stop 'cause of yesterday. Companies change passwords and routing numbers periodically. There are windows for executing before they close, you feel me? I open accounts, let 'em sit a month or two, then deposit these type of checks. No red flags."

Onyx nodded, though his mind was elsewhere. He rose off the sofa and walked over to the desk, settling into the chair to print the checks. He adjusted the seat, angling the monitor just enough to block his view of Stacy, who seemed to shift her hips a little too much, as if trying to seduce him.

. Two hours passed. The condo hummed with the seamless harmony of a finely tuned orchestra—Stacy designing IDs, Amani verifying bank accounts, and Onyx printing checks as if each one were a masterpiece. But despite the steady rhythm of the work, something gnawed at him.

With the final check printed, Onyx handed it to his sister for inspection before heading into the kitchen to make himself a fruit bowl—one he had no intention of sharing. Observing the time, he strolled back into the living room to grab his phone, ensuring he hadn't missed a call or text from 44. Money was on the line, and he was ready to execute. Even with cash in hand, his hunger for more was insatiable.

Unable to focus on the movie as Stacy's silly antics grated on his nerves, he finally gave up and moved to the window, staring out at the skyline. When he wasn't distracted by the sugar gliders' unique, graceful movements, restlessness burned in his chest, his thoughts fixating on 44's invitation. His knees bounced involuntarily as tension surged through him. Unable to sit or stand still, he began pacing the room, his fingers twitching as if trying to suppress the relentless itch in his mind.

"Bruh, why the f**k you pacing like you got ants in your pants?" Amani snapped, side-eyeing him. "Please tell me you ain't done nothing stupid."

"F**k no... no reason," Onyx lied, forcing a half-smile. "Just thinkin'."

Amani rolled her eyes. "Well, sit your ugly ass down or go eat that bitch pussy to calm your nerves. I'm tryna watch this movie."

Stacy giggled, voice dripping with mischief. "N***a, stop stressin'. Just lay down, and I'll put it in your mouth like a bridle. Need me to get you a towel or a bib?" she teased, her laughter bubbling up as she leaned back, watching his reaction.

Onyx raised an eyebrow, shaking his head with a smirk of his own. "You wild as hell, Stacy. Always got somethin' slick to say."

Stacy shrugged, her grin unwavering. "That's why you keep me around, ain't it? Somebody gotta keep you on your toes."

Their laughter burned, but Onyx didn't react. He stared at Stacy a moment too long, his expression blank, before collapsing back onto the couch. His phone buzzed on the coffee table, and he shot forward, heart racing. It was 44. The call he'd been waiting for. He snatched it up, pressing the button—but the voicemail envelope popped up instead. Six thousand on the table, and he'd missed it. How? Frustration simmered as Onyx called back. Voicemail. Again. And again. Voicemail.

"Damn, this some bullsh*t." Frustration boiled over, pushing him to his feet. He walked to the bedroom, hoping for a better perspective. Stepping inside, he grabbed his shirt and sneakers, shoving his phone into his pocket. He stormed out of the condo, the weight of the streets already pulling at him. Needing space to clear his mind, he headed to the elevator. Once inside, he dialed again. Straight to voicemail. "What the f**k."

The elevator doors slid open to the lobby, and Onyx stepped out, his frustration weighing him down with each step. The usual rhythm of the building felt suffocating, and he needed a moment—any moment—to escape the pressure. With nowhere else to turn, his gaze landed on the small flower garden beside the building. The sight of it, tucked away in the corner, drew him outside, where the cool air cut through his skin like a sharp reminder of the world beyond his own chaos. He sank onto a stool, running his hands through his locs, his mind still racing.

For the first time since his release, he truly looked—really took at his surroundings. The flowers danced in the breeze, vibrant and alive, as though they held secrets he couldn't yet understand. Their gentle sway seemed to calm the storm inside him, each delicate petal a quiet invitation to slow down. "Damn, I need to slow down," he muttered, his eyes following the subtle movement of the blooms, as if they held the answers he was too impatient to find.

Sitting there, Onyx watched the residents stroll by—some moving with purpose, others with vacant eyes, their movements sluggish, their noses subtly sniffing. He knew the characteristics well. They weren't just neighbors; they were a different breed. Career-oriented, yet trapped in a cycle of addiction, masking their struggles behind business suits and briefcases. He felt a shift in his gut—an unsettling clarity. These people, they had potential. Real potential. No risks, no desperation. He could see it—he could move product, no hassle, no strings attached. But then the thought hit him, like a punch to the chest: How would Amani feel if he opened that door, right under her nose? Would she even notice? Would she care? The questions lingered, unspoken but heavy, as his mind raced with possibilities.

Onyx wrestled with himself. Money was survival; it was freedom. Handouts wouldn't cut it, but the streets was his chessboard? They called to him like an old friend. Music—his real dream—felt so far away, like a mirage at the edge of a desert. His phone buzzed. Amani. *Come back upstairs.* He sighed, rising to his feet. That's when he saw her.

She stepped out of the building like she owned the earth itself. Tall, statuesque, her hips swayed with purpose. Titian-red hair framed her polished face, her lips soft and full. Power radiated from her. The kind of woman who didn't just inspire a man—she transformed him. The moment he laid eyes on her, it struck him with undeniable force—he had to do better, to rise above it all, because Stacy was never the solution. This extraordinary woman was the wake-up call, piercing and unrelenting, that he didn't realize he'd been waiting for—shaking him awake from a slumber of apathy.

Onyx watched her as she walked, his gaze following every graceful step she took. There was something magnetic about her—a quiet confidence that made her stand out even in the simplest moments. Her strides were purposeful, a natural sway in her hips that caught even the wind's attention. He couldn't help but notice the way the sunlight seemed to dance off her skin, making her all the more alluring. As she approached her car, he admired the way she handled herself, each movement fluid, controlled, as if she were aware of the power she wielded with just her presence.

He watched her pull off, still frozen in place, his body a statue in the stillness of the moment. But then, something else shifted in his peripheral vision. Two boys lingered suspiciously near a Dodge Charger GT, their movements erratic and unnatural—sloppy, desperate, too green. A third kid stood apart from the others, shifting nervously, his puffed-up jacket too bulky, betraying the telltale weight of a ratchet tucked inside.

With a plan brewing and years of street wisdom backing him, Onyx knew he'd found the right pawns to get his hustle back in motion. The petty hustlers posted up nearby were sloppy—reckless—but they had the raw potential he could shape. He strolled toward the parking lot, leaning against a sleek Porsche Macan parked across from them, his gaze sharp, predatory. He watched. Calculated. These kids were younger versions of himself—wild, unpolished, but hungry.

Onyx knew he was playing with fire, putting himself on the line by dealing with their recklessness. Time was tight, and patience wasn't a luxury he had. Without wasting another second, he pushed off the vehicle and stepped in their direction, Onyx's voice tore through the air with a force that demanded attention—raw, commanding, and laced with an authority that left no room for defiance.

"What the f**k y'all lil' n***as doin'?" he barked, eyes locked on them, daring them to answer.

The kid with the strap panicked, bolting into the distance like a deer in headlights. The tall one standing beside the driver's door with his accomplice barked back, trying to mask his nerves with bravado. "Mindin' our f**kin' business, n***a. Fall back." His voice wavered, trying to sound tough but shaking under pressure.

"Bruh, hurry the f**k up! This n***a might've already called the folks!" His eyes darted wildly, the tension in his words clinging to the air.

Onyx remained unfazed, his voice slicing through the panic—calm but firm. "Y'all playin' gangsta with the wrong one, lil' bro. I'm just tryna keep it a buck with y'all—don't make the same dumbass moves I did when I was your age. Out here in broad daylight? Sh*t ain't sweet, and y'all ain't invisible."

He moved slow, intentional, reaching into his pocket to pull out two snake-eyes. The tall one froze, watching Onyx's every move like a hawk. He scribbled his name and number on each bill with the kind of cool confidence that said he wasn't worried. With his other hand still visible, Onyx stepped forward and placed the money on the hood of the Charger.

"First off, cool the f**k down. Stop all that flexin'. I ain't no cop, and I damn sure ain't no snitch. Y'all wanna keep hustlin' small-time, breakin' into cars like some crash dummies? Go ahead. But if y'all serious about stackin' real paper, cop a burner and hit that number. Or keep the cash and keep playin' with your freedom. It's your call."

The Charger's alarm erupted into the empty lot, loud and shrill like a warning siren. The tall one jumped, his nerves shot, and scurried to the front of the car, right hand still tucked beneath his shirt like he was grippin' the strap. Snatching the cash in one swift motion, he yanked open the hood, severed the power cable with practiced precision, and slammed it shut with a heavy clang that echoed through the lot. Meanwhile, his accomplice scrambled into the car, fumbling to get it started.

"Man, fall the f**k back, n***a! Worry 'bout your damn self before you end up on a t-shirt," the tall one barked, but his voice cracked, his false bravado slipping. He shot Onyx a hard look, his mind racing. Who the f**k was this dude? Cop? Some wannabe hero from the building? The paranoia was eatin' him alive. "Hurry up and crank this bitch, shawty!" he snapped, eyes shifting back to Onyx as he crept toward the passenger door. "I'll light this nosey-ass n***a up if I gotta."

Onyx didn't even blink. He could see through the act—the tall one had heart, sure, but fear had him twitchin' like a cornered animal. So, Onyx let him have his little moment. He took a step back and threw out one last question, his voice smooth as ever. "What's y'all name, shawty?"

Silence hung in the air as the passenger door slammed shut, the weight of the question lingering. The Charger roared with a metallic growl. Tires screeched as they peeled out of the lot, smoke curling up from the asphalt. Onyx watched them go, his lips curling into a faint smirk. He didn't need their names. He'd already planted the seed. Whether it grew? That was on them. Right now, Onyx had bigger moves to make.

Walking back toward the entrance as security bolted from the building, his mind churned, gears clicking into place with each calculated step. The streets had always been an option—hell, they'd taught him everything he knew. But deep down, he knew music was his real way out. The problem? The streets kept pullin' him back like quicksand. Then, an idea sparked—something bold.

"Start with what's right in front of you," he muttered to himself, a faint grin tugging at his lips. Throwing a party for the building? That was step one. A way to get his name out, lay down the groundwork, and establish something bigger. Something lasting.

Onyx's steps quickened, his thoughts clear and focused. Thinking outside the box wasn't just a skill—it was his specialty.

Chapter 13

"Checkmate in the Streets"

"Are you serious, bruh?" Amani asked, her voice a mix of disbelief and excitement as Onyx breezed into the condo, already hyping up his idea for a pool party. The way he framed it made it seem like an opportunity to network and gain exposure among the career-driven residents of the complex. But Amani knew better—Onyx was always ten steps ahead, and his plans always carried a hidden agenda. Still, she was game. She wanted her brother to win, even if it meant playing along with his antics.

"*Nakupenda*," he said, flashing a sly grin that softened Amani's skepticism. He always did that—disarmed people with charm, like a master strategist moving pieces on the chessboard of life.

"Man, I see the way you're plotting," Stacy chimed in, sprawled out on the loveseat. Then, with her usual lack of filter, she added, "Come here and let me taste your dick. Gotta see if you been messin' with another bitch—might be tryin' to throw me off, the loose booty bitch with your game."

Amani and Stacy burst into laughter as Onyx shook his head, muttering something under his breath. Stacy's crass humor hit every nerve, yet somehow, it still entertained. Amani leaned over, still giggling, to grab the stack of counterfeit checks off the coffee table to observe once more. With her earbuds in and her watch flashing a reminder, she tapped it impatiently. "Clock's ticking," she said.

Onyx ignored the chaos around him and slid into the kitchen. He poured a glass of cranberry juice, leaning back against the stove as he watched Stacy across the room. She was wild, unpredictable, and down for whatever—a perfect piece for his plan, even if she didn't realize it.

Time was running short. He stepped into the bedroom, threw on his clothes, and kept pushing Stacy off him. He liked the way she made his body react, but his mind was elsewhere—plotting, drained from dealing with Chardonnay's clingy ass all morning after the club, thinking about 44, and stuck on the statuesque woman who had him trippin' more than he wanted to admit. Right now, the mission was clear: stack bread, level up, and keep it moving. Nothing else mattered.

"Man, why the f**k you actin' funny, O?" Stacy demanded, annoyed by his constant rejection.

"Yo, chill. Business come first," he said flatly, barely sparing her a glance. The more she attempted to give him a quick dose of head, the more he realized he needed more than a certified head doctor on his team.

"Man, f**k all that," she snapped under her breath, falling back, knowing when not to push him.

Minutes later, everyone was dressed and ready, each of them clear on what needed to be done. They left the condo with purpose, poised to take action. Onyx sat in the backseat, his mind a blur of calculations, moving at lightning speed as he mentally mapped out each step of their plan. Amani, calm and focused, navigated the city streets, steering the car through the busy daytime traffic with precision. The buzz of the city around them—horns honking, pedestrians bustling—seemed distant to Onyx, his focus locked on the task at hand. But as Amani turned onto Simpson Road, the sight of a flashing roadblock up ahead hit them like a wall. The car went silent, their eyes widening in unison as the weight of the unexpected obstacle sank in.

"Sh*t," Amani muttered, turning down the music. "Stacy, secure the checks." Without hesitation, Stacy slid the envelope containing fake licenses and checks into the hidden compartment under the console. Too smooth. Almost too damn smooth.

When the officers approached with a K-9, Amani rolled down her window, trying to appear calm. But her heart was racing given all the police presence. Why were they being singled out when other cars were waved through? What had her brother done?

"Step out of the vehicle," one officer barked.

Amani hesitated. "What's going on?"

"Step out!"

With a carefully composed face, she unbuckled her seatbelt and stepped out of the car, her movements steady and precise. But beneath the surface, a storm churned. Her fingers, usually so sure, brushed the edge of the doorframe for a moment too long before falling to her sides. Had Onyx done something? Were they about to take him from her again?

Her gaze darted to him, her throat tightening as she watched the officers shove him against the car. They cuffed him with unnecessary force, their hands rough, but he didn't flinch. His expression was calm, almost eerily so, as though he had already surrendered to whatever came next. That quiet acceptance unsettled her more than rage ever could.

Stacy, meanwhile, was a stark contrast—spitting curses and thrashing as they frisked her on the sidewalk. Her fiery defiance seemed to fill the air, loud and raw, but it only made the silence between him and her more deafening. The quiet stretched, wrapping around her like a vice, as if this was the moment the ground beneath her would finally give way.

"What the f**k is going on?" Stacy snapped, her voice dripping with attitude.

"Shut up," the officer growled, ignoring her protests.

After ten agonizing minutes, the K-9 sniffed the car inside and out, and the officers searched every crevice. They found nothing. Reluctantly, they let them go. Amani sat back in the driver's seat, her jaw tight as she glared at the rearview mirror. Annoyance simmered beneath her calm exterior—the way they treated Onyx had her heated, but she kept it together.

"They said they pulled us over 'cause some dude and his sister killed his baby mama and her parents," Amani said, her voice clipped. "Apparently, their car looks like mine."

"Man, that's straight bullsh*t," Stacy snapped, still fuming. "And that cop grabbin' my ass? I should report his nasty ass. Ain't it supposed to be a woman doin' searches?"

"Bitch you've f**ked every n***a this side of the Chattahoochee and you mad 'cause a cop grabbed your ass," Amani said, laughing at her foolishness. "You're stupid!"

Ignoring Stacy's snarky remark, Amani's fingers drummed lightly on the steering wheel, her mind replaying everything. The way the officers moved, their sharp tone, the questions they asked—it all felt off, like there was something they weren't saying, a warning hanging in the air she couldn't quite shake.

The bright sun bathed Amani's face in a warm glow, casting a halo around her as if she were nestled in a bed of petals. Slouched in the backseat, staring out the window with an unreadable expression, Onyx broke the silence with a faint smirk. "That little stash spot came through. Didn't know you had that in the whip. Smart move, sis."

Amani glanced at him through the rearview mirror. "Yeah, well, you ain't the only one who knows how to cover their ass."

Onyx chuckled low under his breath, but his eyes were still distant. "Good thing you do. That could've gone way worse." The weight of his words hung in the car, unspoken fear and relief mingling in the quiet. Amani gripped the wheel a little tighter, her unease still lingering.

Pulling into Washington Park, Amani felt the tension dissolve the moment she spotted her girls, Yoshe and Jasmine, waiting near the curb. She parked and stepped out into the warm sun, her movements relaxed now. Walking over, she greeted them with warm, affectionate hugs.

The air around them filled with laughter and light-hearted teasing, a stark contrast to the chaos they'd left behind. Onyx lingered by the car, watching the trio with quiet admiration. Their connection was undeniable—a sisterhood that was messy, loud, and unshakably strong, built on a foundation of love and resilience. He admired their bond, the way they built each other up despite the constant bickering.

"Onyx, I'm calling you the Black Hole from now on," Jasmine teased, walking over to embrace with a hug.

He raised an eyebrow. "Why?" he asked, shaking his head as he admired the lime green Luxury Villa dress and strap-up stilettos she was rocking.

"Cause that ratchet bitch ain't left your side since you got out," she shot back, rolling her eyes. "Either your tongue or your dick got gravitational pull, bruh. Let up for some air, hoe."

The group erupted in laughter—everyone except Stacy, who threw a look of annoyance. "Bitch, your maggot ass mad 'cause he picked this tight exotic pussy over your stank loose booty ass," Stacy shit back, snapping her fingers and rolling her eyes. "Since you can't stop fantasizing 'bout it sliding back and forth in your throat or that elephant-sized pussy of yours, we can do a threesome once we finish busting these checks if you're 'bowdy bowdy,' bitch. I've told you before, we down to turn your ass out together."

Jasmine shot back, 'Tight exotic pussy, bitch, please. I wouldn't let a toy that's been sterilized after marinating in bleach for a month touch this royal pussy if it had ever been exposed to yours." She opened her arms wide to hug Stacy, while the others laughed at their ridiculous back-and-forth.

The insults flew, but the laughter never stopped. Onyx chuckled, pulling his phone from his pocket and stepping away from the car to snap pictures. "This right here is the sight of unfathomable money," he said, capturing Yoshe leaning against her F-type Jaguar, rocking a peach Cozy Cuddles set.

He had Amani stand with her car door open, showcasing her sexiness in the black-and-champagne Sensual Whisper set she was rocking. With their unbreakable sisterhood chemistry, he snapped Stacy in her white Turks & Caicos dress, standing with her back to Jasmine as she posed in front of her SUV.

"Y'all definitely gonna pay me for this photo shoot," Onyx said, as they stood beside him, admiring the shots—group and solo.

"N***a, whatever I owe you, take it out on your bitch mouth tonight," Yoshe joked, snatching his phone to look at her photos. "It should be illegal for me to look this muthaf**kin' sexy!"

"Bitch, you look like a four-week-old yeast infection," Stacy chimed, rolling her eyes when Yoshe glanced her way.

With business now at the forefront and her stomach still tight from the laughter, Amani walked over to her car. She retrieved the envelope from her secret compartment and tuned out the barbed insults still flying between them. Opening it, she handed out the fake IDs, fraudulent checks, and instructions to each person. Onyx was all in for the hustle, but he wasn't built for walking into a bank—he'd leave that part to the others. No more jokes, no more distractions. The mood shifted, and the lighthearted energy faded into sharp focus. Stacy's jealousy was unmistakable, her expression hardening as Onyx slid into the car with Yoshe. Without another word, they left the park, focused on hitting their marks with surgical precision.

No room for error.

Chapter 14

"Golden Hustle"

The sunlight filtered through the bank's tinted glass doors, catching the sheen of Yoshe's golden hair as it cascaded past her shoulders. Her striking green eyes swept the room, drawing attention as effortlessly as a queen entering her court. The diamonds set into her four open-faced gold teeth caught the light, winking like tiny stars. Heads turned, necks craned—customers, tellers, and even the security guard couldn't help but marvel at her sexiness.

Yoshe was radiant in a peach Cozy Cuddles set that hugged her curves with perfection. The soft fabric highlighted her toned silhouette, the understated elegance of the outfit drawing every pair of eyes in the bank. She approached the counter with effortless confidence, her walk a hypnotic rhythm of grace and power, reminiscent of an Andalusian horse in full stride. "May I speak to the manager, please?" she requested, her voice melodic yet firm. Within moments, a middle-aged man with a receding hairline and a clearance-rack suit emerged, his composure faltering under her gaze as he could do nothing but stare.

"Good afternoon," she said smoothly, extending a manicured hand when the manager arrived. "I'm Lisa Rainwater, CEO of Pinnacle Path."

The manager blinked as if trying to wake from a dream before taking her hand. "Pleased to meet you, Ms. Rainwater. Please, follow me to my office."

Inside, he gestured for her to sit. Yoshe settled into the leather chair, crossing her legs with deliberate elegance. The manager's gaze shifted, barely able to tear himself away from the way the peach fabric draped over her figure. Yoshe ignored his distraction, sliding a check across the desk as her green eyes locked onto his.

"I'd like to deposit this into my business account," she said confidently, then called out the account number in a smooth, melodic voice as he began typing on his computer. Her tone was calm yet commanding, laced with an authority that made the manager straighten in his chair. "Actually, I've changed my mind. I'd prefer to cash it. I feel like doing a little shopping."

The manager's fingers hovered over the keyboard, his usual methodical approach momentarily thrown off by her presence. As Yoshe leaned in closer, her gaze locking with his, a subtle heat spread across his chest. The soft, intoxicating scent of her perfume clouded his senses, making it harder to focus on the details in front of him. Her confidence was disarming, and with each word, she seemed to wrap him further in her influence.

He felt a flutter of unease, his professional instincts warring with an undeniable pull he couldn't quite resist. He knew there was a policy about large withdrawals, but as she continued to smile, her tone smooth and sweet, the rules felt less important. There was something about the way she looked at him—like she knew exactly what buttons to push— and it caused a surge of excitement, mixing with a twinge of guilt.

"Of course, Ms. Yoshe," he said, the words coming out softer than intended. The manager glanced at his screen, noting the account details. The account had been opened just two months prior, with a balance of $21,694. He quickly adjusted the transaction, bypassing the usual checks, too distracted by the pull of her charm to think clearly.

"Is there a problem?" she asked, her voice soft but edged with just enough charm to disarm him completely.

"Not at all," he stammered, quickly rising from his chair. "I'll take care of this personally."

He left the office with the check, a small smile tugging at his lips as he glanced back at her one last time. Moments later, he returned with an envelope, sliding it across the desk toward her.

"$18,375," he said, his voice barely above a whisper.

Yoshe smiled, her green eyes sparkling. "Thank you. You've been incredibly helpful." She slipped the envelope into her designer bag and rose, her heels clicking against the natural stone tile as she left the office.

Exiting the bank, Yoshe strutted across the parking lot, the soft peach fabric accentuating every confident step she took. Her golden hair caught the sun's rays, a halo of silk shimmering as if it had a life of its own. With each step, the light seemed to play in her hair, casting a glow that turned heads even in the busy parking lot. Men paused mid-conversation, their eyes tracking her as she made her way toward her car. She didn't look at them—didn't need to—but the magnetic pull of her presence had them all momentarily stunned.

Sliding into her Jaguar, Yoshe was already texting Amani, her fingers tapping the screen with precision. *"All good. Move the money and close the account."* She smirked as she hit send, her mind already on the next phase of the plan. The engine purred as she pulled out, the growl of the car's power making heads turn as she cruised down the road, perfectly aware of the men trying to get her attention. Some revved their engines in a futile attempt to impress her, while others hung out of their windows, offering flirty smiles or honks. Yoshe didn't even acknowledge them, her focus solely on what lay ahead.

As Yoshe eased off the accelerator and turned onto Roswell Road, the sun hung low in the sky, casting a warm golden hue over everything. Her Audi RS 3 idled by the pump, purring like a sleek predator. Onyx stood casually beside the door, his phone propped in the window frame, video chatting with his mother using sign language. He grinned when he saw her Jaguar pull up, but Yoshe, as always, skipped pleasantries.

She cruised to a halt next to him, lowered the window, and handed him the envelope through the open window. "Here," she said curtly. "Eighteen-three seventy-five. And Onyx—" Her voice dipped, playful yet clear—"don't even think about taking a dime of our money to buy your bitch some antibiotics. And for God's sake, don't f**k her in my car."

Onyx burst out laughing, shaking his head. "Yoshe, you wild."

"No I'm serious," she shot back, her smirk widening. "Keep her infections out of my business. I love my baby, and I don't have time to have her scrubbed down for a month to get the smell and germs out." She revved the engine, her laughter trailing as she sped off toward the next bank.

Onyx slid the envelope into his pocket, a faint grin playing on his lips as he turned around and signed, *I love you. I'll call later,* before ending the call with his mother. Settling into the driver's seat of the Audi, he carefully placed the envelope in the console. Shifting into gear, the engine purred beneath him, low and powerful, as he eased onto the road, the Audi gliding like a predator stalking its next move.

After hours of driving across the city and collecting money from the checks cashed by each crew member who hit their marks, Onyx finally met up with the team at Yoshe's loft off Howell Mill Road. The air was thick with the rich scent of her decadent candles, their soft glow casting a warm, inviting ambiance throughout the space.

Stacks of cash and envelopes covered the table—$138,382 in total. The atmosphere was celebratory, filled with laughter and the buzz of another accomplishment. Stacy got up from the table and wandered into the kitchen, returning moments later, munching on chocolate bars she'd grabbed from the fridge. "We really did that sh*t," she said, laughing as Jasmine, Amani, and Yoshe worked to sort the cash.

"Girl, don't eat that!" Yoshe snapped, jumping up to snatch the saucer from Stacy's hand. "Those bars got THC oil in them, you greedy ass bitch."

The room erupted in laughter as Stacy froze in confusion. "I'm definitely not going nowhere now," she muttered, sitting back at the table. "Y'all not about to laugh at me acting a fool while I'm high."

"You've lost your damn mind thinking you're about to contaminate my spot with your freakiness," Yoshe joked, walking back to the table to grab a stack of hundreds and tossing it at her. **"Your musty, bacteria-ridden ass is getting out of here."**

"F**k you!"

The banter flowed freely, laughter and insults bouncing around the room. Onyx, always one for theatrics, stood in the middle of the loft and started gyrating like a stripper, his exaggerated moves sending waves of laughter through the crew.

"Throw the stacks!" he hollered. "No single hundreds—stacks only!"

Jasmine rolled her eyes. "Ain't throwing sh*t. I'd rather pay the CDC to come quarantine you. Lord knows what Stacy done gave you."

The room exploded with laughter again, Yoshe clutching her stomach as tears streamed down her face. "Facts! Stacy, you and your man toy spreading diseases in my loft like it's a damn epidemic. Time for both of y'all to go."

Stacy fired back with an insult, the exchange growing louder and funnier. Amani chimed in, cross-legged at the table. "Y'all leave my brother alone. It's truly our fault we don't make Stacy wear a biohazard sign around her neck."

Amid the chaos, Onyx's phone buzzed in his pocket. He pulled it out, noting the name on the screen: 44. His smirk disappeared. "Yoshe, can I step out onto the patio to take this?"

"Yeah," she said, waving him off. "But don't touch my plants. Last thing I need is my calla lilies catching whatever STD you're carrying."

More laughter erupted as Jasmine added, "And don't come back until you've been decontaminated!"

Onyx shook his head, stepping onto the patio and shutting the door behind him. He answered the call, his tone immediately serious. "Yo, what happened this morning, fool? I called back, and you ain't answer."

44's deep voice came through, laced with his Jamaican accent. "Mi drop mi phone inna di dish wata, bredren. Been busy—jus' now get a new one."

Onyx rubbed the back of his neck, pacing back and forth as his mind churned through the plan. "A'ight, but listen—I'm throwing this pool party soon. Gonna open both doors, see which way benefits me most. I'll let the game play out, but I'm making sure I'm holding all the cards when it does." His gaze sharpened, a hint of anticipation in his voice. "No mistakes this time. It's gonna be a real test of who's loyal and who's just playing for their own pocket."

"Onyx," 44 said firmly, his tone weighted with wisdom. "Mi know yuh. Yuh nuh need fi open no door back to di street, seen? Stop lookin' fi respect weh yuh already got. Yuh nuh pan di edge—so why yuh a push yuhself?"

"Man, it ain't about that," Onyx argued, though his voice lacked conviction.

"Mi know yuh better," 44 interrupted. "Di streets got nuttin' fi yuh but loss. Focus. Be patient wit' di music. Yuh too smart fi dis foolishness."

The words hit harder than Onyx wanted to admit, but his mind was made up. Before he could respond, an incoming video call interrupted him. He sighed, saying, "Gotta go," and hung up.

When he answered the video call, his breath hitched. On the screen were the two men who had stolen the GT. They grinned, dangling a pair of keys as if taunting him.

"Pawn-pushing time," Onyx thought as he stared at the screen.

Chapter 15

The Foundation

Onyx wasn't just talking about the pool party anymore—he was moving like a man on a mission. Every day since convincing Speedy and Gunna to join Money Bag Mafia, he had been meeting up with them and the twins at a social lounge. It wasn't just about breaking down his vision for a street dynasty or recruiting their help with pulling the party together; it was about testing their sincerity, feeling out their potential, and seeing who was truly down to ride.

Talk was cheap. Onyx knew that. He had spent too many years locked up, hearing promises that never came through, seeing men switch up when the pressure was on. So, he played it differently. To prove his seriousness, he put money in their pockets—$250 each time they met. It wasn't just cash. It was currency in a deeper sense, a sign that he was building something real, something worth their loyalty. Speedy and Shadow weren't stupid; they peeped game, and Onyx could see their trust growing with each payout.

But the money wasn't the only piece. Onyx had his sister Amani, along with Jasmine, Stacy, and Yoshe, all helping him out. They were tapped into a different side of things, plugged into the shifts that had happened in the last decade while he was gone. The streets, the music, the social scene—it had all evolved. Onyx wasn't about to play catch-up; he was about to take over. The pool party was just the start, a way to set the tone for Money Bag Mafia's presence, to turn heads and let people know who was really making moves.

Still, Onyx knew the reality. A party alone wasn't enough. He wasn't about to throw a one-night event just for the sake of fun. He was mentally plotting—every conversation, every handshake, every dollar spent was another brick in the foundation of something bigger. The pool party was bait. A spectacle. The kind of thing that made people watch, whisper, and wonder. But Onyx? He was already thinking ten steps ahead.

Something had to be done. Drastically. The streets weren't forgiving, and Onyx wasn't naive enough to think he could just step in and take what he wanted without resistance. He needed leverage, power, a way to make sure when he moved, people moved with him. This wasn't just about having a good time or making connections. It was about establishing dominance, planting a flag that nobody could ignore.

As he sat back in the lounge, watching Speedy talk with Shadow while Gunna scrolled through his phone, he exhaled slowly. He had the players. He had the plan. Now, all he needed was the right moment to set everything in motion.

Chapter 16

"The Cost of Loyalty"

Amani had always ensured Onyx benefited financially whenever he helped her, but this time felt different. The girls handed him $5,000 each from their share after cashing checks across the city, and Onyx wasn't about to let a single dollar go to waste. Onyx used the funds to invest in his vision. He'd recently put a down payment on a sleek white Chevrolet Camaro and was sparing no expense to ensure the pool party—a critical move in his plan—would be a success.

A few nights ago, after sitting down with Amani and opening up about his true intentions, he'd been at a loss for words when she responded with understanding. She acknowledged the mental struggle he was fighting, though she wished he'd trust himself and exercise patience. Onyx realized that keeping his plan a secret from Amani would have backfired, potentially damaging their bond. Her understanding strengthened their relationship, and he felt compelled to honor that trust.

Feeling grateful, Onyx sent Amani to a spa and headed to Phipps Plaza.

"Excuse me, sir, your total is $1,681.73," the Tiffany store clerk advised politely as Onyx admired a gold Tiffany Triton Clasp necklace displayed in the case. His eyes gleamed with admiration, imagining the design draped around his neck. Still, he didn't want to embarrass himself by returning it if he came up short.

Reaching into his crocodile-patterned messenger bag, he retrieved a stack of cash secured with rubber bands. Counting out $1,700, he handed the bills to the clerk. Though dressed casually yet polished, he didn't realize his demeanor still screamed street. As the clerk processed his order, Onyx's phone buzzed with an incoming call. He answered but was instantly distracted by her megawatt smile and striking violet-colored eyes. Her presence was so magnetic that he barely registered his cousin's voice and hung up without a word when the clerk handed him his purchase.

"Thank you!" Onyx said, his fingers brushing hers as he took the receipt and bag. Her glossy brown skin was as soft as it looked, and for a brief moment, he thought about striking up a conversation. But with time pressing, he held back, though their locked gazes lingered in his mind as he walked out.

Onyx glanced back through the window, silently promising to return. The sight of her parting her sleek black hair with Venus-red nails ignited a spark of intrigue. "Damn, she's sexy as f**k," he muttered, drawing giggles from two women passing by.

"Well, you're handsome as f**k too, brother," one of them quipped, tossing her hair over her shoulder. Onyx blushed but kept walking, focused on his mission.

Onyx went store to store, buying gifts for Amani. Since his return, she'd been more than a sister—she was his anchor. Expressing his gratitude through actions rather than words felt necessary. Amani had opened his eyes—he'd been thinking too small, like a street hustler trapped in old habits. But she'd shown him the bigger picture—security cameras he didn't recognize in the building, strategic blind spots to handle business in, and even the willingness of the building manager to turn a blind eye for a cut. For the first time, Onyx felt like he was strategizing, not just reacting.

As he left the mall, carrying multiple bags, he felt the weight of people's stares. He knew he looked like money, but he also knew the importance of his next move. To level up, he couldn't remain a pawn in Amani's or 44's schemes; he had to define his own path. Glancing at his watch as he reached his Camaro, he shouted into the open sky, "Money Bag Mafia on the rise!"

After loading the bags into the trunk and sliding into the driver's seat, Onyx dialed his cousin back to reiterate the day's plan. Everything had to go perfectly—there was too much on the line. Hanging up, he called Amani to ensure she was still enjoying herself at the spa. With his seat leaned back and Trap music blasting through the speakers, he moved through traffic, his mind racing with thoughts of what lay before him.

Once home, Onyx wasted no time. With the bags in hand, he headed straight to Amani's room. Clothes and shoes were scattered everywhere, so he began tidying up before carefully arranging the three outfits he'd purchased across her bed. Each outfit was complete with stilettos and a matching bottle of perfume.

"I can dress your ugly, fat-headed ass better than you dress yourself, sis," he muttered with a smirk, admiring his work.

When he reached for the Tiffany items to place in her nightstand drawer, he froze at the sight of a collection of sex toys. Groaning, he decided against it. "Your nasty, freaky ass," he mumbled under his breath sliding it back closed without hesitation.

Instead, he laid the items on the mantle beneath her TV. The Tiffany Heart Tag Toggle necklace and bracelet were hung delicately on the wings of a large crystal hummingbird he'd purchased as a symbol of his love for her. **Onyx stepped back, picturing Amani's reaction.** With everything in place, Onyx headed to his room to shower, gearing up for the next step in his plan.

Chapter 17

"Crossroads of Loyalty"

Onyx stepped out of the shower, steam trailing behind him. He toweled off quickly, then slid into an all-black fitted jogging suit, paired with a black T-shirt and matching black shoes. His movements were swift and deliberate as he grabbed his phone off the dresser and headed for the door. Since the food delivery service had sent him a text confirming the order was neatly placed on the doorstep, he unlocked the door and grabbed it.

Also noticing a text from Speedy, Onyx grinned. Four days after initiating Speedy and Shadow into the MBM family, Speedy was already proving himself trustworthy as a capo. The message was short and direct, outlining a successful move with no loose ends—a testament to Speedy's efficiency. Onyx couldn't help but feel a surge of pride. Building Money Bag Mafia wasn't just about loyalty; it was about finding people who could think on their feet, adapt, and execute under pressure. Speedy was checking all the boxes, and Onyx knew he'd made the right choice.

As he unlocked the door and retrieved the food, his thoughts lingered on Speedy's next test. Trust wasn't given lightly, and Onyx had no intention of lowering his guard. But for now, Speedy was on track, and Onyx allowed himself a rare moment of satisfaction before refocusing on the day's challenges ahead.

Onyx rested on the sofa with a lamb gyro in hand, licking his fingers clean as an old episode of Godfather of Harlem played in the background. He answered his phone on the third ring. "Yeah, what's the move, shawty?" Onyx's tone was calm, but adrenaline stirred in his veins.

"Bredda, yuh sure dis a road yuh waan walk? Yuh just touch road, mi yute," 44 said, his voice heavy with concern. "Yuh cyah mek di system grab yuh 'gain, mi nah lie. Yuh nuh tink 'bout di ones who bawl fi yuh when yuh gone?"

"Shawty, you know I don't open doors just to close 'em—I step inside," Onyx replied, his tone hardening as he cleaned up behind himself and grabbed his keys.

"Alright den, mi seh TJ deh pon West End by Popeye's. Him deh inna green Jeep. Watch yuh moves though, mi bredrin. Remember seh Onyx nuh supposed to be Trigga. Yuh a play wid fire."

Onyx nodded and ended the call. He knew 44 meant well, but he couldn't slow down now—too much was already in motion. Deep down, he knew TJ was trouble—'Mr. Double Cross, who was infamous for using women to set up dealers and robbing them blind. But Onyx also knew TJ respected the darkness he carried inside. That was leverage.

As Onyx headed for the door, his phone rang again. He answered without checking the screen. "Yeah?"

"Yo, Onyx, what's good? This Soundwave—the producer from the club. Amani introduced us." The calmness in the voice felt out of place.

"Wassup, fam?" Onyx replied, locking his door behind him. He slipped his keys into his pocket and walked to the elevator, his tennis shoes making soft scuffing sounds against the floor. As the elevator descended, Soundwave's voice filled his ear, talking about music, the exposure he could provide, and the studio time he had lined up. But Onyx's mind was already elsewhere, focused on the game. The producer's smooth pitch barely registered—his focus was heavy with the moves he had in motion. Not in the mood for small talk, Onyx invited Soundwave to the pool party and ended the call.

For a moment, as he stepped out of the building and into his car, he wondered if the call had been a sign to back out. Sitting in the driver's seat, the weight of his choices pressed on him like an incoming tide. His mother's promise came to mind, a reminder of the path he'd once vowed to follow—one that now felt distant. But the pull of unfinished business was too strong, dragging him back into the shadows of the life he couldn't seem to escape.

With a heavy sigh, he tightened his grip on the steering wheel and started the engine, the low hum of the car filling the silence. He couldn't ignore the gnawing sense of dread in his gut, but he pushed it aside. There were no second chances in this world, no time for second-guessing. He'd made his bed, and now he had to lie in it, no matter how sharp the edges.

Nodding to the aggressive beat of Kool-Ace's latest single, he let the music fuel his focus as he rolled through the city, ready to see it all through. Fifteen minutes later, he pulled into Popeye's parking lot, scanning his surroundings. A grayish-blue BMW 735i with chrome rims caught his eye. Behind the wheel sat a woman with caramel skin that seemed to glow under the radiant sunlight. Her thick, coiled hair framed her heart-shaped face, and her full lips moved slightly as she focused on her phone. Her curves filled the driver's seat effortlessly, and the confidence in her body language made Onyx pause.

He considered introducing himself and asking for her number but shook off the thought. Business came first. Spotting the money green Jeep Wrangler parked behind the building, Onyx walked over. He slid into the passenger seat and greeted TJ with a quick dab.

"Look, Trigga, my girl got a GPS on this n***a's car. Dude came down from Memphis last night to cop six bricks from Light-skinned Trent. Now he meeting someone from Stonebrook over at the shopping center on Old National to grab ten bags of White Rhino," TJ said, handing Onyx a handheld tracking device with the mark's location. "A heavyset n***a driving a pine green Lincoln Navigator. Shawty, you gotta murk this n***a. If you don't, my girl get exposed, and you know that means I get exposed."

Onyx nodded, his expression hardening as he absorbed the details. He wanted to tell TJ he no longer went by Trigga but thought against it—this wasn't the time. "No doubt," he said curtly, locking in on the task ahead. With everything he needed, he stepped out of the Jeep, his mind steady and locked on the mission, his focus unwavering as he prepared to move.

Back in his Chevy, Onyx cruised to Pittman Park and pulled up on the hill overlooking the field. After scanning the area for any signs of trouble, he got out and crossed to the opposite side of the street, walking up the sidewalk that led to the back of Parks Middle School. There, he retrieved a hidden key from beneath the bumper of a black Ford Mustang parked beside the curb and slid into the driver's seat.

The glove compartment held a Glock-21, black hat, gloves, and a nylon mask. Onyx pulled the gun out, his fingers working swiftly as he removed the magazine to check for bullets. Satisfied, he slid the magazine back in with a firm click, then cocked the gun, letting the action put one in the chamber. Without a holster, he laid the weapon gently in his lap, the cold steel a steady reminder of the business at hand. A faint smile tugged at his lips as he glanced at the Glock, the weight of it grounding him.

Next, he checked the tracking device, the screen lighting up to confirm the target's location. Everything was in position. His mind drifted for a moment, replaying the conversation from earlier, but he quickly shook it off. This wasn't the time for hesitation. He reached for the black hat and pulled it low over his eyes, adjusting it for a snug fit. The gloves followed, slipping them on like a second skin, and finally, the nylon mask, folded neatly in his lap, ready for when he'd need it.

With a deep breath, Onyx started the car, the engine roared, breaking the silence of the empty lot. The sound echoed briefly before settling into a steady hum. He glanced at the dashboard clock—timing was everything. As the car idled, he allowed himself one last moment of stillness, his fingers drumming lightly on the steel in his lap. Then, with his gear ready and his mind set, Onyx eased the car into drive, merging into the night. The road stretched ahead like a battlefield, and he embraced it, knowing there was no turning back.

Onyx merged onto I-285 East, his pulse quickening as he spotted the Lincoln Navigator up ahead. He eased off the gas, falling in behind a Toyota Corolla to avoid suspicion. His phone rang. It was Amani. "Yo, wassup, sis?" Onyx answered, his eyes locked on the Navigator.

"Big bro! Thank you. I love you—like for real, you didn't have to go this hard for me—especially cleaning my damn room." Her voice was warm, her excitement spilling through the phone.

"Sis, stop playin'. Ain't sh*t too hard for you. You my heart, lil' sis. You know how we rock," Onyx said, his voice softening for the first time all night.

"I mean it, O. You always hold me down, even in ways you have no real idea," Amani's voice cracked, the rawness in her tone reflecting the depth of their bond. "Sometimes I don't even know how to say thank you, but I feel it… deep, like you're the only one who really understands me, who's always had my back, no matter what, even when you were away."

"Shawty, quit talkin' crazy. You got me out here smilin' like a goofy," Onyx said, laughing lightly. "But hold up. What's all this extra mushy sh*t? You a'ight?"

"Yeah, yeah, I'm good. Just wanted you to know I see you, big bro. I appreciate you," she replied, lifting the necklace to the camera to show him. "Look at this! You snapped with the Tiffany Heart Tag Toggle set. You really outdid yourself."

"Just a lil' somethin' to say *nakupenda,* sis. You worth it," Onyx said, merging lanes. The light ahead turned red, and he cursed under his breath.

"Everything cool?" Amani asked, her voice quick with concern.

"Yeah, just tryna stay ahead of this traffic. What you wearin' tonight?" Onyx asked, shifting the tone.

Amani laughed and started holding up outfits to the camera. "Which one, O?"

"Damn, not that one! You tryin' to have these dudes actin' crazy?" he said, grinning as he chose the least revealing option.

"Fine, fine," Amani said, rolling her eyes playfully. "I love you, big bro. See you in a minute, and stay safe, a'ight?"

"Always," Onyx replied, hitting the gas as the light turned green. Hanging up, he dropped the phone into his lap and scanned the road ahead. The dim glow of streetlights blurred past as he pulled into the shopping center parking lot, his pulse steady but his mind racing with possibilities and risks.

He wasn't sure if he was after respect, revenge, or redemption—but tonight, he'd find out soon enough.

Chapter 18

"No Turning Back"

Seeing the Navigator parked on the far end as the GPS indicated, Onyx backed into a vacant spot two aisles over. Cutting the engine but leaving the keys in the ignition, he sat for a moment, letting the silence wrap around him as his eyes swept over the parking lot. He shifted the rearview mirror so he could see the Navigator clearly, his eyes narrowing as the plan began to unfold in his mind.

A small voice in the back of his head nagged at him. This wasn't the life he envisioned when he thought about freedom—every move felt like a calculated gamble with stakes he didn't want to consider. His pulse quickened as he slid on the mask and opened the door, the scent of fried chicken and the sharp tang of exhaust fumes filling his nostrils as he prepared for what was about to go down.

Exiting the vehicle, the crisp night air brushed against his face. Moving quickly and quietly toward the rendezvous point, Onyx walked with purpose. The parking lot felt vast and exposed, but his body language projected confidence as he positioned himself where he wouldn't be seen.

A yellow Ford Explorer pulled up beside the Navigator, and Onyx's gaze locked onto the prey stepping out. "Damn, this n***a too comfortable," Onyx thought, a mix of disbelief and disgust in his chest. The man was completely oblivious, too absorbed in his own world to realize a predator was in pursuit of a crown, and he was a crucial piece in helping him claim it. Fat Boy slid into the Explorer, ready to handle business like it was just another day. Onyx's lips curled into a smirk—this was about to be even sweeter than he imagined. He eased closer, staying low, his eyes tracking every move, calculating how much time he had before Fat Boy finished his business and came back.

Mentally transforming into Tigga, Onyx became one with the darkness, a shadow blending seamlessly between the parked vehicles.

His breathing slowed, every muscle in his body coiled like a spring ready to unleash. His heart hammered against his ribs, but his focus was unyielding, locked intently on the target.

Fat Boy exited the Explorer, his hefty frame illuminated briefly by the glow of the exterior lights as the vehicle drove off, leaving him alone in the lot. Oblivious to the danger lurking nearby, he moved to the rear of the SUV, lifting the hatch with a grunt. The brown bookbag in his hands looked inconspicuous, but Onyx knew better. It wasn't just a bag—it was one key to a move that was about to change everything.

Fat Boy fumbled slightly as he adjusted the bag, placing it carefully in the trunk. Onyx observed every detail: the way the man moved, the way his head turned just enough to check his surroundings without really seeing anything. He was too comfortable, too confident, and Onyx knew he wouldn't see it coming.

Like a predator stalking its prey, Onyx moved with silent precision, his Glock already in hand. He closed the distance in seconds, his movements calculated and unrelenting. The cold steel of the weapon glinted faintly under the pale parking lot lights as he raised it, aiming directly at the back of Fat Boy's head.

"Don't move," Onyx growled, his voice low and dangerous, each word cutting through the noise of the busy shopping center parking lot. Cars passed by, their engines humming, and people chatted as they moved toward the entrance, but in that moment, it was as if the world had narrowed down to just him and the person in front of him.

Fat Boy froze, his hands instinctively rising in surrender. The look in Onyx's eyes was piercing, devoid of mercy—a look sharp enough to carve fear into the bravest soul.

"Turn around slow," Onyx commanded, his voice steady, each syllable carrying the weight of absolute authority. Fat Boy complied, his eyes wide with panic as they met Onyx's.

Fat Boy turned, shocked, his hands trembling as he tried to make sense of what was happening. "What the hell?" he blurted, his voice cracking. His mental rage surged, and Onyx could see it in his eyes— that he wasn't going to comply easily. "Pussy n***a, do ya know who da f**k I am?" he spat, his voice growing more defiant, though the fear was still there.

Onyx didn't flinch. "Give me the keys and get your bitch ass on the ground," he growled, his voice a low, menacing whisper. Every muscle in his body was taut, his focus laser-sharp. He shifted his eyes quickly to make sure no one else was in the SUV, then centered his gaze back on Fat Boy. The air felt thick, the tension almost unbearable.

"Ain't giving…"

Without giving him a chance to say anything else, Onyx squeezed the trigger twice. 'Blocka! Blocka!' The sound of the gunshots rang out, echoing through the parking lot, followed by the sickening splatter of blood as the bullets tore through Fat Boy's skull. His body crumpled, lifeless, before hitting the asphalt. Onyx moved fast, adrenaline surging as he rifled through the man's pockets. Cash. The fob. No gun. His heart stuttered. He scanned his surroundings—then froze. A gray Volvo was approaching, its driver locked onto him with an unnerving intensity. For a moment, Onyx's stomach tightened. Was this backup, or just an unlucky witness?

He didn't hesitate. Without a second thought, Onyx lifted the Glock and fired again. 'Blocka! Blocka! Blocka!' The driver's head snapped back, and the car slowly rolled into the back of a parked vehicle. No more questions. No more witnesses.

Onyx jumped into the Navigator, his hands steady despite the chaos swirling around him. He hit the start button, and the engine came to life with a powerful growl, blending seamlessly with the distant screams and the murmur of the parking lot. Without a second glance, he shifted into drive, his foot slamming into the accelerator as he weaved out of the lot, merging into traffic with calculated precision.

The Navigator felt strange in his hands, like it didn't belong to him. But the adrenaline pumping through his veins drowned out the unease. His eyes flicked to the rearview mirror, scanning for danger. Finding nothing alarming, he quickly dialed T-Roc's number, issuing instructions to move the Mustang as he sped through the light and merged onto the expressway. Hanging up, he texted the gate code to the other twin—

Gunna who already knew the drill. The plan was unfolding, but Onyx remained cautious. He didn't trust TJ—never had, never would. He needed time—time to tear through the SUV, to figure out what was truly hidden inside and what it all meant. Every second counted, but his gut told him to stay alert. He knew TJ had a way of smiling in your face while plotting behind your back.

After exiting the expressway and pulling up to the security gate of a secluded subdivision in Union City, the weight of the situation pressed down on him like a heavy blanket. For the first time, he noticed a security camera fixed above the gate, its unblinking eye recording every move. His stomach tightened, a cold sweat forming on his brow. He shifted uncomfortably in the driver's seat, debating whether to proceed or turn back. The camera's presence was a reminder: no moves could be erased, no shadows could hide him now.

He punched in the code and drove around to the back, parking near the trash area. For a long moment, Onyx just sat there, staring out through the windshield, listening to the faint sounds of life in the distance—the rustling of leaves in the breeze, the distant chirp of crickets, the faint hum of the night air. It should have been peaceful, but there was something about this moment that felt wrong.

He had just killed two people. There was no undoing it. The weight of it sank in—but it wasn't regret. It was power, raw and electric, surging through his veins. He had been behind bars for years—fighting to survive. And now, he was free. Free to make his own choices. Free to take what he wanted. Free to change his life—or to keep slipping deeper into the same choices that had landed him in prison in the first place.

His mind screamed at him to do better, to break the cycle. But every inch of his body was telling him that he was doing exactly what he needed to do. The thrill of it, the control, the power—it felt too good to let go of.

He took a deep breath, the air thick with the scent of exhaust and decay. He wasn't the same man he was before. He was stronger. Smarter. More dangerous. He stepped out of the Navigator, moving with purpose, and began his search, feeling the weight of the money and drugs in his hands as he pulled out the bags in the trunk. 6 kilos. 10 bags of White Rhino. Over $40k in cash.

Onyx was in control now.

Trigga would never have hesitated, questioned the path he was on, or second-guessed his decisions. But that man was gone, buried beneath the scars of betrayal and the lessons of the streets. He had learned the hard way that control wasn't just taken—it was earned, seized, and wielded with precision.

His fingers tightened around the straps of the duffel bags as he scanned the area, his instincts sharp, honed by countless nights like this one. The atmosphere seemed to breathe with him, shadows shifting as if they recognized who he had become. Each step he took carried a confidence that was unshakable, a silent declaration to the world that he was no longer anyone's pawn. This wasn't just proving something to himself anymore—it was domination. Onyx now had the power, the tools, and the will to keep it. And he wasn't about to let anyone take it from him.

After dumping the unnecessary items in the dumpster, he quickly counted out $10,000 and stashed it in the center console. Gunna arrived moments later, parking beside him, his eyes wide with excitement.

"What does it look like back there?" Onyx asked, his voice low, scanning the area.

"Police everywhere, cuz. They were starting to pull in after my bruh dropped me off. If we hadn't been in position like you said, I wouldn't have made it out," Gunna replied, his face lit with a mix of excitement and relief.

"A'ight, we gotta move. Follow me and stay alert. The money in the center console is for you and your brother to split," Onyx said, his tone firm as he grabbed the bookbag and slid into the Mustang. The engine growled as he sped off, dialing Stacy's number.

"Hello!" Stacy's voice came through the phone, nonchalantly and demanding.

"Damn, it don't sound like that mouth, missin' this dick the way you just answered," Onyx teased, his grin spreading across his face as he cruised through the streets.

"Boy, bye, stop playin' with me. Where my gifts at?" she snapped, irritated.

"Listen, I got you. But right now, I need you to come scoop me. I'm stranded by the airport," he said, his voice calm despite the storm inside him. His eyes flicked to the patrol car up the street, a slight unease creeping in. He wasn't outright worried, but he couldn't shake the thought—had the Navigator been reported yet? He didn't trust anyone, not even in moments like this.

"Where your car at? How the hell you get stranded? What bitch you out there with?" Stacy asked, too curious for Onyx's liking.

"Baby, hold on, let me hit you right back, it's my mom on the other line," he lied, cutting the call short before she could press him further. He dialed his cousin T-Roc and gave clear instructions to pick them up. It was a decision he should have made from the start instead of foolishly trying to secure Stacy as an alibi witness.

As the car glided along the streets, Onyx's mind raced. A few weeks ago, he'd been locked up, wondering if he'd make it out alive. Now, he was free, rolling in cash, and controlling his own fate. Six bricks of powder. Ten bags of White Rhino. Over fifty-grand. This was his moment. A part of him reveled in the power, but another part of him couldn't shake the thought of how quickly everything could unravel. This was the life he chose. But it was the only one that made sense now.

"*Nimerudi muthaf**ka… Nimerudi muthaf**ka…*" he muttered under his breath, the words feeling almost like a prayer as he repeated them for the next several minutes. The rhythm of the chant calmed the storm inside him, grounding him in the moment. He had come a long way from the concrete walls of the prison, but the ghosts of his past still lingered—haunting every decision, every choice.

Thinking about his next move as he pulled into the scrapyard, Onyx felt excitement bubbling under his cool exterior. Parking the Mustang, he stepped out and threw up his index finger at Gunna, a silent signal to wait. His tennis shoes crunched against the gravel as he made his way into the yard, his pace quick but calculated. The air was thick with the metallic tang of rust and oil, blending with the steady drone of machinery.

He stopped a few workers, asking where Sam was, his intense gaze sweeping the yard. His eyes eventually landed on him—slouched over a forklift, head bobbing as he teetered on the edge of sleep. Onyx shook his head, a wry smirk tugging at the corner of his lips. Same old Sam. Always unbothered, moving at his own pace, even with chaos buzzing all around.

Grabbing a piece of scrap metal from a nearby pile, Onyx walked up and banged it against the side of the forklift. The clang echoing across the yard. "Sam!" he barked, his voice heavy enough to slice through the noise of the scrapyard.

Sam jolted upright, his bleary eyes blinking against the sudden noise. He looked at Onyx as if he'd seen a ghost, then a grin spread across his face. "Ya ugly muthaf**ka! Damn, my dawg, when they let yo psycho ass outta prison?" He hopped off the lift and pulled Onyx into a tight hug, laughing. "Don't tell me Trigga back at work!"

Onyx laughed, but it was a hollow sound. "I been out a little over three weeks, Shawty. And I need you right now." He pulled out several stacks of rubber-banded cash, watching Sam's eyes widen as the bills shifted between his fingers. Money always spoke louder than words. For a brief moment, Onyx contemplated advising him that his name was Onyx now, not Trigga. The old name carried too much weight, too much blood. But with no intention of ever seeing Sam again, he remained silent.

"I got two rides I need you to crush. Right now. No time to waste." Onyx's tone was firm, leaving no room for negotiation.

Sam's gaze lingered on the cash in Onyx's hand, his fingers twitching with anticipation. "$4500, and I'll make it happen," he said, his voice eager but still respectful. He usually never asked for more than a thousand, but this was Onyx. The man always came through when it counted. But after seeing that much money in his hand, Sam couldn't help but feel the urge to push his luck, trying to take advantage of the opportunity.

Without hesitation, Onyx peeled off the money and handed it over. Sam stuffed the stacks into his pocket with a grin, his eyes darting toward the crusher. "I'll be right back," he said, already moving with purpose. Sam disappeared toward the trailer, his steps quickening with excitement. Exiting the control booth moments later, his grin still wide, the rumble of the hydraulic crusher filled the air. Sam waved his hand, signaling for Onyx to bring the vehicles inside. "Let's get this done!" he hollered.

Scurrying back to the car, knowing every second counted, Onyx motioned for Gunna to follow. He slid into the driver's seat. His movements were swift. Using his rearview mirror, he carefully backed the car into the scrapyard, stopping just a few feet from the compactor. Onyx removed the Glock from his waistband, tossing it into the glove compartment alongside the tracking monitor. He grabbed the bookbag from the passenger seat, his phone clutched in his hand as he stepped out. Turning to Gunna, who had just pulled up beside him, Onyx waved him out of the car.

"Watch this sh*t, cuz," he called over, his voice low and commanding. "But stay alert—it's almost done."

Gunna nodded, his hand brushing against the gun tucked in his waistband. Onyx could see the tension in his body, feel it in the air between them. They both knew they were in dangerous territory. One wrong move, and it could all come crashing down. This was it—the last step to erase any trace of the chaos he had unleashed.

The metallic clang of the crane's arm reverberated through the scrapyard as it descended, gripping one of the vehicles like a predator seizing its prey. Onyx stood still, his sharp gaze locked on the car as it was hoisted off the ground. The crushing machine below loomed, hungry and efficient, ready to swallow the evidence whole.

The violent crunch of metal echoed, a harsh symphony of destruction that vibrated through Onyx's chest. He watched as the car folded in on itself, crushed into a mangled heap. It was a process he'd witnessed countless times, yet it always left its mark—a visceral reminder of how easily problems could be erased.

As the crusher finished its work, Onyx felt a strange mix of satisfaction and unease. The car wasn't just a vehicle anymore; it was a memory obliterated, a loose end tied up. But the finality of it all weighed heavily on him, pressing against the adrenaline coursing through his veins.

This was his reality now. The life he had clawed his way back into after years of confinement. Each choice, each action, pulled him deeper into the current, leaving no room for regret or hesitation. **The scrapyard mirrored the choices that had led him here.**

They moved to the front entrance, waiting for T-Roc to pull up. Sam was beside him, reminiscing about old times, their laughter drifting around them. "Shawty, you remember that time we robbed that n***a on Graham Rd. for them bags of weed, and you set your whole damn face on fire tryin' to burn the stolen car?" Onyx asked, the memory coming back with a strange sense of nostalgia.

Sam laughed loud enough for Gunna to clutch his stomach. "Cuz, this crazy ass n***a face and neck were 10 shades lighter than a bald pussycat. Now look at him. Darker than a motherf**ker!"

Gunna was still laughing when T-Roc's canary Chevy Caprice rolled into the lot, its engine rumbling as it cruised to a smooth stop beside them. Gunna couldn't help but wonder how Sam had managed to burn his entire face off with a car fire he started, but there wasn't enough time to ask. Gunna opened the rear passenger door and slid in, while Onyx moved around to the other side.

"Preciate that, shawty! You already know I f**k with you the long way!" Onyx said, nodding to Sam and throwing up the deuces.

"Love, fam," Sam replied, pulling a cigarette from his pocket and lighting it up.

T-Roc's eyes darted between Onyx and his brother before he asked, "Where your car at, cuz?" He shifted back into drive.

"At the top of Pittman Park, on the field side," Onyx answered, his voice steady, but something darker had taken hold of him. The excitement of the moment was gone, replaced by cold calculation. He looked out the window, the city lights flashing by, but a small, unsettling thought gnawed at the back of his mind. What if another camera had caught his face—one he hadn't noticed before he pulled up to the gate? The possibility crept through him like ice water in his veins. His breath grew shallow as the thought snowballed.

Could the police retrace his GPS movements? The idea made his chest constrict. It wasn't just this camera; it was the trail he might've left behind, breadcrumbs leading them straight to him. Every turn, every stop, every pause—it was all logged somewhere, wasn't it? A simple mistake could unravel everything. He needed to talk to his sister.

Leaning back against the seat, the bookbag between his legs, Onyx sat in silence, reflecting on the chaos he had created. The thrill of freedom had worn off, leaving behind only the brutal reality of what he'd chosen. A cold, relentless path that didn't allow room for mistakes. He had one more stop before he could relax—if he could even call it that anymore.

And with that, he knew—there was no turning back.

Chapter 19

"Building the Empire"

Onyx felt the weight of every decision as he pieced together his empire. He leaned back in the Caprice, his mind playing out each move like a chess game, every piece a consequence of his choices. His blood cousins, T-Roc and Gunna, sat in the car, their energy electric as they talked about the pool party. Their history was carved into scars—loyalty tested in shootouts, robberies, and murders. But Onyx knew loyalty always came with a price. He trusted them, yet trust in his world was as fragile as glass—liable to shatter at any moment.

The twins were reckless, unpredictable, yet Onyx knew they would stand by him no matter what. He also knew better than anyone: even blood ties could be severed when the stakes were high enough. He wasn't naive—he had learned that the hard way.

With T-Roc, Gunna, and two loyal recruits—Speedy and Shadow—the foundation of Money Bag Mafia (M.B.M.) was taking shape. Five members, each with a role to play. T-Roc and Gunna brought a wild, reckless edge, while Speedy and Shadow added muscle and a sharpness that Onyx respected. Together, they formed the core of what Onyx intended to build, and there was no room for mistakes, no second chances—a cold truth Onyx understood all too well.

M.B.M. wasn't just a crew; it was going to be a movement. Onyx envisioned it becoming a name that would resonate through Atlanta's underworld—a force to be reckoned with, feared, and respected. This was the stage where Onyx would prove he was playing a different game than everyone else.

As the three of them sat in the car, Onyx couldn't help but feel a rush of excitement. The pieces were falling into place, and the pool party was the perfect stage—distinguishing checkmate wasn't just the endgame; it was the moment he proved he had made the right decision.

The money, the work—everything had to be handled with precision. Speedy and Shadow were just cogs in his plan, but the twins, were the real stones to structure the empire around. They were the ones who would help establish the family name in the game, moving product, gaining respect, and making sure nothing stood in their way.

"The muthaf**king pool party tomorrow, so let's close this last door," Onyx said, his words laced with a confidence that only someone in control could exude. The sound of tires crunching on the asphalt broke the stillness of the night as T-Roc eased his ride up beside the Camaro, freshly returned from a robbery gone dark. Onyx and Gunna doors swung open, and for a moment, the neighborhood seemed to hold its breath, the only sounds coming from the distant hum of nature around them.

They all shared a brief laugh, the weight of the night lifting for just a second. Onyx leaned forward in the seat, exchanging a few words with the twins before they dapped each other up. With a smooth motion, he grabbed the bag, slinging it over his shoulder as he stepped out of the Caprice.

As he walked around the car, T-Roc caught his eye with a quick nod—a silent signal that everything was cool, the deal done. Sliding into the driver's seat of his Camaro, Onyx turned the ignition and watched the twins pull off, their car cutting through the night, heading in a different direction, now that the mission for the moment was complete.

Sitting in the Camaro, Onyx was already thinking ahead. He dialed TJ, his connection to the bigger players in the game. "Damn my n***a, it's about f**kin' time," TJ said, as soon as he picked up. "What we lookin' like?"

"Everythang… everythang official," Onyx replied with a grin. He knew everything was falling into place. "Where you want to link up at?"

"Bet, pull up to the back of Leila Valley. You'll see my Jeep—just hit me when you're outside, shawty."

Onyx played it cool. "Can't. Had to park the whip. I'm…. in Carver Homes behind Slick David's old spot," he lied, always keeping his edge sharp.

TJ wanted to press but thought against it. "Cool, I'll send my runner, B-Lo. How much you took for?" TJ asked, trying to gauge whether Onyx was going to keep it real or get greedy.

Onyx leaned back in his seat, "Shiddd, he was coppin' the 10 bags when I pulled up, so beside that, I got 4 bricks and $7000 in cash." He spoke confidently, not revealing too much. "I'll give your runner 5 bags of the White Rhino, 2 bricks, and $3000."

TJ's response was quick, almost too quick. "It's cool for an honest day of work, Fam. This a welcome home present. Next time, I'ma get the extras."

"*Pussy n***a, there won't be a next time,*" Onyx thought to himself, smirking as he hung up." Pride ran too deep in his veins to let anyone take advantage of him. But he wasn't sweating it. Moving with precision, he pulled the black trash bag from his pocket—the one Sam had given him—and quickly separated the work. After scanning his surroundings to ensure no eyes were on him, he stepped out, stuffed the bookbag into the trunk, and slid back into the driver's seat.

Never neglecting a thing, Onyx felt he'd just pushed another pawn on his chessboard. With a calm yet determined demeanor, he pulled off, his mind already calculating the next move. The streets were quiet as Onyx parked on the side of the school. The usual crackheads moved through the shadows, hunting for their next come-up. Onyx sat in the car, his mind racing—thinking, plotting. The game was all about timing—now more than ever, he had to stay patient and aware.

After receiving the call from TJ, confirming his runner was parked outside in a silver Chrysler 300, Onyx stepped out of the car, his eyes scanning the area. He moved quickly and quietly, cutting through the back of the apartment complex and emerging four buildings over.

He approached the car attentively, watching as B-Lo rolled down the window. Onyx felt a sense of familiarity, but now wasn't the time for small talk. He handed over the bag with a nod. "Tell TJ the lunch was great, I needed that."

Without waiting for a response, Onyx turned and walked away, his steps steady and purposeful. He glanced over his shoulder, making sure no one was following. Taking a longer route back to his car, he moved cautiously, aware of his surroundings. Once he was back inside the Camaro, Onyx was already thinking ahead. He dialed 44's number, wasting no time once he picked up.

"Yo, it's all smooth," Onyx said, keeping his tone even as he steered the car through the dim-lit streets. "The show went off without a hitch."

Gunfire cracked through the night as Onyx turned onto Pryor Street. "Sh*t," he muttered under his breath as he slammed his foot into the accelerator. The engine roared beneath him. His eyes flicked to the rearview mirror, watching for any signs of pursuit or trouble but saw nothing.

With bricks, weed, and money in the trunk, Onyx knew he couldn't afford to stick around and risk getting caught up in something he didn't start. The streetlights flashed by in a blur as he escalated up Pryor Street, then turned onto University Avenue at the intersection and merged onto the expressway, pushing the Camaro faster. The city was starting to feel smaller, the danger closer, but his light wasn't about to go out now.

"Onyx… Onyx… what was dat? Are yuh okay?" 44's voice yelled through the phone, the sincerity of his concern clear. "Onyx, yuh straight?"

Onyx's eyes narrowed as he swerved past a car, glancing in the rearview. His mind raced, but his hands stayed steady. Despite the chaos, he remained calm. "Yeah. I'm good. I'm out the hood for now. I'll check in once I'm clear."

"Jah bless, bredren," 44 stated, his voice full of reassurance.

Onyx hung up and tossed the phone into the passenger seat, focusing on the road as the street signs passed and his heart slowed. Onyx drove carefully, making sure not to draw attention to what he was transporting. He weaved through traffic with the precision of a getaway driver, every move calculated. He was on the edge of victory—so close to having everything he'd dreamed of—and he couldn't afford to make a mistake now.

As he pulled into the complex and parked, he stepped out of the Camaro, grabbed the bag from the trunk, and kept his focus. His eyes briefly scanned over the women moving through the building, but he immediately turned his attention back to his goal. No distractions. Not today.

Chapter 20

"The King's Gambit"

Inside the condo, Onyx moved with urgency, snatching a bottle of bleach and a garbage bag from the kitchen cabinet before heading to the bathroom. He stripped off his clothes, tossing them into the bag, then turned on the shower. The hot water pounded against his back as he poured the chemical cleanser over himself, scrubbing hard with an exfoliating brush. His hands and arms tightened with every stroke, but he didn't stop until he was sure no trace of gunpowder or evidence remained.

Stepping out of the shower, the pungent scent of bleach clung to his skin as he dried off quickly. Wrapping a towel around his waist, he grabbed his phone from the bed and video-called his sister. Amani's face brought him a moment of peace, her energy lifting the weight pressing on his chest.

"Wassup, big bro? You good?" she asked, her tone light but laced with curiosity.

"I'm straight. Just needed a lil info real quick," Onyx said, his voice steady. He listened as she gave him the answers he needed, her animated expressions softening his hardened mood.

"*Nakupenda*," Onyx said, the Swahili word for I love you rolling off his tongue with warmth.

Amani grinned. "Boy, you stay actin' like I don't know you love me. Now, what club we hittin' later?"

Onyx chuckled but kept it brief, his focus locked on what came next. As long as she was smiling, he could breathe easy, but for now, his mind was consumed with the plan.

The certainty of his success filled his chest as he hung up and got dressed. His gaze shifted to the bookbag and the garbage bag of clothes on the floor—evidence he still needed to dispose of. Not wanting to draw attention to himself by burning them on the patio, he grabbed his phone again and called Gunna, who was in the middle of breaking down buds for a blunt with his brother.

"Put that sh*t down. I need y'all to pull back up. Ima send the addy."

"A'ight, damn. Let me tell T," Gunna replied, his irritation barely concealed.

Onyx ended the call and stuffed the phone in his pocket. He counted out $15,000 from the money in the bag, placing it in a shoe box along with the five bags of White Rhino and a brick of product. He stashed everything else in the back of the closet. "*Ni wakati wangu kung'aa*," he muttered to himself, the thrill of success settling in. "*Bosi amerudi tena*," he added, grinning as he turned around to witness his reflection in the mirror. The joy of it all was beginning to sink in.

As Onyx stepped out of the room, his thoughts drifted to his homies locked up—those long nights spent dreaming big. He remembered telling them he was going to take over the music industry, but deep down, everyone knew he was destined to return to the streets and rule the game. It was in his blood. A grin spread across his face as he thought about those days, realizing that come tomorrow, he'd know who was right.

Onyx pulled the wad of cash from the box, snapping flex shots— a message to his people inside, a glimpse of the freedom that awaited them. Once satisfied, he sent the pics with a message: "*Udugu wa maisha*" (Brotherhood for Life).

Refocused, Onyx glanced at his watch, then split the cash into two stacks—$10,000 and $5,000. He triple-vacuum sealed each pound of weed, making sure the smell didn't give Amani any clues. He wasn't about to disrespect her space. After breaking the kilo down into four 9-ounce portions, he placed 18 ounces into the shoe box with two bags of White Rhino, and tucked the rest—another 18 ounces and three bags of Kush—into the closet with his cash.

The urge to buy his sister a bouquet of red roses crossed his mind as he stepped into her room, his gaze settling on the crystal hummingbird he'd bought as a token of love. Amani always believed in him, no matter the choices he made. She never failed to encourage him to believe in his own potential. Walking over to place the $10,000 stack in the drawer alongside her sex toys, he chuckled at the strange assortment, wondering why she couldn't just get a boyfriend. "Girl, I love your wild, freaky ass," he mumbled to himself as he wrote a note: "*Neno langu ni heshima yangu na nakupenda.*" (My word is my honor and I love you.) He laid the note on top of the money before closing the drawer.

Gazing at his watch once more, Onyx ensured everything was in place. He then cleaned up thoroughly to erase any traces of his actions. Retrieving two department store bags from the kitchen closet, he placed the garbage bag with his clothes into one and the shoe box with the product into the other. **Onyx knew discretion was non-negotiable.** After texting Gunna to meet him at the executive suite, room #1745, in the Skyline Hotel on Virginia Avenue, he left the condo, feeling like he had initiated the king's gambit.

Driving along Courtland Street, the rhythm of Trap music filling the car, Onyx noticed a group of homeless men huddled around a burn barrel fire. He pulled over, grabbed the department store bag with the clothes inside, and approached them, holding out the bag. "Yo… yo, I'll give you $50 to burn this for me," he said, not directing the offer to anyone in particular.

The three men, their hands hovering over the fire for warmth, scrambled for the bag, pushing each other aside in a rush. Not wanting things to escalate, Onyx reached into his pocket and pulled out two additional $50 bills, handing one to each of them after they approached. Their scent lingered like the heavy air of a forgotten graveyard, forcing him to gasp for air after they walked away. Watching closely to ensure they didn't pull the clothes out to wear, he waited before stepping back toward his car and driving off.

Back in the car, Onyx exhaled, the weight on his chest lifting ever so slightly. The memory of their bond around the barrel lingered in his mind, stirring something deeper inside him—a reminder that even in the thick of struggle, unity mattered. Maybe, just maybe, his actions weren't as selfish as he'd convinced himself. As the city lights blurred past, a sense of clarity washed over him, and with it, the thought of what came next.

He pulled up to the hotel with a sense of purpose. Striding through the lobby like a king, Onyx's confidence seemed to command the space itself. The suite awaited, just as he'd imagined—spacious, modern, with a breathtaking view that stretched out to the horizon. The luxurious atmosphere wrapped around him like a tailored suit, each detail confirming that this was the life he'd always dreamed of, the life he knew he deserved. Now, as the one calling the shots, everything was finally falling into place.

Entering the suite and laying the bag down on the kitchen counter, he took in the atmosphere before stepping out onto the patio. The view was stunning, the city skyline stretching before him like a canvas full of opportunity. He pulled out his phone and video-called his mother, signing that he loved her, planned to stop by in the morning, and was just checking to make sure she was okay. The sight of her smile filled him with a renewed sense of life, but after hanging up, he lingered on the promise he had made her—not to turn back to the streets. The weight of that promise now being broken made him feel like he was betraying her, but thinking about the benefits of his actions, he felt she would understand.

Surrounded by silence, he logged into his chess app, playing a few games to distract himself. But his thoughts kept drifting. What would this moment feel like if he were sharing it with the woman from Tiffany's or the mystery woman he'd seen at Amani's condo? He craved someone who could offer him more—someone who could bring depth to his life, unlike Stacy, who offered him nothing but some jaw dropping head.

A sudden knock at the door snapped him out of his thoughts. Their faces lit up with excitement like kids in a toy store as they took in the suite's opulence. The circular staircase and spacious design were nothing like what they were used to. Chuckling, Onyx dapped them both up and locked the door behind them.

"Damn, cuz. This you?" T-Roc asked, wide-eyed as he glanced at the circular staircase and marble countertops.

"Yeah, this me for the night," Onyx said, smirking. "But check this out."

He directed them to the shoe box on the counter. Their fascination with the room faded as their eyes locked onto its contents.

"This right here," Onyx began, his tone calm but commanding, "is the start-up for tomorrow's move. No more small-time sh*t. Y'all take half, split it, and move it without thinkin' like a petty hustler. We makin' chess moves now, not checkers.

As they leaned in, Onyx continued to lay out his strategy. He explained how they would distribute free samples at the party to build a customer base and create a discreet platform within the complex to serve them. "We're about to take this to another level," he said. "Y'all can't move like you do in the hood anymore. These people are connected to folks you don't want on your radar. They're not used to the street antics y'all pull, so don't do it. More importantly, they definitely don't want any attention brought their way. You feel me!"

Gunna nodded, his grin wide. "Say less, cuz. We wit' it."

When his phone buzzed with a call from 44, interrupting him, Onyx stepped out to the patio to take it. Looking at the excitement of the twins through the glass window, he smirked, realizing they were already strategizing and mountains his cousins would move to make sure his plan succeeded. Returning a few moments later, he finished laying out all the details to ensure there would be no mishaps. He emphasized the importance of keeping everything low-key and warned against exploiting the residents' naivety. "We don't squeeze or beat people out of money. We move smart and let the product speak for itself."

Gunna grinned. "I feel you, cuz."

T-Roc nodded. "Definitely, no doubt."

"The party's gonna be lit," Onyx continued. "So, y'all country ass n***as better step your dress game up. There's literally no telling who's gonna be attending, so represent like y'all from zone 3 and not muthaf**kers that have no drip."

His joking insult caused the twins to speak out and defend their fashion choices, which in their minds were innovative. "Hell nah, y'all n***as trippin'," Onyx cut in, interrupting their excited chatter about dressing him for the party. He had no intentions of looking like a clown on a budget for his event.

After setting up a video call with Shadow and Speedy to make sure everyone was on the same page, Onyx advised that, from that moment on, they would move as a family. Every Friday, they would switch their line of communication, and every Sunday, they'd meet for dinner to discuss business, profits, and the re-up. Everyone nodded in agreement.

With the two new recruits still on video, Onyx led the twins out onto the patio, pausing to take in the skyline. "This," he said, gesturing to the city lights, waving his phone so Shadow and Speedy could see what he was referring to, while the twins looked on, "is what we're working toward. Limitless elevation."

As the night settled, Onyx felt it—the power, the control. Money Bag Mafia was solidified. The city was theirs for the taking.

Chapter 21

"The Morning After"

Onyx woke slowly, the murmur of the city filtering in through the massive glass windows of the executive suite. Sunlight poured in, touching everything in a warm, golden glow. He stretched, the soreness in his body reminding him of last night—the clubs, the drinking, and the chaos that always seemed to follow him.

Swinging his legs off the bed, he stood, his designer boxers riding low on his hips as he made his way to the spiral staircase. The polished metal reflected the tattoos covering his chest and arms—testaments to his story, his struggle, and his ambition.

He descended the stairs with ease, his hand sliding along the cool railing. The air in the suite was crisp and quiet, the kind of peaceful silence only found in early mornings. Sliding open the patio door, Onyx stepped outside, letting the city greet him. Atlanta sprawled before him, alive with opportunity and danger. He leaned on the railing, his gaze distant as he thought about the night before.

Last night had been a success. Fat Boy was gone, and with him, one less obstacle in Onyx's path. He wasn't proud of what he'd done, but pride didn't pay the bills, and it damn sure didn't secure a legacy. The pool party today was more than just an opportunity for everyone to have a good time—it was a statement. A reminder to everyone that he was back and stronger than ever.

The growl of his stomach interrupted his thoughts. With his phone in hand, Onyx called the kitchen and ordered room service, requesting a spread big enough for three. Hanging up the phone, the city stretched out before him, alive and buzzing even in the early hours. The faint sound of birds chirping added a layer of serenity to the morning, a rare moment of peace that didn't feel fragile or fleeting.

A few minutes later, a knock at the door pulled him out of his daydream—a life where indulgence had no limits, where pleasure stretched endlessly, unbound by time or consequence. He stepped back inside, crossing the spacious living room to answer it. A waiter stood there with a cart piled high with silver-domed trays, a feast fit for a king, further proving that in this world, desires weren't just met—they were exceeded, over and over again.

"Come on in," Onyx said, holding the door open and gesturing to the dining table.

The waiter wheeled the cart inside, stopping at the table. Setting the trays down with practiced efficiency, his movements were smooth and impersonal, like he'd done this a hundred times before. The soft clink of silverware and porcelain broke the room's silence as he arranged everything neatly. Onyx barely glanced at him, nodding in silent thanks once he was finished, his mind already drifting elsewhere.

Without a word, Onyx turned and headed back up the spiral staircase, the polished metal railing cool under his palm as he took the steps two at a time. His movements were deliberate but restless, the echo of his footsteps reverberating softly in the quiet luxury of the suite. Each step felt like it carried him further from the chaos of the world below, yet the weight of his thoughts followed him relentlessly. By the time he reached the top, the faint aroma of the food lingered behind him, but his appetite had been replaced by a sense of urgency he couldn't quite shake.

Reaching his room, he grabbed a wad of cash from the pocket of his crumpled pants on the chair. Thumbing through the bills, he hesitated. Was this enough? Too much? He shook off the thought, pulled out a crisp fifty, and jogged back down, the faint aroma of the food trailing up to meet him.

By the time he returned, the waiter stood by the door. "Here you go," Onyx said, extending the money. "My bad for the wait."

"No problem at all, sir," the waiter replied with a polite nod as Onyx signed the receipt.

Closing the door behind him, Onyx walked over to the table in the dining area, lifting the lids to let the aroma of pancakes, turkey bacon, eggs, grits, biscuits, and fresh fruit fill the room. The smell alone was enough to wake the dead—or, in this case, his sister and Yoshe. The aroma was making Onyx's stomach rumble again. But first, he had to wake up Amani and Yoshe. "Y'all better get up!" he hollered repeatedly, his voice bouncing off the high ceilings. "Food here! If you don't hurry, I'm eatin' it all myself!"

"Onyx, if you wake me up yellin' like that ever again, I'ma kill your ugly ass!" Amani shouted from behind closed doors.

Yoshe's laugh lingered as she buried her face in the pillow, her body melting into the comfort of the mattress beneath her. "Boy, shut the hell up! Ain't nobody tryna hear your loud-mouth ass this early in the morning!" she shot back, her tone playful but laced with just enough annoyance to make her point clear.

Onyx smirked. "Oh, a'ight. Bet." Grabbing a couch pillow, he sprinted up the stairs and pushed open Amani's door. She was still under the covers, her scarf half-off her head. Without warning, he smacked her across the face with the pillow.

"Aye! Wake your ass up, Amani!"

She shot up instantly, the sudden movement jolting the bed. Her face twisted in a mix of frustration and fury as she reached over, snatching one of her stilettos off the floor. The gleaming heel caught the light just before she hurled it across the room with surprising precision.

"N***a, I ain't playin' with your ugly fat head ass!" she barked, her voice sharp and cutting through the air like the weapon once in her hand. Her chest rose and fell, breaths heavy with raw emotion. Her eyes burned with a fire that warned him she wasn't just blowing smoke.

Onyx ducked, laughter spilling out as he bolted down the hall and burst into Yoshe's room. The door slammed against the wall, and he caught her in mid-attempt to disappear under the covers like a guilty child avoiding trouble.

"You too, Yoshe!" he shouted, grinning as he swung the pillow down, landing a satisfying thwack to the side of her head.

Suddenly, a burst of energy erupted behind him. Amani darted out of the room, her hair slightly disheveled, and without hesitation, leapt onto his back. "Oh, you thought you could just wake me up like that and walk away?" she said, laughing, assuming Yoshe would come from under the covers to help her double-team him.

"Gotcha now!" Amani yelled triumphantly, tightening her grip around his neck.

Yoshe added with a smirk, "Choke his ass, girl."

Yet, before either of them could execute their uncoordinated plan, Onyx shifted his weight effortlessly. With a smooth twist, he flipped Amani off his back and onto the bed where Yoshe had barely removed the comforter to reveal her face. Amani crashed on top of her in a tangle of laughter, their surprised shrieks filling the air.

"Oh, you thought a choke hold would help you?" Onyx teased, grabbing the cushion off the floor. Without hesitation, he swung it with precision, landing soft but firm blows on both of them.

"Stay down!" he joked, his laughter booming as Amani squealed in mock outrage.

"Boy, get the hell outta here!" Amani yelled, flailing an arm out towards him but missing. Her swings were wild and aimless, each one missing him by a mile as he effortlessly dodged her attempts. Yoshe, caught between giggling and half-heartedly defending herself, tried to snatch the cushion from him, but Onyx was too quick.

The room dissolved into playful chaos, filled with shouts, laughter, and the sound of muffled cushion hits. Onyx, still grinning, stood victorious at the edge of the bed. "Y'all gotta come harder than that," he said, tossing the cushion aside with a dramatic flourish. Amani huffed and threw a portion of the comforter over her head, muttering, "You play too damn much," while Yoshe collapsed back into the pillows, shaking her head and laughing.

"Onyx! I swear to God!" she yelled as he turned toward the door to leave. Her voice slicing through the air as she sprang out of bed. The silk sheets slid away, revealing her in a matching bra and panty set that traced her curves with effortless perfection. Her body was mesmerizing—smooth, toned, and sculpted in a way that demanded attention without effort. The soft glow of morning light kissed her caramel skin, accentuating the dip of her waist and the elegant lines of her thighs. She moved with a fiery confidence, every step radiating a sensual energy that made it impossible to look away.

By the time Yoshe gave chase, Amani had joined her, holding another stiletto. Both women followed him down the spiral staircase as he laughed hysterically, narrowly avoiding the second shoe Amani threw at him.

"Y'all too slow!" he taunted, sliding behind the dining table like a kid who'd just stolen cookies.

Both women stopped, out of breath and glaring at him. Yoshe leaned on the chair, shaking her head. "I hate you right now."

"Well my sister love me," Onyx said with a grin, throwing his hands up in surrender. "Now, sit down and eat before it gets cold."

The three of them finally settled at the table, Yoshe shooting him a look as she took a bite of bacon. Her eyes lingered on his bare chest and abs longer than she intended, the attraction catching her off guard.

"Onyx," she said, her tone more cutting than usual, "put some damn clothes on. I'm not tryna shoot your bitch for eyeing your body."

Onyx smirked, leaning back in his chair with a playful glint in his eyes. "Ain't nobody makin' you look, and hell, you showin' more than I am. Better hope you don't wake up Mr. Pleasure, though—'cause if you do, you'll be the one puttin' him back to sleep."

Yoshe rolled her eyes, but her tone softened, teasing. "Boy, bye! Sh*t, depends on how much I drink at the party, O. I might wake up Mr. Pleasure and let that be my excuse to find out if it's actually all you down there… or if you wearin' a cup."

Amani choked on her coffee, laughing. "Hoe, you wild!"

Onyx grinned, his muscles flexing playfully as he leaned in with that familiar cocky grin. "Why wait? You can find out right now." His voice was low, teasing, allowing his eyes to caress the raw sexiness of her body.

He'd always known she was fine, but damn, the way her body responded to the light in the room made his breath hitch. The curve of her hips, the way her bra and panties clung to every inch of her—he hadn't realized just how sexy she was. The intensity in her eyes, the fire she carried in her movements, made his pulse race. He'd loved to test the limits of her affection, feeling that electric tension between them, knowing that every glance, every word, pushed her closer to unraveling. And he was ready to explore every inch of it.

"Boy, stop," Yoshe said, laughing despite herself, the heat in her face undeniable. "Like I said, if—and the emphasis is definitely on if— I get drunk, because otherwise, there's no f**kin' way in hell I'd let you or any other mutherf**ker touch me after laying up with Stacy cross-country pussy slinging -ass," Yoshe said, rolling her eyes with a mix of disgust and irritation. "The alcohol would just be my excuse to see why she follows your footsteps like a damn gnat when it's supposed to be the other way around."

With everyone laughing, the conversation shifted to the pool party, but the undercurrent of tension between Onyx and Yoshe remained. After they finished eating, Yoshe stood up, her movements slow and almost mechanical as she wandered over to the TV, flipping through channels without really paying attention. Amani took a call and stepped toward the patio, while Onyx casually mentioned he needed to get dressed to visit their mother.

But then, Yoshe froze. Her entire body went still, her hand halting mid-air over the remote, like she'd just been struck by a bolt of electricity. She was still in her matching bra and panties, her butt cheeks completely exposed, and she could feel Onyx's eyes on her, staring intently, but all of that seemed irrelevant now. The weight of whatever she was watching on the screen pushed everything else to the back of her mind. Her chest tightened, and the usual confidence she carried with her seemed to vanish in an instant.

"Hold up, y'all," she said, her voice raw and tight, a sharp edge cutting through the air. The playful, seductive energy that usually came so naturally to her was gone, replaced with something darker, more urgent. "Check this sh*t out." Her words hung in the air, heavy with a mix of disbelief, her eyes blazing as she turned toward them, no longer concerned with her exposed skin or how Onyx was looking at her like prey. The news broadcast crackled to life, the reporter's voice carrying an ominous weight.

"Breaking news out of Atlanta," the reporter announced. "A double murder at a shopping plaza on Old National Highway last night. Names of the victims are being withheld pending family notification. The suspect, seen here in surveillance footage, was wearing a black jogging suit and fled the scene in the victim's SUV."

The room seemed to freeze, the air thick with tension. Amani's eyes locked onto the screen, her breath catching as the grainy security footage played. The suspect moved with a calm, calculated precision before slipping into the SUV and driving away. Her stomach churned. The suspect's build and the black jogging suit—it all felt too familiar. Her mind immediately went to Onyx. She shook the thought off, but the seed of doubt had been planted.

Her gaze flicked to her brother, standing across the room, his expression unreadable. Too unreadable. Onyx was leaning back against the wall, his face calm—too calm. Amani recognized the look in his eyes, and a chill ran down her spine. She knew her brother better than anyone. Something wasn't right.

"Onyx," she said cautiously, her voice low but steady. "You know somethin' 'bout that?"

Onyx didn't answer immediately. His jaw tightened as his eyes stayed glued to the screen. The delay in his response set off alarms in Amani's mind. When he finally spoke, his voice was low, almost too casual.

"Nah. I don't know nothin'."

The words rang hollow, and Amani's arms instinctively crossed over her chest. Her expression hardened as she stared him down. "Don't lie to me, O," she said firmly. "You my brother. I know when you ain't keepin' it real."

Her voice cracked ever so slightly, but her resolve didn't waver. She needed the truth, even if it tore her apart. Onyx's eyes didn't meet hers. He stared straight ahead, his face unreadable, but the tension in the room spoke louder than words.

Amani's mind raced, replaying the events of the past 24 hours. She thought back to her late-night video call with him. He'd been dressed in all black, his tone distant, distracted. The image of him pulling off the Old National Highway exit during the call now burned in her mind. Then there was the $10,000 he'd handed her earlier that day, the gesture so out of place it had left her uneasy. Why would he suddenly give her that and where did he get it from? The puzzle pieces started falling into place, and with each click, the pit in her stomach grew heavier.

Her voice shook as she pressed him again. "You ain't tellin' me somethin', O. Why you riskin' it all when you don't even need to?"

Onyx finally turned to face her, his eyes meeting hers. For a fleeting moment, Amani saw something in his expression—a sparkle of guilt, regret, or maybe even fear. But just as quickly, it was gone, buried beneath a mask of indifference. He leaned forward slightly, his tone flat and final. "Sis, I got no reason to lie to you."

The words hit like a brick wall, shutting down the conversation, but Amani wasn't convinced. Her intuition screamed at her, the weight of unspoken truths pressing down like a vice. She knew her brother too well. Whatever he was hiding, it was only a matter of time before it came to light. The weight in his eyes told her everything she needed to know—there was more to this than they were letting on.

Yoshe stood before the TV, her arms casually crossed over her chest, but her eyes darted between Amani and Onyx. She could feel the tension radiating off them like heat waves, the air so dense it seemed to weigh on her shoulders. Her instincts told her this wasn't just a sibling squabble—it was deeper, more dangerous. But she said nothing, choosing instead to let her presence linger without making a sound. Her silence was a message in itself: she was watching, waiting, calculating.

Amani, still locked in a staring match with Onyx, could feel Yoshe's gaze on them. Her frustration flared, but she pushed it down. She needed answers, not distractions.

"I'm serious, O," Amani said, her voice low and cutting. "That footage? That's you, ain't it? Don't play me like I'm stupid."

Onyx let out a slow breath, his expression still unreadable. "You really think I'd be sloppy like that? Come on, sis. You know me better than that.'"

The deflection only made Amani's suspicions grow. She moved closer to him, her voice rising slightly. "Then explain the joggin' suit, O. Explain why you was on Old National last night when I video called you. And don't even start with the bullsh*t about coincidence. The streets don't work like that."

Yoshe shifted her weight. "Y'all need to chill," She finally said, her voice soft but firm. She turned her head to view them. "Whatever this is, handle it smart. This ain't the time for us to be losin' your heads."

Amani snapped her head toward Yoshe, her frustration briefly redirected. "Stay outta this, Yoshe," she shot back. "This is between my lyin' ass brother and I."

Yoshe raised an eyebrow, unbothered by Amani's tone. She held her ground, her voice steady. "I ain't tryin' to get in y'all business, but this back-and-forth? It's only gon' make things worse. Chill out before something gets said that can't be taken back—especially when all you workin' with is assumptions."

Onyx stood straight up, his muscular frame casting a shadow over the room. He looked at Yoshe, then back at Amani, his jaw tight. "She right," he said, his voice low but commanding. "Ain't nothin' good gon' come outta you pressin' me right now. Let it go."

Amani's eyes narrowed, her chest tightening with anger and disbelief. "Let it go?" she repeated, her voice rising. "O, I'm tryna save your f**kin' ass! You think this some kinda game? That footage? That SUV GPS system? You haven't even been out a whole f**kin' month and you already doing sh*t that will send you back forever. That's you, and if it ain't, prove me wrong!"

Yoshe turned around and walked over to stand in between them, her presence a calming but firm barrier. "Enough," she said, her tone leaving no room for argument. "Amani if you ain't got the facts, then you need to stop jumpin' to conclusions. Amani, I get it—you worried, and don't want to lose your brother again. But this ain't the way."

Onyx's gaze lingered a moment too long on Yoshe's body. She noticed he was staring and paid it no mind. Then he turned to Amani, his voice quieter now but no less firm. "You can think what you want,

Amani," he said. "But you ain't gon' pin this on me. Not without proof that doesn't exist."

Amani opened her mouth to argue, but Yoshe shook her head, cutting her off. "We done with this," Yoshe said, her voice final. "Ain't no point goin' in circles."

For a long moment, the room was silent except for the soft drone of the TV in the background. Amani's anger simmered just beneath the surface, but she didn't push further. She glanced between Onyx and Yoshe, her chest rising and falling with heavy breaths. "Fine," she said finally, her voice tight. "But this ain't over, O. Not by a long shot."

With that, she turned and stormed out of the room, the echo of her footsteps fading up the staircases. Onyx exhaled deeply, his face a mask of exhaustion. Yoshe stayed where she was, her eyes fixed on him.

"You better hope she wrong," Yoshe said quietly, her tone carrying more weight than her words. "Cause you know if she ain't, that calm act you just received. It ain't gon' be there when she returns."

Onyx didn't respond, his gaze dropped to the outline of her body. Yoshe lingered for a moment longer before turning and walking away herself, her steps slow and deliberate. She didn't look back, not once, her confidence radiating with every step she took. But Onyx couldn't tear his eyes away, his gaze tracing the curve of her hips and the effortless sway in her stride. It was more than just the way her body moved—it was the way she owned every inch of the space around her, the quiet power in her presence. The thought that she might've entertained the idea of him lingered in his mind, igniting something primal. His hands balled into fists at his sides as desire burned through him, raw and unrelenting. He wanted to follow, to close the distance, to take the risk of saying something that could make her stop and turn around. But he stood frozen, torn between desire and restraint, his pulse pounding in his ears long after she disappeared from view.

Chapter 22

"The Weight of Truth"

Onyx stepped out of the hotel lobby, the door closing behind him with a soft thud, but it wasn't enough to drown out Amani's voice. The weight of their conversation wrapped around him like chains. He exhaled hard, his jaw tightening as he walked to his car, her words echoing in his mind. "You haven't even been out a month, Onyx. A f**kin' month. And already, you're flirting with disaster. I know that's your work."

Her words were still fresh. Her tone wasn't loud, but it didn't need to be. Amani's voice had a way of burrowing under his skin, dragging out every ounce of guilt he tried to bury. "I can't lose your stupid ass again," she'd said, her eyes glassy but steady. "There's nothing out there in those f**kin' streets that's worth you jeopardizing your life and freedom for. We already have everything we need. Why can't that be enough for you?"

Onyx hadn't responded. What could he say? That it wasn't enough? That he didn't feel whole, even with everything she did for him? He wanted to scream that she didn't understand, but the words died in his throat. He didn't have the courage to admit out loud what felt so true in his heart—that he didn't have everything and felt like a pawn in her world. He had nothing. Nothing that was his own, besides what he took last night.

The thought was unbearable, gnawing at him since the day he stepped out of those prison gates with nothing but hand-me-downs to his name. In prison, he'd thrived off the money Amani sent, but instead of using it to build a foundation for his release, he'd squandered it. Now, on the outside, he was still leaning on her, surviving off her generosity, and it was eating him alive. It made him feel like less than a man.

Amani had welcomed him home with open arms, brimming with hope and plans for a brighter future. But Onyx couldn't see it. All he could see was the ghost of who he once was and the hollow shell of what he'd become. He gripped the steering wheel tightly as he slid into the driver's seat. The silence inside the car felt oppressive, but he didn't turn on the radio. He needed to think, to breathe. The streets of Atlanta blurred past him, familiar yet distant. He didn't need directions to his mother's house; the route was etched into his memory like a second heartbeat.

By the time he pulled up to the small, well-kept home, the tension in his chest hadn't eased. He stepped out of the car, his eyes scanning the flowerbeds she tended so carefully, the wind chimes on the porch that danced with every faint breeze. It was a picture of peace, but Onyx felt none of it. He thought of knocking just so she could feel the vibration, but he used his key to let himself in instead.

The savory aroma of cube steaks smothered in onions and served over rice hit him first, wrapping around him like a warm embrace and stirring something raw and familiar deep within. In the living room, his mother sat on the couch with one of her church sisters. She looked up at him, her eyes lighting up in a way that made his chest ache. She couldn't hear him, but she didn't need to. Her smile was enough to replicate the love that swelled in his heart.

"Hey, Ma," he said, raising his hand in a brief wave before switching to sign language. "I didn't know you had company. I wanted to come by and take you out to eat."

She paused, glancing at her friend before signing back, "I'd love to, baby, but I promised Joyce I'd help her clean the church today. We have an event tomorrow." Her expression softened, but there was a hint of concern in her eyes. "You okay?"

Onyx hesitated, his hands still. He hated how easily she could read him, even without words. "Yeah," he signed back, forcing a smile. "I'm good."

She tilted her head slightly, studying him the way only a mother could. Then she stood, motioning for him to follow her into the kitchen. Once there, she grabbed a small vial of holy water from the shelf above the sink. Onyx froze. He knew what was coming. She turned to him, her hands moving deliberately as she signed, "Have you broken your promise to me?"

He shook his head quickly, too quickly. "No, Ma. I haven't."

Her eyes narrowed slightly as she took his hands, her touch firm yet gentle. Signing slowly, she said, "The spirit tells me you're not being truthful… and your eyes confirm it." She paused before continuing, "We're going to pray about this."

Before he could protest, she poured the holy water into her hands and began rubbing it over his, her lips moving in silent prayer. The coolness of the water felt heavier than it should, like it carried the weight of her belief. She moved to his face, dabbing the water across his forehead before clasping his hands together in hers. Her eyes closed as she continued to pray, her brow furrowing with emotion. Onyx watched her, his throat tightening as guilt clawed at him.

When she finished, she opened her eyes and signed, "The spirit has never lied to me, Onyx. If you are lying, I'll have no choice but to remove you from my life. I have prayed too hard to bring you back to me. I won't lose you to the darkness again."

Her words hit him like a hammer, each one landing with devastating weight. He swallowed hard, his gaze dropping to the floor. "I love you, Ma," he said softly lifting it back up so she could read his lips. The words escaping before he could stop them.

She smiled faintly, reached up, and placed her hand over his heart. "Then show me," she signed, her movements calm and clear. She let out a deep sigh, her shoulders rising and falling as if releasing a burden too heavy to carry.

Onyx leaned down and kissed her on the cheek, a gesture of quiet reverence, as they stood in the kitchen. His mother moved with a quiet purpose, her hands gliding over the stove as she dished out two plates of cube steak with rice and gravy, the rich aroma filling the house.

She glanced at him, her expression soft but serious as she signed, "Take this. You and your sister are too thin."

Onyx smiled faintly, taking the plates she had carefully wrapped in foil. "Thanks, Ma," he signed back, watching her with a mix of gratitude and guilt.

Struggling to steady his thoughts, he avoided his mother's gaze as they walked back into the living room, where her church sister, Sister Joyce, was gathering her things. His mother turned to her and signed, "Are you ready to leave?"

Sister Joyce nodded, offering Onyx a kind smile before the three of them stepped outside. The evening air was cool, a faint breeze stirring the chimes on the porch. Onyx carried the plates in one hand and opened the car door for his mother with the other, helping her into the passenger seat.

As she settled in, she turned to him, her eyes locking onto his with a piercing intensity that made his throat tighten. Reaching out, she rested her hand gently on his arm before signing, slowly and with intent, "I love you, Onyx. But I need you to understand something. I won't taint my relationship with God—not for you, not for your sister, not for anyone. If you break the promise you made to me, I'll have no choice but to let you go. You can't ask me to choose between you and God. I won't do it." Her hands trembled slightly as she finished, but her gaze didn't waver.

Onyx swallowed hard, his chest tightening as her hands moved with a clarity that pierced him. He nodded, his own hands trembling slightly as he signed back, "I understand, and I love you, Ma." Leaning down, he kissed her forehead gently and stepped back as she closed the door. He stood there watching the car disappear down the street. With the plates of food still warm in his hand, he stared at nothing for a moment, his thoughts a whirlwind of guilt and frustration.

When he got into his car, he gazed intensely at his hands, still moist from the holy water. The sensation lingered, as if it had seeped into his skin, a reminder he couldn't shake. The guilt was suffocating, pressing against his chest like a vice. To ease his mind, he turned on some Trap music, letting the bass and rhythm drown out his thoughts. The familiar beats pulsed through the car as he pulled out of the driveway, his jaw clenched as he navigated the streets.

Onyx drove across town to check on the twins, ensuring they were set for the pool party. The meeting was brief, mostly transactional, but it gave him a sense of control he desperately needed. By the time Onyx reached the condo, the day had shifted and the sun was starting to decline. The shadows stretched long and low across the pool area, the lights around the patio gradually coming to life. He forced himself to focus on the party preparations, walking through each detail meticulously. The furniture placement, the DJ area, the lights, the catering setup—it all had to be perfect.

But no matter how much he tried to lose himself in the work, the echoes of Amani's voice and the weight of his mother's silent prayers stayed with him.

"The spirit has never lied to me."

As he stood by the pool, watching the water ripple under the lights, he clenched his fists at his sides. Deep down, he knew they were both right. He was teetering on the edge of something he couldn't come back from, the truth stabbing into him like an ice pick.

But the streets didn't give second chances. And Onyx? He wasn't sure he deserved one.

Chapter 23

"White Linen Nights"

The bass from the DJ's speakers hit deep, shaking the air with its rhythm. Bodies swayed and dipped along the pool's edge, the glow from the underwater lights bouncing off the shimmering water. The party was already lit. Guests mingled, danced, and laughed as if the day held no limits. The scent of grilled shrimp and burgers drifted through the air, mixing with the sharp tang of chlorine and the faint aroma of expensive cologne and perfume.

Onyx stood beside the DJ booth, scanning the scene from a distance, taking in the energy. This wasn't just a pool party—it was a statement, his declaration. He adjusted his fitted cap, letting a small grin play on his lips before heading upstairs to prepare for his role as the center of it all.

Inside the condo, the sound of Amani's voice floated through the hallway. She was singing in the shower, her notes soft but smooth, carrying a natural vibrato that always stopped him in his tracks. Onyx chuckled to himself. Her voice had always been mesmerizing, a talent she carried effortlessly. When he stepped into his bedroom, his attention immediately locked onto the shopping bags sitting neatly on the bed. He walked over, curiosity drawing him in. Pulling out the contents, his grin widened. "All-white linen? Okay, sis, I see you."

The short-sleeve linen shirt and matching drawstring pants were crisp and clean, oozing sophistication but with a flair that still felt him. And the loafers? Designer, low-key but sexy, the type of shoes that made a statement without shouting. "Amani, you really went in, Nakupenda!" he said, shaking his head.

"Yo, Precious," he called out to the AI device. "Play some old-school R&B."

The room filled with the soulful croon of Marvin Gaye's "I Want You," setting the mood. Onyx stepped into the bathroom to wash away

130

the work sweat and smoke, the steam from the shower curling around him as he let the warm water relax his body. His mind raced, though. This party wasn't just a celebration—it was a critical chess move. He needed to make sure everything flowed, no slips, no drama.

Once out of the shower, he dressed carefully, admiring how the linen fit against his skin. The loafers added effortless swagger to his look, and for a moment, he couldn't help but smirk at his reflection. As he adjusted the linen shirt on top of the tank top, Amani walked by his door, her hair tied in a towel.

"Yo, sis, come here for a second," he called.

She paused, leaning in with a raised brow. "What you want now?"

"Just come in," Onyx said, nodding toward the bed.

Amani stepped in, pulling the towel off her hair and letting it fall free. She sat on the edge of the bed, arms crossed. "A'ight, what's up, O?"

Onyx leaned back against the dresser, his face serious. "Look, I gotta keep it real with you for a minute."

Amani tilted her head, her playful expression fading. "Oh, so we havin' a real moment now?"

"Yeah, we havin' a moment," Onyx said, his voice dropping. "Sis, lying ain't never been our thing. But you gotta understand—there's certain sh*t that you can't know. And there's certain sh*t you damn sure can't ask me in front of other people. That's not how we move and you know that."

Amani's eyes flashed, her tone cutting. "So what? I'm supposed to just sit back while you turn back to the streets and make dumb ass decisions? You got options, Onyx. You got people who believe in you and people who support you. "Why the hell would you choose a path that could send your black ass straight back to prison instead of a life filled with freedom and peace?"

Onyx exhaled, rubbing the back of his neck as if trying to ease the weight pressing down on him. "Because I gotta build my own foundation, Amani. Brick by brick. I can't live in nobody else's lane, not even yours." His voice cracked, but he pushed through. "Scamming?

That's you. You kill it, and you do it your way. But me? I'm not tryna ride your coattails or 44's. That ain't living, Amani—that's surviving. And I'm done just surviving."

He stepped closer, his eyes locked on hers, filled with a raw vulnerability he rarely showed. "You don't get it. If I don't build this my way, I'll never feel whole. I'll always be at war with myself, asking what kind of man I am. How can I look at myself in the mirror knowing I didn't fight for my own dream, my own legacy?"

Onyx's hand dropped to his side. "Yeah, I know it's risky. I know it could cost me. But what's the alternative? To live a life that ain't mine, depending on you or 44 to carry me like a bitch? That ain't me, Amani. I gotta prove to myself that I'm worth something—that I can make it on my terms." His voice softened, though the intensity in his eyes never wavered. "You've always been there for me, more than anyone, but this is something I gotta do alone. Even if it's messy. Even if I stumble. At least it'll be mine."

Amani looked at him, her anger softening into something more vulnerable. "O, I hear you. For real. But this ain't it. The same streets that sent you away for ten years? You really think they gon' give you peace and glory now? You think they care about what you buildin'? Believe in yourself, O. Pursue the music—that's your f**kin' gift and your way out. That's what you were born to do. That's the foundation you need to build, brick by brick. Stop lookin' sideways at everybody else's path and start buildin' your own. You've got it in you—I've seen it. Now it's time you see it, too."

Onyx's jaw tightened, his voice low. "I ain't got time to worry about what the streets care about, Amani. I'm focused on me. Tonight, I'm gonna find clarity. I'm gonna embrace whatever comes. But it's gotta be my way."

Amani stood up straight slowly, her gaze locked on his. "A'ight, you're going to do your own thing so there's no reason for me to waste my breath," she said softly. "But if you shut me out and lie to me for any reason again? I'mma slap the sh*t outta your muthaf**king big head ass. Straight up. Like them slap competitions you be watching."

Onyx laughed, the tension breaking. "Bet. I ain't tryna get laid out by my own sister."

"And I swear, I'm tellin' Mama if you buck and lay a hand on me!"

They hugged tightly, a rare but needed moment of connection. "Nakupenda," Amani whispered softly, releasing her arms from around his waist. But before Onyx could respond, she playfully mugged him and stepped back, adopting a fighting stance with her fists up and a glint of mischief in her eyes. Her fierceness, though playful now, was a trait that always added a unique spark to her beauty—fiery and unapologetic in a way that was hard to put into words.

Onyx smirked, crossing his arms. 'Sis, you better sit your lil ass down before I show you what I did to the last n***a who disrespected me in prison," he teased, slipping off his loc hair ties, letting his hair fall free.

Seeing Amani in her "war mode" brought back memories of their childhood. It had been years since they'd sparred like this, and the sight of her bouncing on her toes, in her outfit, pretending to size him up, was almost too much. He turned his back to her, spraying on cologne and chuckling to himself.

That's when she struck—like a lioness, yet with the cowardice of someone knowing they couldn't win head-on. With quick precision, Amani snapped him on the butt with her damp towel, the sting immediate and startling. Dropping the towel, she sprinted out of the room, yelling at the top of her lungs, telling her phone to call their mother.

Onyx winced, rubbing the spot where the towel had landed. For a moment, he just stood there, shaking his head, laughing at her antics. He considered chasing her down and popping her back but decided against it—it wasn't worth the energy, especially with her calling their mother.

Ten minutes later, both of them were ready and looking like an unstoppable force. They sat at the table, savoring the plates of food their mother had cooked. Even though he had hired a caterer for the party, nothing could compare to their mother's seasoned cooking. It was a flavor you couldn't set aside for anyone else. Between bites, they fell into old habits—teasing, joking, and laughing. The joyful banter continued as they left the condo and headed back to the pool area.

"Remember that time you let that girl leave hickeys all over your cheeks, neck, chest—hell, even your back? Just so people would think your game was strong?" Amani teased, her laugh filling the room.

Onyx groaned, covering his face with one hand exiting the elevator. "Hell yeah, I was in the 8th grade! How was I supposed to know Mama was gonna see all that and give me the worst whooping of my life? My ass was numb for weeks!"

They both burst out laughing, the memory of that embarrassing moment bringing tears to their eyes. By the time they reached the pool, their bond felt stronger than ever, their laughter a testament to it.

Chapter 24

"The Turning Point Under The Lights"

The party was in full swing when they returned. The pool area had transformed into a vibrant scene straight out of a music video—lights dancing like stars in the night sky, casting a warm, golden glow over the crowd of residents and invited guests. The DJ's bass-heavy beats thumped through the air, shaking the ground beneath them. The grill smoke swirled into the air, filling the space with the mouthwatering scent of charred shrimp, seasoned spices, and burgers. The caterer was working in overdrive, barely able to keep up with the demand. Every platter of shrimp barely touched the table before hungry hands snatched them up, leaving nothing but empty trays and a few stray tails. People were eating them like they were the last thing on Earth, licking their fingers between bites.

Escorting Amani to their personal section, Onyx scanned the scene, his mind already on the next move. He knew it was time to elevate the energy. Without wasting another second, he made his way to the DJ table, grabbing the mic with a confident grin. "Let's turn it up one time!" Onyx shouted, his voice booming over the crowd. The beat dropped, and everyone seemed to feel it. The room pulsed with the rhythm, and just like that, the party was on another level. He dropped a quick freestyle, effortlessly flowing with bars that had the crowd hyped in an instant. The energy was electric—bass thumping, people dancing, laughing, and drinking, their excitement infectious. The whole vibe was like the world was on fire, but in the best way possible.

As he finished, Onyx's eyes caught sight of Stacy walking into the pool area, her loud, brash energy flooding the space. She strutted in like she owned the place, eyes darting around the crowd, making sure everyone saw her. Jasmine followed behind, rolling her eyes in silent disapproval, clearly not wanting to be associated with Stacy's antics.

Onyx sighed, knowing exactly what kind of scene Stacy was about to cause.

He made his way over to Amani, pulling her aside with a serious look. "Yo, get your girl, before she messes everything up," Onyx muttered, nodding toward Stacy, who was already throwing shade and making a scene. He didn't need any drama occurring—especially not with the kind of crowd they had gathered. Amani, sensing his frustration, just shrugged.

"Her ratchet ass always doin' too much," she said with a half-hearted laugh, clearly used to Stacy's behavior. But Onyx wasn't laughing. He had bigger plans for the event.

"I got her!" she said, giving him a reassuring look, while walking off toward Stacy. Onyx took a deep breath, refocusing on the crowd. The last thing he needed was drama distracting him from his grind.

The music shifted, and Onyx didn't miss a beat. He grabbed the mic again and called out, "Who's ready for the next round?!" The crowd went wild, hyped by his energy. They were eating it up, and Onyx knew how to keep them in the palm of his hand. He dropped a track he wrote in prison he called: "Don't Judge Me," flowing effortlessly over the beat, and the crowd responded with a roar.

Meanwhile, Yoshe had been making her rounds, talking to a few people, but it was clear where the party's attention was. She didn't even have to try. When she removed her kimono and made her way to the pool, the entire space seemed to pause. She slipped into the water with ease, her movements graceful, seductive, like she was born to be in the spotlight. Her two-piece swimsuit clung to her perfectly sculpted body, and the kimono she was wearing in an attempt to conceal her curves was almost like an afterthought—an accessory to her natural beauty.

Onyx caught himself staring, his breath hitching as she emerged from the pool, water glistening along her curves. When she adjusted her swimsuit, the simple movement made his pulse spike. He hated himself for thinking it, but he couldn't help it—he regretted choosing Stacy that night. Yoshe had a vibe about her that was undeniable. She wasn't just about the flash; she had that quiet confidence that drew people in, something he admired more than he wanted to admit. She had the grit of the streets but the finesse to move in any room. Sharp enough to help a man build an empire, Yoshe had all the qualities of a true boss bitch— just like his sister. And the longer he gazed at her, the more he regretted letting his sexual desire cloud his judgment that night.

"Yo, y'all actin' thirsty!" Amani said, her voice cutting through the crowd as she approached, shaking her head at the men openly ogling Yoshe. But it was no use. The guys couldn't take their eyes off her. Onyx knew what that felt like. He was drawn to her energy, even from a distance.

As the day wore on, Onyx was in his element. Every hour, he grabbed the mic, taking the crowd to another level with a mix of his personal tracks and freestyling that kept them on the edge. His voice dripped with confidence, the energy he radiated pulling everyone in like a magnet. Each time he stepped up, the crowd grew louder, their excitement contagious, rapping along to his hooks, chanting his name. The party wasn't just a party—it was his stage, and everyone there was a part of the performance.

Leaving Amani, Stacy, and Jasmine, Yoshe went to get herself a plate of shrimp and a margarita. She stood at the bar, effortlessly drawing attention as she ate and sipped on her drink. The silk fabric of her kimono fluttered with each movement, brushing against her sun-kissed skin. Her curves were sculpted yet effortless, the tie of her kimono cinching her waist just right. Under the lights, her skin seemed to glow, and her wet curls framed her face in a way that made it impossible for anyone to look away. She moved with natural, effortless confidence, and every step she took was purposeful yet fluid, making sure no one could take their eyes off her. Her smile was warm, inviting, but there was always a hint of something just out of reach, leaving the crowd wanting more.

Stacy stood a few feet away, clutching her drink like a lifeline, while Jasmine ignored her altogether. She watched Yoshe, her tight smile barely masking the raw jealousy simmering underneath. Every laugh, every glance Yoshe received from the men only stoked the internal fire.

Stacy's grip on her glass tightened, and she took another sip, trying to mask the heat rising in her chest.

"That bitch thinks she all that, don't she Jas?" Stacy muttered under her breath, loud enough for the guy passing in front of her to hear as well. Her eyes narrowed as Yoshe laughed at something Onyx whispered to her, her voice dripping with irritation. "The bitch can have all of his attention now, but it'll be my pussy those lips will fall asleep licking on."

"He's networkin', Stacy," Jasmine snapped, her patience worn thin by Stacy's jealous whining. "Hoe, you know damn well she doesn't want Onyx. And she'd never f**k anyone who's been with your biohazard ass."

Her focus on Onyx and Yoshe was so intense that it rendered her speechless.

Onyx, oblivious to the tension, was in his element, soaking up the attention. He worked the crowd between sets, dapping up guests, making everyone feel like they were part of something bigger. But it was the twins that had the real control over the party. They moved like shadows through the crowd, slick and smooth, exchanging quiet words with the residents who knew exactly what to do. Every so often, one of them would slip off to a secluded corner or a bathroom, disappearing for a few minutes, only to return with a new energy that was unmistakable.

With Amani breathing softly, her head resting against her brother's shoulder, Onyx leaned back against the bar, a cold drink in hand, his gaze scanning the room like a chess player setting up his next move to execute. He liked how the twins worked the crowd—nothing too obvious, just enough to keep things moving without raising suspicion. The way the residents would disappear for a few minutes and come back with that extra bounce in their step was almost an art. It was controlled chaos, and Onyx respected the precision of it.

"This party hittin', huh?" a guy said, sliding up next to Onyx with a nod toward Stacy.

"Hell yeah," Amani replied, smirking. "Ain't nobody do it like my bruh. You see how they eatin' that shrimp like it's gold? The caterer lookin' stressed as hell tryin' to keep up."

The guy laughed, nodding as another empty platter was whisked away by the server, only for a new one to take its place, the shrimp disappearing just as fast. Standing there, he noticed the crowd's energy was still electric, fueled by the music and the people. Shockwave—the local producer—was hanging around, his eyes on Onyx, clearly impressed. After another one of Onyx's sets, Shockwave made his move, sliding up to him with a knowing grin.

"You got talent, man," Shockwave said, his tone low but serious. "I wanna work with you. I've got a show comin' up, and I need you on that stage."

Onyx's heart skipped a beat. He knew this was it—the opportunity he had been waiting for. His eyes lit up as he nodded. "Say less. Let's make it happen."

The rest of the night flew by in a blur, the energy never fading. People kept coming up to Onyx, showing love, but his mind was already elsewhere. As the crowd began to thin out, he stood by the pool, watching the last few guests wrap up their night. It had been a perfect mix of business and pleasure. He had made the connections he needed, kept the crowd hyped, and the night was still far from over.

Onyx felt like he was exactly where he needed to be—on the verge of something big. All the pieces were falling into place, and as the sound of the last few people leaving echoed in the distance, he knew this was just the beginning.

"The Mirrored Consequences of Our Choices"
"10 Months Later"

Chapter 25

"Power and Perception"

"Ten months after that wild pool party at Amani's spot, the city didn't just know Onyx's name—they felt his presence, like a storm rolling in, unpredictable and impossible to ignore. He had carved out a reputation that extended far beyond the streets, solidifying himself as a force that couldn't be overlooked. Onyx wasn't just hustling for survival anymore—he was building an empire, one calculated move at a time. His crew, loyal and efficient, followed his vision, leaving a trail of respect and fear in their wake. Every decision he made, every risk he took, pushed him closer to the throne he knew was his."

The orchestrated hits they pulled off to maintain their rise were legendary: 27 bricks from a Jamaican stash house, 17 more off some Mexicans in Gwinnett, and 15 snatched clean from some country dealer out in Griffin. But it wasn't just the bricks that gave them recognition. Nah, it was the way they handled business—shootouts over turf, strategic moves that left rivals shook. Money Bag Mafia (M.B.M.) wasn't just surviving; they were dominating.

And now? Young hustlers from East Point to Bankhead were begging for a seat at the table. The family was tight—12 deep. Loyalty wasn't just a word they threw around; it was stitched into their very existence. Each one of them understood the rules: eat together, move together, win together. Onyx made sure everyone benefited. He kept his crew looking sharp, rolling in used luxury cars that still turned heads, each one polished to perfection. They rocked diamond-encrusted M.B.M. pendants—a gleaming symbol of their unity and growing power. And the parties they threw? Legendary. People didn't just attend; they experienced them, retelling every detail like they'd been to a sold-out music festival. From the pounding bass to the exclusive guest lists, the vibe was undeniable—Onyx and his crew were rewriting the rules of the game.

But Onyx always stayed sharp, never letting the hype cloud his judgment. "Keep flexin' like y'all untouchable, and the Feds gon' pull up like they RSVP'd," he'd tell them, his tone a firm blend of warning and wisdom. He understood the game too well—flash too much, and you became a target. Onyx wasn't about to let reckless moves bring down everything he'd built.

That morning a little after 11 o'clock, the vibe in Onyx's Buckhead condo was electric. The scent of peppercorn butter melting over swordfish steaks wafted through the air, blending with the soft hum of conversation. The dining room was a statement—sleek and modern, with a massive glass-top table that reflected the golden light pouring in from the floor-to-ceiling windows. Outside, the Buckhead skyline stretched like a promise of success, glittering against the crisp winter sun.

The crew was gathered, their laughter and banter bouncing off the high ceilings. Speedy and Shadow were cracking jokes while Cle and Lil B debated about the best spot in the city for wings. Onyx sat at the head of the table, his presence commanding without effort.

"Y'all remember this ain't just dinner," he said, his voice cutting through the noise. "This business. Always gon' be business."

The laughter quieted, but the energy didn't fade. They knew what he meant—this wasn't just about breaking bread. It was about keeping the foundation solid, but Onyx's mind wasn't on the food or even the jokes. He pushed his chair back and stood, the metallic scrape of the legs against the floor silencing the room for a beat. "Gotta handle somethin'," he said, his tone casual but firm.

He slipped away to his office, closing the door behind him with a soft click. The air inside was cooler, quieter, the faint buzz of the city was barely audible through the thick glass windows. The space reflected his duality—clean, minimalist, but with just enough flair to remind anyone who walked in that they were standing in the presence of someone who moved with purpose.

Onyx sank into the leather chair behind his desk, his fingers tapping lightly against the polished wood. The phone was pressed to his ear as he waited, the silence on the other end heavy with potential. This call wasn't just important—it was everything to the survival of M.B.M.

A week ago, during a video call with his homies still locked up, Onyx had caught a glimpse of a familiar face in the background—Diego, his Colombian homeboy. Seeing him again stirred a memory Onyx hadn't revisited since his release. He recalled Diego mentioning that his father had once said, "If you're ever serious 'bout movin' like a king, call me." Back then, Onyx had smiled and brushed it off, focused on walking a straight line and staying out of trouble. But now, with pressure mounting and his options dwindling, those words hit him differently, carrying a weight he couldn't ignore.

The crew's demand was growing by the day, and scraping together bricks from local dealers was no longer enough to keep up. Robbing other crews wasn't a sustainable plan either—it was messy, reckless, and painted a target on their backs. Then there was TJ, his primary connect, a relationship that felt more like a leash with every deal. Onyx had wanted to cut TJ off months ago, even toyed with the idea of killing him, but without a solid connect, TJ remained an asset he couldn't afford to lose.

Now, the chessboard was shifting, and Onyx knew he needed to think four moves ahead. Diego's father might just be the key to flipping the game entirely—and for the first time, Onyx was ready to take the risk. The call came together quickly. Diego's father had agreed to talk, but nothing was guaranteed. Although Onyx had saved Diego's life in prison and felt the connection was owed to him on merit alone, this conversation was his opportunity to prove he was worth the investment—a chance to lock in a reliable supplier who could stabilize their entire operation.

"Señor, I appreciate you takin' this call," Onyx said, his tone steady but carrying the weight of respect. He leaned back in his chair, his free hand gripping the edge of the armrest as if grounding himself for what was to come.

The voice on the other end was calm yet firm, laced with the kind of authority that only came from years of wielding power. "Understand this, joven. This is not just business—it's trust, it's family. You misstep, even once, and there will be no second chances."

"I feel you on that. I move the same way, señor. This is bigger than just moves though—it's about loyalty, trust. I ain't here to waste nobody time or play no games. If y'all give me the lane, I'm gon' handle it right. Straight up." Onyx nodded, though he knew the man couldn't see him.

The call ended with a simple promise of a meeting—no dates, no locations, just the subtle confirmation that Onyx's name was now in the conversation. He leaned back in his chair, the gravity of the moment pressing down on him. This was the move he'd been waiting for, the one that could solidify everything. Without a steady supply, the money, the music, the reputation—it all meant nothing.

Sliding his phone back into his pocket, Onyx stood and headed toward the dining room. The sound of clinking glasses and bursts of laughter spilled into the hallway, a sharp contrast to the intensity of the call. As he stepped into the room, he allowed himself a small smile, soaking in the fleeting moment of normalcy before the weight of his next move would inevitably take over.

"Ay, Cle," the Godfather said, cutting through the loud debate about the best strip club in Atlanta as he leaned back in his custom chair at the head of the table. His voice carried the weight of authority, silencing the room. "I see you out here holdin' it down. Joyland was chaos after that shootout, but you kept it solid. Real good work."

Cle grinned, raising his glass in a lazy toast. "Appreciate that, Godfather. But you already know—I ain't lettin' naw f**k n***a stop me from feedin' the family."

"*Udugu kwa maisha!*" Lil B shouted, raising his glass high.

"*Udugu kwa maisha!*" the crew echoed, their voices overlapping in a rare moment of unity.

For Onyx, it was more than a toast. It was a reminder of why he did what he did. The streets were unforgiving, but this? This family? It was everything. Still unable to fully surrender to either music or the streets, he clung to both, as if they were the paths fate had forged for him.

The energy in the room settled after the toast, but the laughter and chatter picked up again as the crew polished off their plates. Onyx watched them, quietly observing the dynamics. There was pride in the way they carried themselves—a swagger that came from knowing they were part of something bigger than themselves. But Onyx saw the cracks forming—some lacked the discipline to balance success with restraint.

"Y'all ready to lose some money?" the Godfather asked, rising from his seat with a smirk. He pulled off his shirt, revealing a canvas of tattoos and a chiseled physique, his tank top clinging to his powerful frame. Reaching into his pocket, he pulled out a thick wad of cash and waved it in the air with a cocky grin. "Ante up, y'all know what the f**k it is."

Not wanting to be outdone, despite his wiry frame resembling a starving chicken, Speedy ripped off his shirt and dropped to the floor, banging out 20 push-ups as if sheer effort could make his physique rival that of the Godfather. The crew erupted into laughter, shoving their chairs back as they followed him into the foyer.

Tossing quarters had become their weekly competition, a game designed to keep the playing field even since Gunna dominated them each time they shot dice. This game, however, required precision, a steady hand, and just the right amount of finesse to land the coin closest to the wall without hitting it—an art that leveled the playing field, no matter how much bravado or muscle someone had.

The polished floors gleamed under the soft glow of recessed lighting, while the faint jingle of coins in the Godfather's hand echoed through the space, building anticipation. The crew gathered around, eyes on the first toss, the tension in the room electric with the unspoken challenge. "A'ight, y'all know the rules," the Godfather said, standing by the front door. "Hundred a throw. Closest to the door takes it. No cryin', no excuses. And I'm takin' all side bets."

The game was simple, but the stakes made it serious. Everyone lined up, pulling crumpled and crisp bills from their pockets to toss into the growing pile. Malik, the newest member, had been talking big all week, claiming he was the one to beat.

"Man, I'm takin' all y'all f**kin' money today—side bets, whatever. Godfather, you talk that money talk, now show it," Malik said, a wide grin spreading across his face as he dropped $300 on the Godfather's shoes with a cocky flick of his wrist. Casually flipping a quarter in his hand, the metallic clink echoed through the foyer, drawing everyone's attention. His eyes gleamed with confidence, a bold challenge written all over his face, daring anyone to step up.

"Yeah, a'ight," Cle shot back, narrowing his eyes. "Don't let that east side confidence get you embarrassed, shawty. A n***a from the 6 can't whip me at sh*t."

The first few rounds were lighthearted, filled with trash talk and laughter. But as the pile of cash grew, so did the tension. Gramz, the youngest in the crew, dominated the game, consistently landing his quarter closest to the door. By the eighth round, he had racked up close to $10,000 with side bets.

"Godfather, this lil' n***a cheating or somethin'," Cle said, shaking his head after another one of his tosses bounced off the doorframe and rolled out of competition. "Ain't no way you hittin' that sh*t every f**kin' time."

Gramz grinned, sliding another stack of bills into his pocket with a smug swagger. "Skill, big bruh. You gotta get like me. Y'all already know a n***a from Zone 1, 4, 6, or wherever can't beat a Zone 3 n***a at sh*t," he said, leaning back with his arms crossed like he'd already won the whole game.

He glanced around the room, letting his words hang heavy in the air, his smirk daring anyone to challenge him. "I think it's somethin' in our muthaf**kin' water, ya feel me? Our hustle and swag built different. This sh*t like a robbery with no strap, y'all might as well hand over that money now, save yourselves the continuous embarrassment."

The crew laughed and jeered, tossing playful insults back, but Gramz didn't budge, his confidence unshakable. He grabbed another quarter off the table and flicked it between his fingers, letting it shine under the lights like a trophy. "Y'all can try, but this game already mine."

The Godfather laughed, despite losing, as he leaned against the wall, watching him toss—quarter after quarter—flowing through the air with the precision of someone who'd perfected it into an art. "Rep that spot, shawty," he said, his voice clear, and everyone understood exactly what he meant. "Gramz didn't stutter."

For a brief moment, everything felt easy, almost normal. But the weight of the earlier phone call still hung in the back of his mind. He needed that connection, and the uncertainty, the waiting, was slowly gnawing at his peace of mind. After losing seven more times without even winning a single side bet, his smile slowly faded. He stepped back, leaving the crew to their game, and made his way to his office, with his chest growing heavier with every step.

Back behind his desk, Onyx pulled out the ledger and tablet, scanning the numbers with a critical eye. Something wasn't adding up. The books weren't clean, and he knew exactly whom to ask about it. Reaching for the intercom, he pressed the button and spoke calmly. "Marko, I need you to stop and come to the office. Bring Bishop and Gunna with you."

Minutes later, the door opened, and the three men walked in. Marko looked uneasy, while Bishop and Gunna were still caught up in a video on Bishop's phone. "Bruh, look at shawty right here," Bishop said, pointing to the screen and laughing. "She's thicker than a bowl of f**kin' oatmeal."

"Man, shut up," Gunna muttered, nudging him. "We in the boss's office."

The Godfather didn't even glance up. His focus stayed on the ledger as he tapped a pen against the desk. The immediate silence in the room grew more suffocating as the seconds stretched. Finally, the Godfather spoke, his voice low and measured.

"Marko, why haven't you locked down that store on 4th yet? And why did you only deposited a hundred bands when the numbers say it should've been one-fifty-seven?"

Marko swallowed hard, his eyes darting to Gunna and Bishop for support, but neither of them spoke. "Uh… the money still bein' cleaned through the laundromat, and uh… the storeowner won't sell," he stammered.

Onyx's pen stopped tapping. He leaned back in his chair, his eyes narrowing as he stared Marko down. "Didn't you tell me the same bullsh*t last week?"

Marko nodded slowly, the color draining from his face.

"So what you sayin' is, you can't handle the job," Onyx said, his tone sharp enough to penetrate. "You tellin' me I was wrong to grant you a position in this family?"

"Nah, Godfather, it ain't like that," Marko said quickly, his voice trembling. "The owner refuse to sell—stubborn as hell. But I swear, I'll get it done. Just need a few more days, and them papers will be signed. I promise… I promise."

The Godfather studied him for a long moment, the silence heavy. Finally, he nodded. "Three days. No excuses. If that store ain't ours by Wednesday, you gon' wish you never stepped foot in this family."

Marko nodded again, his hands trembling as the Godfather issued final instructions, his tone leaving no room for questions. One by one, they exited the room, the door closing with a soft click. The Godfather leaned back in his chair, rubbing his temples as the weight of it all settled over him. Weak links were a liability—then, now, and always. As the crew expanded, so did the risks, and he knew that with more people came more chances for mistakes. Everybody wanted to eat, but few understood the discipline and precision it took to keep the table from collapsing.

He stood and walked to the window, looking out at the city below. The lights stretched for miles, a glittering reminder of the power he held—and the danger that came with it. "Loyalty and work," he muttered to himself. "That's all that matters. Keep moving, or get left behind."

As the day wore on, Onyx rejoined the crew, reminding them to stay sharp and united before they headed out. Once alone in his condo, he walked through the newly decorated space, his eyes taking in the luxurious details. The transformation was complete—the interior designer had outdone herself. Black-and-gold accents gleamed against sleek, minimalist furniture. The open floor plan felt expansive, but intimate, a perfect blend of sophistication and comfort. Everything was polished, like a reflection of himself—powerful, untouchable, yet still grounded in something raw and real.

His gaze shifted to the large steel-clad fireplace, where a set of crystal M.B.M. letters was affixed, catching the light and casting reflections that danced across the room. It was a subtle reminder of his empire—his name, his brand, his world. He paused for a moment, letting the stillness of the space sink in, before moving forward.

His eyes then fell on the 100-gallon circular tank against the southeast wall, a centerpiece in the living room. The Australian Flathead Perches swam lazily, their sleek bodies gliding through the water, oblivious to the world outside. Onyx watched their effortless movements, the way they drifted with ease—a sharp contrast to the chaos ruling his life. For a split second, he allowed himself to imagine a life where this was all he had to worry about—the beauty, the peace, the freedom. But that fleeting moment shattered with the shrill ring of his phone.

Chapter 26

A Narrow Escape

The crisp Augusta air kissed Amani's skin as she and Stacy stepped out of the Clubhouse Restaurant at Sugar Creek Golf Course. The meeting with Major and Vot had gone off without a hitch, leaving a sense of triumph hanging between them. With every step, Amani exuded an irresistible blend of power and allure, her Sassy Girl set perfectly sculpting her figure and accentuating the graceful curves of her hips. The soft, clingy fabric of her skirt hugged her in all the right places, while its hemline framed her toned, shapely, honeyed legs that seemed to glide effortlessly with each stride. Every movement was a captivating symphony of elegance and sensuality, drawing eyes like moths to a flame and leaving an unspoken promise of confidence and poise in her wake.

Heads turned as the two women walked toward Amani's red BMW M5. Conversations stalled, and even the gentle whir of passing golf carts seemed to fade into the background. Men stared unabashedly, captivated by the magnetic energy Amani radiated. She didn't have to try—her presence was enough. Every sway of her hips and flick of her glossy hair radiated confidence and power, daring anyone to approach.

Beside her, Stacy was no less striking, her mocha-colored Be Mine set hugging her curves with equal precision. Her caramel-toned skin gleamed under the afternoon sun, and her defined features carried a quiet intensity. Stacy moved with an air of effortless cool, her piercing eyes daring anyone to challenge her. Together, they were a vision of beauty and danger, two women who knew they owned the room—and now the parking lot.

Interrupting their laughter, a golf cart zipped to a halt in front of them. Inside sat two white men, their faces a mix of awe and intrigue. The driver, an older man with a receding hairline and flushed cheeks, leaned forward, his gaze locked on Amani.

"Ma'am," he said, his Southern drawl thick and slightly trembling, "I don't mean to be forward, but… your feet are stunning. Could I—uh—take a picture of them?"

Amani stopped mid-stride, arching a perfectly groomed brow. Her lips curved into a smirk, her voice laced with amusement. "You serious right now?" she asked, letting the moment hang in the air.

The man nodded eagerly, his face reddening. "I swear, I've never seen anything like them. They're just… perfect."

She let out a soft laugh, disbelief woven into it. "Well, I guess there's a first for everything." With effortless poise, Amani extended her foot in her strappy stilettos, showcasing skin so flawless it seemed almost airbrushed. She angled her foot slightly, letting the sunlight glisten off her freshly polished toes. "Go ahead, get your shot."

The man fumbled for his phone like a nervous schoolboy, his grin spreading as he captured the image. Meanwhile, Stacy couldn't help but play along. She circled to the passenger side of the cart, where the younger man sat, his eyes glued to her every move. With a sly smile, she leaned down, so close he could feel her breath on his skin.

"If you were mine," she murmured, her voice a velvet whisper dripping with seduction, "you'd go to sleep and wake up drowning in my throat." Her finger traced his jawline, lingering just enough to make him shiver before stopping above his chest, her touch sparking a fire in his veins.

The man visibly squirmed, his hand instinctively reaching for his wallet. "What do I need to do to make that happen?" he stammered, his voice shaking.

Stacy tilted her head, letting her eyes sweep over him with a calculated slowness. "Baby, you couldn't afford it," she said with a wink, turning on her heel and sauntering away. Her hips swayed deliberately, teasing the men and anyone else who dared to look.

Amani, amused by the whole scene, shook her head as she slid into the driver's seat of the BMW. "Bitch, you're a damn mess," she said, grinning as Stacy climbed in, her smirk satisfied.

As they pulled out of the parking lot, the bass-heavy music blasting through the speakers matched the energy in the car. They laughed, recapping the absurdity of the interaction, the weight of the business meeting fading into the background. Bouldercrest Road stretched ahead, a familiar route lined with trees and the occasional businesses. But their lighthearted mood shattered with the sharp, unmistakable crack of a gunshot.

Amani gripped the wheel tighter. "What the hell was that?" she asked, glancing in the rearview mirror.

Before Stacy could respond, another shot rang out, and the car jolted violently as something struck the rear panel. Stacy twisted in her seat, her voice rising in panic. "They're shooting at us!"

Amani's pulse spiked. "You've gotta be f**kin' kidding me! Who? Why?" she yelled, her foot slamming on the gas. The sleek BMW roared forward, but the engine behind them grew louder. A cactus-colored Durango came into view, its menacing presence filling her mirrors. It surged forward, ramming into the back of the BMW with a thunderous crash. Amani gritted her teeth, her hands gripping the steering wheel tightly as she fought to keep the car under control, the tension in her fingers mirroring the adrenaline coursing through her veins.

"They're trying to run us off the road!" Stacy screamed, gripping the dashboard, as another shot shattered the rear windshield, spraying glass across the back seat. The bullet zipped past Amani's ear, heat trailing in its wake. Her heart pounded like a drum, her mind racing.

The Durango swerved recklessly, its driver moving like a maniac as he pulled up alongside them after unleashing another deafening round of gunfire. The passenger leaned out of the window, his face twisted with malice as he aimed the gun directly at Amani's face.

Stacy screamed uncontrollably, clutching the door as panic overtook her. Amani was frozen with terror, her eyes darting frantically between the street ahead and the barrel of the gun. Her breath hitched, her chest tightening with every passing second, yet she forced herself to stay in control, locking her focus on the road as chaos closed in around them.

For a breathless moment, her world shrunk to the gun barrel aimed at her face. Time seemed to freeze. She could see every detail—the cruel smirk curling his lips, the icy gleam in his eyes, and the cold metal of the gun reflecting the afternoon sun. Her heart pounded as his finger curled around the trigger, fear crashing over her.

But instead of pulling the trigger, the man tilted the gun upward and fired a single shot into the sky, his mocking grin widening as he watched them flinch. Stacy's scream pierced the air, and Amani's knuckles ached as she gripped the wheel tighter, her entire body trembling as the sound of the gunshot echoed through the chaos. It was a cruel reminder of how close they were to death, the man's facial expressions reflecting in her mind like a taunt.

"Motherf**ker's playing with us!" Stacy yelled, tears streaming down her face.

Amani slammed her foot into the accelerator harder, the engine screaming as the car shot forward. But the Durango wasn't letting up. It rammed them again, the impact jarring Amani so hard she almost lost control. On the third collision, the BMW skidded off the road, grass and dirt spraying in all directions as it careened into a ditch.

The airbags exploded with a deafening pop, knocking the breath from Amani's lungs. Stacy clutched her seatbelt, sobbing uncontrollably. For a moment, everything was silent except for their ragged breathing. The Durango skidded to a stop, and the passenger leaned out one last time, firing a few precise shots at their tires. The hiss of deflation was followed by mocking laughter as the Durango sped off, leaving them stranded, shaken, and exposed.

Amani sat frozen, her mind reeling, her chest rising and falling with heavy, uneven breaths. Her body trembled, adrenaline still coursing through her veins like fire. The aftermath was eerily silent, broken only by the faint creak of the battered car settling deeper into the ditch.

Her hands shook violently as she unbuckled her seatbelt, the metallic click echoing louder than it should in the stillness. Her fingers fumbled as she reached for her phone, slick with sweat and barely able to hold onto it. The weight of what had just happened bore down on her chest, threatening to crush her.

Her lips parted, and when she finally spoke, her voice was raw—a fragile mix of fear and simmering fury. Each word carried an edge that betrayed just how close she had come to breaking.

Stacy stumbled out of the car, her legs shaking as she steadied herself on the uneven ground. She stared down the empty road, her expression hardening. "This ain't over, muthaf**ker," she muttered.

"No," Amani said, her voice hard as steel. "It's just f**kin' beginning."

Chapter 27

"Blood in the Water"

"Yeah?" Onyx answered, his tone sharpening, his mind snapping back to reality.

The voice on the other end came fast, urgent, causing his jaw clenched. It was time. The cold weight of the Glock rested against his hip—both a comfort and a warning. Today could go either way. That brief taste of peace? Gone. The air in the Black House felt different now, the polished surfaces and luxury around him suddenly sterile, lifeless. The walls seemed closer. This wasn't home. This was just a pause before the storm.

No more hesitation. Move.

"Bruh! Where the f**k you at?!" Amani's voice burst through the speaker, raw with anger, laced with something shakier—panic. Her breath came fast, erratic, like she'd been running.

Onyx took a slow sip from his glass, unbothered. "I'm at the Black House. Why? Wassup?"

"Bruh, this bitch-ass n***a just shot at me and Stacy, then ran us off the damn road!" Amani spat, her voice climbing an octave as her anger boiled over, the words coming out clear and fast. "That n***a straight up acted like my life don't mean sh*t! You should've seen it, O—we barely made it outta there alive! Stacy's cryin', my car's all f**ked up, and this n***a just sped off like it was nothin'!"

She paced, her chest heaving as the scene replayed in her mind. The screech of tires, the splintering glass, the gunshots, the terror in Stacy's screams—it all felt too raw, too real. Her thoughts were interrupted by the sound of sirens growing louder, and seconds later, the flashing red and blue lights illuminated the street as the police pulled up. Amani stopped in her tracks, her anger still elevating, trying to steady her breathing as the weight of what had just happened settled heavily on her shoulders.

"I swear, O, this ain't just some random beef. This was personal. He wasn't tryin' to scare me—he was tryin' to end me. I'm not lettin' this slide. Hell no. What we gonna do about this?"

Without hesitation, his hand went to his waist, fingers grazing the Glock—but that wasn't enough. Not for this. He needed more power. Moving fast, he scurried to his bedroom, yanking the steel from his waist and swapping it for the FNX-45 from the safe. Its weight settled against his palm like an unspoken promise. This was war. He tucked the heavy frame into his waistband, his pulse steady, his mind locked in. Whoever had dared to play with his sister's life was about to feel the full force of his wrath.

He snatched his keys off the dresser, the metallic glint flashing in the dim light before vanishing into his grip. "Where the hell y'all at?" His voice was sharp, edged with impatience.

Onyx's veins bulged beneath his skin, tight like they might burst. His pulse pounded in his temples, each throb feeding the slow-burning rage bubbling just beneath the surface. The silence on the other end stretched too long. His grip tightened around the phone, knuckles darkening as he scurried toward the door. His mind raced, chasing worst-case scenarios before he could stop them.

"Shell Gas Station down the street from McNair High School," Amani said, her voice trembling but steady. In the background, Stacy's biting words sliced through the noise as she tore into someone, brushing off a hustler's unwanted advances with the fiery intensity of someone who refused to be messed with.

"I'm on my way." Onyx hung up before Amani could respond, anger simmering beneath his skin like a lit fuse. He stormed out the front door, hitting T-Roc's line as he paced toward the elevator. "Yo, put everybody on high alert and meet me at the Shell on Bouldercrest now," Onyx barked, his voice rigid with authority. "Someone just shot at Amani!"

"F**k nah! A'ight, bet," T-Roc replied without hesitation.

Riding the elevator down to the garage, Onyx's thoughts spiraled into a storm of rage and calculation. Whoever had disrespected his sister hadn't just crossed a line; they'd signed their death warrant. But was this personal, or was someone trying to send him a message? The unanswered question gnawed at him, tightening the knot of tension in his chest.

As the elevator doors slid open, Onyx stepped out with purpose, scanning the dimly lit garage. He wasn't sure if he'd need to handle business, but he wasn't taking any chances. He chose the Impala he had for emergencies—a sleek, unassuming ride with a history as dead as the person it was registered to. The paperwork was clean, a perfect ghost car for dirty work and escape.

He slid into the driver's seat and scrolled through his playlist until he landed on some old-school B.G., the grimy beats and raw lyrics syncing with his mood. The music blared through the speakers, sharpening his focus. His fingers drummed on the grip of the .45 resting in his lap as he rolled toward the garage gate. The steel carried both promise and peril, a silent vow that the day's outcome rested on his next move. The metal barrier arm groaned, dragging upward at a snail's pace, testing his patience.

The moment the gap was wide enough, Onyx hit the gas. The tires screeched against the concrete, and the Impala shot out of the garage like a bullet. He weaved through the sparse afternoon traffic, driving with the intensity of a man on a mission—or like the devil himself was right on his tail.

Exiting off I-285 and turning left onto Bouldercrest, Onyx's teeth ground together once he spotted Amani's car half-sunken in a ditch. He eased off the gas, the knot in his stomach tightening as he pulled to the side of the road. The damage was bad—busted windows, a mangled driver-side door, dented bumper, and deep gouges along the side of the car that looked like battle scars. This wasn't just a random accident. This was personal. It wasn't just a hit—it was a message.

Onyx sat for a moment, his eyes scanning the scene as his pulse quickened. The faint smell of burnt rubber still lingered in the air, and shattered glass sparkled on the asphalt like broken promises. He climbed out of his car, slamming the door shut with more force than he intended, and stalked toward Amani's wreck. His mind raced with questions and anger, every step making his fury grow hotter.

This wasn't just about Amani. This was about him, about someone testing his resolve, daring to cross lines they had no business even approaching. He crouched beside the car, running his hand along the jagged metal. Whoever did this wasn't just sending a warning—they were picking a fight. And Onyx was more than ready to answer.

"F**k n***as gon' pay the piper tonight," he muttered under his breath, the words spilling out like a dark prayer as he turned away from the wreck. Sliding back into his car, he fired off a quick text to Gunna, his fingers moving fast. *See which crew's available for some havoc tonight?* The engine roared to life, and Onyx peeled away from the scene, his mind racing as he planned his next move.

Cruising through the intersection, he pulled into the gas station lot, his eyes sweeping the area like a hawk on the hunt. The tension in his chest tightened when he spotted Amani and Stacy near the pumps, talking with two officers. He eased the car to a stop, his gaze locking on them. Amani's stance was unyielding, her chin high, her arms gesturing sharply as she spoke. Stacy, in stark contrast, stood frozen, her lips pressed into a thin line, her silence speaking volumes.

The sight hit Onyx harder than he expected—not with fear, but with a white-hot fury that rippled through him. This wasn't just an attack on Amani and Stacy; it was an attack on him, his family, his name. Whoever thought they could pull this off clearly didn't understand who they were dealing with. Onyx promised himself this wouldn't end here. Not tonight. Not ever.

Onyx parked by the air pump, his hand brushing against the .45 in his lap. His phone buzzed, snapping him out of his thoughts. It was Gunna.

"Yeah, I'm here," Onyx said curtly, giving directions to Gunna, Cle, Lil B, and Savage. Within minutes, they all pulled up in a tight line behind T-Roc's SUV, engines rumbling like a storm brewing in the night. The convoy was more than a show of force; it was a declaration. Each rider was ready to defend Amani's honor, even if it meant spilling blood—or losing their own. The Godfather's crew stayed in their vehicles, their presence silent but heavy. He didn't need them drawing more attention—not yet.

The officers finally left, and Onyx began texting Amani. "*SNITCH*"—the word repeated in every message until she stormed toward him, heels clicking like gunfire against the pavement.

"I ain't no muthaf**kin' snitch," she snapped, jabbing her finger into his forehead as he held the passenger door open for her. Her glare was molten fury, but she nodded at the crew in acknowledgment before collapsing into the passenger seat. Amani had the heart of a lioness, but the streets weren't her jungle. "You better stop tryin' me before I show everyone your big head ass have a glass jaw."

Onyx ignored her jab, turning his attention to Stacy as she hesitated at the back door. Though they'd cut ties months ago, he reached out, guiding her into the seat with an unspoken truce. This wasn't about their past—it was about protection. With the girls momentarily safe, Onyx lingered, his keen eyes scanning the area for any signs of prying eyes or threats lurking in the shadows. The harsh afternoon sun cast long shadows across the pavement, but nothing seemed out of place—at least not yet. Satisfied for the moment, he turned and made his way over to Salvage '87 Buick Grand National GNX.

"I need you to call a tow for her car," the Godfather said, his tone firm yet calm as he handed Salvage a folded stack of cash—five crisp $100 bills. "I don't want it sittin' back there for vultures. Handle it." His voice dropped slightly, colder now. "And make sure word hits the streets. Everyone needs to know what happened—because whoever did this? They won't be breathing by morning."

His gaze was unflinching, steady, and deadly serious, the weight of the situation pressing into every word. There was no room for misunderstanding; the Godfather's orders weren't just commands—they were promises.

Salvage nodded. "Bet."

After imparting street wisdom and laying down orders for the Money Bag Mafia, Onyx strode back to the Impala. He slid behind the wheel, shaking his head as his gaze hardened. His voice came low and steady—the calm before the explosion. "Now tell me what happened, sis."

Amani's tough exterior cracked as she leaned across the console, wrapping her arms tightly around him. Her breath hitched, and for a moment, she just held on as if trying to anchor herself in the chaos. "Bruh, I thought they were gon' kill us," she whispered, her voice trembling, barely audible. They were shootin' at us, O. Then they stopped, like they were tryna decide somethin'. I literally heard one of the bullets whiz past me before it punched a hole clean through the windshield."

Her grip tightened as her voice broke. "I ain't never been that scared in my life. My hands were shakin', my heart was poundin' so loud I thought it might stop." But it wasn't just that..." She pulled back slightly, her eyes glossy but burning with a mix of terror and fury. "They weren't just shootin' to scare us, O. They were tryin' to take us out for a moment it seemed. The way they kept comin', the way they stopped just long enough to let it sink in—like they were tryna make a point. It wasn't random."

Leaning back into the seat, her eyes locked with his, wide with a mix of fear and anger. "When they pulled alongside me, they stopped shootin' and started ramming us more. Over and over, like they didn't care if we flipped or died. I couldn't do nothin', O. I had no choice but to run off the road."

Onyx sucked his teeth as her words hit him like unseen blows. This wasn't just an attack—it was a message. And whoever sent it was about to learn the cost of crossing a line they should've never touched.

Her hands gripped her knees as if steadying herself, tears threatened to fall, but she wiped them away quickly, reclaiming her edge. "I've never felt that helpless, like my life didn't mean a damn thing to them. But now? Now I want them to feel what I felt. I want 'em to know what it's like to be hunted."

Onyx sat in silence, the fire in his chest burning hotter with every word she spoke. His heart twisted at her vulnerability. He reached for her hand, squeezing it tightly. His eyes darted to Stacy in the rearview mirror, her silence louder than any scream. "I got y'all," Onyx said, his voice a promise and a warning. "Whoever did this gon' pay."

Onyx knew he was the rock she needed, the one person who could steady her in the storm. The way she had breathed against him, he could feel her fear, but also her trust. In that moment, he understood that his true power wasn't in the violence he was capable of—it was in the way he could lift her up, calm her, and make her feel safe again. As he gently caressed her hand, fighting the urge to let his anger take the wheel, he struggled to keep his anger composed, knowing he had to be the strength she needed, even when everything else felt like it was falling apart.

The car fell silent as they drove down Moreland Ave., tension thick enough to choke on. Amani leaned against him at a red light, her grip on his hand firm and desperate. "*Nakupenda*," she whispered, her Swahili soft and raw amidst the chaos.

"Ride or die for life," Onyx murmured, his voice steady as steel. He wrapped an arm around her, anchoring her while maneuvering through traffic.

As they approached the bridge crossing I-20, the heavy silence hung in the car like a storm cloud. Amani, desperate to break the tension and distract herself from the chaos still replaying in her mind, glanced over at Onyx. "You figured out what songs you gon' spit tonight, bruh?" she asked, her voice softer than usual, laced with an attempt at normalcy.

Onyx smirked, his eyes narrowing with purpose. "Headshots," he replied, the word dripping with intent. "F**k that show. Headshots gon' be my anthem tonight—for every f**k n***a that disrespected you and those associated with them."

Before Amani could protest, Onyx's phone buzzed again, Malik's name flashed on the screen. Without hesitation, he picked up. "Yeah," Onyx answered, his tone firm, his expression hardening as he listened to whatever Malik was saying on the other end. After a brief pause, he replied curtly, "Make sure it all checks out," then ended the call, his jaw tightening as he slid the phone back into his pocket.

As the storm loomed, Onyx prepared to confront it directly. Every inch of him was on edge, but he kept his demeanor calm, like a predator who knew the hunt was near. Atlanta hummed around him, but in that moment, the stillness carried an eerie weight, like the world holding its breath before the inevitable strike. His mind raced with possibilities, the faces of those who'd dared to disrespect his sister flashing like car blinkers in his head. Adrenaline surged through his veins, a controlled fury ready to consume anyone who got in his way.

Onyx knew the rules of the game. You hit hard, but you hit smart. Patience wasn't just a virtue; it was a weapon. His eyes shifted to the rearview mirror. The atmosphere was tense, saturated with the promise of violence, but Onyx wasn't just angry; he was calculating. Every move, every decision mattered now more than ever. **He wasn't just going to retaliate—he was going to make them regret ever crossing him.**

As the Impala cruised through the streets, the afternoon sun filtered through the windows, casting faint shadows on the pavement, giving the city a muted, almost ominous glow. It was a different kind of heat today—not the kind you could feel on your skin, but the kind that simmered deep in the soul. Onyx's mind played out a thousand scenarios, each one more brutal than the last. He thought about the people who may be behind this—what they stood for. But more importantly, he thought about the message he needed to send. He couldn't afford to leave any loose ends. This wasn't just about Amani's safety anymore; it was about sending a message loud and clear that no one f**ked with the Godfather, not his family, not his crew, and not anyone who thought they could get away with disrespect.

The weight of his promise to Amani—the promise to protect her and make things right—hung in the air, heavy and unspoken. She was still shaken, still trying to process what had happened, but Onyx saw the resolve in her eyes. He knew what he had to do. He could feel it in the tension between them—the unspoken understanding that he had to take action, to fight back. But Amani, fierce as she was, didn't want him to lose himself in the process.

Her voice echoed in his mind: She didn't want him to be consumed by the violence, to let it swallow him whole like it had so many before. She wanted him to focus on something bigger—the opportunity that was sitting right in front of him tonight, the one that could finally close the door on his street life for good. She didn't want him to throw everything away for revenge, but at the same time, she craved justice—she wanted whoever was behind it all to feel the full wrath of Money Bag Mafia.

Onyx understood. He understood her fear, her love, the way she didn't want him to become what she feared most—the man who couldn't escape the streets. But in that moment, the streets didn't want to let go of him. It was a part of him, like blood in his veins, and it was calling him to finish what had been started. The pull was too strong, and the rage too deep.

Onyx was a man of extremes. To him, family, loyalty, and respect left no room for a middle ground. The storm wasn't just inevitable—it was his to command.

Chapter 28

"The Room of Mayhem"

Onyx chose not to question Amani further after receiving another phone call. The information he and Malik shared had already sent his thoughts into overdrive. Instead of taking the interstate home, he crossed over the I-20 bridge. The steady purr of the Impala blended with the backdrop of the city. Turning off Moreland Avenue onto a quiet side street that led into Edgewood, he backed into the driveway of a house neither Amani nor Stacy recognized.

"Give me a moment," he said, stepping out of the car, his tone leaving no room for questions.

As Onyx approached the house, frustration sharpened his movements. He pulled out his phone and started dialing Bam-Bam, the man responsible for safeguarding the location. Before the call connected, the front door opened, and two massive Cane Corsos bolted out. Their deep, thunderous barks startled Stacy, who screamed his name from the car.

"Onyx... Onyx watch out..."

Turning his head, the dogs reached him before he could steady himself, their sheer size and energy nearly knocking him off balance. "Easy, boys. Easy," the Godfather said, his voice calm but firm as he rubbed their heads and scratched their necks. Their tails wagged, their aggression quickly replaced with enthusiasm. "Wassup, my boy!"

Once they settled, the Godfather climbed the steps with the dogs circling around him, eager for more of his attention. In the doorway, Bam-Bam appeared, his expression calm but watchful. The Godfather acknowledged him with a brief nod before commanding the dogs to enter and stepping inside.

The house's peeling paint and weathered porch revealed nothing of what lay inside. Bam-Bam's hulking frame moved out of the doorway, his expression serious. "Follow me, Godfather," he said, his voice low.

The faint creak of the floorboards followed their steps as Bam-Bam led him down a narrow hallway, dimly lit by a single overhead bulb.

At the end of the hallway stood a reinforced steel door, its thick frame and keypad lock giving away its purpose. The weight of the door alone hinted at what lay beyond. The Godfather reached into his wallet, pulling out an RFID card and swiping it against the reader. The lock clicked with a heavy sound, and he pushed the door open, revealing a small, secure room that exuded controlled power.

The walls were lined with an arsenal of weapons—assault rifles, pistols, shotguns, and ammunition, all meticulously organized on racks. Each piece gleamed under the cold fluorescent light, reflecting the care and precision that had gone into this operation. On one side of the room, a heavy safe stood bolted to the floor, its combination dial gleaming. Nearby, a workstation held a laptop and blueprints, scattered alongside stacks of cash bundled in rubber bands.

The Godfather stepped inside, his eyes scanning the room as a wave of satisfaction settled over him. This wasn't just a stash—it was a fortress, a testament to his growing empire. Bam-Bam leaned against the doorframe, arms crossed. "Everything's in place, boss," he said, his tone steady.

Onyx nodded, running his fingers along the barrel of a rifle before turning back to Bam-Bam. "Good. I need this place locked tighter than ever. Ain't no room for slip-ups."

Bam-Bam straightened, his expression unreadable. "You know me, Godfather. This place is untouchable."

The Godfather took a slow breath, the tension in his shoulders easing as he ran his eyes over the collection. "This," he said, his tone calm but edged with menace, "is the Room of Mayhem. Anybody dumb enough to cross us will find that out the f**kin' hard way."

Still leaning against the doorframe, watching the Godfather move through the room like a curator inspecting his prized collection. He ignored the vibration of his phone as he focused on the task at hand. Opening the closet, he retrieved two tactical rifle bags and began carefully selecting weapons with precision.

Thanks to his military connections, the options were plentiful. He picked up a MCX Spear, running his hand over its sleek frame before setting it aside. Next, he selected two CZ BREN 2s, four Beretta ARX160, two

MR556A1s, two AM-17s, and four KS-1s. One by one, he placed each rifle carefully on the table at the center of the room, creating a formidable display of firepower. "That should get my muthaf**kin' point across loud and clear," he murmured to himself.

Bam-Bam raised an eyebrow as Onyx unlocked the ammunition case and handed him boxes to match each weapon. "What are we doing, Godfather? Robbing a bank?"

Onyx's gaze didn't waver. "This isn't about money, lil bro. It's about respect. People need to know where we stand. Someone disrespected my sister like she was nothing, like they meant to send me a message—and trust me, I got it. Now it's my turn to make a move on the chessboard."

Bam-Bam leaned against the table, his face hard, eyes narrowing as he took in the Godfather's words. "Sh*t, say less, boss," he said, his voice gritty and cold. "Ain't nobody finna play us like that and walk away breathin'. I'm ridin' with whatever move you make. Folks gon' learn real quick not to cross Money Bag Mafia, 'specially not your blood. Just say the word, Godfather—we'll make 'em regret ever thinkin' they could step."

With everything carefully chosen, the Godfather and Bam-Bam packed the weapons into two large tactical bags. They moved with precision, making sure every piece of gear was accounted for— magazines and spare ammunition tucked in snugly. The bags were hefty, but they carried them with ease, each step steady and cautious. Once outside, they loaded the gear into the back of Bam-Bam's rugged Ford Bronco, its matte black finish blending seamlessly into the quiet surroundings.

Returning to the house, Onyx double-checked the vault, ensuring that no trace of their preparation was left behind. Satisfied, he secured the high-security, reinforced steel door, the keypad lock reader blinking green as it locked with a heavy, mechanical click.

Moving to the kitchen and pausing, the Godfather grabbed a cold bottle of water from the refrigerator, twisting off the cap as he pulled out his phone. Dialing Gunna, he let it ring as he leaned against the counter, taking a long swig of water to steady himself.

The low rumble of the dogs' growls drew the Godfather's gaze to the living room window. They stood poised in front of the glass, their sharp eyes following his every move. Without a word, he gave Bam-Bam a quick nod and stepped outside, the dogs immediately falling into step beside him. Their quiet, watchful presence offered a kind of reassurance that no weapon ever could. The chill of the evening air brushed against his face as he walked toward the Impala, his mind focused and clear. This was the calm before the storm, and he was ready to set everything in motion.

As he pressed redial and the call connected, Onyx's attention shifted to a purple Monte Carlo rolling slowly down the street toward the driveway. "Hold on," he said into the phone, pausing at the front of his car.

The young hustler eased his car to a stop at the driveway and rolled down the window, his movements smooth but purposeful. "What's poppin', Godfather?" he said, his voice carrying a mix of respect and ambition.

The Godfather gave him a slow nod, his expression unreadable. "You still serious about wanting a seat at the table?" His tone was calm but firm, each word intentional.

"Fo' sho'! Always," the hustler replied, leaning casually against the door, his posture betraying his eagerness to prove himself worthy of standing as a solid member of Money Bag Mafia.

"Then here's your chance," the Godfather said, locking eyes with him. "Find out who's pushing that cactus-colored Durango SRT Hellcat sitting on deep-dish concave 24-inch Forgiatos with floating caps," he said, his voice edged with authority. "I want a name. Bring it to me before I find it myself—'cause if I do, y'all gon' wish you got to me first."

The weight of the task hung in the air for a moment, but the young hustler didn't flinch. His smile widened as he nodded. "Bet. I'll handle it."

Without saying another word, he revved his engine and pulled away, the determination in his eyes matching the urgency of his exit. The Godfather stood there for a moment, watching the car disappear down the street, the afternoon sun glinting off its polished surface. With a measured breath, he turned back towards his car, his mind already shifting to the next move. With Gunna still on the line, the Godfather's tone sharpened. "Everything set?" he asked Gunna.

"Locked down tight," Gunna replied. "But what's the move? Those wild-ass Bama Boys are already en route to handle some business, so I told them fools outta Carrollton to hit the road. They should be at the safe house in 'bout an hour."

Payback's a bitch, cuz," the Godfather said, his voice low and laced with finality. "And tell that crazy-ass black hillbilly Cletus it's time to wake up the Hulk. He'll understand. Also, make sure everyone meets me back at the Black House," he locked eyes with Stacy for a moment, the gravity of his command hanging thick in the air before sliding back into the driver's seat.

The Godfather exhaled deeply, the weight of his plans settling on his shoulders like a heavy cloak. His mind raced through the details— who would move, when, and how cleanly it all needed to be executed. This wasn't just about getting even—it was about sending a message that couldn't be ignored.

The drive home was tense, the silence in the car nearly suffocating. Amani sat stiffly in the passenger seat, replaying the chaos in her mind. Stacy sat in the back, arms crossed, her gaze flicking between the passing cars and Onyx's unreadable expression. The only sound was the steady hum of the engine, the faint rhythm of the tires against the asphalt, and the low, haunting bassline of a rap track playing softly through the car speakers, its lyrics almost blending into the tension that filled the air.

Finally, Amani broke the silence, her voice small but steady. "So, what happens now? We just wait for 'em to come back? Or do we hit first? Do you think this could be a setup? A distraction to catch you off guard?"

Onyx's expression was unreadable, his eyes fixed on the road, unwavering. "It crossed my mind, but ain't no waiting, sis," he said, his voice sharp, leaving no room for doubt. "This ain't just payback—it's a message. Whoever thought they could play with y'all is about to find out, in the worst way, exactly who they're dealing with."

The car dipped into a turn, the weight of his words hanging in the air, heavier than the tension itself. "Until I know what's going on, both of you are staying with me."

"I don't have clothes at your place," Stacy said, her tone casual, though the idea of being near Onyx clearly thrilled her.

"I'll handle it," Onyx said, his voice steady as he cut across lanes, ignoring his usual exit ramp. His jaw flexing as Amani's wrecked car weighed on his mind. Someone had the audacity to play with his sister's life, and that wasn't something he could let slide. It wasn't just about the car—it was her safety, her pride, and a blatant message that someone thought it was amusing. The Godfather wasn't about to let them get away with it.

Spotting the Lennox Mall and Phipps Plaza exit ahead, he made a split-second decision, veering off and pulling into the lot. He found a spot near the entrance, cutting the engine as his mind raced. Once the engine died, he reached into his pocket and pulled out two thick stacks of cash. Turning to Amani and Stacy, he counted each of them $1,000 in crisp bills. "A'ight, go do what y'all need to do. Whatever. Just keep it quick," he said, his tone firm, leaving no room for debate.

Amani looked at the money and frowned. "Bruh, you ain't gotta do this."

Onyx shot her a look. "Sis, don't start. Take it. I said what I said."

Stacy was already grinning, flipping through the bills like she was counting blessings. "Say less! You ain't gotta tell me twice." She hopped out the car, already plotting her shopping takeover.

Amani sighed and followed, shaking her head. "Bruh, you can't spoil a bitch that's already spoiled."

"Well, I can add to it, sis," Onyx replied, leaning back in his seat as they swayed their hips across the pavement. The car was silent, but Onyx's mind raced. He unlocked his phone, skipping the car listings, and went straight to his new source. Tapping on a familiar contact name, he waited. The line barely rang before a smooth voice answered.

"Godfather, my brother! What can I do for you?" Zaid greeted, his thick Arabic accent wrapping warmly around his words.

Onyx didn't waste time. "Zaid, I need a favor. My sister's car got wrecked, and I need a replacement. But not just anything—it's gotta be sexy, safe, fast, and untouchable. You got somethin' that fits?"

Zaid chuckled lightly, a sound that was equal parts amusement and confidence. "For you, my friend, always. Let me think… I just got a Ferrari, a Lamborghini Urus, and even a G-Wagon. Or do you want something more subtle? Tell me your vision."

Onyx thought for a moment, tapping his fingers against the steering wheel. "Send me some pics. I'll pick today."

"Of course. Consider it done," Zaid replied smoothly. "And Onyx, whatever you choose, I'll make sure it's perfect. You will have it by tomorrow, in sha Allah."

"Bet. Appreciate you," the Godfather said before hanging up. He exhaled, staring out the windshield as the weight of his plans settled in. This wasn't just about replacing Amani's car—it was about showing the streets that his family wasn't to be played with. About half an hour later, Amani returned with a few bags in one hand and a smirk on her face. "You do too much sometimes, you know that? I'm a bigger and richer boss than you, so stop wasting your money on me, bruh," she said, her tone sharp with playful confidence, climbing into the passenger seat. "And never ever forget—on the chessboard, the Queen dominates."

Onyx gave her a rare smile, but his response carried more weight. "You right, the Queen dominates," he said, his tone steady, locking eyes with her. "But don't forget who protects the Queen. That's me, Amani. Always has been, always will be. You might not need my money, but you gon' always have my loyalty, my strength, my respect, and my love. We breathe from one soul, and ain't nobody gon' mess with that."

Amani's smirk softened into a genuine grin. "You right. *Nakupenda.*"

"Where Stacy at?" He asked, looking around with a hint of impatience.

Amani rolled her eyes and gestured toward the plaza. "Still in there actin' like she shoppin' for Fashion Week. You know that's my girl, but she so extra for no damn reason."

Onyx checked his watch, sighing. It was nearly twenty minutes till 4 when Stacy finally appeared. He could do nothing but shake his head as she sauntered toward the car, arms overflowing with bags, and hips swaying with deliberate exaggeration. "Yo, you done or nah?" Onyx called out, stepping out of the car.

Stacy grinned, tossing her bags into the backseat, after he walked around and opened the door. "I just wanted to make sure I looked good and smell good in case you tryin' to go to sleep or wake up with your dick in my throat."

Onyx didn't respond, his focus narrowing as he slid back into the car. His eyes immediately caught sight of a gray Escalade parked a few spaces over, its engine idling. Two men sat inside, their gaze fixed on him, unwavering and intense. A tight knot formed in his chest, and instinctively, his hand reached for the .45 lying beside his phone on the console. The cool metal of the gun felt reassuring in his grip, its weight grounding him.

The Escalade pulled out of the parking spot, its tires grinding against the asphalt. As it crept forward, the two men inside still locked onto Onyx with their unblinking stares. Onyx's body tensed, his instincts kicking in as his hand gripped the .45. Every muscle tensed, ready to spring into action.

As the Escalade slowly disappeared from view, Onyx's grip on the gun loosened. He exhaled, realizing he had been holding his breath. The tension slowly drained from his shoulders as he carefully placed the weapon back where it belonged, his fingers lingering just a second longer than necessary, double-checking its presence and the calm it brought with it.

Taking the back streets to avoid being followed, Onyx navigated through the quiet neighborhoods, his thoughts drifting to the chaos he was about to unleash. He didn't know who had crossed the line, but they were about to learn what it meant to provoke him.

Chapter 29

"Unspoken Tensions"

Backing his car smoothly into his parking spot, Onyx killed the engine and leaned back, a deep sigh escaping his lips. The weight in his shoulders eased slightly as the soft vibration of the engine faded into stillness, but his mind stayed restless, replaying the day's events. He rubbed the back of his neck, his eyes closing for a moment, hoping to find clarity in the stillness.

As he opened the car door and stepped out, the cool evening air hit him like a splash of water. He stood there for a moment, staring up at the building, the weight of his next move pressing down on him. The sound of Amani's heels clicking against the pavement was the only thing heard until Stacy's voice cut through his thoughts.

"Amani, we plannin' on workin' tomorrow or nah?" Stacy asked, tugging at her panties to adjust them while closing the passenger door. She shot Onyx a playful side-eye, her tone teasing but he ignored making eye contact.

"I'on know right now, Stacy. That's not important or on my mind," Amani responded, her tone clipped as she brushed off the question.

Onyx's eyes darted to his neighbor's pink Mercedes GLA parked nearby, the sight hitting him like a sharp reminder. In the chaos, he had forgotten the long-stem roses he'd planned to buy as a surprise—a small gesture to show his thoughtfulness, something she wouldn't have expected.

"Sh*t," he muttered, tapping the trunk in frustration. He stood there for a moment, his thoughts churning. Forgetting the roses was bad enough, but with Stacy hanging around, things could get messy. His neighbor might think he was a liar—or worse, not single. The idea made his chest tighten, a mix of guilt and frustration bubbling under the surface.

"Sh*t," he muttered again, running a hand over his face as he tried to shake the uneasy feeling creeping in. Unlocking the trunk, he grabbed his sister's bags as Stacy started to follow Amani toward the building door. They stopped in disappointment, turning to glance back at him, realization dawning that they couldn't get in without his building security card.

"Y'all ain't gon' make it far without me," Onyx teased, walking up and swiping his card against the reader. The door unlocked with a smooth click, and they stepped inside, their footsteps echoing faintly against the glossy porcelain floor. The air-conditioned lobby carried a faint scent of bergamot, with a soft herbal undertone of rosemary, a stark contrast to the humid afternoon heat outside.

The three of them stepped into the elevator just as an elderly couple shuffled in behind them. Onyx leaned back against the wall, his eyes fixed on the ascending numbers on the screen. His mind was racing, silently praying that today wouldn't be the day he crossed paths with his neighbor. Of course, the thought of seeing her—the captivating beauty with her flawless poise and piercing gaze—was always a mix of anticipation and dread.

Even though they were strangers, she had a way of exposing his vulnerability and sensitivity, unraveling parts of him he wasn't ready to face. She made him desire a life, not just a dream—something real, something tangible. Yet, he couldn't help but admire her.

She carried herself with a quiet integrity that demanded respect, and without even trying, she pushed him to think beyond the narrow lines of his usual world. Her presence was a lesson in self-reflection, a mirror showing him who he was beneath the surface—and who he hoped to become.

Still, no matter how much he admired her, she never let him forget where he stood. Every attempt he made to get close was met with the same measured rejection: 'Boy, bye! You're not mentally ready for a woman of my caliber. I'm a natural champion, not a thot like the ones you're accustomed to.'"

Her words lingered in his mind, a constant reminder of the gap he had yet to bridge. And though the sting of her rejections never fully faded, there was something magnetic about her honesty—something that made him want to rise to meet the standard she set, even if it felt unattainable.

The elevator dinged softly as the doors slid open, and Onyx's eyes darted up and down the hallway, scanning with the precision of someone who couldn't afford to miss a detail. The coast was clear, but his body remained tense, moving with a controlled urgency that he tried to mask.

He stepped out first, positioning himself to block Stacy's view of the hallway. Without breaking stride, he handed Amani the key, his voice low and steady. "Go 'head, unlock it," he said, nodding toward the door with a quick glance.

Amani arched a brow, sensing the faint edge in his tone, but said nothing as she walked ahead. Onyx's movements were deliberate but unhurried, an act of calm meant to avoid raising suspicion. Behind him, Stacy followed, her heels clicking faintly against the polished floor as she adjusted her handbag.

Reaching his door, Onyx shifted the bags in his hand, his movements quick and precise as he glanced over his shoulder once more, scanning the hallway. He leaned slightly toward Amani, his voice barely above a whisper. "Make it quick," he urged, his eyes still wary. Though everything appeared calm, he couldn't shake the nagging feeling that his neighbor might step out—or be watching from her peephole.

The moment they stepped inside, Stacy let out an appreciative whistle. "Damn, it smells good in here," she said, spinning around to take in the sleek bachelor pad. She ran her fingers across the marble countertop before flopping onto the couch. "Onyx, this bitch is nice as hell. I swear, I could suck your dick in every room of this joint." she said, a mischievous grin tugging at the corner of her lips. Her words were playful, but the underlying confidence in her tone made it clear she wasn't just talking—she meant it.

175

Onyx brushed off Stacy's suggestive remarks, his mind elsewhere as he walked over to his sister, who was clearly impressed by the decor the interior designer had chosen. The space was elegant, every detail meticulously arranged, and Amani stood there taking it all in with a look of quiet admiration.

Leaning in close, Onyx spoke softly, his voice laced with urgency. "Amani, please do me a favor and keep Stacy contained. I really don't want her here, you know that, but I can't have her ratchet antics messing up the vibe." His tone was serious, though he tried to keep it low.

He straightened up, then lowered his voice even further, making sure only she could hear. "And, uh, can you please order some long-stem roses for my neighbor? Make sure they're elegant, nothing cheap. I forgot to grab them while we were out." He glanced at her, hoping she'd understand the unspoken request.

"Anything else, Godfather?" Amani said with a mock bow, her voice dripping with sarcasm as she toyed with him.

Onyx smirked, shifting the bags in his hands as he leaned slightly to one side. 'So, you're a comedian now? I wonder what Mom would say if I told her I asked for your help and got nothing but sarcasm in return.'" He raised an eyebrow, the playful challenge in his voice clear, despite not being able to cross his arms.

Amani rolled her eyes, taking a playful swing at him but missed. "I don't know what she'd say, but I'd say you're a damn snitch. A damn fat head ass snitch too."

Onyx chuckled, dodging easily. "Damn, you're funny and slow. That's a rare combo, sis." With that, he turned away, shaking his head as he carried their bags to the guest room—the one he had the interior designer decorate to her taste, just in case she ever stayed over.

Satisfied, he headed to his office, pulling out his phone as he dropped into the chair. Dialing Gunna, he leaned back with a grin. The moment the call connected, his smile widened, already anticipating the conversation. 'Are the Carrollton misfits here yet?' Onyx asked, his tone business-like.

"They still en route," Gunna confirmed. "And the sticks of candy? Locked in tight."

"Bet," Onyx replied, his mind already shifting to other business affairs.

Chapter 30

"Into The Fire"

After about 20 minutes of scanning the books and making phone calls, Onyx's eyes began to blur from the constant back-and-forth, his mind growing heavy with uncertainties and possibilities. The quiet of his office was interrupted only by the occasional ringing of his phone, the tapping of his fingers on the desk, and the soft hum of the air conditioner. He shifted in his chair, rubbing his temples, trying to shake the restless feeling that had settled in.

Then, the doorbell rang—an abrupt, insistent chime that broke him away from his therapeutic moment. Straightening in his chair, he glanced at the monitor to ensure it was his boys and not his neighbor, which would have been an ultimate surprise. As he rose from his seat, the familiar creak of the chair filled the room. He left the office and walked toward the door. His footsteps padded quietly on the hardwood floor as he approached, his mind already shifting into a new gear.

Peering through the peephole, he saw the familiar faces of Speedy, Cle, Lil B, Marko, and Bishop. It was his crew, just as he had anticipated. Speedy's grin was wide as usual; Cle stood with his arms crossed; Lil B had that cocky swagger; Marko's eyes were sharp; and Bishop's presence was as steady as ever.

Onyx opened the door, stepping back to allow them inside. He gave a small nod, acknowledging their arrival. "What's good, fellas?" His voice was calm, but there was an edge to it—business, as usual.

Speedy was the first to step in, his usual high energy filling the air. "You know we're here to handle business, right?" he asked, his tone light but carrying an undertone of seriousness. "So what's the word, Godfather? You find out who disrespected my big sister? I'm ready to see what kinda holes my Glock 17 put in a n***a's ass."

Cle followed with a quiet nod, his eyes scanning the room as he always did, assessing everything. Lil B swaggered in, tossing a quick glance at the Godfather before setting his attention on the space around them. Marko and Bishop entered with a more measured pace, their quiet confidence filling the room.

Onyx closed the door behind them, his movements steady and calculated. He chuckled dryly, his expression shifting from calm to focused as he motioned for everyone to sit in the living room. The room fell into a quiet focus as the team spread out, the tension of the moment settling in. With other members still en route, he sank into his personal recliner, playfully snatched the remote from Lil B, and flipped through channels until the doorbell rang again.

Without looking up, he said to Bishop, 'Get that.'"

Bishop went back to the foyer and swung the door wide open, ushering in more of the family. One by one, they filed in, each person's presence adding to the weight of the moment. The condo, once calm, now buzzed with energy. Murmured voices blended with the clinking of keys, the shuffle of feet, and the rustle of jackets. There was an undeniable shift in the atmosphere, a sense of anticipation settling over everyone as they gathered.

Onyx scanned the room from the counter, then walked to his office to retrieve his tablet. "A'ight, let's get to it," he said, his voice steady and businesslike. "We've got work to do, and I need all of you on point. Focused."

After a moment's hesitation, Onyx pressed the intercom button. The soft, familiar buzz filled the air as he leaned back slightly against the counter, his mind already shifting gears for what was to come. "Yo, sis, Stacy, can y'all come to the living room?" he called into the speaker, his voice calm but laced with an underlying urgency.

He waited for a moment, then the sound of footsteps could be heard in the background as the women moved toward the room. The silence that followed was thick with the anticipation of their arrival, and Onyx straightened up, ready for the conversation ahead. It was time to handle business, and he needed them to be on the same page.

Amani's eyes narrowed at the crowded sofas. "So nobody gon' be gentlemanly enough to let me sit?" Amani asked, her tone dripping with sarcasm. "Damn, the family only breeds thugs?"

Cle tapped Marko's arm. "C'mon, bruh. Let the ladies sit."

"'Preciate y'all," Stacy and Amani said in unison, taking the freed-up space.

Onyx moved back to his recliner and leaned forward, resting his elbows on his knees. His voice dropped, steady and commanding. "Sis, I know this sh*t probably hard to replay in your mind, but I need you to run everything back. What happened earlier? What the streets sayin' gotta line up with what y'all saw. Description of the n***as, the car they were in—all of it."

As she voiced how the event replayed in her mind, Amani's face crumpled, her composure cracking as tears welled in her eyes. The room fell into a heavy silence, the weight of her pain settling over everyone like a dense fog. Noticing her distress, Speedy quickly darted to the bathroom, returning with tissue, which he handed to her. She dabbed at her face, her voice trembling as she whispered, "After he pointed the gun at my face and shot in the air, he started back ramming his ugly-ass sh*t into mine until I lost control and ran off the road. Bruh... am I even safe anymore?"

The family responded in unison, their voices overlapping in a chorus of reassurance.

"Hell yeah."

"F**k yes."

"Damn right."

"Safer than my grandma's EBT card in her big-ass drawers," Shadow said with complete sincerity, his deadpan expression leaving no room for doubt. The words hung in the air for a second before the entire room erupted into laughter, the absurdity of it all hitting everyone at once.

Marko shook his head, his mouth open in disbelief. "You're a real stupid muthaf**ker." He couldn't help but laugh, though, as he threw a playful jab at his friend.

Before Shadow could respond, Amani's voice cut through the noise, her teasing tone biting as she turned to her brother. "You're not gonna let him get away with that, are you?" she asked, grinning.

Onyx, who'd been listening quietly, finally laughed. "Nah, I'm letting it slide this time," he said with a chuckle, shaking his head. "But don't make me regret it, Shadow."

The room calmed down, but the laughter still lingered in the air, the camaraderie between them all thicker than ever. Onyx sat there, his jaw clenched tight, his eyes fixed with a determined intensity. Then, his voice cut through the room like hot steel, firm and resolute. "Sis, I'd tumble a mountain with my bare f**kin' hands for your peace of mind and safety."

His words weren't just an expression; they carried the weight of every promise he'd ever made to protect her, to keep her safe at all costs. The members in the room mumbled in agreement, each voice adding its own quiet affirmation to the truth of his words—"Yeah, that's real," "No doubt," and "We got you." The sincerity in his tone left no room for doubt.

Amani nodded, her tears slowing. Stacy chimed in, her tone thoughtful. "Look, it was like them n***as was lookin' for somebody with a car exactly like Amani's. And I swear I know that driver from somewhere."

Onyx stood after speaking his mind, he paced toward the patio door. The skyline stretched before him, the late afternoon sun casting long shadows across the city. His mind raced with a storm of questions, each one sharper than the last. Who crossed the line? Why now? Was someone in the family trying to make a move? Was this TJ's attempt to distract him? The weight of the situation pressed heavily on his chest, tightening with every unanswered thought. His eyes scanned the horizon, but all he saw was the blur of everything that had been building up to this moment.

Amani followed him outside, her steps soft on the cool wood floor. She hesitated, then wrapped her arms around him from behind, pressing her cheek against his back. The warmth of her embrace was a stark contrast to the cold thoughts running through his mind. "Is everything okay, bruh?" she asked, her voice low and laced with concern. Her breath was steady, but Onyx could feel the subtle tremor in her grip, the tension in her touch.

He didn't answer right away, lost in the web of his thoughts. Onyx closed his eyes, trying to pull himself together, but the questions wouldn't stop. They were like daggers, each one digging deeper. He inhaled deeply, forcing himself to focus.

"No," he muttered, his voice thick with frustration. He gently pulled away from her, turning to interlock their eyes. "I don't know what the hell's going on, but I think someone's tryin' to make a move, and I feel it's someone whose eyes should have been closed. And if that f**k n***a TJ has anything to do with it, then I'ma pour gas down his throat before tossing a match in his f**kin' mouth," he said with extreme intensity, his voice low and full of menace. The words hung in the air, heavy with his anger. It was as if the simmering rage inside him had finally reached its boiling point, and now it was spilling over, raw and unfiltered.

Amani remained silent, watching him with a calm, steady gaze. She knew him better than anyone, and she could see the storm brewing behind his eyes. "Bruh, don't react out of pure anger," she said softly, her voice steady and grounding. "You know the truth always comes to light, and whoever's behind this will be exposed."

She took a deep breath and stepped closer. "But don't let this situation push you into making a rash decision that could cost you—and the family—everything. You've got bigger things to focus on. It was hard enough getting those security cameras wiped at the subdivision and the scrapyard before the police had a chance to investigate. You don't need more trouble piling up right now."

Her words hung in the air, a reminder of the delicate balance he was walking. But Onyx's eyes were distant, clouded by payback. The anger burned in him like a fire that couldn't be quenched, and every part of him wanted to see it through, to make whoever had crossed him feel the full force of his wrath.

He exhaled forcefully, shaking his head as if trying to clear his thoughts, but they clung to him like oil. Then, all of a sudden, his eyes softened just a fraction—the fire in them dimming but not completely extinguished.

He didn't speak for a long moment, as though weighing her words against the fury that still boiled inside him. Finally, he let out a long breath.

Chapter 31

"The Weight of Loyalty"

From the patio of the Godfather's condo, the city looked alive—vibrant with energy and endless possibilities—but inside, his chest felt tight, as if the walls were inching closer, stealing the air from his lungs. His hands gripped the railing tightly as his mind spun in circles. Adrenaline coursed through him, a restless tide fed by the urge for revenge, the weight of family, and the pressure of building his business and music dreams. Each demand fought for dominance in his mind, a storm he was struggling to silence.

Beside him, Amani stood with a calm, steady presence, her quiet strength anchoring him in the moment. She leaned lightly against the rail, her gaze sweeping over the Atlanta skyline, her understated beauty amplified by her unshakable composure. Without a word, she reached for his hand, her touch firm yet soothing, and lifted it toward the glowing expanse of the city. "Look," she said softly, her voice carrying the weight of unspoken reassurance.

"Bruh, you've come a long way in such a short time," she said, her voice soft yet edged with purpose. "Out of anger, I said you should make those responsible regret crossing us—but I don't want you letting some meaningless street code or pride be the thread that unravels everything you've worked for. Look out there." She gestured toward the skyline, her gaze focused. "See that skyscraper? And that little corner store tucked beneath it? You know what separates the two?" Her tone steadied, breaking through the weight of the moment.

Onyx had always admired his sister's uncanny ability to compartmentalize her emotions, even when she was shattered inside. She could transform from a woman ready to torch the entire city just to carve out a path, to someone willing to extend a hand and feed the very person who had disrespected her, if it meant fortifying the foundation she'd built. It was a balance he struggled to understand but couldn't help but respect.

As he stood there, his mind spun, trying to grasp the comparison she had drawn. He thought about size, wealth, ambition—everything that separated a corner store from a skyscraper. One was temporary, easily replaceable, while the other demanded time, vision, and endurance to stand tall. "There's a lot that makes them different, sis," he said finally, his tone measured as he searched for the right words. He wanted to show he understood the weight of her point without getting lost in the details.

Amani nodded, her voice steady as the golden rays of the sun cast a warm glow over their faces. "Exactly. A short building settles for the view it has, but a skyscraper? It's built to reach higher, to take risks, to stand above everything else. Bruh, you can't keep tying yourself to street-level thinking. You've got to elevate. Your music—it's your way out. But rising to where you're meant to be takes sacrifice and the courage to see the world from a higher perspective."

Her words hit him hard, piercing through the armor he wore to protect himself from the world. Amani always had a way of reaching the parts of him he tried to hide—even from himself. For a moment, he was quiet, his eyes scanning the skyline as her words sank in. He knew she was right. To rise above the command of ignorance, he'd have to let go of some things, break free from the familiar. But this? This wasn't something he could let slide. Whoever had disrespected his sister wasn't going to get away with it.

Breaking the brief silence, Amani smirked and added, "Even though it's also about having vision, knowing when to be disciplined is just as important, Onyx. Knowing when to move and when to stand still. But I know your ugly, big-head ass ain't hearin' a word I'm sayin'. You just standin' there contemplatin', lookin' dumb as hell, and with the sunlight hittin' your face like that… damn, you the spittin' image of Mama."

"I'ma tell," Onyx cut her off with a laugh, already pulling his phone from his pocket. "I'm definitely about to call her and let her know you said she's dumb as hell and ugly like me."

"I'on care, and I ain't say that sh*t, snitch. I said you look like her," Amani shot back, her voice dripping with mock annoyance as she slapped him lightly on the back of the head before reaching for his phone. Her attempt was pointless—he was too strong—but she wasn't about to let it go. "Don't make me knock your ugly ass out on your own damn patio. Snitches get f**kin' stitches, O. You know the rules. Remember that!"

Onyx dodged her swing with ease, still laughing as he stood there, fake dialing their mother's number and pretended to press call. To sell the act, he stepped back after blocking another one of her punches and made an exaggerated attempt at sign language, only for her wild swings to leave him doubled over with laughter. "Sis, stop playin'. You ain't nothin' but a Chihuahua, and I'm a damn Kangal—the biggest, baddest dog walkin' this f**kin' earth.

"Try me then," she shot back, her grin fierce as she leaned in, bouncing lightly on her toes like a pro fighter, her stance sharp and steady. She tilted her head, ready to imprint her soft knuckles square on his jaw. Their playful bickering filled the patio, stretching out as Amani's energy sparked in the air, daring him to make his next move.

After toying around for a few minutes, with the eyes of his crew observing from behind the glass that separated them from the living room, they finally broke into laughter. The weight of everything seemed to lift for just a moment. But then Amani's tone shifted, her gaze dropping to the streets below as she leaned over the rail. The stretching tension caused her voice to harden again.

"For real, O, what you gonna do about the show?" she asked, her words cutting through the momentary lightness. "I noticed Shockwave called you twice while we were in the Fifth Plaza parking lot waiting on Stacy, and you ain't answer. And now here you are, out here searchin' for answers the damn sky ain't gon' give you instead of gettin' dressed? You really gon' let this music thing slip through your fingers? Just to react how some fool wants you to react?" She paused, her gaze sharp as she turned to meet his. "A tall building only rises when it lets go of the ground beneath it, O."

Onyx's grip on the patio rail tightened, "Sis, f**k that performance. Ain't no stage, no opportunity, no amount of money worth more than you. You're my priority, Mani. Your respect, your honor, your safety— that's what matters to me."

Amani's eyes widened, a mix of understanding and frustration flashing across her face. "Boy, bye. You trippin'. God protects me, O. You really finna throw this opportunity away? Performin' at Lakewood Amphitheatre? Do you even hear yourself? Industry heavyweights gonna be there—real shot callers. This ain't just a performance, it's your chance to shut the streets out for good. And you out here talkin' about throwin' it all away over me? For real?" She shook her head, her voice softer but still firm. "Yeah, I'm mad as hell. That sh*t is f**kin' with me, but it ain't worth the cost of your future. Them lames can still get handled, but don't let that sh*t ruin the doors you worked too hard to get open."

His eyes burned with intensity as he locked onto hers, the unspoken weight between them almost suffocating. "They f**kin' shot at you, Mani! Ran you off the damn road like you didn't even matter! And you expect me to just let that ride?" His voice cracked, the raw anger barely holding back the storm beneath. "How you think I'm supposed to perform with that on my mind?"

Amani knew exactly who her brother was—the head of Money Bag Mafia, a man bound by the code of the streets and the reputation he'd worked so hard to build. She understood the rules he played by and the expectations that came with his position. But she also saw what he couldn't: the chance to stand in front of music industry power players, the very people who could help him escape the life he was so tied to. She wanted him to see beyond the rage blinding him, to understand that retaliation in her name wasn't worth losing everything he'd built. Her safety mattered, but not at the cost of his future—or his life. Retaliation meant nothing if it cost her the one person she couldn't bear to lose, especially now, when the spotlight of the music world was finally beginning to shine on him.

Stepping closer, her voice softened, but her resolve was unshakable. "Yeah, O, they did. And I'm still here. Shaken, scared as hell—even though I'm surrounded by bloodthirsty muthaf**kers who'd go to war for me—but I'm alive. You go out there chasing revenge, and I might not get to say the same about you. Is that what you want? For me to bury my brother or watch him rot in prison because he couldn't see past his own anger? Because he let the streets fool him into thinking rage was power instead of showing the strength in his intelligence?"

Her words hit him like a punch to the kidney. He turned away, his gaze drifting to the skyline, searching for clarity. "It ain't about revenge," he muttered, his voice low. "It's about respect and you know that better than anyone. If I don't handle this, they'll think they can keep coming at us. Next time, it might be worse."

Amani grabbed his arm, and pulled him back to face her. "You think this is about respect? Bruh, it's about control. They want you to react, to lose focus, to throw away everything you've worked for. Don't give them that power. You're better than this, O. Let them have the streets. You're meant for something greater. Be that skyscraper, not the corner store."

Onyx swallowed hard as her words cut through the fire in his chest. He wanted to argue, to clap back and defend his pride, but the truth in her words hit harder than he wanted to admit. Still, the streets didn't let things slide. He was already moving pieces on the chessboard without her knowing, calculating his next move, but he needed her to validate the storm brewing inside him. "You know I can't just let it go, Mani," he muttered, his voice low but unyielding. "That's the sacrifice that keeps me from being a complete skyscraper. Not reacting—it ain't just a choice, it's a risk. To you, it might look like strength, but in my world, it's a sign of weakness. You don't understand because our paths don't run the same. Not reacting makes me more vulnerable—it opens the door for them to try me again."

"And you really think slidin' on them gon' fix all this?" she snapped, her voice laced with urgency but steady enough to cut through his storm. "You've always been the one to carry sh*t, to fight for us. But this ain't just your fight, O. It's bigger than you—bigger than us. You got a gift, bruh. That music? That's your real power. Don't throw that away for some petty-ass payback. You say you the Godfather, right? Then act like it. Lead. Show everybody in the Black House a way out, not a way straight to the grave or a prison yard. F**k the streets, O."

Onyx rubbed his hands together, his jaw tightening as he shook his head. Deep down, he was composed, addressing the situation with the calculated mind of a boss. Yet her words stirred something volatile inside him, making him want to release the pressure in his chest—to punch a wall, to let the storm brewing within bleed out somehow. But her words lingered, looping in his mind, hitting harder with every replay. He wasn't a fool, and he hadn't come this far by acting like one. He understood the consequences of his actions, but no matter the logic she brought, no matter the vision she wanted him to see, his decision was already made. Someone was dying tonight, and only God Himself could stop it.

Amani's voice softened, her hand resting firmly on his arm as if trying to hold him steady. "I just… I can't believe you right now. But it's like Mama always said—the hardest prison to escape is the mind of someone too stubborn to see past their own walls. You can't win this fight on their terms, O. You gotta think bigger. Rise above it. Show them you're untouchable—not by stooping to their level, but by rising above it. Retaliation might feel good for a minute, but it won't stop the next one from trying you. Or the one after that. Build a life where you don't have to keep looking over your shoulder."

Onyx started to respond, but Amani wasn't done. Her voice dropped, low and serious, carrying a weight that froze him in place. "If you don't wanna do it for yourself? Fine." She paused, her eyes locking onto his. "Then do it for your baby. Stacy's pregnant."

Her brother froze, his grip on the patio rail tightening as Amani's words hit him like a freight train. "What the f**k you just say?" His voice cracked, his wide eyes locking onto hers, searching for any sign that this wasn't real.

Amani's expression didn't waver, calm but unyielding. "You heard me. Stacy's pregnant. She didn't wanna tell you 'cause she thought you'd feel trapped. Said you might even try to convince her to get rid of it. That's why she been so quiet and distant. She's scared, O. Scared you ain't ready, scared you'd force her to make a choice she don't wanna make."

He swallowed hard, her words slamming into him like body blows. His chest felt tight, his breath uneven, as if the air had been snatched right out of him. His eyes flicked toward the sliding glass door, where Stacy sat on the couch in the living room. She shifted slightly, her gaze darting toward him for a moment before she quickly looked away.

His heart pounded like a drumline. He hadn't even been able to truly look at Stacy since she embarrassed herself at a cookout, and now Amani was hitting him with this. A baby? His mind spiraled, trying to piece together a timeline, trying to figure out how the hell he'd missed this. He turned back to Amani, his jaw clenched so tight it ached. "Nah, nah, you can't be serious right now. Pregnant?"

His voice cracked again, and he felt the weight of the moment threatening to crush him. "How the f**k... I mean..." He trailed off, shaking his head as his thoughts ran wild. His hand dragged down his face as he started pacing. "Mani, I ain't ready for this! I got too much on my damn plate already. A baby with her of all people? You know what this means for me? For us?" His voice rose, the frustration and disbelief spilling out as his composure slipped further.

Amani stood still, watching him unravel, her expression unreadable. But then, a faint twitch at the corner of her mouth stopped him mid-step. His pacing ceased, his eyes narrowing as her sly grin broke through.

"Boy, I'm just playin'," she said, her tone dripping with amusement. "Ain't no baby."

Onyx froze, his jaw dropping as her words sank in. "What the— Mani, don't f**kin' play with me like that!"

Amani burst out laughing, doubling over as tears of amusement glistened in her eyes. "O, you should've seen your damn face! Had you out here thinkin' you were the dumbest n***a in Atlanta for knockin' up the city's *f**kin' playground pussy!*"

Onyx stared at her, disbelief and irritation mixing in his expression as she cackled uncontrollably. "Sis, you play too damn much," he muttered, shaking his head, though a small smirk tugged at the corner of his mouth despite himself.

Amani, still laughing, stepped backwards as Onyx tried to shove her, but his reflexes were too quick. She swung back, aiming a playful slap at his face, but he stepped out of reach with ease, a smirk tugging at his lips.

"Too slow," he teased, though his thoughts were far from light. The joke had landed harder than he wanted to admit, stirring a mess of emotions he wasn't ready to face. His mind churned, tangled in the weight of decisions he couldn't afford to get wrong.

Amani straightened, wiping tears from the corners of her eyes, her grin still bright. "Bruh, you too uptight. You gotta learn to laugh sometimes. Ain't nothing in life worth all that tension you carryin' like a badge of honor."

Onyx didn't answer as he stepped to the side and slid the glass door open with precision, his movements measured. He called into the condo, his voice cutting through the noise. "Lil B! Get over here!"

Amani raised an eyebrow, her laughter fading as she leaned against the railing. "Now what you callin' Lil B for? Don't tell me you mad over the baby joke. Damn, my big ugly ass brother sensitive?"

Onyx ignored her, his eyes cold and focused as Lil B jogged into view, his usual energy faltering at the sight of Onyx's expression.

"I need you to escort Amani to the door now," Onyx said, his tone calm but laced with authority. "She ain't takin' nothin' but her phone."

Amani's jaw dropped, and mock outrage flashed across her face. "Oh, so now you tryna kick me outta my own sh*t? My family sittin' right in there, O. You done lost your damn mind! I'm the boss bitch, remember that?"

Lil B hesitated, confusion etched on his face as his gaze darted between the siblings. "You serious, Godfather?"

Onyx's glare sharpened, his voice slicing through the air. "You questioning me now?"

Lil B threw his hands up in surrender, his voice stumbling. "Nah, nah. I'm just sayin'… You got us sittin' in there ready to ride for Amani, and now you tellin' me to put her out? I don't know what kinda test this is, but Godfather, I ain't tryna fail it—and I damn sure ain't tryna die over somethin' stupid!"

Amani doubled over laughing again, her infectious energy filling the patio as she jabbed a finger in Onyx's face. "See? You don't run sh*t, O! I'm the f**kin' boss of Money Bag Mafia! They fear me! They loyal to me! I run this sh*t, n***a!"

Onyx shook his head, his serious demeanor slipping as the corners of his mouth twitched into a smirk. With a low chuckle, he gave both of them a playful shove, sending Amani stumbling into Lil B as their laughter rang out in unison.

"Y'all wild," Onyx muttered, shaking his head as he turned back toward the open sliding glass door. The weight on his chest eased slightly, though it still lurked beneath the surface, ready to erupt. For now, the streets could wait. Family came first—establishing loyalty, calling out betrayal, and understanding where everyone stood was his priority.

Amani had played him like a pawn on his own chessboard, and the thought lingered: did others think she was untouchable simply because she was his sister? He needed clarity—who was solid, who was loyal, and who was truly ready to ride for whatever came next.

Onyx stepped into the doorway and called out to the Money Bag Mafia crew lounging in the living room. "Blick check! Blick check! Y'all know what it is." His tone was calm, almost casual, but the intensity in his gaze betrayed the weight behind his words. His sharp eyes cut through the room, sizing everyone up, silently demanding answers without having to say more.

Chapter 32

"The Shift in Power"

As Onyx stepped into the living room, the atmosphere shifted immediately. Every member of Money Bag Mafia was locked in, gripping their pieces with a readiness that screamed they were prepared to move without hesitation. No need for explanations—just a target. The block check wasn't some routine drill; it was a declaration of war, and the charged energy in the room was palpable. All eyes were on him, anticipation crackling like static electricity as they waited for confirmation, assuming he'd uncovered who had dared to disrupt Amani's peace. Onyx smirked at their intensity, but the gravity of the moment kept his expression steeled.

Bishop, posted against the far wall, cocked his head with curiosity, his finger brushing the trigger of his Glock like a musician testing a string. "So, you found out who did that to Amani?" he asked, his voice low but charged with anticipation. The thought of action lit a dangerous glint in his eyes, as though he was itching to pull the trigger.

Onyx shook his head, his expression darkened. "Not yet," he muttered as he stepped into the center of the room, his eyes scanning every face. His tone carried heavy authority. "But we've got a serious issue to deal with."

The room fell silent. It wasn't the kind of silence that came with peace—it was sharp, tense, and alive. If anyone focused hard enough, they could probably hear their own heartbeat. Even the faint murmur of Amani and Lil B's laughter from the hallway felt out of place, a cruel contrast to the heavy mood. "I need y'all to escort Amani and Lil B out of the Black House," Onyx said, his voice cold and firm. His next words shattered the unease like glass: "Now."

Heads turned, glances exchanged, and confusion rippled through the crew like an unspoken question. Cle hesitated, the strain etched across his face, before finally stepping forward and gripping Lil B's arm with a firm resolve.

"Man, what the hell? Y'all serious right now?" Lil B protested, pulling back against Cle's hold. His face twisted in disbelief as he tried to free himself. Shadow stepped in, grabbing Lil B's other arm, but the younger man wriggled and yanked, forcing them to struggle to keep him under control.

"Godfather, boss, you really doing this?" Lil B shouted, his voice laced with desperation as his feet dragged against the floor.

"Take him out—and her too," the Godfather barked, his tone ripping through the rising unease like a gunshot. "There's no forgiveness for betrayal." His gaze swept the room, cold and calculating. He needed no further words. He needed to see who was truly loyal to the brotherhood—who would follow his orders without hesitation, without questioning the consequences. This was the moment that would reveal who accepted his word as law.

"N***a, you better not break none of my sh*t with all that scuffling you doin'," the Godfather barked, his voice laced with an intensity that left no doubt—he wasn't playing. As Cle and Shadow wrestled Lil B toward the door, all eyes shifted to Amani. Unlike Lil B, though, she didn't move, and no one took a step toward her.

"Onyx, what's going on?" Stacy asked, her voice tinged with unease as she sat, baffled by the scene unfolding before her. She couldn't believe he was ordering his tightly-knit group of misfits to kick his own sister out of his condo.

"Not right now," Onyx snapped, his patience wearing thin. "Y'all think I'm playin'? I said escort Amani out of the f**kin' Black House too!" His voice boomed, the aggression in his tone leaving no room for doubt.

Even though the Godfather's word was law and everyone knew there were consequences for defiance, only stares grazed the soft fabric of her skin. Amani stood tall, her hands planted firmly on her hips, her head tilted ever so slightly as if she were sizing up the entire room. Her expression was a mix of amusement and disdain, confidence radiating from her as though she were untouchable.

"I wish one of you motherf**kers would touch me. Y'all must've forgot who the f**k I am," she said, her voice smooth and dripping with arrogance. "And y'all let Lil B go before I have both of you tossed off the patio without a second thought. Let me make myself clear—Money Bag Mafia? That's my name on it. I run this sh*t."

Shadow and Cle instantly released Lil B, their hands falling away as if burned by the weight of unspoken rules. The fear of defying the Godfather's sister was etched across their faces, their loyalty tangled in the web of respect and confusion Amani had spun around them. They turned toward the Godfather in unison, their expressions clouded with uncertainty, silently seeking guidance from the man who had built this empire but now seemed locked in a battle of wills with his own blood.

Amani's stance didn't waver, her hips tilted in defiance, and her presence commanded every inch of the room. She let out a soft giggle, shaking her head as though the entire situation was beneath her. "Now, y'all go ahead and keep playing the soldier for my brother, but we all know who the real muthaf**kin' boss is," she arrogantly stated, staring intently at Onyx while struggling to maintain a straight face.

The crew exchanged uneasy glances, unsure whether to make a move or stay rooted in place. The laughter from earlier had died, replaced by a heavy silence. Onyx's jaw flexed as he stared her down. Every word she spoke felt like a slap in the face. "Amani," he said, his voice low and dangerous. "You really think you're f**kin' untouchable?"

"I don't think, Onyx. I know," she shot back, her eyes glinting with challenge. "You can puff your chest all you want, but at the end of the day? They follow me. They loyal to me. They fear me. Money Bag Mafia."

Her words lingered in the air like a loaded gun, daring anyone to challenge her. No one knew what was truly going on. Was she really the boss? Some hesitated in doubt. Still, no one moved to escort her out of the Black House. Eyes darted nervously, and heads turned cautiously, as if searching for answers in the room.

Breaking the silence that hung in the air like an eternity, Lil B raised his hand with three fingers and echoed the words, "Money Bag Mafia."

Amani's lips curled into a smirk, one that made the room feel hotter. She tilted her head, letting out a soft, mocking laugh. "Y'all heard him," she said, her voice dripping with arrogance. Though his words were meant as a confirmation of his allegiance to the brotherhood, they felt more like an acknowledgment of betrayal to the Godfather and a declaration of loyalty to Amani. One by one, each member followed suit, repeating the phrase until every voice in the room had spoken it.

Onyx's body trembled with a fury he could barely contain. His eyes burned with disbelief as he stared at his crew, each one of them now seemingly pledging loyalty to his sister instead of him. The audacity, the betrayal—it felt like being hit with a sledgehammer in the dark.

"Y'all deadass serious right now?" he spat, his voice raw with rage. "I told y'all to do one thing, one f**kin' thing, and none of y'all had the balls to follow through. Instead, y'all standin' side by side chantin' Money Bag Mafia like she's the damn boss. Y'all n***as don' lost y'all minds!" His chest heaved as he pulled his phone from his pocket. "I'm definitely gon' make examples of all y'all betrayin' muthaf**kas. Talk to me."

"I told you, n***a," Amani shot back, her voice sharp and cocky. "I'm the boss, bitch. Money Bag Mafia is my crew now." She couldn't hold her composure any longer and burst out laughing, wagging her finger at him like she was daring him to defy her. A ripple of nervous laughter spread through the room. Some of the crew chuckled nervously, while others couldn't hide their amusement.

Chapter 33

"Collateral Moves"

Gunna's southern drawl poured through the phone, laced with excitement and urgency, each word carrying the weight of something monumental. "Godfather," Gunna began, his tone edged with anticipation. "The Carrollton Boys are posted up at the safe house, but I just sent you some pictures. See if Amani and Stacy can confirm if that's the cactus-colored Hellcat that shot at them and rammed them off the road."

The Godfather's lips curled slightly, the faintest glimmer of satisfaction glinting across his otherwise stoic face. "Bet. Hold on." Turning his back to the crew, he moved toward the kitchen, washing his hands before plucking a navel orange from the counter with calm precision. His voice remained smooth but measured. Seconds later, a buzz followed, signaling the arrival of the images. He tapped the screen, his gaze narrowing as he studied the photos—a cactus-colored Durango, its front and passenger side marred with dents.

"Amani, come check something out real quick," he called, his tone steady and commanding.

The muted thud of Amani's heels on the carpet shifted to a sharper rhythm as she stepped onto the kitchen tile. Her expression tightened the moment her eyes locked onto the phone. "Yeah, that's the one. Ain't no doubt, bruh."

The Godfather motioned with a subtle wave, signaling Stacy to join them. She approached without hesitation, brushing close enough for her cheek to graze his chest in a fleeting, charged moment that felt intentional. Her left hand slid lightly along his back, her touch lingering with an intimacy that seemed second nature. "That's it. No question," she said, her voice steady as her eyes focused intently on the images.

The Godfather's expression didn't waver—a masterclass in control, his face revealing nothing. His voice, low and firm, maintained a tone that offered no clues. His gaze swept over the Money Bag Mafia crew, who stood and sat in complete silence, their eyes locked on him, waiting. The room felt alive with tension, as though every breath held the weight of the moment.

The Godfather finally nodded, a trace of satisfaction slipping through his cold exterior. Lifting the phone back to his ear, he spoke with quiet menace, the kind that hinted at inevitability. "Both confirm that's it." His words carried the weight of a decision made, the consequences already set in motion.

Hearing the confirmation, Gunna's voice dropped an octave, laced with intent. "A'ight, listen. Word on the street is, the f**k n***a who owns the Durango Hellcat go by Monster. They say he gettin' a lil' paper out there in Decatur, got a crew 'bout like seven or eight ridin' with him, and he runnin' a trap house over on Daniel Avenue."

The Godfather sucked his teeth as cold fury dripped from every word he spoke. His mind raced, piecing together the audacity of it all—Monster, the corny dude he had humiliated in front of everybody just last month. It was a laid-back Saturday afternoon at Major's new spot, the atmosphere was relaxed and untroubled. Amani stood by his side, her presence effortless as always, while Yoshe, Stacy, and Jasmine laughed and floated between the patio, pool, and yard, the warm buzz of conversation filling the air. But Monster? Monster was different. He couldn't just blend into the vibe. Instead, he kept running his mouth, pushing boundaries like he thought he was invincible—like he believed his own hype as some kind of untouchable legend.

The memory remained vivid, etched into his mind like it had happened yesterday. Yoshe, the picture of elegance and grace in her Brandi Mini Dress, had brushed off Monster's repeated advances throughout the day with calm confidence. Her disinterest was unmistakable, yet she handled him with a politeness that left no room for disrespect. But Monster couldn't take it. Rejection hit his ego like a slap, and he snapped in an attempt to salvage his pride. His tone turned venomous as he spat out, "Stuck-up bitch," before gripping her face and shoving her back with a rough push, his hostility radiating the wounded pride of a man desperate to reclaim his sense of power.

The Godfather didn't waste time with warnings or words. Stepping away from the DJ table, his movements were swift and precise, like a flash of lightning in the calm before a storm. Without hesitation, he struck, his palm connecting with Monster's face in a slap so forceful it pierced through the music, ringing out across the backyard like a cracking whip. Monster stumbled back, his body betraying him as he hit the ground. His eyes fluttered, caught in a haze between consciousness and unconsciousness. The world around him seemed distant—a blur of muffled voices, blurred faces, and a dull throb reverberating in his skull.

Conversations died mid-sentence, drinks hovered frozen in midair, and even the music seemed to fade into a stunned silence. All eyes were locked on Monster as a few people rushed to help him up. He swayed slightly, disoriented, blinking hard as if trying to steady the spinning world around him. The weight of humiliation pressed down on him like a physical force.

When Monster finally steadied himself, he didn't lash out. There was no rage, no defiance—no pushback or bark. Instead, he stood there, his eyes darting to every face in the crowd, his expression a mix of shame and barely concealed fury. His face burned red, the sting of the slap and the humiliation etched across it for all to see.

The Godfather watched him closely, chalking the lack of reaction up to fear—or perhaps respect for Major's house. Either way, Monster had folded, and that was enough for the Godfather to leave it alone. Later, when Major had pulled him aside and assured him the issue was squashed, he suppressed it in his thoughts. For the Godfather, it was over. For Monster, though, it was far from finished.

But now it was clear: Monster hadn't let sh*t slide. He had been stewing, plotting, waiting for his chance to strike. This wasn't just petty revenge—it was a test. A challenge. Monster was trying to make a move, to show he had weight to throw around. That was his mistake. A fatal one.

The Godfather's resolve solidified, cold and unyielding, the kind that came with the certainty of a decision already sealed. His eyes darkened as the fury inside him hardened into something more focused, more calculated. This wasn't a man toying with grudges; this was a man about to deliver a lesson. Monster wanted to see what power looked like? Onyx was about to show him, in no uncertain terms, why challenging the Godfather was a game no one survived.

"You checked his trap spot yet?" he asked, the Godfather's voice steady but loaded with menace, already suspicious of the amount of weight Monster might be moving and the steps needed to shut it down.

"Nah, not yet," Gunna replied. "But T-Roc already posted outside. Says there's a steady flow of customers comin' through. I'm sittin' outside the house where the Hellcat's parked. N***a ain't moved much. Barely seen him."

The Godfather's gaze swept the room, his eyes settling on each member of his crew. Their expressions were taut with focus, their bodies coiled, ready to spring into action now that the target who had violated his sister's peace had been identified and located. He gave a purposeful nod, then spoke into the phone, his voice steady, commanding.

"A'ight, Gunna. You know what to do. Tell the team it's time to execute. I want both houses demolished—wipe that bitch ass n***a and his whole crew off the map. No loose ends. After I transfer the paper, you and your brother get dressed and come here. We all going to leave for the concert together."

"Yes, sir, but I thought you weren't gonna perform, boss," Gunna asked, curiosity lacing his tone.

The Godfather lips pressed into a hard, grim line. "I wasn't, not while this sh*t was still up in the air. Protecting the family comes first. I couldn't focus with that unknown threat hanging over us. Had to make sure everyone was safe before anything. But now that it's about to be handled, I'm about to burn that bitch to the ground. Us being there? It's our damn alibi, airtight. No ties. No questions."

"Got it, boss," Gunna said before the line went dead.

The Godfather slid his phone into his pocket and gestured for Amani to follow him toward the office. "Sis, log into that crypto account you set up for me," he said, his tone calm but laced with authority as they stepped inside. The door clicked shut behind them, sealing the room in tense quiet. Grabbing the tablet off the desk, he turned to her, his gaze locked on hers with an intensity that demanded obedience.

"Transfer $50,000 to this address please." His voice was low but firm, each word carrying the weight of urgency and control, leaving no room for hesitation. He handed her a folded piece of paper, the wallet address scrawled neatly across it. His expression was unflinching, his eyes focused with purpose, making it clear this was an important request.

The silence in the room stretched out until Amani's voice sliced through it with a teasing edge. "So you lied to me?" She lifted her eyes to lock with her brother's, a playful smirk tugging at her lips.

"What the hell you talkin' about?" Onyx replied, his confusion flashing briefly across his face.

"You said you wasn't gonna perform, but I heard you tell Gunna to meet you here 'cause you want everyone to go to the Amphitheater together. And that your ugly ass gon' burn the damn place down." Her voice was biting, but her fingers kept typing.

"Why the hell you ear hustling on my convo? Didn't Mama used to spank your ass 'bout that? Your nosy ass something else." Onyx gave her a side-eye before continuing, "But yeah, I am now that I assume you and the guys are safe." His smirk took the bite out of his words, a flicker of relief settling behind his usual bravado.

"N***a, I can't step out lookin' like this—not with my sh*t at the house and Jasmine and Yoshe flexin' them fly-ass designer fits. You foul as hell for this, bruh." Amani shot back with sarcasm, trying to slap his face but missing.

"Told you, you too slow. And no matter what any bitch wear, you still gon' outshine 'em. What's the issue?" Onyx chuckled, enjoying the way her face scrunched up in response. "I'll have Shadow and Cle take you home so you can change. Then y'all meet up here afterwards with your crybaby ass."

Amani flipped her hair over her shoulder with a smirk. "You know I don't waste fits. Thought I was gon' have to get my crew to toss your ugly ass over the patio." She laughed as she moved toward the door. "Money's sent, by the way."

"If it wasn't for Mama, I'd lay your lil' poor body ass out right here—and any n***a dumb enough to cross me for you," Onyx said, his voice low and simmering with controlled aggression, each word carrying the weight of a threat he was ready to back up.

"You could try, but best believe my whole crew would toss your ass around like bread dough," Amani shot back, raising her hand and flashing three fingers. She strutted down the hallway like she owned the world, untouchable. Then, without missing a beat, she yelled, "Money Bag Mafia!"

As the chant of "Money Bag Mafia" thundered from the living room, Onyx's expression hardened. Shaking his head, he pulled out his phone and dialed Shockwave. When the call connected, his voice was calm but resolute. "My bad, dawg. Had an unexpected family situation that threw me off for a minute. But my commitment to performing? That ain't changed."

Ending the call, Onyx's thoughts shifted immediately to retribution. His mind raced, already piecing together the steps to ensure those responsible for the betrayal paid the price. Exiting the office and stepping back into the charged atmosphere, Onyx's eyes fell on his sister lounging in his recliner, legs crossed like she'd already claimed his throne. She looked every bit the boss, and it struck a nerve he'd address later. For now, he shoved the thought aside, refocusing on the task at hand.

The humor drained from his voice, replaced by an air of absolute authority as he reclaimed control of the room. "A'ight, y'all betraying-ass n***as, listen up," he said, his tone cutting through the tension like the edge of a katana. "Plans just changed. We ain't stayin' here no more. We hittin' the Lakewood Amphitheater tonight. I'm performin' after all."

The room erupted into a wave of protests, confusion and frustration rippling through the crew like a rising tide. Every man was strapped and ready, fully expecting the night to end with a statement carved into the streets—a statement that crossing Money Bag Mafia was a death sentence. Yet here was the Godfather, cool as ever, telling them they were headed to a concert instead of handling the business they'd been primed for, even with the target in their sights.

The disbelief hung in the air like smoke, heavy and suffocating, but no one dared to outright challenge him. The Godfather's word wasn't just law—it was survival. They might grumble under their breath, but they all knew better than to question the man who held both their loyalty and their lives in his hands.

"First off, I ought to make all y'all show up to the concert as is— that'd be the consequence for disobeyin' me earlier. Betrayal!" The Godfather voice boomed, carrying the weight of his authority. "Y'all got my crazy-ass sister thinkin' she's f**kin' untouchable, but lucky for y'all, I'm feelin' generous tonight."

"I am untouchable," Amani shot back with a smirk, deliberately annoying him as she threw up three fingers to rep Zone 3. "And I am the boss bitch!" she declared, her voice cutting through the tension.

"Money Bag Mafia!" she shouted next, her energy infectious. The crew, caught in the moment, echoed her words with fervor, their chant filling the room with renewed intensity.

The Godfather pinched the bridge of his nose, shaking his head, unimpressed but let it slide. "A'ight, y'all done?" he asked, his tone flat but laced with the kind of warning that made it clear his patience had limits. The crew immediately quieted, the energy in the room shifting back under his control. The room stayed silent, everyone hanging on his every word.

"Y'all got two hours ppl," he continued, his tone firm and final. "Go home, change, do what you need to. But your asses better be right back here, ready to move, before the clock run out. Don't make me regret this." He scanned the room, daring anyone to test him. No one did. The energy shifted, their frustration simmering down as they absorbed his words. It wasn't just an order—it was a reminder of why he was the one in charge.

The Godfather turned to Cle and Shadow, his tone precise. "Y'all, escort my sister to her spot and back. Don't waste time—just grab your clothes and head right back here to get dressed." His tone left no room for debate as his gaze shifted to Malik and Bishop. "Same goes for Stacy. Make sure she's good. Move quick." He paused, letting his words sink in before continuing, his eyes scanning the crew. "As for the target," he said, his voice calm and commanding, "I'll brief everybody once you're back. The clock's ticking, so don't make me wait."

The crew grumbled as they filed out, frustration etched on their faces. Postponing retaliation didn't sit right with them—they craved the raw adrenaline of a shootout, the chaos of proving Money Bag Mafia's dominance. As the condo slowly emptied, the charged atmosphere began to settle, replaced by a faint sense of anticipation. Stacy slipped off to the bedroom to grab her purse, the soft click of her heels breaking the quiet. When she returned, her energy shifted, her stride confident as she approached the Godfather.

Her voice dropped into a sultry tone, her hands pressing lightly against his chest as she leaned in, her lips hovering near his ear. "Look, I know we ain't together no more," she started, a playful smirk tugging at her lips, "but since I gotta stay here tonight... you gon' let me slide that dick in my throat the way you like?"

The Godfather chuckled, tossing a slice of orange into his mouth as he leaned back against the counter. "Girl, you wild as hell," he replied, his grin widening. "Depends on whether or not I catch some action at the concert. Maybe, maybe not."

Stacy pouted dramatically, crossing her arms with a teasing glint in her eye. "N***a, you know damn well I'm down with sharin'."

The Godfather shook his head, laughing as he pushed off the counter, his casual swagger carrying him toward his room. "You somethin' else, Stacy," he said over his shoulder, leaving her grinning slyly, the spark of mischief still lighting her eyes.

Chapter 34

"Country Chaos"

The low growl of Gunna's tangerine-colored '69 Chevrolet SS 396 with white stripes rumbled through the quiet Atlanta street as he pulled up to the safe house. The two-story, run-down house looked like it belonged deep in the woods, not in the middle of the city. With some idle time before their next assignment, the Carrollton Boys lounged on the porch, exuding their usual swagger—beer cans in hand, dip tucked in their cheeks, and laughter booming loud enough to rattle the thin walls of the house.

Parking the SS, Gunna stepped out smoothly, adjusting his chain as his focused gaze swept over the group, absorbing every detail. The out-of-town crew was a rough-looking mix of Black and white country boys, their faces weathered by long days under the sun, eyes squinting against the afternoon light. They were clad in mud-streaked jeans, scuffed boots, and flannel shirts that hadn't seen a wash in weeks, each one bearing the stains of hard labor and countless nights spent around campfires or in smoky bars. Their beards were thick and unkempt, and the faint scent of tobacco and sweat lingered to their clothes like a second skin.

These weren't men who worried about appearances—their clothes told their story: rugged, unpolished, and tough as hell. The quiet confidence in their posture suggested they were no strangers to trouble, their eyes darting warily between Gunna and the road as if waiting for something to jump out of the shadows. Their conversations were low and clipped, but there was a sense of unity in the way they carried themselves—a bond forged through years of brotherhood and survival in a world that didn't give a damn about them.

Every now and then, one would grunt, offering a half-smile or a nod, acknowledging Gunna's arrival without needing to say much. It was clear they weren't here for small talk, but for business. And in a place like this, under the weight of the silence between the distant murmur of the city and the noise from the nearby woods, that business was only a moment away from becoming dangerous.

Gunna knew this crowd—tough, loyal, and unpredictable—but they weren't the type to rush into anything unless boredom set in. And right now, they were nearly drowning in it. He glanced at the crumpled, bent beer cans scattered across the porch, the overgrown weeds fighting for space around the house, and the junked-up cars littering the yard. This wasn't the kind of place a man like him would stay long. But he'd learned not to judge a book by its cover; this safe house was off the grid, and these boys could get sh*t done when they needed to.

"Yo, Gunna," a gravelly voice called from the porch. A tall, wiry guy named Hank, always the first to speak, waved him over. His eyes were bloodshot, his face rough from too many late nights, but he had a certain raw charisma that made you listen. "You bringin' that heat or what?" he asked, grinning wide.

Gunna gave a short nod and tossed a glance over at the two men playing cards at the rickety table. Their eyes barely moved from their hands, focused on the game, but they acknowledged him with a quick nod of their own. He could tell they were ready for whatever came next.

"Yeah," Gunna said, his voice steady but with a hard edge. "We got work to do. Y'all ready?"

Hank leaned back, resting his boots on the edge of the porch. "Always," he said with a shrug, popping open another beer. "But you know we ain't in no rush. Just keepin' low 'til it's time."

Gunna didn't have to say much more. The Carrollton Boys operated like a well-trained tactical unit—calculated, precise, and lethal when the time came to strike. It was one of the things Gunna respected most about them. They weren't loud unless they meant to be. Every move, every glance, spoke a language of precision and purpose.

He hadn't planned on staying long—these gatherings weren't his scene—but they had a way of pulling him in. The atmosphere buzzed with a quiet intensity, where the only thing louder than the occasional bursts of laughter was the oppressive silence that followed. It was the kind of silence that made your chest tighten, the kind that hinted at conversations unspoken and deals yet to be struck.

Cigarette smoke hung thick in the air, the fading light casting crawling shadows on the walls. Gunna adjusted his stance, leaning against the edge of a worn-out lounge porch rail, his eyes scanning the faces around him. These weren't boys pretending to be gangsters. These were men born into the game, and it showed. Gunna pulled out a box of Black and Mild, lit one, and took a long drag, letting the smoke curl up and dissipate in the air. As the sun dipped lower, the creeping shadows from the trees seemed to pull the house deeper into itself, wrapping the scene in a strange, muted calm. But Gunna knew better than to mistake calm for safety.

"Let's handle this," Gunna muttered under his breath, flicking the ashes from the Black and Mild. The weight of what was coming settled in his gut. This wasn't just another job, not just another day waiting around for some easy cash. No, today the air carried something darker. And it was only a matter of time before the storm hit. "Y'all ready to handle business?"

"Hell yeah," Billy Jack shouted, spitting a stream of tobacco juice into a styrofoam cup. "Been itching to make some noise since we left the house, city boy. Looks like Atlanta's missin' some of our fireworks."

Suppressing a smirk, Gunna motioned for two members to follow him to the car. The scuff of their boots against the weathered concrete mingled with the whispers of nature—the rustle of leaves, a distant dog barking, and the faint hum of the streetlights. It was a symphony of nature's mystery, wrapping the moment in an uneasy calm.

Gunna strode toward the car, his steps measured and unhurried. He slid the key into the trunk lock, twisting it with a metallic click. With a firm pull, the trunk lid creaked open, revealing two large tactical bags resting inside. The dim amber glow of a nearby streetlight spilled over the canvas, emphasizing the bulging weight and the grim purpose they carried.

"Go on," Gunna said, his tone calm but edged with authority, each word a subtle command. "Grab 'em." His eyes flicked toward the bags, unreadable but expectant, leaving no room for hesitation.

The two men exchanged a quick glance, their eyes glinting with curiosity and anticipation. They didn't need to ask what was inside—whatever Gunna brought was always worth their attention. The men stepped forward, their movements careful, as if the bags themselves held secrets too heavy to disturb. With a grunt, they heaved the bags into the house, their weight causing their arms to strain.

As the bags thudded onto the living room floor, the sound reverberated like a gunshot. Heads turned, conversations paused, and the air thickened with a collective sense of expectation. "What you got for us this time, G?" one of the men finally asked, his voice tinged with eagerness.

Gunna walked over and crouched down, taking his time as he unzipped the first bag. The deliberate pace was part of the show, and he knew it. All eyes were on him now, the room holding its breath. He glanced up briefly, his smirk returning. "Something that'll make y'all more dangerous than last time," he said, his tone as crisp as the glint of metal inside the bag.

"Boss said when y'all slide, make sure the whole city feel it so they know to fall in line," Gunna said, his tone cold and cutthroat. "Ain't no loose ends. No witnesses. Clean sweep. These untraceable pieces are yours once the job's done."

Hank bent down and unzipped the other bag, his eyes widening like LED headlights in the dark. Inside were assault rifles he'd never seen before, each one outfitted with extended magazines, and enough ammunition to arm a small militia. "Damn," he whistled, pulling out a KS-1 and an AM-17. "This here's some serious heat. I wanna stick both of these in somebody's mouth and let it rip."

Cletus, a burly Black member, chuckled low as he stepped forward, pulling an IWI Carmel from the bag and loading it with ease. "Ain't nothin' like the smell of gun oil. Reckon we'll see some bodies twistin' tonight."

Shaking his head and chuckling at their thick country drawl, which he could barely understand, Gunna strolled over to where Billy Jack stood, fixated on the AM-17 as he loaded fresh rounds into the magazine. Gunna held up his phone, the glow of the screen casting a faint light on his face. "Crypto's in your account. Addresses are in the file," he said, his tone clipped. "Y'all better handle this right. No screw-ups. I'll text EXECUTE when it's time to move."

Billy Jack nodded, a sly grin tugging at his lips as another member approached, with a KS-1 slung under his arm. "Don't worry, city boy. We'll turn this whole town into a damn war zone if it comes to that. Last time didn't go smooth, but we still got it done."

Gunna smirked, dapping up several members before making his way outside. "Yo, Cletus, for real—handle this sh*t right," he called over his shoulder as he descended the porch steps, his tone half-serious, half-joking.

From the doorframe, Cletus hollered back with a grin, his thick southern drawl almost impossible to understand. "Shiiit, boy, I got this! Ain't no thang but a chicken wing! Ain't no messin' up when I'm in charge… I'll make sure it's hotter than a two-dollar pistol on a summer day!"

Gunna paused for a second, trying to decipher the words, then shook his head with a chuckle. "A'ight, Cletus, just don't blow sh*t up this time. We need precision, not just chaos."

Cletus just waved him off, his laughter echoing through the air. "Precision? Ha! I'm like a damn storm, boy—ain't no stoppin' me when I get rollin'!"

Gunna shook his head, rolling his eyes as he slid into the driver's seat. The engine fired up, the bass of the exhaust pulsing beneath him as he hit the gas. Cletus's wild energy was a force in itself, but Gunna had learned to roll with it. Tonight would be no different. As he pulled away, the house lights dimmed into the darkness behind him. Gunna tapped his phone screen, dialing his brother. The line clicked, and T-Roc's voice came through almost immediately.

"Yo bruh, boss' orders are in motion," Gunna said, glancing in the rearview mirror as if the chaos was already catching up to him. "Them crazy-ass country boys 'bout to light sh*t up. I swear, they were all dropped on their heads as babies."

T-Roc's laugh boomed through the speaker. "Bruh, you crazy as hell. But, hey, they might be dumb and rowdy, but they get the job done—every time."

"Yeah, you right, chaos like a muthaf**ker," Gunna muttered, shaking his head. "A'ight, bruh, meet me at the apartment. Boss said we gotta roll to the concert together, need to be at his spot in two hours."

T-Roc smirked. "Bet. I'll be there in twenty. But he told me he wasn't gonna perform about an hour ago."

Gunna furrowed his brows. "He changed his mind. Said he'll let everybody know what's up once we're there. So stay alert and put your foot in it."

"Fo sho'! And bruh, tell Godfather he better not leave me hangin' like y'all lame asses did last time," T-Roc shot back.

"Relax. Just be on point tonight. Move your ass," Gunna said, hanging up and tossing the phone onto the passenger seat. The streets stretched ahead of him, Atlanta's hazy skyline loomed on the horizon. It was gonna be a long night, but that was nothing new.

Chapter 35

"A Father's Joy and the Devil's Whisper"

The sun dipped low, its golden rays bleeding into the darkening sky outside Monster's charming Tudor-style house. Shadows stretched long across the soft, plush carpet as Monster sat cross-legged on the living room rug. His daughter, Crystal, nestled in his lap—a tiny bundle of energy wrapped in a pink onesie. The distant chirp of cicadas drifted through the open windows, blending with the soft rustle of leaves outside. Duke, Monster's pit bull, lay still beside them on the carpet, his amber eyes fixed on Crystal, guarding her every move.

Crystal's tiny fingers stretched toward Monster's chain, her soft palms brushing against the thick gold links that rested against his chest. Her eyes sparkled with curiosity, her brows furrowing as she clumsily grasped at the shiny prize.

"You think this yours, huh?" Monster said, his deep voice carrying the playful drawl of the streets. "Lil' shawty, you gon' jack Daddy's chain now? You wild."

Crystal babbled confidently, her lips moving with the confidence of someone who believed her words held meaning. Then, as if she caught on to the humor in his teasing tone, she squealed with laughter, her whole face lighting up. Her tiny shoulders shook with joy, and for a moment, the room seemed to glow, her giggles wrapping around Monster's heart like a balm for every dark day he'd ever faced.

Monster grinned, his laughter rolling through the room. "Man, you somethin' else, lil' mama." He scooped her up, holding her high above his head while she giggled uncontrollably. "Duke," he called, glancing at the pit bull. "You see this? She ain't even one and already actin' like she run the crib."

Duke gave a lazy wag of his tail, his amber eyes flickering with interest before stretching out his massive paws. His broad chest rose and fell in a steady rhythm, exuding quiet confidence, as if to say, Y'all got this under control. Unbothered, he kept his watchful gaze on Crystal, a silent guardian basking in the peaceful moment.

But the peace didn't last. Monster had been tossing Crystal gently in the air, her tiny arms stretching out with each lift like a baby bird testing its wings. Her giggles cascaded through the room, a melody so pure it rose and fell like the sweetest notes of a violin. The sound was infectious, filling the air and softening everything it touched, as if her laughter could weave harmony from chaos. On the fifth toss, however, he froze mid-laugh, his nose twitching as something unpleasant registered, breaking the symphony.

"Aw, hell no, Crystal," he said, holding her at arm's length and squinting at her as if the truth would reveal itself in her wide, innocent eyes. He sniffed the air again, this time for confirmation, and groaned loudly.

"Yo, you really did me like this? Right now? You ain't even gon' warn me?" he groaned, his shoulders slumping as he brought her down carefully onto the soft blanket in front of him. Crystal's tiny legs kicked playfully as if she had not a care in the world, her bright smile deepening his dramatic sigh.

"Why you couldn't wait 'til I dropped you back off tomorrow? We was vibin', girl!" he said, shaking his head while reaching for the diaper bag behind him on the sofa. Crystal gurgled in response, her tiny face lighting up with a toothless grin. Her little hands flailed in all directions, her laughter a melody of innocence and mischief. She stretched out on the blanket, legs kicking with the same carefree rhythm, lost in her own joy.

"A'ight, lil' troublemaker. Let's get you cleaned up," he said, his voice a mix of exasperation and amusement. Gently, he unfastened the buttons of her onesie, peeling it off to reveal the warm glow of her bare skin and her wiggling legs. "You way too comfy for somebody causin' this much drama."

Monster carefully set the onesie aside and braced himself, his shoulders sagging with the resigned patience of a man who knew this wasn't just a routine diaper change—it was a full-blown mission. As he peeled back the diaper tabs, the reality of the situation hit him, and his nose wrinkled in disbelief. "Oh, nah," he muttered, shaking his head at the sheer scope of the mess. Quickly, he refastened the diaper, deciding this would require reinforcements.

"Keep an eye on her, Duke," Monster said, pushing himself off the floor. The dog perked up at the sound of his name, tail wagging as he barked and stepped closer to Crystal, keeping his watchful eye on her. Monster jogged upstairs to grab another blanket and a full cleaning kit, muttering under his breath about the unpredictability of babies.

When he returned, armed with supplies, he gave Crystal a playful kiss on her belly, eliciting a soft gurgle and a toothless smile. "A'ight, princess, let's get you cleaned up for real this time," he said with a smirk, lifting her gently to swap out the blanket for a fresh one, just in case it got messy while cleaning her. Crystal's tiny legs kicked in the air as he settled her down, completely oblivious to the chaos she'd just created.

Monster sat back on his knees, letting out a dramatic sigh before grinning. "You're lucky you so cute," he teased, tickling her belly briefly before getting to work. Her giggles softened into a happy gurgle as she lay on the blanket, completely unbothered while he wiped her down, carefully cleaning every crease and fold. Her tiny fingers stretched toward the air, as if reaching for something only she could see.

"Girl, you went crazy in this diaper," Monster said, shaking his head with a grin. "You ain't even care, huh?"

He grabbed a clean diaper with one hand and the baby powder with the other. "You think this funny, huh?" he teased, his grin softening as he gently dusted the powder across her soft skin. Her giggles bubbled up again, her tiny legs kicking with pure joy, filling the room with her sweet, infectious energy. It was a moment of peace and love, the kind that made all the chaos melt away.

Satisfied she was clean, Monster slid a fresh diaper under her, adjusting it with precision. He leaned over, playfully tapping her tiny nose, a smirk creeping onto his lips. Just as he moved to pull the diaper up between her legs—

PSSHHH!

A sudden, warm stream shot straight onto his forearm and chest. Monster froze, eyes widening in disbelief as Crystal erupted into laughter, her little body wriggling with pure mischief, as if she knew exactly what she'd done. His head fell back with a groan, one hand thrown up in exaggerated frustration.

"Yo! Crystal! Nah, you wildin' now!"

But as her joyful giggles filled the air, Monster couldn't help but laugh too. "A'ight, a'ight, you got me," he said, shaking his head with a smile, the mess forgotten as he leaned in to kiss her forehead. It was messy, it was chaotic—but it was theirs, and in that moment, his heart swelled with an overwhelming love only she could bring. He grabbed another wipe to clean himself off, shaking his head. "A'ight, this the last time. You ain't gon' catch me slippin' again."

Crystal just giggled louder, her little feet kicking in delight, completely unrepentant. Monster chuckled despite himself. "Yeah, yeah, laugh it up. You lucky I love you, troublemaker."

Duke lifted his head at the commotion, his ears perking up and his tail wagging as if he were in on the joke. Monster swiped at the cascading fluid on his chest with a mix of disbelief and humor. "You got me lookin' crazy," he muttered, shooting a mock glare at Crystal, who giggled again, completely unrepentant. He glanced at Duke, who tilted his head in curiosity. "I swear, you and Duke probably plottin' on me together."

Duke let out a small bark as if confirming the accusation, while Crystal's laughter rang out like a tiny bell. "Yeah, that's what I thought," Monster said with a smirk, shaking his head as he tossed the wet wipe and soiled diaper into a bag for the trash. "Y'all ain't right for this, teaming up on me like that." Despite his words, the warmth in his voice betrayed his amusement as he glanced between the dog and his daughter, both clearly enjoying his plight.

Just as he settled back with Crystal, his phone buzzed on the coffee table. He adjusted her on his lap and reached for it, glancing at the screen. Slim. A dealer with weight moving steady through both the east and west sides of the city. Monster let the call ring for a beat, his thumb hovering over the screen before he finally answered.

"Yo, what's good?"

Slim chuckled nervously on the other end, the kind of laugh that always came before bad news. "Word is, you and Baby J was out in the Hellcat earlier, wildin' like some f**kin' amateurs. You of all damn people. N***as talkin', bruh. Sh*t all over the streets."

Monster leaned back against the sofa, his face softening with rare joy as he watched his daughter squirm on the blanket, her tiny hands grabbing at the air while she giggled at nothing in particular. For a moment, her innocence pulled him out of the weight of his world. But Slim's voice through the phone dragged him back into it.

Slim had a knack for knowing things, like the streets had their own secret language, and he was the only one fluent in it. It was as if invisible cameras were always rolling, feeding him angles nobody else could see. Monster didn't fully trust him—Slim was too slick, too connected—but his intel was usually solid. Keeping his voice steady, controlled, he leaned into the phone.

"Yeah? What's the word?"

Slim hesitated before letting out a strained laugh. "Man, word on the street is, your dumb ass was drivin' while Baby J's goofy ass hangin' out the window, shootin' at some dime and her homegirl, then you rammed 'em off the road like you auditionin' for a damn Fast & Furious flick. That what we doin' now?"

Monster's grip on the phone tightened as he sat up straighter, his shoulders squaring. His voice dropped—lows, sharp, heavy with warning. "What the f**k you just say to me, n***a? Watch your mouth before I remind you who you talkin' to. Don't let this phone make you brave."

As he spoke, his daughter started climbing up his legs, her tiny fingers gripping at his pants with determination. Duke, sensing the shift in the room, got up and trotted over, lowering his face to meet Crystal's. She let out a delighted giggle, reaching out and grabbing Duke's nose with both hands. The dog stood perfectly still, his big eyes blinking patiently as she gave his nose a few enthusiastic squeezes. Her laughter breaking through the tension, light and unbothered, as if nothing in the world could weigh it down.

Slim didn't miss a beat; his voice dropping. "Nah, bruh, don't hit me with that gangster sh*t over the phone. You know I stay strapped, just like you. F**k all that noise—ain't nobody scared."

His grip on the phone tightened slightly, his free hand instinctively resting on his daughter's back as she continued her playful assault on Duke. He exhaled slowly, his voice dropping even lower. "N***a, like I f**kin' said," Monster growled, his tone dark and unyielding. His eyes shifted to Crystal, still giggling as she played with Duke's nose, her innocence a stark contrast to the heat of the conversation. "You better watch how you speak on my name. You know I don't give second warnings. Now, say what you gotta say, and make it worth my time."

Slim let out a humorless chuckle, the kind that carried more weight than words. He wasn't the type to puff his chest or seek validation by running his mouth. He'd earned his respect the hard way, grinding his way up from nothing, and everyone knew the only one he feared was God. "A'ight, shawty," he said, his tone calm but laced with a seriousness that couldn't be ignored. "But like I said, y'all got the streets on fire right now. Do you even know who you shot at and ran off the damn road?"

Monster smirked into the phone, arrogance dripping from his voice. "I don't f**kin' care? What, she some lawyer? A city council bitch? A cop? N***a, I don't give a f**k who the two bitches were. They both should be glad Baby J's no-aim having ass didn't hit one of 'em before I actually realized they weren't the ones I was looking for and told him to stop. So miss me with all that sh*t."

Slim paused, his tone shifting to something more serious. "You a fool for real. That 'sexy ass bitch' in the driver's seat, whose life y'all played with, since you acknowledge you don't give a f**k? That's *the Godfather's sister.*"

Monster froze, his breath stalled mid-inhale. Even Duke, stretched out at his feet, lifted his head, sensing the shift in the air.

"The Godfather's sister," Monster repeated, his voice low and rough, the words heavy in the air. He could feel the blood draining from his face, but his expression didn't falter. The same Godfather he'd crossed before—the one who had humiliated him, stripped him of his dignity, and yet, in Monster's mind, was only still breathing because he had allowed it. That memory clawed its way back into his mind, the bitterness and shame tightening his chest like a vice.

He replayed the events, the missteps that had led to this moment. The thought of reaching out, of trying to defuse the situation, flickered in his mind for a split second before his pride crushed it. *Nah, never that.* He knew he'd exposed himself, shown weakness where there should've been none, but there was no way he'd bow now. He wouldn't fold—not completely. His arrogance wouldn't allow it.

"F**k him. And f**k her too," Monster growled, his voice sharp, but the weight behind the words didn't land. They felt hollow, even to him, like an empty attempt to convince himself he was still in control.

Slim sighed on the other end, his tone laced with warning but edged with a hint of resignation. "A'ight, shawty, I'm just putting you on game. But you better go on and lock that door, 'cause you know Money Bag Mafia don't play. You threw the first shot, so now you gotta sit back and see how they spin it."

Monster didn't respond. He ended the call with a sharp jab of his thumb, tossing the phone onto the sofa as if it burned him. The room sank into shadow, the sun long gone, with only the faint glow of streetlights filtering in. Duke let out a low whine from the corner, his eyes flicking between Monster and Crystal, sensing the shift in energy.

Monster sat in silence, his chest rising and falling, thoughts churning. He leaned back, dragging a hand over his face before resting it protectively on Crystal's tiny back as she entertained herself beside him. She was oblivious to the storm brewing outside, her giggles soft and carefree, a cruel contrast to the weight crushing his mind.

Monster stood abruptly, a surge of defiance propelling him to his feet. His frame loomed in the darkened room as he grabbed his gun, scanning the quiet streets below.

"Ain't nobody folding over here," he muttered, his voice laced with arrogance, masking the doubt creeping beneath. He knew they'd come—it wasn't *if* but *when*—and he was ready for whatever.

Chapter 36

"Rolling the Dice"

Turning into the apartment complex, the thunderous growl of the engine melded with the pounding rhythm of music that filled the car like a living pulse. Gunna eased into a parking spot. The low rumble of his classic '69 Chevrolet SS 396 reverberated against the surrounding buildings. He killed the engine but let the music ride, the bass-heavy beats shaking the interior like a heartbeat in sync with his own. Reaching into his pocket, he pulled out a sandwich bag of kush and a blunt wrap, his fingers steady despite the surge of energy coursing through him. His heart thumped harder with every note, anticipation mixing with the electric rush flooding in his veins. This was his sanctuary—a moment of raw energy and control, behind the wheel of his pride and joy.

The car gleamed under the dull streetlights, its tangerine paint catching the eye of anyone nearby, especially the young kids eager to grow up too fast, idolizing his status. Breaking the buds down on top of the blunt wrap, Gunna lifted his eyes to briefly survey the area. His gaze landed on his twin brother T-Roc's pristine '69 Buick Electra 225 parked in its usual spot. "Deuce and a Quarter," they called it—a car so clean it looked fresh off the showroom floor. Gunna smirked, satisfied that T-Roc was finally making an effort to be on time. For once.

But his excitement evaporated in an instant. Just as he raised the blunt to seal it, Gunna caught sight of four Drug Squad vans creeping past the entrance to the lot. The vehicles' dark, unmarked exteriors blended into the shadows, giving them an almost ghostly presence. Gunna froze, his chest tightening as if squeezed by an invisible vice. The way they moved in formation, silent and calculated, sent a wave of unease rippling through him. He wasn't about to end up face-down on the pavement—or sprinting through the complex, especially not tonight, strapped and carrying weed.

He leaned back in his seat, lowering the music until the bass was nothing more than a faint vibration. His eyes stayed locked on the vans as their tires slowly crunched over the uneven asphalt. The streetlights glinted off their tinted windows, concealing the prying eyes undoubtedly scanning every inch of the complex. Gunna sat motionless, barely breathing, until the last van crossed the intersection and melted into the distance. Only then did he let out the breath he'd been holding, sealing the blunt with a swift lick and lighting it to steady his nerves.

"Not tonight," he muttered, his voice low but firm, the words more a prayer than a declaration.

The twins' punctuality had been slipping lately, something that didn't sit right with Gunna. They were already skating on thin ice, and the timing couldn't be worse—not when the Godfather was waiting. Even though they pulled in solid money overseeing the daily operations of Money Bag Mafia for the Godfather, the twins couldn't bring themselves to leave the hood. Mechanicville was more than just home; it was their essence, their identity. To move out would feel like cutting off a piece of themselves. They'd grown up in the chaotic symphony of Atlanta's projects, and they thrived on it—the noise, the hustle, the survival. It wasn't just where they lived; it was who they were.

As Gunna stepped out of the car, the cool evening air wrapped around him, carrying the rich aroma of exotic weed mingled with faint motor oil and the biting tang of crack fumes. He blew out a plume of smoke, adjusting the heavy chains draped across his chest, each link glinting under the uneven glow of the unreliable streetlights above. Crossing the lot, he moved with quiet confidence, nodding at a group of hustlers posted on the step entrance of a building. Their watchful, calculating eyes scanned the area as they worked, their presence were a constant reminder that the streets never slept. The energy in the air was raw, electric, and familiar—this was home.

Approaching his building, he passed a dice game just starting to heat up. The clack of dice on concrete was like music to his ears. Gunna's weakness was dice—it wasn't just a game to him; it was an obsession. He paused, promising himself it'd be just one quick bet, something light to keep it moving. But he knew better. His veins were already pulsing with the adrenaline.

Pulling out a wad of cash thick enough to choke someone, Gunna flashed a confident grin, his gold grill catching the light. "Aye, I got fifty on a side bet. Shawty's point is eight. What y'all on?" he said, his voice smooth but firm, the swagger in his tone undeniable.

The scene buzzed with energy as money passed from hand to hand, bills dropping to the ground like confetti, only to be scooped up in the frenzy. The air brimmed with anticipation, tension crackling like static. Gunna kept puffing on his blunt, the rich, sweet aroma of exotic kush weaving through the crowd. It was a magnet, pulling in attention from everyone nearby, each inhale a reminder of his status—untouchable, in control.

"Aye, bruh, let me hit that. I know you smokin' that top-shelf sh*t from the way that smell," a voice called out, rough and eager.

Gunna smirked and shook his head, exhaling a cloud of smoke that hung heavy in the air. "Naw, shawty. This right here? This that exclusive. You gotta level up first," he said, laughing as he waved the young hustler off.

With money still changing hands and bets stacking up, the energy climbed higher. Gunna wasn't just another dude at the dice game—he had a finesse that made him untouchable. When the shooter hit four straight craps, the frustration in the air was so intense it felt like it was weighing on your skin. But Gunna didn't flinch. He stayed cool, eyes locked on the dice like a hawk zeroing in on its prey.

"Run it back! I'm still taking all side bets against six and eight! Let's see what's what! Who like it?" he called out, slapping his stack of cash onto the ground, the bills smacking the concrete with authority.

The dice rolled, tumbling across the ground as the crowd leaned in, their breath caught in collective anticipation. When the dice landed on a five and a two, the energy detonated like fireworks, the crowd erupting in a roar of disbelief and excitement. Fists pumped in the air, and Gunna felt a fiery surge race through his veins. Money flowed like a river when the shooter handed him the dice. Now it was his turn to prove why he ran these streets.

The pressure didn't faze him—it gave him life. He cradled the dice in his palm, feeling their weight as he gave them a quick roll between his fingers. With a flick of his wrist, he launched them onto the ground, the bounce and clatter sending a ripple of excitement through the crowd. One hit, then another, and another. Gunna's stack grew, the money piling up until it was too much to hold in one hand.

The crowd buzzed with a mix of awe and envy, but Gunna just kept puffing his blunt, calm and collected. "Y'all see it," he said, his voice low and steady, the confidence in his words undeniable. This was his zone, and tonight, the streets were his for the taking.

"Damn, shawty chomping on that f**kin' gum like she tryna seduce a n***a," one of the hustlers muttered as three women strolled by, their bodies swaying with effortless confidence. Each curve was accentuated by their tight outfits—crop tops clinging to torsos, mid-thigh skirts, and sheer leggings that left nothing to the imagination. Their skin glistened under the dim streetlights, demanding attention. As they passed, the scent of cheap perfume lingered. They tossed a few teasing glances back before disappearing into the shadows, heading for the weed man.

Lost in the thrill of the game, Gunna barely noticed time slipping away. He'd won over three thousand dollars before his phone buzzed in his pocket.

"Where you at, bruh?" T-Roc's voice cut through the noise.

Reality struck Gunna like a splash of cold water as his eyes dropped to his watch. The concert. The Godfather. Time was slipping, and he couldn't afford to mess this up. The kush and the dice game had pulled him in, but now they felt like distractions he couldn't afford.

"F**k!" he yelled, throwing his hands up. He snatched up his winnings, stuffing the bills into his pockets. "Y'all gon' have to finish without me. I'm out."

The group erupted in groans of protest, voices rising in frustration as tempers flared. Demands for their money back echoed in the air, but no one dared to press the issue. Gunna's name carried too much weight, his reputation a warning in itself. Everyone knew better than to cross him or Money Bag Mafia—he wasn't just respected; he was feared.

Racing up the stairs, Gunna reached his apartment, his heart pounding like the dice he left behind. He burst through the door, greeted by the chaos that was his shared world with T-Roc. The twins had always been inseparable—clothes, shoes, even women; everything was shared. The apartment, a peculiar mix of project grit and luxury ambition, held a living room decked in high-end furniture, but Gunna's room was the opposite—scattered clothes and chaos. He didn't care. His mind was on the night ahead.

T-Roc, already dressed to impress in designer threads, strolled into the room and casually perched on the edge of the bed, adjusting his watch as it caught the dim light, gleaming like a trophy. He looked like a bar of gold, polished and ready for display. Gunna had no time to match that shine with a shower. So he grabbed a clean outfit from the closet—one of the few items not strewn across the floor—and threw it on. A few spritzes of cologne masked the mix of sweat and smoke clinging to his skin. Satisfied with the mirror's reflection of someone who looked like money, he nodded to T-Roc. "I'm ready."

T-Roc smirked, locking eyes with him in that twin connection. "Let's get it."

Choosing to ride together, they locked the door behind them, leaving the mess and the grind inside. As they sprinted back to T-Roc's car, the sounds of the dice game still echoed in Gunna's mind like the ticking of a bomb. Sliding into the passenger seat, he exhaled sharply and passed T-Roc the blunt. The flick of a lighter followed as T-Roc cranked up the car and pulled out of the lot, the engine's growl a backdrop to Gunna's quick glance at his phone. Nothing yet from the Godfather, but tonight wasn't just about dice or pride—it was about survival, about proving they weren't the ones to f**k with.

The smell of weed filled the car as they sped through the city, headlights bouncing off buildings that held stories of dreams lost and hustles gone wrong. Gunna leaned back, the blunt now between his

223

fingers, his thoughts flickering between the stakes of tonight and the life they were clawing through.

"Twin," T-Roc said, breaking the silence. "You think about how long we can keep this up?"

Gunna didn't answer immediately. He took a long pull from the blunt, exhaled, and stared out the window at the blurred city lights. "Ain't about how long, bro. It's about what we do while we here. Streets don't owe us nothing. Gotta take what's ours, but we gotta be smart. All this flossin' don't mean a thing if we ain't got our priorities straight."

T-Roc glanced at him, nodding slowly as Gunna's words sank in. The car roared onto the highway, the city falling behind them. "Out here, it's two choices," Gunna added, his voice low but firm. "You either lead or get led—ain't no in-between. But if we don't move right, all this?" He gestured to the car, their clothes, the imagined power they chased. "It's just a setup, twin. Streets don't play fair, and the clock don't stop ticking."

T-Roc unlocked his phone, scrolling until he found the video he was looking for—a group of bad thots who'd be at the concert, ready to turn up. Smirking, he angled the screen toward his brother. "We gon' freak them after," he said, amusement lacing his tone.

Gunna watched, anticipation stirring as the beat thumped through the car, the blunt burning down to its final inches between his fingers. He took one last pull before flicking it out the window, watching the ember vanish into the night. "Tonight, we shine," Gunna said, as he leaned forward, his eyes locked on the road ahead. "But tomorrow? We gotta figure out what's real, or these streets gon' take us under."

The air in the car grew heavier, not from the smoke but from the unspoken truth in his words. Tonight was theirs to own, but the weight of their world demanded more than just fast money and fleeting fame. It demanded choices—ones that could either free them or bury them.

Chapter 37

"All Eyes on the Godfather"

The Godfather's condo pulsed with electric energy as members of Money Bag Mafia filed in one by one, each arrival dripping with swagger. Their high-end outfits turned the living room into an impromptu runway, every piece radiating luxury. Bold logos, flawless fits, and rich fabrics made it clear—they weren't just stepping into the room, they were making statements that demanded attention.

Their M.B.M. diamond-encrusted pendants sparkled under the glow of the condo's chandelier, the stones refracting light like miniature fireworks. Every move they made seemed calculated to draw attention, from the way they adjusted their chains to how they leaned casually against the pristine white walls, exuding an effortless swagger.

As always, the air was thick with the scent of high-end colognes, mingling to create a heady mix of power and wealth. Conversations buzzed in the background, punctuated by bursts of laughter and the occasional boast about whose fit was representing the most. Whether someone was flexing the watch they purchased, adjusting their shades (even though they were indoors), or bragging about the cost of the shoes they had on their feet, the one thing that was certain was that Money Bag Mafia was on a high level.

A few of them posted up by the bar, pouring drinks, the repeated clinks of ice against glass adding to the ambiance. Bottles of premium liquor lined the countertop—all untouched, waiting for the night to begin. Despite the show of camaraderie, a subtle tension lurked beneath the surface—a quiet acknowledgment that tonight wasn't just about looking good.

The Godfather's presence loomed large, even as he remained unseen in his office. Everyone knew this wasn't just a gathering—it was a call to action. The condo was their safe haven, but it was also the war room, a place where plans were made and lives were decided.

As a few more members trickled in, the group grew louder, their voices bouncing off the high ceilings. It wasn't long before the Godfather's office door creaked open, and the room instantly fell silent. With everyone except Lil B and Speedy accounted for, the Godfather stepped into the room, his mere presence commanding respect.

His fit embodied Atlanta's street fashion royalty—a crisp designer white shirt with subtle embroidery peeking from under a quilted black vest with gold accents, paired with dark, distressed denim that fell effortlessly over a pair of clean black-and-gold Nike Air Maxes. His M.B.M. pendant, heavy with diamonds, rested on his chest, glinting with every move, while a perfectly tilted all-black Atlanta Falcons fitted cap completed the look. The glint of his diamond-studded pinky ring, paired with a sleek gold chain-link bracelet and a two-tone Audemars Piguet on his wrist, made it clear he was the boss. Every detail was sharp, street, and undeniably Atlanta, reflecting his status without a word.

Standing in the doorframe, scanning the room, he couldn't help but admire the extraordinary lineup of stunners he had assembled to represent Money Bag Mafia. Each one of them looked sharp, their energy palpable, ready to move at a moment's notice. "Y'all know the drill," the Godfather said, his smooth but commanding voice slicing through the chatter. "Office. Now."

The group followed him back into his private office, the air taut with anticipation. Once inside, the Godfather leaned against his desk, his eyes staring at something on his tablet. "Listen up," he began, his tone measured but firm. "It's imperative we stay focused tonight. Y'all enjoy yourselves, but represent the way we do. I've done a lot at the last minute to make this happen, and honestly, I don't know how it's all gonna play out. But for now, keep it clean and tight. Got it?"

"Got it," came the chorus of responses, though one voice stood out.

Gramz sat in the corner, clenching his jaw and crossing his arms, his eyes burning with frustration. "So what about the f**k n***a that violated Amani? We just gon' act like that sh*t didn't happen,

Godfather? This bullsh*t ain't adding up. Since when we start letting disrespect slide? Hell nah, we ain't 'bout to start now."

The room tensed. Everyone had been thinking it, but Gramz had the nerve to say it out loud. The silence that followed was thick, oppressive with unspoken words and raw tension. Eyes shifted between Gramz and the Godfather, waiting for a response. But the Godfather didn't flinch. He remained unbothered, cool as ever, his gaze steady and unwavering.

"Some sh*t should be understood without needing to be spoken by now," the Godfather said, his voice low but carrying the weight of authority as it cut through the room. "We don't let disrespect slide on any f**kin' level, but with the heat on us after the Joyland shootout, I'm handling this situation from another angle—one that ensures we stay protected. So tonight, let's enjoy ourselves without worrying about it."

His gaze locked onto Gramz, his tone calm yet commanding enough to break through the tension. "But if you or anyone else in here has a problem with my decision, we can make that the mission to focus on. Just say the word." The room remained silent, the Godfather's words settling over the group like a heavy cloud, daring anyone to challenge him.

Gramz kept his arms crossed, his stance unyielding, his eyes narrowing with quiet fury. "A'ight, Godfather, but don't act like we ain't all seein' the same sh*t. You know ain't nobody scared to put in work when it's time. Just don't expect us to ignore what's right in front of us."

"Y'all eager for vengeance without an awareness of the consequences," the Godfather said, his voice cold and cutting. "If any of you wanna go out there half-cocked and light up the streets for my sister's honor, then remove those letters from your neck and lay them on the deck, and do as you wish. Just know that you'll be dead in the water before the night even starts."

The room was dead silent. No one moved, no one spoke. The Godfather's eyes shifted slowly from one member to the next, his gaze piercing, demanding respect.

"And Gramz," he continued, his voice unwavering, "when you can beat me at chess, I'll step down and crown you the f**kin' king. But until then, don't ever question me. What happened to Amani and Stacy will be handled, accordingly. Right now, I need y'all to leave all your straps here and get ready to roll."

The tension in the room was charged, but no one dared challenge the Godfather. One by one, they placed their weapons on the desk, the weight of their movements laden with anticipation. Every pair of eyes remained fixed on him, silent, waiting for his next command. The Godfather didn't speak until the final weapon was laid down. With a slow, deliberate motion, he locked everything into the office safe, his gaze never leaving the room.

The office door swung open. One by one, the members of Money Bag Mafia filed out, the weight of the conversation lingering in the air. The tension of not retaliating, of letting things slide for now, lingered, but the night was young, and everyone was ready to enjoy it. As they made their way down the hallway towards the living room, Stacy stepped into view, a glass of Chardonnay in hand. Her dazzle-me jumpsuit sparkled under the lights, the rhinestones catching every bit of glow in the room. With each step, the room paused, every gaze locked onto her.

Everyone knew not to flirt with her because of her connection to the Godfather, but that didn't stop the stares. Stacy's curves had them mesmerized, and the way her body moved in the shimmering fabric had heads turning in unison. They all watched as she glided past, each of them silently acknowledging her presence, but no one dared say a word. She was beautiful, confident, and they all knew better than to disrespect the unspoken rule. Despite the respect they had for her connection to the Godfather, the men couldn't help but feel the stirrings of desire, even if they kept it buried beneath the surface.

Stepping out of her room just as Stacy reached the end of the hallway, Amani couldn't help but giggle at the way the crew was eyeing Stacy like she was some kind of irreplaceable treasure. They were so obvious, their gazes locked on her as if they couldn't get enough.

"Damn, y'all that thirsty?" Amani uttered, a teasing grin spreading across her face. It was hard to miss the way the men were practically drooling, but Amani wasn't fazed. She was used to the attention, though she always found it amusing how n***as in the city knew Stacy had slept with almost everyone in Atlanta, yet the men still couldn't hide their reactions when they saw her.

Amani was flawless in her red She-In-Moment set, the fabric flowing around her body as if it were custom-made for her. The soft material hugged her curves in all the right places, highlighting her figure with effortless grace. The outfit gave off a vibe of casual elegance, but there was no mistaking the quiet confidence that radiated from her as she moved. She didn't have to try to be noticed; it was natural, like a magnet pulling the eyes of everyone around her.

As she made her way down the hallway toward her brother, Amani stood tall, her head held high, exuding a calm and composure. There was a spark in her eyes, a subtle challenge to anyone who might think they could underestimate her. With a faint smirk, she passed the men in the hall, who, despite their attempts to play it cool, couldn't help but watch her intently. She noticed, but it didn't faze her. She had bigger things on her mind than dealing with their stares.

"Bruh, I'm so happy you changed your damn mind and decided to perform," Amani said, flashing a grin as she caught his eye. She moved closer, giving him a quick once-over and offering a teasing suggestion. "You need to change that shirt, though. You can't be stepping out with me like that."

Stacy, never one to miss an opportunity to stir the pot, sidled up to him with a mischievous glint in her eye. "He need to let me perform. I just wanna rock the mic," she said, her voice playful and bold. Without missing a beat, she started to act out for his amusement, twerking provocatively as the crew cracked up, egging her on. "All I need is one mic… one mic… deep throat it all night," she sang, her body moving to an invisible beat as the laughter and hype grew louder around her.

Amani, shaking her head at her friend, couldn't help but add her own playful jab. "Bitch, your freak ass gon' pollute the air if you keep it up," Amani joked, pushing Stacy away with a grin, while her brother just stood there shaking his head, half-amused by the antics.

The lighthearted moment filled the hallway, but it was clear that, despite the jokes, everyone was primed and ready for whatever came next—business as usual, but with a little fun mixed in. "Y'all ready sis?" the Godfather asked, his tone softening slightly.

"Always," Amani replied with a smirk, brushing past him toward the living room.

The condo was a whirlwind of motion as the crew grabbed their things. Designer duffels were slung over shoulders, diamond pendants sparkled under the overhead lights, and conversation buzzed in low murmurs. The Godfather, calm and composed, gave a nod that signaled it was time to roll out.

They moved as a unit down the hallway, their presence commanding. Stacy followed near the rear, swirling her glass of Chardonnay as the rhinestones on her jumpsuit shimmered with every step. Amani walked beside her brother, her quiet confidence matching his, her gaze fixed ahead.

As they approached the elevator, the doors slid open, revealing Speedy standing inside. His usual grin was replaced with a tense expression, and the energy in the hallway shifted immediately. His shoulders were stiff, and his eyes darted to the Godfather. "What's good, Speedy?" the Godfather asked, stepping into the elevator, a few of the crew trailing behind him while the rest waited for the next one.

Speedy exhaled deeply, his voice low but steady. "Just got off the phone with Lil B. They rushed his grandma to the hospital. Docs saying she ain't got much time."

The elevator fell silent, the news landing heavily. Amani stepped closer, her voice soft but sincere. "We'll keep her in our prayers, Speedy."

The Godfather gave a firm nod, his tone steady. "Tell Lil B to take care of what matters. Family first. Always."

Speedy nodded, appreciating the sentiment. The ride down was quieter than usual, the weight of Lil B's absence hanging over them. But as the elevator doors opened to the lobby, the energy shifted back.

Their swagger returned as they exited into the crisp night air, the glow of Atlanta's skyline casting shadows on their designer fits. Parked at the curb were two sleek black Sprinter vans, their tinted windows shimmering under the streetlights like polished obsidian. The side doors slid open with a smooth hiss, revealing a custom interior that reeked of luxury. Plush leather seats were arranged in a way that encouraged conversation, while soft LED lighting glowed from the floor and ceiling, bathing the space in a futuristic ambiance. A minibar was tucked neatly into the corner, stocked with top-shelf liquor, and a state-of-the-art sound system filled the cabin with bass-heavy tracks that made the van feel like a mobile nightclub.

The crew split up and piled into both vans, their energy palpable as the night began to take shape. Amani slid into a plush leather seat beside her brother, her poised demeanor radiating quiet confidence for what lay ahead. Across from her, Marko leaned back with his signature grin, cracking jokes that had the group erupting in laughter, the tension from earlier melting away with each punchline.

Near the door, Gunna claimed a spot, scrolling through his phone with an air of nonchalance, though his keen eyes missed nothing. Gramz, on the other hand, sat stiffly with his arms crossed, his frustration still simmering beneath the surface but held in check. The soft hum of the luxury van surrounded them, the dim ambient lighting casting a cool glow over the group as the city lights blurred past the tinted windows. It was a night full of promise, and everyone could feel it.

Relaxed yet commanding, the Godfather surveyed his crew—his gaze a silent reminder of who called the shots. The van glided through the city, Atlanta's vibrant lights flickering across the tinted windows as the crew vibed to the music and chatted amongst themselves.

He joked with his sister about taking pictures of her and sending them to their mother so she could see how she was dressed. The

Godfather grinned as Amani shot him an elbow, then tried to slap him but missed.

"I'll beat your damn ass and tell everyone you were on First 48 if you do that shit," she whispered, trying to look serious, but he only chuckled in response.

The sudden buzz of his phone drew his attention away from her fake gangster act. He glanced at the screen, and then shifted his eyes to Gunna, giving him a subtle nod. He understood immediately what it meant, pulling out the phone and typing a quick message: *EXECUTE*. He hit 'send,' removed the SIM card, broke it along with the burner phone, and gave a faint smile before leaning back into his seat, his focus shifting back to the road ahead.

As the Sprinter vans pulled up to the Lakewood Amphitheater, the energy shifted. The music from the venue spilled out into the night, blending with the anticipation inside the van. One by one, the crew stepped out, their movements smooth and calculated, their presence impossible to ignore.

The Godfather was the last to exit, adjusting his designer vest and smoothing the creases on his pants. His calm confidence was unshakable, his aura magnetic. Tonight wasn't just another performance—it was a declaration. Atlanta was his stage, and by the end of the night, the city would know exactly where the power resided.

Chapter 38

"Blood in the Night"

With no confirmation to proceed on the target they were paid to eliminate, the tension in the air was pressing down on them like an oppressive fog. Every minute felt like an hour as they waited in silence, their nerves tightly wound.

"Man, this here waitin' is killin' me dead," Hank muttered under his breath, his thick drawl drawing out each word like molasses.

"Keep ya damn head on straight," Billy Jack growled, his eyes narrowing as he shot Hank a hard look. "We ain't movin' till the word comes down. Patience is what keeps us breathin', boy."

The weight of his words settled over the crew, silencing any further complaints. Each of them knew what was at stake—one wrong move, one step out of sync, and the entire operation could unravel.

Time stretched endlessly. The silence was heavy with tension, every second dragging like eternity. The air was taut, buzzing with the weight of unspoken possibilities, until finally, the abrupt buzz of Billy Jack's phone shattered the stillness like a gunshot. The sound was jarring, commanding attention as every set of eyes snapped toward him, the room frozen in anticipation.

Billy Jack's gaze locked onto the screen, his breath hitching as he read the notification in bold, unflinching clarity—EXECUTE. A surge of adrenaline coursed through him, intense and electrifying, his pulse hammering in response. The simple word carried the weight of finality, a command that demanded precision, action, and ruthlessness.

Without a word, Billy Jack's fingers moved with practiced efficiency as he opened his email to retrieve the address. His eyes scanned the screen, the faint glow casting shadows across his sharp features, reflecting the steely resolve in his expression. Once he had the information, he quickly jotted both addresses onto a piece of paper. With a muted thud, the phone dropped into his lap. He tore the paper in half and shoved one addresses toward Cletus. The room seemed to hold its breath as he fixed his crew with a hard stare, his eyes burning with a dangerous focus that demanded their unwavering attention.

"Alright, boys, time to git! Showtime!" he hollered, his voice twangy and brimming with excitement.

The Carrollton Boys didn't need to be told twice. They sprang into action with precision. No words, no hesitation. Just the cold efficiency of warriors on a mission. Billy Jack's fingers were already working over his weapon, checking the chamber, ensuring the ammo was loaded. There was no room for error tonight.

The crew pulled their tactical gear over their rugged, country clothes—faded flannels, tattered jeans, and boots stained with mud and grease. The smell of smoke and sweat clung to them, a testament to days spent living rough. But once the black vests and masks were secured, they transformed, no longer ragged country boys but men ready for war.

Stepping out of the safe house, their boots crunched against the concrete walkway as they moved in unison toward the vans. The damp night air mixed with the metallic tang of their gear. Without a word, they climbed into the two black cargo vans, their dark paint blending into the shadows and windows tinted so dark they were nearly opaque.

The vans rumbled awake, engines growling low as if echoing the intensity inside. As the vehicles rolled out, the darkness enveloped them, leaving nothing behind but the faint scent of gasoline and the promise of chaos. The streets were alive with the usual buzz of city life—distant car horns, the faint hum of streetlights, and the soft chatter of people on sidewalks. But inside the vans, the air was tense, broken only by the deep purr of the engines as they cut through the night. The crew's focus was absolute as they sped through the city, each turn and acceleration adding to the growing anticipation for what was about to unfold.

Gliding through the dimly lit streets with purpose, Billy Jack's squad arrived at their target location first. The trap house on Daniel Avenue was the destination marked for destruction. The night sky above was moonless, with the only light coming from the distant street lamps, casting their faint glow and stretching jagged shadows across the cracked sidewalks. This added an air of menace to the tense journey, while the lighters of crackheads flickered in the dark like fireflies.

As planned, he parked two houses down, the weathered asphalt crunching under the tires as he killed the engine. The sounds of the night settled over the street, broken only by the occasional flash of headlights from a passing car on the adjacent road and the shuffling of crackheads approaching the house to buy drugs. Billy Jack instructed the others to stay low, scanning the area with the calm composure of someone who had done this a hundred times before. With a fluid motion, he retrieved his phone and dialed Cletus's number without hesitation. The line clicked, and Cletus's voice came through, rough and steady as ever, like the growl of a bear in the woods.

"We in position," Billy Jack said, his gravelly drawl carrying a tone of certainty, like a man who knew his crew was always on point.

"Hold yer horses, we almost there," Cletus fired back, his southern twang thick and unhurried, like he had all the time in the world. The line went silent, the kind of hush that stretched forever, brimming with the kind of anticipation only men like them could stomach—men who lived for trouble and didn't flinch at the thought of blood.

Billy Jack leaned back into the seat, watching as some scrawny fella staggered away from the trap house window, standing smack-dab in the middle of the street to spark up whatever junk he'd just bought. The flicker of the lighter briefly illuminated his hollow features, casting grotesque shadows on his face before the darkness swallowed him once more

Finally, Cletus's voice crackled back over the line. "We here now. Let's git this done."

Both men spoke with a deep, slow southern drawl, each word heavy with the weight of their roots. Their accents were thick—enough to make outsiders pause, straining to catch every syllable. Behind them, three rough-around-the-edges country boys lingered, ready to follow orders and bring havoc to anyone who crossed their path.

Billy Jack's lips curled into the kind of grin that only surfaced when blood was about to spill. "A'ight, boys. Let's make it rain and add to our kill counts."

With those electrifying words spoken, the team exited the van, charged and ready to bring mayhem. The rhythmic thud of their boots echoed against the cracked sidewalk—a grim warning that death approached—yet unheard by the world. Every step was calculated, every breath measured.

At the front of the house, Billy Jack raised a fist, signaling for his crew to fall into position. They lined up across the sidewalk, standing shoulder to shoulder, their bodies slightly swaying with the rhythm of their steps. In perfect sync, they moved as one, each man locked in with a singular focus, eyes scanning every shadow, every corner, ready for whatever came next. The sidewalk beneath their boots was a silent witness to the storm that was about to break.

From a side street, a crackhead—looking disheveled and jittery—approached, her eyes darting around as she neared, clearly hoping to score some drugs. Her gaze landed on the group, but before she could move or make a sound, one of the men, his hand steady and gun raised, locked eyes with her, barrel aimed. He placed his index finger over his mouth in a clear, silent warning. The message was simple: stay quiet, or else.

The crackhead froze, eyes wide in terror as the weight of the moment hit her. Her breath quickened, her body trembling with primal fear. She took one slow, cautious step back, her feet shuffling against the cracked pavement, desperate to put distance between herself and the looming danger. Her gaze darted between the men, then into the darkness of the night ahead. With a final glance over her shoulder, she bolted, disappearing into the shadows as if she'd never been there at all.

Then, without warning, Billy Jack's Kalashnikov AM-17 erupted with gunfire. The deafening roar of gunfire shattered the stillness of the night, its sound like thunder in a storm. Billy Jack's team followed suit, opening fire with ruthless precision. A torrent of bullets tore through the front of the house, splintering wood and glass, and shredding whatever else stood in their way. The chaos was unrelenting. The rapid crack of assault rifles echoed down the block, drowning out the distant hum of the city, leaving only the sound of destruction in its wake. The night, once still and quiet, was now a battlefield.

Inside the house, chaos exploded. The heavy thud of bodies hitting the ground mixed with the screams of people who hadn't known what hit them. The walls were no match for the firepower that tore through them. Bullets shredded drywall, splintering wood and sending glass flying in every direction.

The first man took the brunt of the gunfire—his chest burst in a gruesome mess as he collapsed against the wall. Blood sprayed across the floor, pooling in a crimson puddle. Another man, scrambling for cover, managed only a few steps before the next volley of shots hit him square in the back, sending him sprawling to the ground with a sickening thud.

A third man, desperate for escape, bolted for the front door. His hand gripped a pistol, the weapon more of a liability than protection. He barely made it outside before the bullets found their mark, the impact of the rounds sending his body jerking back violently. His face twisted in agony as he crumpled onto the porch, body convulsing while bullets still found their mark.

Meanwhile, across Decatur, Cletus and his crew weren't wasting a second. Moving with tactical precision, they exited the van and advanced down the street in formation, their boots crunching against the weathered asphalt. Two of the men broke off, climbing onto the hood of a Dodge Charger parked in front of Monster's house. With quick, practiced movements, they hoisted themselves onto the roof, their combined weight making the car creak. Then they began bouncing, the intentional motion sending shockwaves through the vehicle until the alarm blared to life, slicing through the night like a scream.

That was the signal—a clear warning that whoever was inside the house would snap to attention, rising to their feet, either to peer out the window or bolt for the door to see what was going on.

In unison, the entire team raised their rifles and squeezed the triggers. The first volley of gunfire ripped into the house with brutal precision, the deafening roar of the rifles reverberating through the neighborhood. Bullets shredded walls, wood and drywall exploding like shrapnel. Windows shattered in violent bursts, spraying shards of glass across the lawn. The house groaned under the relentless assault, as if it knew its fate and was begging for mercy. But mercy wasn't on the agenda.

Cletus stood firm, his rifle steady as he directed the storm of destruction. Inside the house, chaos erupted as furniture was obliterated—tables, chairs, lamps—all disintegrating into fragments and debris, the shattered remnants scattered across the floor. High-velocity rounds punched through walls like they were paper, leaving gaping holes in their wake. Sections of the ceiling cracked and caved in, spilling insulation and dust into the air like confetti. The acrid smell of gunpowder mixed with the unmistakable odor of burning wood and plastic as sparks flew from exposed wires.

Flames licked at the edges of the wreckage, casting a fiery glow over the scene of utter devastation. The chaos roared louder with each passing second as the once-peaceful night erupted into a cacophony of shouts, splintering wood, and the relentless staccato of gunfire. The unyielding onslaught tore through the house, leaving it a skeletal shell. Debris flew in every direction, carried by the force of the assault, while thick, acrid smoke began to choke the air.

The noise was overwhelming—a deafening symphony of destruction that announced the wrath of the Money Bag Mafia with brutal clarity. This was no mere warning; it was a declaration, delivered in blood and fire. No one crossed them and lived to tell the tale.

As the final clip emptied, silence followed—thick, weighed, carrying the promise of death. This wasn't peace; it was the oppressive quiet that followed chaos, heavy with the echoes of violence. In the distance, voices rose in alarm, urgent and panicked, cutting through the still night. Porch lights flickered on in every direction, illuminating the once-dark neighborhood like a stage set for disaster.

The shift was instant. Without a word, they bolted—boots pounding against the debris-littered pavement, adrenaline surging through their veins. Their eyes swayed nervously, instinctively aware that the violent racket they'd just created would draw attention. Billy Jack cranked the engine in one swift motion, slamming it into drive. The screech of the van's tires shattered the night—a desperate, reckless escape from the destruction they'd left behind. The sound echoed through the still streets as they sped off into the darkness.

As the van peeled away, the men pressed their backs against the cold metal, breath heavy in the night air, hands moving quickly to reload their weapons, just in case the law came sniffing. Stoppin' wasn't an option. Not now, not ever.

The city hummed behind them, but ahead, only the black void remained—as if the night had swallowed every damn thing they'd done. The engine's low thrum was the only sound as they tore through the streets. Cletus reached for his phone and dialed Billy Jack to check on the crew. His voice crackled through the speaker, laden with that familiar southern drawl.

"Y'all good?" he asked, his fingers tight on the wheel, his eyes scanning the rearview.

"Hell yeah, we good," Billy Jack replied, his voice steady but edged with tension. 'We're in position, just waitin' for y'all to catch up. If the law catches wind, we'll be ready."

The streetlights were flashing in the rearview mirror like fading memories, each flash dimming as if the past itself was being erased. The night devoured them, pulling them deep into its shadows until they were nothing more than whispers on the wind. Behind them, the air was thick with the stench of gunpowder, and fear—an unspoken warning left to linger in the empty streets. By morning, the city would be buzzing with speculation, rumors swirling like smoke. But tonight—tonight, they were ghosts, slipping unseen through the veins of a city that would never know their names.

In the distance, the wail of sirens began to rise, but they were already gone, swallowed by the night, their mission complete. Inside the van, silence settled like a heavy weight, the kind that needed no words. Each of them sat with their own thoughts, their own reckoning. The streets they left behind would remember them, if only for a while. Soon, it would all fade into another forgotten memory—until the next time the Carrollton Boys came to collect.

Chapter 39

"Shadows in the Glow"

Finally, after soothing his one-year-old daughter into a quiet slumber, Monster gently placed her tiny body on the bed. He pulled the corner of the sheet over her and tucked her in with a tenderness that softened his otherwise hardened demeanor. Leaning down, he kissed her forehead, his lips lingering just long enough to feel her warmth.

The soft glow of the moonlight streaming through the window illuminated her peaceful face, casting a serene beauty that tugged at his heart and brought an unexpected smile to his lips. She was his greatest blessing—the only thing in his life untouched by imperfection.

"I love you, princess," he whispered, his voice low and filled with conviction. With one last glance, he stepped out of his brother's room, closing the door softly behind him, carrying the weight of her innocence out into the night.

Monster strolled quietly into the living room, rubbing the soreness from his neck before sinking onto the sofa. His gaze fell on his older brother and his kids, who were offering their tahajjud salat, their devotion a stark contrast to the turmoil stirring within him. For a brief moment, he wondered if his life might have found a greater purpose had he not traded Allah's love for street notoriety. He knew it was ash-shirk-al-khafi to feel inward dissatisfaction with the destiny Allah Ta'ala had ordained, but the thought lingered, persistent and unrelenting, given his circumstances.

Growing up, everyone thought Monster's deep love for animals would lead him to become a veterinarian. But everything changed after his father was falsely accused of rape—a crime he couldn't have committed because he was working in another state at the time—and was brutally killed in prison before he could be exonerated. Shattered, Monster stopped praying, dropped out of high school, and sought solace in the streets. Rebellion became his armor—a desperate attempt to numb the pain and redeem his family's name.

He never cared about how others admired him—the aquiline nose that complemented his sharp cheekbones, the granite jaw, and Titan-like shoulders that spoke of strength. He never craved admiration—only legend status, a man wielding leonine power. Yet, in this moment, as anger and frustration swirled, he felt something entirely different: embarrassment and violation. Sitting there, consumed by thoughts of retaliation, his blood pressure spiked, rage pulsing through him. His chest tightened as the weight of his fury pressed down on him, feeding the storm that brewed within.

"As-salamu alaikum wa rahmatullahi, Uncle Monster," his nephews chimed in unison as they approached after finishing their prayer.

"Wa alaikum as-salam wa rahmatullahi wa barakatuh," he replied calmly, giving each of them a pound and a quick hug before they launched into an impromptu kung-fu battle. Monster did his best to block and weave against their uncoordinated chops and kicks while remaining seated on the sofa. Their relentlessness eventually forced him to surrender. Grabbing both of their small arms, he pulled them into his embrace and squeezed them playfully.

"Fahim, Luqman, go get ready for bed," their father instructed, folding their prayer rugs and placing them neatly on a nearby stool. He then walked into the kitchen, returning moments later with two glasses of chamomile tea.

"Here you go," Sabir said, extending a glass to Monster as he sat down beside him on the sofa. His eyes lingered on his younger brother, watching him closely.

"Why you starin' at me like that?" Monster asked, taking a sip of his tea, eyes glued to the TV to avoid making eye contact.

"Actually, I'm lookin' at you wonderin' what happened to my brother, which has me offering du'a, not judging," Sabir said, his tone calm but firm, his gaze steady as if searching for the brother he once knew. "The selfish, senseless decisions you keep makin' have me wonderin'—are you literally insane?"

"Du'a? Man, what for? I'm straight," Monster shot back, pulling his phone from his pocket to check the incoming call. "I don't need nothin' but my muthaf**kin' strap. I'ma spin that pussy n***a when I catch him. Who the f**k does he think he is, sprayin' up my spot, takin' out my boys? I'ma muthaf**kin' legend out here in these streets."

"No, you not a legend; you're a damn fool. And I've asked you not to curse in my house," Sabir countered, his voice cool but firm. Leaning forward, Sabir grabbed his Qur'an from the coffee table and flipped it open, as if searching for something specific. "You think life is a game? Those three young men are dead because of your nonsense, and you sittin' here actin' like someone else is to blame. When are you gonna realize there's always consequences for your choices? And there's always somebody hungrier and more ruthless than you out here. Does watching your daughter grow up hold any meaning for you?"

"You say you're not judging, but what do you call this, huh? I didn't come here for this." Monster muttered, his voice tinged with defiance, though a spark of doubt flashed in his eyes.

"This ain't judgment, little brother. This is a reality check," Sabir said, looking at him with steady eyes. "You started something without thinkin' about the aftermath. Ain't nobody gonna respect you for gettin' people killed over your pride. "

"Bro, what the hell are you talkin' about? Are you even hearin' yourself right now?" Monster shot back, his voice drenched with frustration, rising from the couch to pace in front of the TV. Curious due to the elevation of his voice, his nephews peeked from behind the doorframe, unaware of the storm brewing in the room. Monster's rage was a raw, overwhelming thing, spilling out like a floodgate that had been forced open. His friends and workers were dead, and the blood of that loss was on his hands. The houses had been shot up, money lost, and the police definitely had questions they needed answered. His life was unraveling—but it didn't matter. He couldn't let anyone see that. He couldn't let anyone think he was weak. He was a legend in Decatur. That had to remain unshaken. If it didn't, the shame would swallow him whole.

"Bro, that pussy ass n***a could've killed my daughter. If I hadn't taken her out back while Duke was using the bathroom, she'd probably be dead right now. He violated the hell outta me—had me crawling and running through the woods like I was some damn Viking, with my baby girl in my arms, while they shot up my sh*t like it was routine target practice."

Sabir's eyes stayed steady on his brother, though his expression didn't shift. Calm. Controlled. "Akhi, like I told you when you showed up two hours ago with my niece all dirty like y'all had been fighting wolves, and just a moment prior, watch your language. Respect my house, akhi or leave. It's bad enough you're putting my sons' lives in danger by coming here, but at least respect that they're in the other room and don't need to hear the negative energy you're spilling out right now." Sabir's voice was low, but each word hit like a weighty truth. "Instead of letting this be a turning point for you, you're standing here talking about how you're gonna outdo someone in the street instead of putting your daughter first. That's what you need to focus on. Your loyalty should be to her, not to the streets. Whoever shot up your houses ain't playin', and you need to take heed before this gets worse."

Monster's anger flared, his voice climbing. "That n***a decimated my house with bullets, and you have the audacity to say I should use this as a turning point in my life. Have you lost your damn mind, Sabir? Has Islam blinded you to life? It's his fault my princess got hurt. She's got a scar on her face now, and you wanna talk about turning points? I ain't got no choice but to empty the clip on this fool." Monster roared, storming over to the window. He yanked a few of the blinds down with a sharp tug, peering out into the darkness, his jaw clenched, eyes blazing.

Sabir's face remained unreadable, his calm demeanor unshaken as he sat with the Qur'an open in his lap. His voice was steady, carrying the weight of centuries of wisdom. "Imran," he began, the name suppressing the tension rising between them, "in case you've forgotten your birth name and its meaning—because you're too busy trying to distinguish yourself a 'trap lord' instead of a father—Surah Al-Baqarah, verse 190, has something to remind you."

Sabir's finger traced over the sacred text as he read aloud, each word intentional. ***"Fight in the way of Allah those who fight you, but do not transgress. Verily, Allah does not love transgressors.'"*** The room seemed to hold its breath, the verse hanging heavy in the air. Sabir's eyes, dark and penetrating, finally lifted to meet Monster's, challenging him without a single word beyond the scripture he'd just recited. It wasn't just a verse; it was a mirror, forcing Monster to confront the choices he'd made and the man he'd become.

"You said yourself you made a mistake by assuming that guy's sister was the one who gave your worker counterfeit money and ran off with your product. Instead of stopping to make things right, you chased her through the streets assuming that was his girl, shot at her, ran her off the road, and then drove off like you didn't care. And now look at you—losing money, losing lives, and causing the police to put you on their radar. How many times you gonna keep making it worse? How many more people gotta die 'cause of your pride?"

Monster's jaw tightened as he glared at Sabir, but the words hit him like a jab he wasn't expecting. "You need to grow up, Imran. Stop trying to act like you're someone you're not. A true leader wouldn't be out here, plotting on revenge like this. A real leader would pick up the phone, make amends, and try to fix the situation before it gets out of hand. You've got a chance to change things, but you're too engulfed with proving a point to everyone else instead of being the father Crystal needs."

Sabir paused for a moment, letting the weight of his words sink in. "If you could swallow your pride when the same dude who had your house shot up slapped you in front of everyone you're trying to impress now, then you can do it again—for your daughter more importantly. Remember, there's a hadith in Al-Bukhari that mentions the Prophet (SAW) said: ***'O people, do not desire to meet the enemy, but rather ask Allah for safety. If you meet your enemy in battle, be patient and know that paradise is under the shade of swords.'*** You need to understand what that hadith means, akhi. You're so caught up in chasing this ideal street image that you can't even see what it means to be a father. It's not about your pride, Imran. It's about your family. It's about your responsibility. Stop putting yourself first and start putting Crystal at the center."

Frustrated that Sabir missed the point entirely, Monster stayed silent as his brother left the room. His nephews' wide-eyed curiosity gave them away—their little heads peeking around the corner got them caught eavesdropping on grown folks' conversation. With his brother ushering the kids to bed, Monster peered back through the blinds again, his attention caught by movement on the street—a black Buick Regal creeping past the house. The sight made his stomach tighten. It didn't stop, didn't speed up—just cruised. Monster stood motionless against the wall, watching, making sure the vehicle never returned.

Time crawled. His mind churned with possibilities—none of them good. Was it a coincidence? Or a message? Had Money Bag Mafia discovered where his brother lived? The thought of reaching out to the Godfather and acknowledging his careless mistake crossed his mind again, but he refused to be seen as a coward again. Weak. He shook his head, killing the thought before it could take root.

Monster's chest tightened, weighed down by unanswered questions. Taking Sabir's advice felt like a cop-out, but he needed a reset. Stripping off his shirt as he walked to the bathroom, he stepped into the shower, letting the water drum against his tense shoulders. Steam blurred the glass door as he stood, hands braced against the wall, battling for silence in his mind.

With nothing but a towel to conceal his nakedness after stepping out and drying off, he invaded his brother's drawers and closet for some fresh clothes, given they were the same size. Exhaustion began to nip at his heels, but sleep didn't come easy as he stretched out on the sofa. Restless thoughts clawed at him, dragging him in and out of broken sleep. Eventually, a faint mottling of baby blue and white broke through the blinds, blending with the pale grey of morning.

Groaning as he opened his eyes and pushed himself up, the stiffness from a night spent journeying through the woods and then tossing and turning had him dreading any movement. The house had a peaceful vibe, though his nephews were in the middle of a heated competition on the living room video game. The scent of his brother cooking breakfast filled the air, but the calm made his instincts itch. Rising off the couch to check on his daughter, the sound of his brother's voice hit him like a wave, stirring something deep inside—an overwhelming rush of emotion he hadn't expected.

"She's right here, Imran," Sabir called from the kitchen as he fixed a breakfast plate for him. "As-salamu alaikum wa rahmatullahi. Oh, and—I had a ukhti from the masjid stop by this morning. She brought a bottle and some food for Crystal, since you were too busy plotting revenge to notice."

"Wa alaikum as-salam wa rahmatullahi wa barakatuh," Monster responded, his voice rich with warmth and sincerity as he walked over and gently lifted his princess from Sabir's arms. The weight of her in his hands settled him, grounding his racing thoughts. Grabbing the plate, he gave a slight nod of gratitude, his heart swelling with unspoken appreciation. "Shukran, akhi."

After sitting at the table, eating breakfast with his family, and watching the morning news, Monster's stomach twisted when the reporter mentioned that the police were seeking him for questioning. His eyes narrowed as the words settled in. The measly amount of cash he had left on his living room table, along with the three bodies discovered in the trap house, told him everything he needed to know: the streets were about to go into overdrive, and he needed to move like a ghost until he could balance everything out.

The weight of the situation gnawed at him. His need for retaliation was strong—anger, unresolved and burning inside him—but the uncertainty of the police's next move, coupled with his daughter's scar, gnawed at him. He couldn't let his emotions dictate his next steps.

Grabbing his phone, he texted his location to one of his boys, requesting to be picked-up. Deep down, Monster knew it was a bad idea. Exposing his safe haven wasn't smart, but he couldn't let the streets think he was afraid to show his face or take action. From the couch to the window, he walked back and forth for an hour, peeking through the blinds repeatedly, waiting for confirmation. Finally, he saw the white Mazda3 parked where it was supposed to be. He grabbed his daughter and moved toward the door.

"Imran, I know you weren't foolish enough to tell someone where I stay," Sabir said sternly, his voice laced with concern as he walked over to the window to look out. "Have you literally lost your mind, given what's going on?"

"Success requires no explanations; failure permits no alibis," Monster replied nonchalantly, brushing off his brother's worry like it was nothing. He stepped out the front door with the kind of confidence that only comes from feeling like you hold all the answers.

As he reached the car, he glanced back at Sabir, fully aware that the weight of his decision was both selfish and disrespectful. Yet, more than anything, he felt an overwhelming need to make his presence known. He'd just betrayed his brother's trust, and his pride kept him locked in his own perspective, blind to how far he'd strayed from the flawed but honest man he once was.

Chapter 40

"Tensions and Shadows"

With no car seat to secure Crystal in, Monster held her snugly in his lap after getting inside the car, dapped up Tre as he slid into the driver's seat. He instructed him to drive carefully, given the circumstances, and Tre complied, sticking to the speed limit and making sure to stay attentive. Their first stop was a store where Monster picked up a few essential items for his daughter before heading to the stash apartment on Amanda Drive.

When they arrived, Tre parked near the adjacent building. Monster scanned the area carefully, his eyes darting for any signs of danger before stepping out. He tossed Tre the door key through the window and instructed him to take the bags inside. Meanwhile, Monster remained vigilant, cradling Crystal tightly against his chest. His daughter's safety was his top priority, and he needed to ensure no one was lying in wait to ambush them.

Once Tre returned, Monster hurried upstairs, holding Crystal close, shielding her from the world. Inside the apartment, he bounced her gently in his arms while peeking out the living room window for a full ten minutes, scanning for anything suspicious. Only then did he begin to feel a small measure of security. In his mind, he was on a mission, taking nothing for granted. He didn't consider himself scared, only cautious.

The soft, gentle touch of Crystal's hand against his face as he made his way to the bathroom deepened Monster's longing for the freedom to move without constantly fearing for her safety. As he filled the baby tub with warm water, he playfully blew on her stomach, before washing away the remnants of the previous prior. The radiant smile she flashed after he rubbed lotion on her delicate skin and dressed her spoke volumes of pure joy, filling his heart with overwhelming warmth.

"Daddy loves you, princess," he whispered, his voice rich with emotion, pressing a tender kiss to her soft forehead. Monster lifted her high into the air, her giggles filling the room like music that wrapped around his heart. In that moment, nothing else mattered. She was his world, his reason, and he silently vowed to shield her from every struggle, every storm he'd ever faced.

As he held her close, her tiny fingers curled around his thumb, and for the first time since before the chaos, something inside him settled. A warmth he didn't realize he was missing filled his chest, grounding him. "I got you, baby girl," he murmured, his voice low but steady. "Daddy's always got you."

Determined to make her feel safe, he moved with quiet purpose, retrieving a comforter from the bed and spreading it across the living room floor, creating a soft play space. Gently, he set her down with the toys he'd picked out, watching as her little hands explored them, her face lighting up with wonder. A smile tugged at his lips, and he crouched beside her, brushing a stray curl from her face. "You're my sunshine," Monster said softly, his voice almost breaking. "The best thing I've ever done."

Even as his mind raced with the weight of everything he still had to do, the sight of her playing grounded him in a way nothing else could. She was his source of peace, his center in a chaotic world. Leaving Crystal on her blanket, he headed to the kitchen to prepare a few bottles, glancing back every few seconds to check on her. He wanted to be ready for her every need, to prove to her—and to himself—that he could be the father she deserved.

Once the bottles were set aside, he activated his new phone and sank into the sofa, letting out a deep breath. His eyes stayed locked on her, a soft smile playing on his lips. The way she babbled to herself and clapped her little hands made his heart swell. She was a light in his darkness, a reminder that love could be pure and unbreakable.

As he waited for her mother to arrive, he leaned forward, resting his elbows on his knees, and whispered again, "I love you, Crystal. More than you'll ever know."

Hearing a knock at the door, Monster paused for a moment, his gut tensing. He moved to the peephole and looked through, saying nothing. He already knew the storm on the other side was about to hit. He opened the door and stepped aside as Lyric stormed in, her face twisted with anger and worry. Her eyes locked on Crystal, who was sitting on the comforter with her toys, and the bruises on her baby girl's soft skin broke something inside her.

"What the hell, Monster?!" she yelled, her voice shaking with rage. She scooped Crystal up, cradling her close, as if her touch alone could erase the pain. "How you gon' let this bullsh*t happen? You out here playin' gangster, and now look at our baby! Look at her!"

Monster stood still, his jaw tightened. He'd braced for this, but the weight of her words still landed like punches. He clenched his fists at his sides, forcing himself to stay calm. He knew damn well what Lyric was capable of when she got like this. The last thing he needed was the neighbors getting nosy.

"Lyric, chill," he said, his voice low but firm. "I ain't finna argue wit'chu right now. You already know what happened. And you already know I'm gon' address that sh*t."

"Chill'?!" she snapped, her voice rising. "N***a, you think I'm 'bout to chill when my daughter look like this?! You supposed to protect her, Monster! But nah, you too busy out here actin' f**kin' stupid, like you ain't got nobody dependin' on your black ass!"

Her words struck like daggers, each one slicing deeper than the last, and Monster's mask shattered as his fury erupted. "What the f**k you talkin' 'bout, Lyric?!" he snapped, his voice cracking with raw, unfiltered rage. His chest heaved, each breath coming in sharp bursts, like a storm raging just beneath his skin. He stepped closer, his presence towering, his tone laced with a deadly edge. "You think this sh*t don't eat me alive? You think I don't feel every f**kin' ounce of her pain? Don't you dare come in here actin' like I'm some deadbeat ass n***a who don't give a f**k! Nah, I'm finna show this pussy n***a why they call me Monster. He gon' learn, Lyric. For her. For us. Believe that."

"Fix it?" she fired back, her voice cracking under the weight of her anger and pain. "You don't fix nothin', Monster! All you ever do is make sh*t worse! You don't even see what you're puttin' her through—what you're puttin' us through!"

The air was suffocating with tension. Monster's fingers twitched as he fought the urge to lash out. Instead, he reached for her arm, gripping it firmly but not roughly. His eyes locked onto hers, cold and unyielding. "Watch yourself, Lyric," he said, his tone calm but deadly. "I'm lettin' you vent, but you ain't gon' disrespect me in my own sh*t. Take my daughter and get the f**k out. But don't forget who you talkin' to."

Lyric froze, her chest heaving as she met his gaze. The fire in her eyes dimmed slightly, replaced by a spark of fear. She yanked her arm free and turned toward the door, clutching Crystal tightly. Monster's voice softened as he looked at his daughter, her innocent eyes staring back at him from her mother's shoulder. "I love you, princess," he said, blowing kisses toward her. His heart ached as she smiled faintly, her tiny hand reaching out for him.

Lyric scoffed, shaking her head. "Whatever, wit'chu lame ass," she spat before storming out, the door slamming behind her. The sound echoed in the room, leaving Monster in tense silence. For a moment, he stood there with his jaw clenched, listening to her hurried footsteps fade away. Instead of escorting them to the car, he stepped over to the door, twisting the lock with focus, then moved to the window. Peering through the blinds, he watched their car pull off, ensuring they were safe before turning his attention inward.

He leaned against the wall, chest rising and falling under the weight of it all. Chaos. Anger. Unresolved vengeance. His mind raced, his actions instinctual. Monster pushed off the wall, headed to the kitchen, yanked a drawer open, and grabbed a knife. The blade gleamed under the dull overhead light as he strolled back into the living room, his movements sharp and precise. Monster slid the sofa away from the wall, the legs scraping faintly against the carpet, then dropped to his knees.

Pressing the knife against the carpet's edge, he pried it free from the tack strip, peeling it back to expose the hidden floorboards beneath.

With practiced precision, he lifted three floorboards, exposing his stash spot. The bundles of cash and kilos of product didn't calm him—they sharpened his focus. He counted quickly, his mind already calculating his next move.

Four bricks, seventy-four racks," he muttered under his breath, the numbers barely registering in the storm of his thoughts. He grabbed one kilo and $13,000 in cash, setting the items on the carpet beside him. As he replaced the boards and smoothed the carpet back into place, his mind churned with the pieces of a plan. He didn't just need revenge—he needed firepower, muscle, and a plan to remind the streets why they called him Monster.

Chapter 41

"Love and Loyalty"

The overhead lights emitted a faint buzz, blending with the rhythmic beeping of the machines connected to Lil B's grandmother. She lay motionless in the hospital bed, her frail frame barely rising with each shallow breath. The smell of antiseptic and fresh flowers lingered, heavy in the air. Lil B sat close to her bedside, arms crossed tightly, his gaze fixed on his grandmother. The usual fire in his demeanor was extinguished, leaving behind a quiet, simmering grief that weighed heavily on his shoulders.

The door creaked open, and Cle, Bishop, and Malik stepped in, catching Lil B off guard. Their presence was a statement in itself—solid, unspoken, and undeniable. Each man was dressed to impress, like kings of the streets, sporting fresh sneakers, crisply pressed jeans, and the glint of their signature "MBM" diamond-encrusted pendants resting on their chests. Their usual swagger remained intact, but the weight in their steps was impossible to miss. This visit wasn't just about Lil B—it was about honoring his grandmother, a pillar of family, sacrifice, and resilience.

Cle adjusted his cap, taking a seat in the corner. Bishop leaned against the doorframe, his gold chain catching the sterile light. Malik, the quietest of the crew, pulled a chair up to the bed and sat forward, elbows on his knees, staring at Lil B's grandmother with a deep frown.

Lil B spoke, his voice low and thick. "Docs say she's got multiple organ failure. Only a couple of days left." His throat caught, but he swallowed hard, refusing to let tears fall. "She raised me, man. All I have."

Cle nodded from the corner, his silence speaking louder than words ever could. It was an unspoken truth among them—a shared understanding that ran deep. Every man in that room had a story, a chapter in their life where a woman's love had been their anchor when the world tried to drown them. It wasn't just about being saved; it was about the quiet strength of women who sacrificed, endured, and built something out of nothing, holding them down when no one else would.

Malik, still staring at the bed, muttered, "She's strong, B. Real strong. Look like she been through worse and still here."

The room settled into silence again, the weight of it all settled on them like a shroud. A soft knock broke the stillness. Bishop turned, his hand instinctively brushing his waistband before glancing through the small window in the door. A man in a courier uniform stood outside, holding an oversized fruit basket wrapped in shimmering cellophane.

"Yo," Bishop called out. "Come through."

The door opened slowly, and the courier entered. His face was partially hidden behind the oversized basket. "This for Miss Barbara Hill," he said, his voice wavering slightly as he glanced around at the imposing group of men.

Cle rose from his seat, his movements calm and purposeful as he motioned toward the bed. "Right here," he said, his voice steady yet soft, acknowledging the courier's uncertainty with a subtle nod. The weight of the moment hung heavy in the air, and even this small act carried an unspoken respect.

The courier placed the basket on the small rolling table near the foot of the bed and handed Lil B a card attached with a ribbon. Lil B looked at it for a moment before flipping it open. He didn't read it out loud, but the message hit him in the chest: *"To Miss Barbara Hill, the heartbeat of her family. From one family to another, our prayers and love are with you. – The Godfather and Money Bag Mafia."*

Lil B's eyes lingered on the signature before he folded the card and slid it into his pocket—a small gesture brimming with meaning. The words resonated deeply, acknowledging the profound role his grandmother played in her family's life. Her unwavering support and unconditional love had been the foundation upon which her family stood. The gift and message from The Godfather weren't just a gesture to Lil B; they were a testament to the respect and solidarity among them, honoring the strength and sacrifice of grandmothers like his.

He stared at the basket—overflowing with fresh fruit, chocolates, and even a small, plush blanket. It was extravagant, perhaps too much, but the sentiment wasn't lost on him.

Cle placed a steady hand on Lil B's shoulder, grounding him in the moment. His voice was calm but carried a weight that only years in the streets could forge. "Real ones recognize real ones," he said, locking eyes with him. "The Godfather know what family mean. That's respect."

Lil B nodded slowly, his jaw tight as he fought to keep his emotions in check. His chest rose and fell with uneven breaths, the storm inside him threatening to spill over. He glanced down, his voice barely audible, raw with conviction and pain. "She deserves it," he whispered, more to himself than to Cle. "She deserve all of it."

The words lingered in the air like an unspoken promise, a heavy truth that neither of them dared to unpack in the silence that followed. Malik reached into the basket, plucking out an apple and tossed it lightly in his hand. "This how we move. When one hurt, we all show up. Ain't no halfway love in this."

Bishop tilted his head, his voice a low rumble. "You know that. It's us against the world. But don't matter how big we get, this right here"— he gestured to the bed—"this the real wealth. Ain't no replacement for family."

The room fell quiet again, each man lost in his own thoughts. The monitors beeped, a quiet reminder of time slipping away. Lil B leaned closer to the bed, gently taking his grandmother's hand. Her skin was cool, her fingers delicate against his calloused palm.

"I'ma hold it down, Grandma," he murmured, his voice cracking under the weight of his promise. The words trembled as they left his lips, raw and unfiltered, carrying the depth of his pain and love. "I'ma make sure your name lives forever."

A deep ache settled in him, and for the first time, the armor he wore so well began to crumble. The vow wasn't just words—it was a lifeline, a purpose carved out of grief, spoken to the one person who had always believed in him.

Cle, Bishop, and Malik shared a look, the kind of glance that spoke louder than words. In that moment, each man silently made the same vow. This wasn't just about Lil B—it was about her. What she stood for. She would be more than a memory; she was a symbol of resilience. Strength, carved from struggle. Sacrifice that demanded respect. The unyielding love of a woman who had built something out of nothing, pouring her soul into the people she cared for.

The weight of her legacy settled heavily over them, binding them together in an unspoken pact. This wasn't just about standing for Lil B—it was about honoring everything she'd poured into their lives during the brief but unforgettable time they were fortunate enough to share her presence.

Her impact wasn't measured in years but in how she had quietly stitched herself into their souls, leaving behind a mark that time couldn't erase. She'd given them more than moments; she'd given them purpose, strength, and a reminder of what true sacrifice looked like. And now, they carried that with them, a bond forged in her name.

They stayed until the nurse came in to check the machines, quietly slipping out of the room one by one. In the hallway, they stood for a moment, the gravity of the situation settling between them.

"Let's hit the streets, see what's up with this Monster situation," Cle said, his eyes fixed on the glowing screen of his phone. His tone was intense, no room for hesitation. "We need to make sure them country-ass n***as handled what needed to be handled. Ain't no room for loose ends right now."

Lil B nodded, his expression stone-cold, the fire in his eyes burning low but steady. "I'm stayin' by her side, but keep me in the loop. Anything goes sideways, you let me know first."

"Bet," Cle said, the word heavy with unspoken resolve.

The group stood for a moment longer in the sterile, fluorescent glow of the hospital hallway. The weight of the moment pressed down on them like a heavy blanket. Cle slipped his phone into his pocket, his jaw flexing as he gave a short nod. Bishop adjusted his jacket, his gaze shifting toward the exit as if already preparing for the next step. Malik stood rigid, his hands at his sides, his tension palpable, ready to erupt at the smallest spark.

This wasn't just business—it was personal. The air was thick, charged with the weight of unspoken emotions they carried. Every movement was a reflection of their bond, one forged in loyalty and hardened by shared pain. They moved in unison, their footsteps echoing down the hallway. The soft beeping of machines and the murmur of distant voices faded into the background as they approached the exit. Cle pushed open the heavy hospital doors. Cool air rushed in, a sharp contrast to the weight they carried inside.

The parking lot stretched out before them, dimly lit by flickering overhead lights. Cle led the way, his steps firm and measured, his shoulders squared with quiet resolve. Bishop and Malik fell in beside him, scanning their surroundings, ever-watchful, their movements purposeful and in sync.

The world outside was cold and indifferent, but their purpose burned brighter. Their bond was unshakable, their path carved by grief, loyalty, and a promise they intended to keep—no matter the cost.

Chapter 42

"I Need Information"

Trying to make the most of his time after reaching out to his lawyer and receiving bad news, Monster transformed the kitchen—once a place for meals and family gatherings—into a cold, clinical drug-cooking lab. His movements were precise, almost mechanical. The weight of the entire situation pressed on him, but he couldn't afford to slow down. He had no choice but to keep his mind focused and his hands busy.

Monster sliced open a kilo of powder, carefully measuring out 504 grams on the triple-beam scale he kept beneath the counter. He then split it into four 126-gram piles, each a precise step in his process. With practiced skill, he transformed each pile of cocaine into a crystallized pancake of crack, each weighing 164 grams or just a little more to maintain that straight-drop potency. Every motion, every swirl of his wrist, felt like part of a well-rehearsed ritual.

The harsh chemical smell filled the air, forcing him to crack the window for ventilation. The cool breeze swept in, offering a brief respite from the stench. But he knew it wouldn't last. Once the batch was done, it would be back to the drawing board.

As the product dried on glass saucers, Monster moved on to separating the remaining 504 grams of powder into single ounces. Every step was purposeful, each action calculated. Once the first batch finished drying into its final form, he sliced and measured out 7-gram quarters from each one, bagging them meticulously, the plastic crinkling under his fingers. Monster wasn't just showcasing his craftsmanship; he was assembling a weapon. This wasn't about street cred or proving anything—it was about survival. And in this game, survival meant money. Money meant power, and power meant revenge. The Godfather may have initiated this war, but Monster knew, without a doubt, he would have the last laugh because he refused to be dethroned.

Monster's hands moved with grace, his mind keen under the mounting pressure. After wrapping the last of the quarters, he stepped back to survey his work. It was flawless—no errors, no shortcuts. He couldn't afford to slip up now. Money Bag Mafia might be the talk of the underworld, but he was gearing up for a fight they weren't ready for. With every ounce and quarter bagged, his resolve hardened. This wasn't just about retaliation; it was about reclaiming what the Godfather could never take from him: control.

Once the work was done, Monster meticulously cleaned the Pyrex pot and wiped down every inch of the kitchen surface, leaving no trace of his actions behind. He grabbed a brown grocery bag from the closet and carefully loaded the product that had been spread across the counter. As he headed into the living room, his phone buzzed incessantly—calls from people checking in and clients eager to re-up. Monster ignored them all, dialing Tre in a cold, clipped tone. No small talk, no pleasantries, just an order: "Come get me."

After hanging up, Monster transferred all his contacts and data to the new phone before strolling back to the kitchen. Not taking any chances with the police tracing his old device, he removed the SIM card and placed the phone in the sink. With a steady hand, he used his blowtorch lighter to burn a hole straight through it. The plastic curled and melted, obliterating any chance of recovery. With a fresh number activated, he sank back into the sofa, meticulously composing messages to the select few he trusted for business. Each message was intentional, ensuring the right people had the digits they'd need.

Monster's thoughts were already racing ahead. There was product to move, honor to reclaim, and a city waiting for a reckoning. The pieces were falling into place, but Monster knew the real game was just beginning. With his impatience growing, every minute felt like a countdown, and Tre was late. Monster paced, his mind spiraling with thoughts of revenge. He had told Tre to stay close, but the damn fool drove all the way to Thomasville Heights to visit some thot. Trying to contain his anger, he stood at the window, envisioning all the ways he'd make the Godfather suffer—but none brought relief. Paranoia gnawed at him, each step around the apartment only making it worse. Finally, a text buzzed on his phone: "I'm outside."

Monster's eyes narrowed as he walked back to the window, scanning the parking lot for any signs of suspicious activity. Shadows flickered in his peripheral, playing tricks on his mind, but nothing seemed out of place. Satisfied, he grabbed the brown grocery bag and his keys, double-checking the locks on the door before stepping out of the apartment. The air was warming up, but it still carried a crispness that hinted at the lingering hours of the morning.

The quiet rhythm of the neighborhood was broken only by the occasional bark of a dog, birds chirping, and the distant rumble of an engine. The brown grocery bag in his hand felt heavier than it should, the weight of its contents a constant reminder of the fight ahead. His mind swirled with possibilities as he descended the steps. At the car, he opened the door and crouched slightly to slide the grocery bag under the passenger seat, making sure it was out of sight but within reach if the police got behind them.

Still standing in the open door, he popped the glove box, retrieved the 10mm he'd told Tre to bring. A quick check confirmed the magazine was full—he slid it back in, chambering a round. With Tre sitting in the driver's seat, eyes darting between the rearview mirror and the lot ahead, Monster finally felt secure and slid into the passenger seat, his movements intentional. He leaned back, ignoring the seatbelt, his instincts telling him to stay unencumbered and ready.

"Let's move," he said, his voice calm but firm, as Tre nodded and eased the car out of the lot, the bright morning light reflecting off the windshield. As they left the apartment complex, Tre needed no instructions—he knew the drill and understood what was at stake. They moved carefully through Decatur, making one beneficial stop after another at different locations like they were a legit drug delivery service. The streets buzzed, but Monster couldn't shake the feeling of something closing in. Every passing car he stared at as though he expected it to be an undercover cop or a member of Money Bag Mafia. He needed more information, and fast. He needed to release some frustration.

After an hour of phone trapping with street hustlers he knew was solid and falling short on intel about Money Bag Mafia, they pulled up outside a house tucked on the outskirts of Decatur, a place Monster knew he could trust—one of the thots who kept her ear to the street. She always had the latest gossip and wasn't afraid to expose everyone's secrets. Monster's hand rested firmly on the chrome 10mm, but he didn't plan on using it. Not yet, anyway.

Adjusting his chain, he stepped out of the car, leaving the brown grocery bag tucked under the seat as he approached the door. Ringing the bell, the door creaked open seconds later, revealing the familiar face of the woman who'd seen him in and out of situations too many times to count. She gave him a quick once-over before letting him inside.

"What's good, Monster?" she asked, her voice low, eyes shifting to his private area in hope for an unexpected visit of intimate pleasure. Monster wasted no time with pleasantries.

"Bitch, ain't nothing good but your head," Monster stated arrogantly, his tone cold and direct. He didn't care if she was still in her pajamas or if there was a n***a she was serving in the other room. He wasn't there for small talk. He needed answers, and he needed them now. "I need to know what the streets sayin' 'bout my house and the trap getting shot up last night. Who they sayin' did it?"

Tired from a night of heavy drinking, she leaned against the hallway wall, crossed her arms, and stared with an unreadable face. "Yeah, I heard about it on the news this morning but haven't heard nothing directly 'bout it from the streets," she said, giving a casual shrug. "Shiddd, I was at the Lakewood Amphitheater concert last night and didn't get in till five this morning. After the show, Money Bag Mafia had a wild ass after-party at Club Elite. Monster, that muthaf**ker was super lit."

Monster's patience wore thin. He stepped closer, his voice dropping low. "I need you to find out where any of them Money Bag Mafia n***as hanging at or rest their heads. I don't care who you gotta talk to or f**k, just get me something. ASAP! I got ten bands if you can get it before the night is over with."

A smile crept across her face each time Money Bag Mafia was mentioned, and it instantly pissed Monster off because she didn't even smile or flinch at the mention of the money. She grinned like she was concealing a secret or like she thought the whole thing was a game. "Bitch, what's so f**kin' funny?" Monster demanded, his tone sharp.

She giggled, leaning in. "Ain't nothing funny. I'm just thinking about how that boss-ass n***a and his crew represented for Zone 3 last night. The Godfather set the city on fire with his performance. That's all people been talking about online—especially that song, 'Headshot.' You shoulda been there, Monster. It was crazy."

She turned away, leaving Monster standing there as she went to grab her phone. Returning, she tapped the screen, and a recorded video clip of The Godfather's performance lit up the display. The raw energy of the moment pulsed through the tiny speakers as the lyrics from Headshot blasted:

**"One shot, two shots, bet he drop slow, Brains on the curb, make the block glow. Talk like a boss, he is not though—Infrared kiss, watch his heart fold.

Swear he a legend in Decatur streets, But legends fall quick when the Reaper speak. Ain't no love when the lead pop, After the headshot—too late to regret the mistake you made, opp!"**

"Headshot, headshot—lights out, flatline, Aimin' at his temple, make his soul backslide. Headshot, headshot—no talk, just fire, Now his name on a shirt, boy, your legend expired."

The words hit like a gut punch, the beat pulsing like war drums in Monster's ears. His stomach turned, fury boiling under his skin as she rapped along to the hook. The Godfather? Performing at the concert? That could only mean one thing—either his crew lit up his spots, or The Godfather paid someone to handle it. But Monster didn't need proof. He felt it in his bones. It was him. No doubt.

His jaw locked, teeth grinding as his pulse hammered in his ears. He didn't give a damn about no concert, no flashy performances, no afterparty flexes, or none of that sh*t. The Godfather could keep all the glitz and glam.

Monster was after blood.

He needed answers.

And a target.

Fast.

The fact she kept chanting the hook stoked fire in his chest. His anger simmered, a fuse ready to ignite. He took a deep breath, trying to hold it together, but every second her words lingered in the air made it harder to stay calm, because he knew the song was about him. The rage was coming for him, and it wasn't going anywhere.

"Bitch, shut the f**k up and figure out where they at," he snapped, his voice steady but laced with venom. "And let me make one thing real clear— I don't give a f**k who you gotta go through, step on, or screw to get that information. Just get me some f**kin' answers and stop wasting my time."

She held up her hands in mock surrender. "A'ight, a'ight. I got you. I'll hit up some people and see what I can dig up."

Monster didn't actuallywait for her response. He spun on his heels and stormed out of the house, not sparing a single glance back. As soon as he reached the car, he slid into the passenger seat, slamming the door shut with frustration. "Let's ride. We're not done yet," he muttered to Tre.

Tre didn't say a word. He just nodded, started the engine, and pulled away from the curb. The fire that was currently burning inside of him blazed hotter than ever as they sped through Decatur, searching for the answers that would lead them to the next move. Monster was determined to make his response legendary, and not even the police were going to stand in his way.

Chapter 43

"Abandoning His Roots"

Marko leaned back in the driver's seat of the blacked-out SUV, eyes fixed on the modest corner store on 4th Street as traffic and sirens muffled the music spilling from the speakers. The store sign cast a cold glow, illuminating its worn brick and grime-streaked windows. After Mr. Ray rejected the Godfather's offer three times, Marko sat there replaying each encounter like a bad dream, the weight of his obligations pressing down on him. He knew the Godfather's message was clear—failure was not an option. If he didn't close the deal by Wednesday, his mother might end up burying her son—something he wasn't trying to let happen.

Marko checked his watch, exhaling sharply as the seconds dragged. "This stubborn-ass old man acts like he doesn't fear death," he muttered, scanning the street with the quiet focus of a predator.

In the passenger seat, Gramz leaned back casually, rolling a blunt of the indica-dominant Biscotti strain with the kind of effortless precision that came from years of practice, his fingers working the wrap like it was second nature. He didn't glance up, but smirked at Marko's growing frustration. Decked out in designer gear, Gramz made even a casual moment feel like a statement. Marko's oversized graphic hoodie, distressed jeans, and spotless Air Force 1s gave him the effortless look of someone who merged street style with a touch of luxury. "This dude thinks he untouchable, I'm tellin' you," Marko added, his tone cold and unwavering.

Gramz licked the edge of the blunt, sealing it without looking up. "Guess we 'bout to find out how much fight he really got," Gramz said.

Marko nodded, his hand steady as he reached for the door handle. "Let's do it."

The sky was ablaze with the last kiss of daylight, streaked with fiery hues that clung to the horizon. The air carried the faint scent of exhaust and fried food—a lingering testament to the neighborhood's grit—as the two men stepped out of the SUV. Their sneakers scraped against the pavement, each step measured, their thoughts sharp with intent.

The bell above the door jingled crisply as they entered, strutting as though the establishment was already a part of Money Bag Mafia's empire, its soul quietly reshaped under their influence.

The owner, Ray Stein, looked up from behind the counter. His piercing blue eyes didn't waver as he took them in. He didn't flinch, didn't show a lick of fear. "What do you want? I've told you several times that I'm not selling, so why do you keep wasting my time by returning?" he asked, his tone curt as he turned around to sit on the cases of cigars he'd been restocking, crossing his arms. His voice carried the weight of a man who wasn't in the mood for threats and knew how to stand his ground.

"Evening, Mr. Ray," Marko said coolly, a faint smirk on his lips. He stepped forward, his presence commanding the room as he glanced at Gramz, who stood silently by his side, attempting to light his blunt. Marko's voice was smooth but edged with the certainty of a man who wasn't taking no for an answer again. "You've been saying no for a while now. But that's about to change, trust me."

"You can't smoke that in here," Mr. Ray snapped as Gramz took a few hard drags.

Gramz chuckled, puffing out a thick cloud of smoke, unfazed by Ray's resistance. He leaned against the counter like they were casual acquaintances. "My pops can't tell me what the f**k to do, so you think I'm 'bout to give you respect? We here 'cause the Godfather wants this building. You need to sign those papers. I got better things to do—like hittin' the strip club and gettin' my dick sucked—than standin' here tryin' to slap some sense into your old ass." Gramz took another drag from his blunt, letting the smoke swirl around him like he had all the time in the world.

Ray's gaze hardened, and for a brief moment, he considered the last person who'd tried to pressure him into selling. Those who underestimated him learned the hard way that he wasn't one to back down. "Over my dead body," he said, his voice steady, with the weight of someone who had dealt with adversity his whole life. "You boys have no idea who you're dealing with. I suggest you leave before you make a mistake."

Marko smirked, his smile cold as ice. "See, I was hopin' the fourth time would be the charm. Thought maybe we could get past all this rejection. But if that's how you wanna play it..." He leaned in closer, his voice dropping low. "I know you live in Ansley Park, right? Big house, nice yard, your wife and daughter... all good things." He paused for a moment, letting the silence fill with the threat. "If you don't sign those papers, someone's gonna show up at your house in the next ten minutes. They're gonna do things to your family... things you'd never imagine. And you? You'll be forced to watch."

Ray didn't flinch. His voice remained unwavering and direct, his narrowed eyes showing no fear. "Do whatever you want," he said, his tone like a blacksmith's knife slicing through the tension. "You think I'm scared? You think you can hold my family over my head? This store's been in my family for three generations. I'm not giving it up. Not to you, not to anyone. You can hurt my wife and daughter all you like. But nothing you do will ever make me sign those papers."

Marko exchanged a glance with Gramz, who raised an eyebrow. His expression was unreadable, but his body language made it clear he was ready for whatever came next. The tension thickened in the air, every moment hanging like a breath held too long. Marko's lips curled into a cold smile as he slowly straightened up from the counter. The weight of the moment settled over him like a heavy cloak. "A'ight," he said slowly, his voice laced with a quiet menace. "Guess we gotta do this the hard way."

Taking another puff while walking over to lock the store's front door, the loud click echoed through the cramped space. Ray's eyes shifted toward the sound, but his stance remained firm and unwavering as he stood up, his voice booming with authority.

"Unlock my damn door. You boys are persistently trying to open a door that I'm warning y'all not to," Ray said, his jaw clenched, his tone cold and unyielding. "Y'all need to seriously work on your intimidation skills, because this ain't it. Now unlock my door and get out."

Marko let out a dry chuckle, empty of humor. "Gramz, close the blinds," Marko ordered, his voice filled with aggression. Ray stood his ground, his eyes narrowing, refusing to show any sign of fear. He'd seen it all—the violence, the threats, the deals made in dark corners—and he wasn't about to back down from a couple of young black punks. His life had been built on grit and survival, and nothing was going to shake that resolve. But something in Marko's cold, calculating demeanor told him this wasn't a game. Marko wasn't here for small talk and fake threats.

As Gramz moved to close the blinds, cutting off the outside world, Ray's instincts kicked in. In a smooth, calculated motion, he lunged for the baseball bat hidden behind the counter. His grip tightened, and with a swift swing, he aimed for Marko's head. The bat whistled through the air, but Marko was quick, ducking low as the bat crashed into a shelf of liquor bottles. Several of them shattered, sending shards flying and a wave of alcohol spilling across the floor.

"Oh, so we fightin' now?" Gramz growled, stepping forward, his eyes hardening.

Ray didn't hesitate. He swung again, this time aiming for Marko's ribs. But Gramz was quicker. With a grunt of effort, he caught the bat mid-swing, using his brute strength to rip it from Ray's grip, sending the old man stumbling back. Marko seized the opening, stepping forward and driving a precise punch into Ray's stomach. The blow sent Ray doubling over, gasping for breath, but he didn't crumble. Instead, he straightened slightly, his eyes blazing with defiance.

"You've got heart, old man," Marko said, a sly grin spreading across his face as he flexed his hand. "But guts won't get you out of this."

Ray's breathing was heavy, but his resolve never wavered. He fought to protect everything—his legacy, his family, his roots, his blood. He landed a few solid blows, catching Marko off guard and staggering him back a step. But the two younger men were relentless, their combined strength overpowering Ray's defiance.

With a crushing left-hand kidney shot from Gramz, Ray dropped to his knees, clutching his side as a groan of agony escaped his lips. They didn't waste a second. Moving like a well-rehearsed machine, they overpowered him, dragging his struggling frame toward the back office. His curses and threats ricocheted off the walls, defiant and laced with fury, but they only seemed to fuel their momentum. The office door slammed shut with a deafening finality, sealing him inside the dimly lit room. The air thickened, heavy with unspoken threats and inevitable violence.

Inside the office, Gramz rifled through the cluttered desk drawers until he found a roll of electrical tape. Working quickly, they bound Ray's wrists and legs to the office chair, ensuring he was firmly restrained. Ray struggled, his breaths coming in short, ragged bursts as he glared at them. His chest rose and fell with each inhale, but his determination to show no weakness was evident. He kept his eyes locked on Marko, his defiance burning bright.

Marko stepped forward, his tone calm but cold. "You can keep fighting all you want, old man. But you're gonna sign those papers. And if you don't, we'll make sure you regret it." His words hung in the air like a loaded threat, heavy with intent and impossible to ignore.

Ray's sneered. "I'd rather die than sell to you."

Marko's smirk deepened. "That can be arranged. But I'm a patient man. I like to play with my food before I eat it."

Gramz leaned in, his voice low and menacing. "You've already lost, Ray. The Godfather's influence stretches further than you think. Sooner or later, you'll see that. But the question is, how much are you willing to suffer before you realize it's over?"

Ray's eyes burned with contempt, but the sweat beading on his forehead betrayed the doubt creeping into his mind. He was a man who had lived through violence, but this—this was different. Marko and Gramz weren't playing by the rules. They were willing to do whatever it took to win. And that made them dangerous. Ray's jaw clenched. "You won't get away with this. You think those weak punches and tying me up are supposed to scare me?" he spat, blood flecking his lip. "I've dealt with tougher than you two amateurs. My grandmother, rest her soul, had more fight in her than the both of you combined!"

Gramz's lips curled into a sneer, but Marko held up a hand, signaling him to wait. Marko crouched in front of Ray, studying him like a predator sizing up his prey. His face betrayed nothing, but the dangerous glint in his eyes spoke volumes. "You're an old, stubborn muthaf**ker, huh?" Marko said, his voice low, his tone carrying an edge of menace. "A'ight, let's try somethin' else."

He nodded toward Gramz, who stepped forward, cracking his knuckles loudly enough to echo in the small office. The sound was like a gun cocking—a grim promise of what was to come. "Last chance, Ray," Marko continued evenly, his gaze locked on the older man. "Sign the papers, and this all ends now. Keep playin' tough, and you'll wish you hadn't."

"Go to hell! You're both going to regret this—I swear it on my family's name and everything they've built," Ray snarled, his voice biting and defiant, locking eyes with Marko before spitting in his face.

Marko froze for a split second, the room going dead silent, then snapped. His fist shot out, landing a brutal right hook to Ray's jaw, whipping his head to the side. The crack of impact echoed in the tight space. Ray spat blood and chuckled dryly, turning back to Marko.

"That's all you've got, boy? My great-grandmother hit harder than that in the shtetl," he mocked, the defiance in his tone cutting through the pain.

Tired of the tough-guy act, Gramz shoved Marko aside with calm intensity—a stark contrast to the escalating tension. He grabbed Ray's left hand with the precision of someone who'd carried out this grim work before. Without a word, Gramz yanked Ray's pinky back, the sickening crunch of bone snapping filling the small office like an explosive crack. Ray's breath caught, his body jerking in agony, but his face remained defiant, eyes locked on Gramz as he gasped for air. Ray's laughter morphed into a guttural scream, his face twisting in agony.

"That's one," Gramz said coolly, his tone almost conversational as he moved to the next finger. Ray's chest heaved, his breaths uneven, but his eyes still burned with defiance. Gramz broke another finger, the sharp snap reverberating like a gunshot in the confined office. Ray howled in pain, the sound raw and primal, but he still didn't beg.

"Still feelin' tough?" Marko asked, his tone almost casual as he leaned against the desk, watching Ray writhe in pain.

"F**k you!" Ray spat out through gritted teeth, his face twisted in agony as the pain radiated up his arm. Tears began falling from his eyes, but he refused to let go of his legacy. His stubbornness, forged by years of struggle and survival, was as much a part of him as the blood running through his veins. After the third broken finger, Ray continued to show no weakness, though tears poured down his face and his breathing grew shallow and ragged.

Gramz paused, eyeing Ray with a calculating glare. It was clear the man's defiance wouldn't crumble under brute force alone. He needed to break him in a way that went beyond physical pain—a method that would tear at his pride and dignity. Gramz leaned in close, his dark eyes narrowing as he locked his gaze on Ray's trembling form. The air in the room seemed to shift, heavy with unspoken threats, as the older man's defiance burned like embers refusing to die. Gramz exhaled slowly, his voice low and measured, carrying a weight that made each word feel like a blade pressed against the skin.

"Old man, you really don't get it, do you? This ain't about business no more. This is personal now."

Forgetting about Marko for the moment, Gramz unfastened Ray's belt, letting it slide free with a menacing hiss. Then, with unyielding intent, he unbuttoned his pants, tugging them down along with his underwear to his knees, exposing himself. The move was raw, primal, meant to shift the balance of power entirely.

Fishing a lighter from his pocket, Gramz flicked it to life, the flame crackling softly as it danced, casting fleeting shadows across the room. Without hesitation, and with an air of unshakable menace, he pressed the searing flame directly against the exposed head of his dick. The acrid scent of burning flesh filled the air, a brutal, calculated act that froze Ray in place, his eyes widening in sheer, unrestrained horror.

271

"A'ight!" Ray screamed hoarsely, his voice breaking as the searing flame grazed the sensitive skin of his dick, the unbearable heat radiating toward his scrotum. The flame hovered dangerously close, its heat licking at him before grazing just enough to scorch the surface. The pain shot through him like a live wire, his body instinctively jerking in a futile attempt to escape. The sheer brutality of the act shattered his resolve, sending a wave of visceral terror coursing through him and tearing down his final shred of defiance. "Fine! I'll sign!" he shouted, his voice cracking with anger and humiliation. "Just stop this madness! But mark my words—you'll regret this for the rest of your miserable lives!"

Marko's lips curled into a smile as he stood up and pulled the contract from inside his hoodie pocket. He swiftly cut the tape binding Ray's right hand and placed the document in front of him, along with a pen. "Smart man."

The ink on them stood in stark contrast to the dim lighting that surrounded them. Marko's eyes glimmered with a cold intensity as he waited, arms crossed, watching the man in front of him. Ray's eyes darted between the papers and the imposing figures looming over him. He could feel the weight of the decision pressing down on him, knowing the consequences of his actions. A part of him wanted to continue resisting, to continue fighting, but the reality of the situation was undeniable. These men weren't going to stop.

The silence in the room stretched on. Finally, Ray's shoulders sagged in resignation. His resolve cracked, just enough for him to see the futility of the fight. Slowly, he reached forward, his fingers trembling as they hovered over the papers.

Marko's gaze stayed locked, a satisfied smile curling his lips. "Smart choice, Ray. You're not as dumb as you look."

With a final, reluctant sigh, Ray signed the papers, his signature scrawled across the contract in shaky strokes.

Marko snatched the papers, slipping them into his hoodie pocket with a satisfied smirk. "That wasn't so hard, was it?"

Gramz clapped Ray on the shoulder, his grin wide and mocking. "Next time, you might want to consider our offer a little sooner."

Ray didn't respond, his face locked in a grim mask of anger and humiliation, though the excruciating pain in his mangled hand and scorched dick betrayed him. Each pulse of his heartbeat sent fresh waves of agony rippling through his body, his broken fingers throbbing like they were ablaze, while the lingering burn on his dick felt like a searing brand pressed against his flesh.

The sensation was relentless, a cruel reminder of the flame's touch that refused to fade. Sweat mixed with blood on his lip, but his glare never wavered. He clenched his jaw, determined not to let them see how much it truly hurt, even as the relentless ache clawed at his resolve, threatening to shatter it entirely.

Inside, his mind raced. He knew how he was going to get revenge— he could already envision it—and he swore they'd regret breaking his fingers, torching his manhood, and taking his store. These bastards thought they'd won, but they had no idea what was coming. For now, though, all he could do was sit there, bound to the chair, stewing in a volatile mix of pain, fury, and cold determination.

Once Ray was freed from his restraints, Gramz moved through the office and store with mechanical efficiency. He wiped down every surface for prints, grabbed the security footage, and turned off the cameras, erasing any trace of their visit. As Marko and Gramz turned to leave, Marko glanced back one last time. "You made the right choice, Ray. Don't make the mistake of thinking you can fight back now. You're out of your league."

With that, they exited the office, leaving Ray alone in the dimly lit room, the weight of defeat pressing down on him like a heavy stone. His body ached, his pride shattered, but he knew one thing for sure: this wasn't over. It couldn't be. But for now, Marko and Gramz had won. And the Godfather's empire continued to expand, one building at a time.

The cold night air hit them as they stepped back into the darkness of the streets. Marko lit a cigarette, the faint glow illuminating his face as he inhaled deeply. He glanced over at Gramz, who was already relighting his blunt with a cool, detached expression.

"Think he'll try anything?" Marko asked, exhaling a cloud of smoke.

Gramz's lips twisted into a cold, mocking smile as he took a slow, intentional drag from his blunt, the ember glowing ominously in the cold light of the glowing sign. He held the smoke in his lungs for a beat, exhaling a thick cloud that swirled lazily around his face before speaking. "Not with those busted fingers, he won't," he sneered, his voice low and taunting. "But me? I stay ready for the smoke—anytime, anyplace." His words hung in the air, laden with menace, as the faint scent of weed trailed after him as they walked toward the SUV.

Chapter 44

"Blood in the Air"

Monster answered his phone on the first ring as they cruised down Covington Highway, immediately launching into a heated conversation with someone who refused to give up information on the Money Bag Mafia. His voice was taut with irritation as he threatened the individual, "If I don't have my money tonight, I'm puttin' a bullet in your f**kin' head. Act like you think I'm jokin'," Monster threatened, but the caller stayed tight-lipped, loyal to the street code of silence. Monster ended the call with an irritated growl and dialed another number.

"Pork-Chop, meet me at the pool hall on Canton Road in thirty minutes," he instructed, his tone steady but urgent. "Hit up Prime and Rex, and tell them the same. Make sure y'all ain't f**kin' followed. Ain't no tellin' how this sh*t gonna play out."

His eyes darted to a patrol car speeding by. His grip tightened around the gun, the moment hanging heavy around him. Monster knew that pulling the rest of his crew together was a gamble, but he had no choice. The clock was ticking, and second-guessing wasn't an option.

The streets were alive with danger, and every move felt like walking a tightrope over a pit of snakes. He had spent the entire day scouring the city, searching for answers, but all he encountered were dead ends and silence. The hustle was unforgiving; all day, he felt like the hunter had become the hunted.

When they pulled into the parking lot, Tre parked and stepped out, scanning the area while Monster stayed in the car, his eyes shifting between the lot and the rearview mirror. He couldn't afford to get caught off guard. A few minutes later, Tre returned and assured him everything was clear. He grabbed the wad of cash Monster handed him in a bag and stuffed it into his jacket pocket.

Still choosing to play it safe, Monster stayed put, scanning the surroundings for ten more minutes. Patience was key, and being cautious had kept him alive this long. Finally, satisfied that the coast was clear, he slid out of the car, tucking the 10mm into his waistband and assuring the safety was still off.

A heavy bass line reverberated through his chest as he stepped into the pool hall. The walls seemed to hum with its pulse, filling the air with energy. The place was busy—locals, regulars, and a handful of unfamiliar faces scattered throughout. Some looked friendly; others had eyes that lingered too long. Monster scanned the room, locking eyes with a few men, silently sizing them up. Undercover cops? Rivals? He wasn't sure, but he wasn't taking any chances.

He quickly paid the desk clerk for two tables in the back left corner, making sure he had a clear view of the door, the windows, and the entire room. Moving with a confident swagger, he crossed the floor, chest out, signaling he wasn't there to play games. But as anxiety continued to buzz through his body, he realized it was making him stand out more than he wanted. To blend in, he approached the restaurant window and ordered two platters of wings and tenders, giving himself something to do while keeping his guard up. His mind, however, was anything but casual—it was racing, burning with thoughts of what could unfold.

After setting the food down on the table, he and Tre grabbed a couple of pool cues and shot a few games to kill time. The crack of the balls echoed through the room each time, but his focus remained keen, scanning for familiar faces.

One by one, his crew began to arrive, each stepping through the door within minutes of the last, moving with an unspoken rhythm that made it seem as though they'd planned it. They naturally gravitated toward Monster's table, their presence commanding attention as they formed a loose circle around him. Rex lingered on the outskirts, as inconsistent as ever, his jittery energy radiating the same unreliability Monster had come to expect—and distrust.

The two hitmen from East Atlanta stood closest to the food, their hands darting to the platter with the kind of hunger that made Monster's stomach turn. He watched them with a wary eye—he didn't trust them, but he had no choice at the moment. This wasn't a battle he could fight alone, especially with him not knowing the weight of what could be coming.

"What the f**k is goin' on, Monster? 'Cause none of this sh*t makes any sense," Pork-Chop growled, tearing into a tender like he was ready to bite through a bone. His eyes narrowed as they slid over to the two hitmen, who were devouring the food with reckless intensity.

"You tellin' me the Money Bag Mafia shot up the trap and your spot—which, okay, I get, since you and Baby J, rest in peace my n***a, shot at the Godfather's sister—but the whole damn crew was at the concert last night, vibin' with me and Prime. We even hit the after-party they threw. So how the f**k does that make sense? How they know it was you so quick? What the f**k is really goin' on?" Pork-Chop's voice was low, dangerous, his words laced with frustration and suspicion.

Prime didn't let the unease linger. He steadied his hand on the pool table, his gaze tracking the ball as it rolled across the felt. "He right, Monster. This sh*t ain't addin' up. Something's off." His voice was calm but carried an edge, dancing on air like a warning.

Monster's frustration simmered, barely held in check, as he listened to them brag about partying with the enemy. While he'd been dodging bullets and their so-called homies were getting killed, these fools were out popping bottles and trading laughs with the same people responsible. He couldn't believe it. Their smug indifference poured gasoline on the fire in his chest, cutting deeper than he thought possible. And now they had the nerve to question him? Him? The one who'd been holding it all together when things got ugly? It was a spit in the face.

But what pushed him closer to the edge, past fury and into a cold, simmering wrath, was their claim of knowing nothing. They swore up and down they had no idea where Money Bag Mafia moved their work, no idea where they hung out—yet somehow, they'd managed to kick it with them all night. That wasn't ignorance; that was betrayal wrapped in excuses.

Monster's jaw clenched so tight it felt like his teeth might crack. He gripped the pool stick, twisting it as if trying to snap it in two. His muscles coiled with the urge to swing it across the room—or smash it into their faces. Every word they spoke cut deep, hard and stinging, each one piling on the pain of the last.

"Y'all really out here playin' house with the opps while we out here bleeding for this?" His voice was low, a menacing growl that carried enough weight to make even the boldest man reconsider. But the intensity? That hit like a shotgun blast. His eyes burned with fury, locking onto each of them, daring anyone to meet his glare—and none of them dared to hold it for long.

Prime, the skinniest one of the bunch and always the first to fold under pressure, tried to laugh it off, his gold chains jingling as he shifted uncomfortably. The music blasting from the jukebox—something bass-heavy and rowdy—drowned out the murmurs in the room, but it couldn't mask the tension swelling between them. Prime's chuckle sounded forced, shaky, like he knew he was digging himself into a hole he couldn't climb out of.

"C'mon, Monster. It ain't even like that, bruh," Prime said, his voice fighting to be heard over the thumping beat and the crack of a pool cue beside them. "It was business, you know? Networking and sh*t. How we supposed to know…"

Monster's eyes narrowed, the fluorescent lights above making them look like burning coals. He stepped forward, his tennis shoes brushing against the sticky tile floor, the sound swallowed by the pounding music that filled the pool hall. He didn't care about the blasting bass, the laughter, or the overlapping conversations—his presence commanded the room.

"Networking?" Monster interrupted, his voice breaking through the noise with cold precision. His laugh followed, low and dangerous, like the growl of a predator right before the kill. "You call rubbin' shoulders with the same n***as that put Baby J, Spanky, and Dee in the ground networking?" He leaned in closer, his pool stick still in his hands but gripped now like a weapon. "Networking is puttin' every last one of them pussy n***as in a body bag before the sun rises. That's what the f**k networking is."

The room didn't go silent—it couldn't, not with the bass rattling the walls and drunken voices shouting in the background—but it felt like the energy shifted. Laughter softened, and even the players at the far end of the room paused, subtly turning to watch. Eyes darted between Monster and Prime, and even the music couldn't erase the suffocating weight of the moment.

Prime swallowed hard, his bravado slipping under Monster's glare. His chains jingled again as he shifted back, trying to put some distance between them. But there was no escaping the weight of Monster's words or the fury radiating off him like heat from a furnace.

Pork Chop, broad-shouldered and built like a bulldog, shifted against the pool table, lifting his drink to his lips with an air of defiance. He sipped slow, smacking his lips afterward, then squared up, glaring at Monster with a smirk that begged for trouble. "Man, f**k all that. You poppin' off like it's our fault when you and Baby J started this whole f**kin' mess. Yeah, we balled last night. So f**kin' what? N***a, I ain't your bitch. We get money together, that's it. Don't get it twisted." His voice dripped with arrogance, his boldness filling the space between them as everyone else in their presence shifted uncomfortably.

Prime, emboldened by Pork Chop's stance, jumped in. "Yeah, shawty. This your f**kin' fault. Y'all shot at the Godfather's sister? What the hell was you thinkin'? Why the f**k would you do some dumb sh*t like that and not expect a reaction?"

Admitting to them that the entire incident had been a mistake felt like a blade pressed against his throat. The mere thought of it cut deeper than any bullet ever could. The truth wasn't an option—it was poison. It had been his call, his decision, his arrogance that had put them in this position. Letting Baby J take the shot had been reckless, and now, it was a colossal mistake. One that had cost lives, money, and painted targets on their backs.

But Monster wasn't built to fold. The truth of why had perished with Baby J, and that's precisely where it would decay. Standing there, his presence radiated a warning—his mistake wasn't the problem anymore; hunting down every single person responsible was. He needed them, not for alliances forged through weakness, but for retribution. Bowing at the feet of the Godfather for peace? That wasn't just impossible—it was insulting. Not now. Not ever. Ignoring their questions, he let his fury coil, ready to strike. He couldn't let them see the cracks in his armor, couldn't let the guilt seep out, thick and pungent like blood in the water, drawing predators to a wounded prey.

He shifted his weight, his gaze burning holes through the three men in front of him. "Y'all sound like y'all tryna give these n***as a lap dance or somethin'." Monster growled, his voice low and menacing. "Them f**k n***as killed our partners, and y'all too busy playin' checkers while they out there playin' chess. I ain't got time for this soft sh*t."

Pork Chop's lips parted, his body leaning forward as if ready to fire back, but Monster moved first. He stepped forward, the pool stick in his hand now raised slightly, his frame casting a long shadow over the group. "You think I give a f**k what the streets is sayin'? Baby J's gone. Spanky's gone. Dee's gone. And instead of being ready to put in work, y'all wanna stand here questionin' me like I'm the f**kin' cancer? That's why Money Bag Mafia keep winnin'. 'Cause y'all too busy actin' like hoes to stay focused. Let me make one thing clear—if I find out any of y'all standing under the moon light with them opps again, I'ma handle you the same way I 'bout to handle them."

As the bass pulsed through the room, vibrating against their skin, Prime and Pork-Chop locked eyes on Monster, their unyielding anger simmering, teetering on the edge of explosion.

The atmosphere remained thick and heavy as the words settled over them, a stark reminder of the stakes they were playing for. Noticing Prime was more focused on the text message on his phone than the gravity of the situation, Monster's patience snapped. He slammed his fist on the table with a force that rattled the glasses nearby, his veins bulging, a grimace twisting his face.

"Yo, Prime! You think this sh*t a joke?" Monster barked, his voice booming through the pool hall. "This sh*t ain't no damn game. Every move they make, it's all a power play, and that's how it's gonna be 'til we check 'em. Y'all gonna ride for our dead homies, or y'all gonna keep standin' there actin' like them n**as saints? We need to make a statement! The Godfather crossed the line, so now we hit him where it hurts—take his f**kin' mom out. That's how we send a message."

The words hung in the air, charged with raw emotion, daring anyone to challenge him. Monster's eyes burned as they locked onto Prime, waiting for the slightest hint of defiance.

Pork-Chop shook his head, unimpressed, but his voice was dead serious. "Have you lost your f**kin' mind, Monster? That's some hoe sh*t, and I ain't down for it. You wanna go after his mom just to get back at the n***as who killed our people? Nah, that's weak. That's a bitch move. We need the truth. We need a plan, not some reckless ass vendetta bullsh*t just 'cause of y'all history. If the Godfather really behind it, I'll murk him and the whole damn Money Bag Mafia family my damn self, but I ain't movin' till I know the truth. Monster, if we don't think this through, we could end up in a body bag, right next to them, and I ain't tryin' to meet my maker today."

One of the hitmen nodded, his expression cold and unflinching as he mulled over the ruthless stories circulating about the Money Bag Mafia. "Yeah, I ain't with that either," he muttered, his voice low but firm.

Prime spoke up, his tone matching the gravity of the moment, steady and unflinching. "Man, ain't no principles or no morals in that sh*t. We gotta keep our heads straight, Monster—not retaliate with stupidity. His mother ain't did sh*t to me or any of us. We start goin' after families, we just as dirty as them n**as we tryna check. That's how you lose respect in the streets, and once that's gone, we ain't got nothin'. You wanna send a message? Then hit the Godfather, not his family. Keep it about what's real, not no emotional-ass moves that'll leave us lookin' weak or reckless. First, you shot at his sister to start all this bullsh*t, and now you wanna kill his mom? You really think that's the answer? Nah, that ain't leadership—that's chaos, and we ain't built for that."

Monster's blood was boiling now. The rejection of his idea felt like a slap in the face. He slammed the pool stick on the table with a force that made everyone flinch. His eyes were locked on Pork-Chop's, the tension between them palpable. "I'm done talkin', homie. This f**k-ass n***a nearly killed my daughter, and y'all standin' here worried 'bout principles and codes? I'm out for blood, and I don't give a f**k how this sh*t look. Somebody gon' pay today."

The tension around the tables thickened, wrapping the atmosphere in an air of unease. One of the hitmen didn't flinch, his face set like stone, but the other grabbed a few more wings, stuffing one in his mouth as he casually walked toward the door without glancing back or saying a word. Q-Ball, the hitman who stayed, leaned against the pool table, his expression cold and calculating. He wasn't one to question the morality or complexity of a job—all he cared about was the payday.

"Shawty, you already know I'm down for whatever," Q-Ball said, his voice steady as Tre sunk a ball into the corner pocket. His eyes gleamed with a detached hunger. "I'll take out his whole damn family for that paper. Don't matter to me who did what—just break me off, and it's done."

Monster turned to Tre, his voice dropping to a low, venomous growl, his frustration boiling over. "Hand me the money."

Tre hesitated before pulling a crumbled Wendy's bag from his jacket pocket and sliding it across the table. Monster picked it up, pulling out stacks of crisp bills. He grabbed a handful and tossed it onto the table with a thud.

"I got $10,000 for whoever brings me solid info on the Godfather and the Money Bag Mafia by tonight," Monster spat, his voice intense and commanding. "I'm talkin' addresses, any spot he runnin', any move Money Bag Mafia makin'. By midnight, I need some f**kin' answers— or I'm gonna assume every last one of y'all workin' for the Godfather."

Their section went still. Eyes shifted, but no one spoke. Monster's gaze swept over the group, searching for any sign of hesitation or weakness. His pride was on the line, and he wasn't about to let anyone test him. He could see Pork-Chop itching to flex his muscle, but a part of him was relieved he didn't. He needed him now more than ever. Confident his words had landed, Monster snatched up the remaining cash and tossed it back to Tre, pulling out a few extra bills and slamming them onto the table. "That's a tip—for anybody who steps up and does the damn job."

Q-Ball smirked, reaching forward to grab the cash before anyone else could. "Guess I'll be busy tonight."

The tension lingered in the air as Monster spat, "Tre, we done here," stepping away from the table with a cold finality. Without a second glance at Pork-Chop, Prime, or Rex, he stormed out of the pool hall, his steps heavy with frustration and rage. The door banged shut behind him, and the night air struck him like a jolt. He slid into the passenger seat, slamming the door shut as he leaned back, the weight of everything pressing down on him like a ton of bricks.

"Take me to my baby mama's house," he ordered, his voice cold and curt.

Tre didn't utter a word; he just nodded and pulled off. The car ride was suffocatingly quiet, the air filled with unspoken thoughts. Monster's jaw clenched and unclenched as his mind raced through scenarios. He had to strike the Godfather, but he wasn't reckless enough to risk the rest of his crew without solid intel. Every option felt like a ticking time bomb, and the pressure was mounting.

When they pulled up to the modest house, Monster's eyes burned with intensity. He didn't bother going inside. Instead, he called her, barking, 'Come outside,' irritation sharp in his voice. Lyric stepped out of the front door, her expression guarded as she approached the car. Monster didn't give her the chance to ask questions. He just shoved the bag of cash into her hands, his face set like stone.

"Put this in the safe. Don't touch it 'til you hear from me," he said gruffly, his voice carrying the weight of finality. He didn't explain, didn't soften his tone, and didn't stick around for a conversation.

Lyric opened her mouth to respond, but Monster had already started raising up the window, while signaling for Tre to drive. As the car eased forward, he let out a frustrated sigh, dragging his hand down his face.

"Damn," he muttered under his breath, his voice tinged with regret. "Should've gone in and kissed my princess."

Tre glanced at him, his tone cautious. "You want me to turn around?"

Monster shook his head, his eyes fixed on the dark streets ahead. "Nah, I'll see her later." His focus had already shifted. The Godfather was all he could think about now. That snake had to pay, and Monster's patience was stretched to the breaking point. He pulled out his phone, dialed a number, and cursed under his breath when there was no answer. Continuing to curse under his breath, he fired off a text to TJ: "Pull up at Club Velvet Trap. We need to talk."

Monster knew TJ's girls had ears and eyes in places most people didn't even know existed. If there was any dirt on the Godfather and Money Bag Mafia, they'd find it. He didn't care how much it cost—he was ready to pay whatever it took. As Tre navigated through the city, Monster's gaze stayed locked on the streets, his mind a whirlwind of plans and rage. Time was slipping through his fingers, and he knew there was no room for hesitation. This wasn't just about revenge anymore; it was about survival.

Chapter 45

"The Set Up"

Q-Ball didn't ask questions—he followed the money. And right now, there was ten grand floating in the streets for any soul reckless enough to spill about Money Bag Mafia. He wanted all of it. And in his world, a street bounty meant one thing—dead or alive.

As a goon-for-rent, he didn't see people—he saw targets. And tonight, he wasn't hunting just one man. He was after an entire crew. Q-Ball left the pool hall on a mission, tapping into every hood, every plug, and every street corner, searching for the right intel. Money Bag Mafia wasn't just some small-time clique—they were a force. Well-connected, well-respected, and heavily armed. But in the streets, loose lips always led to bodies.

It didn't take long for reckless words to spill. A thot from Grady Homes—one he kept around for pleasure—let something slip without even realizing it. When he called, running his mouth about how he couldn't wait for the next Money Bag Mafia party and wished he had a way to stay tapped in, she tossed out a name like it was nothing.

"Oh, my homegirl from Ellenwood messin' with one of them dudes—some n***a named Salvage."

She had no clue she'd just put a man's life on a countdown. That was all Q-Ball needed. He didn't react, didn't let on that she'd just handed him a priceless gift. Instead, he kept his tone easy, smooth like idle conversation. "Word? Bet. We should link up with them sometime, make a night out of it."

It sounded casual, effortless—like he was just going with the flow. But every word was calculated, steering the conversation exactly where he wanted it to go. She took the bait without hesitation, her excitement bubbling over as she hung up and immediately called her girl. Giggling and playing it smooth, she finessed the details with ease. A little back-and-forth later, she had the drop—Salvage and his girl were posted up at the Movie Tavern on Lavista Road. Wasting no time, she hit Q-Ball right back.

As soon as she mentioned Salvage and his girl were together, Q-Ball didn't miss a beat. His tone stayed easy, his words casual, like it was just another night. He offered to scoop her up without letting on that he had no idea what Salvage looked like or what kind of car he drove. It didn't matter. Looks didn't mean a thing to him—only money and murder did.

On the other end, she felt a rush, knowing she'd just given him something useful. She wanted to impress him, to make herself valuable. If this got his attention, if this made him see her differently, then it was worth it.

Before heading to Grady Homes to pick her up, he swung by the trap in Eastwick, grabbing two eight-balls of powder. He needed to heighten his senses, to bring himself to that razor's edge where hesitation didn't exist. Sitting in the car, he chopped a line on the back of his hand and inhaled it fast, feeling the burn tear through his sinuses before dripping down his throat like gasoline. His heart jackhammered, his breathing quick and uneven as the rush slammed into him, sharpening his focus and sending a restless tremor through his fingers. His pupils blew wide open, and a raw, electric energy coiled through his body, making his skin prickle with anticipation.

He pulled off, a flood of sensation crashing over him—his thoughts firing off too fast to catch, his nerves tingling, his muscles wound up like springs. The city around him felt louder, brighter, moving in a rhythm that matched the surge inside him. Every sound was crisp, every detail sharp, but nothing held his attention for long. His tongue darted across his lips, his teeth grinding as that raw, electric buzz settled deep in his bones. All he could think about was what came next— money, murder, and making sure the night ended on his terms.

By the time he pulled up outside her spot, the high had settled into him, making everything feel clearer, more urgent. He sent her a quick text—*outside*—and when she slid into the passenger seat, he leaned over, pressing a kiss against her lips, brief and meaningless. His mind was already somewhere else. No small talk, no conversation—just the $10,000 waiting for him and the body he had to drop to get it. Fuck collecting intel like a snitch.

When they pulled into the lot, he kept the conversation light, playing it cool—just another curious onlooker, interested in how a member of the Money Bag Mafia moved. But the moment she pointed out Salvage's car, that was all he needed. The rest was just keeping her occupied.

After parking and stepping out of the vehicle, he played the part flawlessly—walking her inside the tavern with their fingers laced, his demeanor smooth and unbothered. He bought her a ticket without hesitation, loading up on popcorn, candy, and a drink like a man settling in for a real date. He even escorted her to a theater, sinking into a seat as if he cared about the movie—but he didn't. His mind was locked on the real reason he was there, the movie her girl was in, and the fact that it was about to end soon. Every move was deliberate, natural, seamless.

Ten minutes in, he casually checked his phone, his expression shifting just enough to sell the act. Urgent call. A quick, smooth excuse. He leaned in close, whispered something reassuring into her ear, then slipped away without hesitation. Now, it was time to work. Time to get in position.

The night air was thick, heat clinging to his skin as he moved through the parking lot with quiet precision. He slid into position between two parked cars, muscles coiled with anticipation. Reaching into his pocket, he pulled out the baggie and took another sharp snort. The burn hit instantly, flooding his system with a raw, electric rush. His pulse surged, his senses heightened, but his movements stayed smooth, controlled.

A quick scan of his surroundings—no eyes on him. Confident he was in the clear, he slid a hand to his waist, fingers wrapping around the Glock 19. With a steady grip, he drew the weapon, his mind locked in. It was time.

People started trickling out of the building, their chatter and scattered footsteps filling the air—a clear sign that a movie had just let out. Q-Ball took notice but stayed low, his focus locked on the tavern entrance.

Then—there they were.

A dude draped in designer, his every step screaming money. A fat, diamond-studded M.B.M. pendant swung from his neck, catching the parking lot lights with every movement. Beside him, a chick strutted with confidence, her eyes locked on the same car Q-Ball's thot had pointed out. Then—flash.

The headlights lit up, revealing a satin black Jeep Grand Cherokee Trackhawk, sitting low on 26-inch Rucci forged wheels, their deep-dish design gleaming under the lights. The wide-body kit gave it an even more menacing stance, the blacked-out grille and tinted windows making it look like a street predator, built to move fast and flex even faster.

Q-Ball slipped from between the cars like a phantom emerging from the void, his movements swift, calculated—death in motion. The darkness clung to him, his presence barely more than a whisper against the night until—

BOOM! BOOM!

The muzzle flashed like a strike of lightning, the suppressed silence of the lot shattered by the violent roar of gunfire. The Glock kicked in his grip, sending a lethal piece of lead screaming through the air, hungry for flesh. The explosion of sound echoed off the surrounding cars, a thunderous death knell for whoever stood in its path.

The first shot punched through the girl's chest, her breath escaping in a sharp, shuddering gasp. A crimson bloom spread across her shirt, her body jerking as she staggered back. Before she could even clutch at the wound, a second round tore through her throat, splintering bone and flesh, silencing her forever. A strangled gurgle died in her throat as her knees buckled, her body collapsing in a boneless heap. Lifeless eyes, wide with shock, locked onto Salvage, as if accusing him even in death.

But Q-Ball wasn't finished. His grip on the gun was steady, his face unreadable as he pivoted without hesitation, lining up his next target. The muzzle flared again—three rapid shots tearing through the air, each one aimed to put Salvage in the dirt before he had a chance to react. The crack of gunfire echoed, spent casings clinking against the pavement like cold, metallic raindrops.

Salvage wasn't a regular target—he moved different, instinct honed from years of survival. The first bullet grazed his ribs, a searing flash of pain tearing through his side, but he didn't falter. The impact twisted him back, adrenaline numbing the wound before his mind could register it. His gun was already in his grip, muscle memory taking over.

Then—he saw her.

His girl.

She lay sprawled on the pavement, her body eerily still. Blood seeped beneath her, dark and final. Her lifeless eyes found his, frozen in time, as if she had one last thing to say. A whisper lost in death. A goodbye never spoken. His chest tightened, something sharp and unforgiving ripping through him.

And then, something inside him broke. The world slowed. His pulse pounded in his ears, drowning out everything—the unknown shooter, the gunfire, even the pain in his side. All that remained was the cold, consuming rage curling through his veins. Death meant nothing. Revenge was everything. It burned in his eyes, clenched in his heart as he pushed himself up, his breath ragged but steady.

Salvage's grip on the Sig Sauer P320 tightened around the polymer frame. His trigger finger moved before his mind could catch up, pure instinct guiding him. The gun bucked in his hands, the muzzle flashing like a promise—one sealed in blood. A promise to end this.

BOOM! BOOM! BOOM! BOOM!

Gunfire ripped through the lot, each shot from Salvage's P320 snapping the air like a whip. Q-Ball hit the pavement hard, the impact jolting through his bones as he rolled behind a car just in time. Bullets punched through steel, glass exploding into deadly shards that rained down like daggers. Alarms shrieked in protest. The stench of burnt gunpowder thickened the air. This wasn't some wild shootout—this was an execution. And Salvage wouldn't stop until Q-Ball's body was sprawled out lifeless on the asphalt.

Q-Ball didn't hesitate. He pushed off the ground and took off, adrenaline launching him forward. Salvage was right there, gun bucking in his grip, muzzle flashing as round after round sliced through the night. A bullet hissed past Q-Ball's ear, so close he felt the heat kiss his skin. Death wasn't just knocking—it was breathing down his neck. A single inch, a fraction of hesitation, and his brains would've been sprayed across the concrete. But he was still moving, still alive. As long as his legs worked, as long as he had breath in his lungs, he had a chance.

As bullets tore through tires, sending chunks of rubber flying. Windshields shattered, glass cascading like deadly confetti. The lot turned into a war zone—screams, alarms, the scent of metal and blood thick in the air. Q-Ball weaved through the carnage, darting between cars, his every step fueled by survival. Salvage wasn't letting up. His P320 smoked, every shot fired with raw vengeance. Q-Ball vaulted over a car hood, tucking his body tight as another round whizzed past his skull. The pavement met him with a brutal scrape, but he kept rolling, kept moving. Sirens blared in the distance, but they were nothing more than background noise. Help wasn't close enough. The only thing between him and death was speed—and luck.

Salvage didn't hesitate. His clip ran dry, but he was ready—he always was. The Godfather had warned them to stay alert, especially with Monster still breathing. That advice sat heavy in his mind as his hand moved with precision, reaching inside his jacket for the spare mag. A swift click, a smooth reload, and the P320 was live again. He raised it, locked in on Q-Ball, and let off another flurry of shots, the sharp cracks splitting the night air.

He wanted death. Needed it. Every bullet carried his rage, his thirst to end this. Q-Ball ducked low, barely making it behind cover before the rounds shredded the car in front of him. Salvage's breathing was rough, his chest rising and falling in sharp bursts, but he didn't stop. He couldn't. Not until Q-Ball's body was sprawled out.

But then—red and blue flickered in the distance. The wail of sirens cut through the chaos, growing louder, closer. His stomach twisted. He cursed under his breath, turning back toward his car, but his feet hesitated. Just for a second.

His girl lay a few feet away. Motionless. The sight punched him in the gut, knocked the breath from his lungs harder than a bullet ever could. The girl he laughed with, rode with, held close—now nothing more than a crumpled body on cold concrete. He had seen death before, been the reason behind it plenty of times, but this was different. It was her. His fingers twitched against the grip of his gun. His vision blurred for a fraction of a second, but there was no time to grieve, no time to kneel beside her. The cops were closing in.

Breathing hard, his chest burning, he forced himself to move. With one last look, one last painful imprint of her lifeless body in his mind, he turned, yanked open his jeep door, and threw himself inside. The engine roared as he slammed his foot on the gas, tires screaming against the pavement. He shot out of the parking lot, weaving recklessly into traffic, his hands gripping the wheel like a vice.

Lavista Road blurred past him in streaks of neon and headlights. His pulse pounded in his skull, but his focus stayed razor-sharp. No flashing lights in the rearview—yet. He didn't slow down. Didn't even blink. Instead, he pulled out his phone, thumb flying over the screen as he hit the call. T-Roc picked up on the first ring.

Sh*t just went left, bruh. Some f**k n***a just tried to take me out,"* Salvage said, his voice sharp, breath still ragged. "I upped and let off. My b*tch dead, so you already know it's finna bring heat."

A pause. Then T-Roc's voice, low and steady. "Where you at?"

"I just hopped on the e-way off Lavista, pushin' to the city now," Salvage said, mashing the gas, the needle jumpin' on the dash. "F**k n**a was duckin' my shots like he had some Terminator sh*t in him. Whoever that shooter was, Roc, I gotta drop that pussy n***a. Ain't no way I'm lettin' that slide."

Chapter 46

"Shadows and Sunshine"

The golden rays of sunlight spilled through the windows, bathing the room in a warm glow that blended seamlessly with the cheerful chirping of birds outside. Amani trudged into the kitchen, her tired eyes puffy from a long night spent researching identities and verifying business account numbers. She opened the freezer, grabbing a few ice cubes as fragments of the previous day's chaos replayed in her mind— the tension, the uncertainty, and the lingering fear that had crept into her every thought. Shaking her head to clear her thoughts, she spotted the tray of freshly made salmon croquettes.

The aroma was irresistible, a savory blend of spices that had her stomach growling despite her fatigue. Glancing over to make sure Stacy wasn't paying attention, she snatched a broken piece of croquette and bit into it, savoring the flavorful crunch. As the flavors hit her tongue, she let out a soft sigh of satisfaction, the rich taste momentarily distracting her from her thoughts. With the ice cubes pressed against her aching right eye, she made her way to the living room, chewing thoughtfully as she tried to shake off the weight of the incident. Flopping onto the plush leather sofa, she released a contented sigh, the comfort of the cushions pulling her into thoughts of booking a spa day to soothe her exhaustion.

"I saw that, with your greedy ass. Don't think your ugly ass is that slick," Stacy called from the kitchen, her voice carrying a playful edge. "And how many times do I gotta tell you? Nobody eats before my Onyx."

Amani smirked, brushing off the comment as Stacy moved through the kitchen with unyielding grace. She pulled a tray of buttered bread from the oven and added the final touches to Onyx's plate. Though their relationship was no longer intimate, Stacy relished the chance to treat him like a king. His kindness and unwavering respect made her feel valued, and she always sought ways to show her gratitude.

After pouring a glass of apple juice, Stacy slipped off her silk pajama set, revealing a daring black lingerie ensemble that hugged her curves with precision. The delicate lace traced her caramel-toned skin, accentuating her full hips and the smooth arc of her waist. The sheer material offered teasing glimpses of her toned thighs, while the high-cut design emphasized her long legs. Her confidence radiated as she moved, each step causing her round, firm butt to bounce slightly, the motion natural and enticing.

Carrying the meal to the bedroom, she moved with a sultry grace, hoping her provocative display would capture Onyx's attention as much as the carefully prepared breakfast. Moments later, she returned to the kitchen, wiping her mouth with a playful, satisfied expression. Phone in hand, she chuckled softly, her smile lingering as she leaned against the counter, basking in the glow of her quiet triumph.

"Hey, greedy! Yoshe and Jasmine are on the phone—they want to know if the paperwork's ready and if you're down to meet them at District 12 Cigar Lounge when they're finished," Stacy called out, stepping into the room with a plate in each hand after washing her hands. She handed one to Amani before placing her own plate on the coffee table, her movements quick and seamless. With a slight sway in her hips, she headed back to the kitchen to grab their drinks, her voice trailing off as she hummed a familiar Coco Jones song.

Stacy returned moments later with two glasses in hand and settled into the loveseat. She sat relaxed, one leg tucked under her, exuding a lighthearted and casual energy as she sipped her drink, glancing occasionally at Amani with a knowing smirk.

"Tell them to come on; we'll be done by the time they get here," Amani finally said, taking a bite of her breakfast. With the morning unfolding in an easy rhythm and her body starting to shake off the tiredness from a lack of sleep, Amani sank deeper into the sofa, feeling the tension ease with each passing moment.

"I don't know if it's safe for us to leave yet, but you can if you want," Amani said, tearing off a piece of the salmon with her fingers and popping it into her mouth after Stacy hung up the phone. She paused for a moment, the weight of the previous day's incident creeping into her thoughts again. She hated feeling vulnerable, especially after everything she'd been through. But she couldn't shake the unease that had settled in her chest. She knew she had to stay alert, stay focused.

She shook her head, forcing herself to focus on something else, trying to shove the anxiety aside. It wasn't the time to dwell on it. Not when there was food in front of her and the day was just starting to unfold. Rising from the sofa to retrieve her phone ringing in the background, she jokingly muttered, "Damn, bitch, what the hell is this? Your triflin', Section 8 ass tryin' to give me a stomach virus or somethin'? I see now why nobody wanna wife your no-grip booty ass."

"Ho, stop frontin' with your Dollar Tree-lash-hatin' ass," Stacy shot back, her tone dripping with sarcasm. "You know damn well I do my thing in the kitchen. That's why you walkin' away suckin' your fingers harder than you do your dildo."

"Bitch, please!" Amani snapped, brushing past her brother as he playfully shoved her out of his way in the hallway, completely absorbed in an intense phone conversation. She shot him a sideways glance, her eyes narrowing as she rolled her shoulders back. "Boy, don't make me mess up your outfit with your own blood." She smirked, her voice dripping with challenge, fully aware that Onyx didn't take threats lightly.

He chuckled dryly but was too absorbed in his call to take her empty words seriously. His voice boomed with anger as he verbally dismantled whoever was on the other end. As she continued down the hallway, she could hear his low chuckle behind her, but she wasn't backing down. She knew he'd never let anyone disrespect her, but that didn't mean she wouldn't remind him who was the real boss around here—especially when it came to physical combat. She trusted in her own skills, even against her brother's size and strength.

As she returned from the guest room, the frustration in the air was palpable. A part of her wanted to tell her brother to cool it, but she knew better. His business wasn't hers to interfere with, and she had learned long ago to pick her battles wisely. Someone had messed up badly, and from the way he was talking, there were about to be some serious consequences.

Sinking back into the leather sofa, she just stared at him for a moment, silently hoping the situation wasn't beyond his control to fix, before turning her attention back to Stacy. "Seriously, though, you really outdid yourself with this one," Amani said, her tone light yet laced with her signature sass as she glanced at her friend. "But I swear, if feeding me like this is just some sneaky way to poison me so you can keep my brother all to yourself, I'll accept—as long as you keep it up every day." She took another bite, the flavor dancing on her tongue, though she kept her gaze fixed on Stacy, who smirked knowingly, as if she had a secret Amani wasn't in on. Amani rolled her eyes but couldn't suppress a grin. Whatever the game Stacy was playing, she'd figure it out eventually. For now, the food was too good, and she wasn't about to let paranoia ruin her morning.

Stacy giggled, her eyes crinkling at the corners as she leaned back into the loveseat. "Girl, let me set the record straight—I don't need to poison you to get your brother's attention," she said, her voice dripping with playful arrogance. "And as for toys? Ho' please. I'm not wasting my time teasin' myself. I need that certified USDA Prime to grow inside me—I don't do plastic games."

She took another bite, savoring the flavor before tossing a cushion at Amani with a playful smirk. The lighthearted banter filled the air as they continued eating, both of them falling into an easy silence. The sun streamed through the windows, casting a warm glow across the room, and for a moment, it felt as if the outside world didn't exist. Amani, still half-focused on the food in front of her, let herself savor the comfort of their routine, a rare pocket of calm untouched by the chaos waiting beyond those walls.

Stacy wiped her mouth with the back of her hand, setting her plate aside as she leaned forward, her expression shifting. "I think I'm gonna step out with Yoshe and Jasmine. I can't stay cooped up like this." The thought of getting out for a while seemed like a breath of fresh air. Amani nodded slowly, chewing her food as she mulled over the idea. But her thoughts quickly returned to the caution she had been feeling.

"Until my brother says it's safe, I'm staying here," she replied, her voice steady but edged with quiet resolve. "That sh*t was too real the other day, and I'm not about to be anybody's target just to get at him. Going to the concert gave me a little comfort, knowing we were all together and the police were there, but..." Amani trailed off, her thoughts growing heavier, her fingers brushed the sofa arm, as though she were anchoring herself. "Getting shot at doesn't just go away. It's like the fear lingers, no matter how normal things seem."

"I know exactly how you feel, but bitch, you need some sunlight and your pussy ate backwards, which none of your toys can do, 'cause you starting to look real malnourished just laying around all day watching TV," Stacy said with a playful mix of compassion and sass, reaching over to slap Amani's hand. She tried to catch pieces of Onyx's conversation as he reentered the kitchen, but he disappeared back into the bedroom before it was quite enough to understand what he was saying. " Your hungry ass was hatin' on my skills, yet you keep stuffin' your face like it's your last meal."

Laughing mid-bite, Amani could only blush as she chewed. "Your stank ass know I mess with your campaign. Even though it tastes like some Salvation Army giveaways," she teased, lifting another forkful.

"F**k you!" Stacy shot back just as the doorbell rang, sending them both into a fit of laughter.

Curiosity filled both of their minds as they watched Onyx walk past the room to answer the door, his footsteps steady and purposeful. He returned seconds later, strolling past the room with T-Roc and Gunna, each of them carrying a black bookbag in one hand. The twins didn't acknowledge either of them, their silence hanging in the air. Stacy, unable to resist, raised her left hand and shot a bird in their direction, a small act of rebellion that only made Amani giggle more at her friend's antics. She knew Stacy craved attention, and it irked her when she wasn't the center of it.

As the laughter subsided, Amani caught sight of the clock on her phone. Time was slipping away, and she had business to handle before Yoshe and Jasmine arrived. Lifting the last portion of food to her mouth, she finished the last bite and rose from the couch, plate in hand. Without a word, she placed it on Stacy's lap, who gave her a look of mild confusion. Amani, unbothered, grabbed her laptop off the coffee table and flopped back down onto the sofa. "I might need you to bring me a plate back if you do decide to step out," she said, half to herself, as she opened the laptop and began tapping away at the keys.

"Bitch, do I look like your personal sink?" Stacy shot back, raising an eyebrow as she stared at Amani.

Amani grinned, " Nah, you look like a walking chlamydia PSA with that outfit on," she teased, her laughter echoing. "You're my brother's housekeeper, secret sexy toy, and portable cum catcher. So where else you expect me to stash it?"

"I bet I poison your no-good, ugly ass the next time I cook," Stacy said sarcastically as she rose from the sofa, gathering both of their plates to take to the kitchen.

Amani giggled, her eyes scanning the screen as she sifted through people's identity information. Her stomach grumbled in protest, reminding her that the small meal hadn't quite satisfied her hunger. Leaning back into the cushions, she let out a sigh, typing away as her mind bounced between tasks. The craving for something fresh and juicy lingered in the back of her mind, but she pushed it aside for now.

With the necessary details aligned on the templates for the checks to be printed, Amani stood up from the sofa and walked out of the room, giving Stacy brief instructions on what to do. As she passed the oval floor mirror in the bedroom, she ignored her girlfriend's earlier sarcasm and took a moment to admire herself in the white powerpuff shirt dress. "Malnutrition my ass bitch," she muttered under her breath, then made her way to the bed, connecting the MICR Laser Printer to her laptop.

For the next 37 minutes, Amani sat cross-legged in the middle of the bed, focused on perfecting her craft. The safety of her girls was her priority over money, so she meticulously checked the account and routing numbers for accuracy, ensuring everything was perfect. When she was confident the information and checks were flawless, she printed five, while Stacy worked on designing the identification cards for Yoshe and Jasmine.

Despite the recent incident forcing her to lay low from the streets, Amani refused to let it stop her from profiting from her skills. She tuned out Stacy's chatter and lifted her phone to call Yoshe. But before she could make the call, Onyx's voice cut through the air, followed by a knock at the door. "Come in, bruh!" she called, glancing toward the door as it opened.

"Can you come to the office for a second? I need your assistance," Onyx asked from the doorway, his gaze fixed steadily on his sister.

Amani glanced at him briefly, then focused back on the last check, carefully double-checking the watermark symbols. Satisfied, she eased off the bed, slipped on her house shoes, and slid the check into an envelope with the others. Handing the envelope to Stacy, she gave her a quick nod before turning to assist her brother.

"Well, I'll be sitting right here stretching my jaws just in case my throat gets desired," Stacy purred seductively as Onyx paused at the door, throwing her a quick glance over his shoulder.

"You need to stretch your disease-ridden ass to the nearest CDC office," Amani quipped, brushing past her on her way out of the room.

"Eat my ass," Stacy shot back without missing a beat, her tone dripping with mock defiance.

Chapter 47

"Balancing the Scales"

Curious about what new adventure he had in store, Amani followed Onyx into his office, the faint scent of leather and cologne invading her nostrils. She offered a polite greeting to her cousins as she entered the room, then snapped at them for not speaking when they arrived.

"Y'all rude asses couldn't say hello?" she barked, her tone brisk but playful.

Her eyes widened as they landed on the sight before her: stacks of crisp $100s, $50s, and $20s spread across the desk in a chaotic display of wealth. The twins sat comfortably in their chairs, methodically sorting and counting the bills, their movements precise and practiced. It wasn't the money that caught her attention—scamming had already made her a six-figure boss in her own lane—but there was something satisfying about seeing her brother thrive. A small, proud smile tugged at her lips as she leaned against the doorframe, silently admiring the scene.

Onyx had fought through betrayal, setbacks, and the constant grind to get here. Yet, he was steadily building an empire brick by brick. He was finally becoming the man he had always envisioned—resilient, calculated, and respected.

"This you, huh? Big boss moves?" Amani teased, folding her arms as her gaze shifted between the money and her brother.

Onyx chuckled, shaking his head. "Gotta stay ten steps ahead, sis. You know how it is."

She nodded, her smile fading slightly as her thoughts drifted to the dangers that came with the life they lived. But as always, Onyx had a plan.

"Sis," he said, his tone turning serious as he leaned back in his chair, "I need you to ride with me if you don't mind. I'm about to meet a Colombian boss, and I need you there to translate anything they might

299

say in secrecy. We're meeting him at a restaurant in Woodstock. The twins will be watching our backs from a distance."

Amani raised an eyebrow, her curiosity piqued. "A Colombian boss? So he's finally allowing you a seat at the table? What kind of business we talking about?"

"Just chill," Onyx replied, his voice calm but firm. "We just talking. You already know I ain't gon' play 'bout your safety, Amani." He leaned forward, his eyes locked on hers, exuding confidence. "The twins gon' be surveying the whole area with Hannibal's awareness. Ain't nobody gon' catch us slippin'."

Amani studied his face, searching for any cracks in his confidence. She knew her brother wasn't one to take unnecessary risks with her safety, but the weight of the situation wasn't lost on her. "A'ight," she finally said, her tone laced with caution. "But if something don't feel right, I'm out. You know I ain't about to die for nobody's ego."

Onyx smirked, nodding. "Fair enough. But trust me, sis, I got this. Just need you to do what you do best."

She sighed, crossing her arms as she walked over and leaned against the desk. "Fine. But you better make sure those two damn knuckleheads"—she gestured toward the twins—"don't get too trigger-happy out there."

The twins paused in their counting, exchanging a glance before Gunna chuckled. "You know we got it, cuz. Quit playin'."

Onyx stood, adjusting his chain with a grin. "It's gon' be smooth. You'll see."

Despite Onyx's reassurance, Amani couldn't shake the feeling that this meeting was far from simple. Still, she pushed her unease aside, forcing herself to step into whatever world her brother was navigating. His words sank in, leaving her momentarily numb. She stared into his eyes, hoping her hesitation would say what she was too afraid to voice. Amani's fiercely guarded independence wasn't ready to leave the safe bubble of healing that his home was providing. Yet her love for Onyx made her fears a faint hum in the back of her mind—present, but not loud enough to stop her.

"You know I always got your back," she muttered, leaning over his desk. Her voice wavered slightly as she reached out, her hand trembling as it lifted a couple of rubber-banded stacks of hundreds from one of the piles. "Ion even got nothin' to wear, though, bruh. But…" Her lips curved into a faint smirk as she glanced at the money in her hand. "I can definitely find me somethin' to match your drip wit' dis."

The silliness of Amani's action made T-Roc chuckle, his broad grin exposing his amusement as he watched the Godfather shake his head. "You sure that's enough, given all the sauce you be exposing, cuz?" T-Roc teased, lifting the bookbag off the floor. He unzipped it and turned it toward her, revealing loose bills balled up and folded inside. "You need mo'?"

The Godfather smirked, tossing a stack of 50s at him. "Once again, I see y'all country-ass n***as' loyalty is to my sister and not to the family," he said, his tone playful as he grabbed his phone to check a text message. Turning his attention back to Amani, Onyx's expression softened. "For real, though, sis, after this meeting, I'mma give you several of them stacks. And just so you know, I already assumed your answer would be yes, so I took the liberty of hittin' up Yoshe. She's picking up somethin' for you to wear, plus a few other things you might need. I heard Stacy's loud-ass mouth—saying her and Jasmine was on the way over here, so I hit her up. And let's be real, Yoshe knows your bougie ass better than anyone."

Amani nodded in silence, absorbing her brother's words and the weight of his expectations. She didn't have the strength to protest, nor did she want to. Slowly, she placed the stacks of money back on his desk and turned to exit the room. The unexpected acknowledgment of it all was too much to handle at once, so she needed a moment—time to collect herself. Ignoring Stacy's nosy comments as she reentered the bedroom, Amani gracefully walked to the bathroom and locked herself inside.

The muffled sounds of Stacy's voice faded as Amani turned on the shower, the water rushing out in a steady surge. She needed the sound and warmth to drown out the chaos swirling in her mind. Sitting on the edge of the tub, she buried her face in her palms and cried. The raw emotion poured out, a mixture of fear and frustration. Fear not just for herself, but for the life her brother was dragging her deeper into. She had always stayed on the sidelines, supporting him from a distance, but now, standing on the edge of something she couldn't undo, she felt exposed and vulnerable.

"Why can't you just focus on music and close the door to this life?" she whispered between sobs, her voice raw. She hated how helpless she felt. The life he lived wasn't hers, and yet, here she was, stepping further into it with every passing moment.

But in the quiet of the bathroom, with the water running steadily, Amani realized that her strength was something she had to claim for herself. She wiped her eyes, forcing herself to stop spiraling into the storm of her thoughts. She couldn't let it win—not the fear, not the doubt. Standing up, she pulled her Powerpuff shirt dress over her head, letting the cool mist of the water hit her bare skin, a sharp contrast to the heat coiling inside her. She stepped into the tub, not ready to shed the weight of her underwear just yet. The cold water shocked her body, but it was just what she needed—each droplet a tiny spark, forcing her to wake up, forcing her to feel something other than fear.

After a few minutes, she needed to shed her discomfort, her clothes, and her doubts all at once. She undressed, letting the wet fabric fall in a puddle at her feet, revealing the curves of her body. She reached for the loofah, lathering it with body wash, the warm scent filling the air. Shifting the water to lukewarm as she began scrubbing, the rhythm of it grounded her, bringing her back to herself.

The steady rhythm of the water soothed her frayed nerves as she scrubbed, kneading out the tension that had settled deep in her muscles. The rich scent of vanilla orchid and amber from her body wash filled the small bathroom, calming her further. Amani leaned her forehead against the cool tile wall, closing her eyes as the water cascaded over her. She knew this wasn't the life she wanted, but it was the life she'd been given. Onyx's world wasn't hers, but his blood ran through her veins, binding her to him in ways she couldn't escape. He had always been her protector, her anchor. Now, it seemed the roles were shifting, and she didn't know how to navigate this new reality.

Amani thought of the superhero Vixen, imagining herself as someone unbreakable. She wasn't a coward, but she wasn't a street soldier either. She understood survival had many layers, and for now, she would be the woman who could hold her own, even if it meant stepping outside of her comfort zone. Her hand slid down the wall, hitting the knob. The sudden blast of cold water snapped her out of her spiraling thoughts. Shivering, she turned off the water and grabbed a towel, wrapping it tightly around herself. She wiped the fog from the mirror and stared at her reflection, taking in the vulnerability in her eyes. "You got this," she whispered to herself, her voice barely audible. "You always do."

"Open the door, stank," Yoshe teased, repeatedly turning the knob, causing Amani to laugh despite herself.

Shaking her head with a smile tugging at the corners of her lips, Amani slipped into her robe, tying the belt tightly around her waist. She walked toward the door, unlocked it, still chuckling. "Ion told your nasty ass I ain't with the licky sh*t, so ain't no reason for you to be tryin' to come in here, ho," Amani said with a playful tone, opening the door to find Yoshe standing there with a wide grin on her face. Despite the fear lingering inside her, Amani knew she was a survivor and would keep her head above water—physically, emotionally, and mentally.

"Bitch, I wouldn't lick that sea turtle-smellin' pussy of yours with Stacy's contaminated-ass tongue to save my grandmother's life," Yoshe snapped sarcastically, shooting a one-finger salute at Stacy, who was already preparing her counterattack with verbal fire of her own. "Here are your clothes, with your ungrateful ass."

They both burst into laughter at the absurdity of Stacy's endless verbal battles, a back-and-forth they had all grown accustomed to. Amani stepped out of the bathroom, her mood lifted by the playful exchange, and walked over to pull her girl into a hug. "Appreciate you, Yoshe," she whispered, snatching the bags from her hands with a smirk before setting them down on the floor beside her bed. She leaned forward to grab the envelope, the business awaiting her attention before she could fully indulge in the comfort of her friends. Pleasure came after priority.

As she settled back onto the bed, Amani quickly shifted gears, launching into an explanation of their business dealings. She addressed Yoshe and Jasmine with the seriousness of a seasoned professional, ensuring they understood the accounts they were withdrawing from, the importance of keeping everything smooth, and how to avoid drawing unwanted attention. "No shortcuts," she said firmly, locking eyes with each of them. "Your freedom is at stake, and we can't afford mistakes. You need to remember what not to do or say to raise red flags, and how to execute the checks with each bank. Perfection isn't a choice; it's necessary."

She made sure they fully understood every detail before moving on to the lighter side of their friendship. The air lightened as they began to reminisce, joking and teasing each other in a casual rhythm, the weight of the world momentarily lifted. But then, glancing at the clock, Amani felt the pressure return.

"Stacy, escort them to the door please," Amani said, her tone now taking on a no-nonsense edge as she stood, grabbing the bags from the floor. "I need to get ready for my brother's meeting. Yoshe, you and Jasmine need to blend in with that lunch-hour traffic, so the mangers will rush y'all through without playing close attention." Her voice carried a quiet urgency, the weight of responsibility hanging in her words. She wasn't just preparing for the meeting; she was orchestrating every detail. With a final squeeze of her girls, she turned toward the task at hand, the balance of business and friendship never more apparent.

After seeing their friends off, Stacy's jealousy flared the moment she stepped back into the bedroom and noticed the clothes Amani had unpacked and spread across the bed. Her eyes immediately locked onto Amani, who was carefully inspecting the outfits Yoshe had chosen for her.

"Girl, who in the hell you tryna flex on in that sh*t?" she demanded, her narrowed eyes full of suspicion as she took in the luxurious pieces sprawled across the bed.

Amani's eyes flashed with a sharpness that came from years of dealing with Stacy's constant digs. "Ho', it definitely want be with a n***a you have f**ked," Amani snapped, startled by Stacy's sudden intrusion.

Stacy's insecurities spilled into Amani's space, with her jealousy intensifying as she watched Amani's poise and confidence. It was like a mirror to everything she felt she lacked. "Bitch, don't nobody care to see your bougie ass over me," Stacy retorted, strutting over to the bags and peering inside.

Amani sighed, staring at the outfit draped over her arm as she studied her reflection in the floor mirror. The rust-colored ballerina mini dress would hug her curves with understated elegance, while the black love flame dress would exude bold sophistication. She held each one against her body, tilting her head as if the right angle might help her decide. After a moment, she folded both outfits carefully and placed them back in the bag with a resigned shake of her head.

The last thing she wanted was to hear Stacy complain about not being invited. Stacy's constant complaints about feeling neglected were getting on her nerves. Amani's thoughts swirled with the words she wanted to say but didn't dare voice: *Stacy, you don't have the charisma, intellect, or class to move in spaces outside the hood.* But she swallowed them, knowing that no matter how true they might be, she couldn't bring herself to hurt Stacy's feelings—not intentionally, anyway.

Instead, she grabbed her phone and stepped away, her mind already shifting to the next task. It wasn't worth the argument, and Amani had bigger things to focus on than soothing Stacy's bruised ego. Quickly retrieving a seamless thong and half bra from her drawer, she headed back into the bathroom, locking the door behind her. Amani set everything on the counter before opening her playlist and selecting H.E.R. The soft melodies filled the space as she cleaned up behind herself and dressed, finally sinking into the calming atmosphere she'd created.

"Damn, gurl, what you in there doing? Playin' with yourself? Livestreaming?" Stacy yelled, knocking on the door about fifteen minutes later. She didn't like being ignored, and boredom, made her seek attention. It was clear she was itching for something to occupy her time, something beyond reruns and aimlessly sitting around. Knocking harder the second time, she let her frustration show. Her jealousy brewed like a flower unfurling in her chest, especially once Amani opened the door, looking effortlessly flawless.

"Shouldn't you be doin' tongue and neck exercises?" Amani quipped, her voice laced with sarcasm as her eyes caught Stacy's raised brows and thinly veiled annoyance. The tension in the air was palpable, but Amani breezed past her, choosing not to linger on the exchange. She strode confidently into her room, dropping the bags on the closet floor with a soft thud before turning her attention to tidying up.

She carefully stowed away her work items, her movements precise, a soothing ritual to steady her thoughts. The weight of the upcoming meeting loomed in her mind, but she pushed it aside, focusing instead on the small act of adorning herself. Amani selected a pear-shaped, 3-carat diamond pendant set in gold, the delicate chain catching the light as she clasped it around her neck. The subtle elegance of the necklace felt like armor—a statement of her worth and resolve.

With a final glance around the room, she adjusted the pendant, ensuring it sat perfectly against her collarbone. The soft click of the door behind her signaled her departure as she stepped out, exuding quiet confidence. Each step carried her closer to the meeting ahead, her mind sharpening with determination to face whatever awaited her.

Chapter 48

"The Right Bitch for the Job"

The strip club felt like a world of its own, the air thick with smoke, sweat, and the sharp bite of cheap perfume and spilled liquor, laced with the scent of crumpled cash and raw ambition. The floors gleamed under dim, colored lights, while the low murmur of conversation blended with the pounding rhythm of the music, a steady undercurrent to the spectacle unfolding. It was midday, but time held no weight here—only movement, money, and desire. Dancers moved effortlessly between poles and laps, their bodies bending and twisting with hypnotic grace, catching the shifting hues of light like a living kaleidoscope.

Monster lounged in a worn leather booth, a fortress of calm amid the chaos. His face betrayed nothing, but his stillness spoke volumes— anger simmered just beneath the surface, coiled and ready to strike. He sat like a king surveying his domain, the chaos around him seemed almost choreographed, a wild dance of temptation and frenzy.

Women filled the space with undeniable energy, their bodies moving as if possessed by the rhythm. Hips swayed in perfect time to the heavy bassline, a hypnotic push-and-pull that commanded attention. Titties bounced with unapologetic allure, barely restrained by outfits designed to tease and tantalize. Each movement caught the flickering strobe lights, making them glisten like forbidden treasures. Booties popped and dipped to the relentless beat, their curves spelling power as they moved with practiced ease, each motion daring onlookers to look away.

A light-skinned dancer with curves that could stop traffic sauntered up, her smile as bold as the rhythm she moved to. She leaned in, offering a lap dance with a tilt of her head, but Monster wasn't interested. He waved her off with a flick of his hand, his eyes locked on the room— scanning the faces and the exit. Everyone noticed him. Staff whispered behind the bar, patrons stole nervous glances, and even the dancers seemed to keep one eye on him. This wasn't just a booth in the corner; this was his throne, and the club around him was a kingdom of unspoken rules and dangerous alliances.

This was where power shifted, where trust dissolved, and where Monster planned his next move. But in the chaos of the flashing lights and pounding music, the question wasn't whether he'd strike first—it was whether he'd see the knife coming before it was too late.

A group of women gathered near the bar, their laughter rising above the music, smooth and warm, like honey dripping over the beat. They leaned into one another, their outfits a mix of street-savvy edge and high-end flair, each exuding their own distinct energy. One rocked a cropped Fendi hoodie paired with sleek, body-hugging leather joggers, the designer monogram catching the strobe lights with subtle flashes. Her white Air Jordans, spotless despite the crowded floor, hinted at a purposeful, blend of style and comfort. Her nails were long, perfectly sculpted, and painted a bold neon green, tapping against her diamond-studded clutch as she laughed.

Beside her, a white woman with platinum-blonde hair exuded effortless confidence, dressed head-to-toe in high-end urban designer fashion. She wore a cropped Balenciaga bomber jacket paired with tailored, wide-leg Louis Vuitton monogrammed pants that hugged her hips before flaring at the ankles. A sleek, layered gold chain adorned her neck, catching the light as it rested against the ribbed fabric of her fitted black crop top. Her straight hair, parted down the middle, swayed with every subtle movement she made, her stride fluid and commanding, as though the crowd parted naturally in her presence.

The third woman, in stark contrast, seemed almost misplaced in the scene but owned her space with quiet confidence. She wore a floor-length gown made of shimmery black silk that flowed like liquid as she moved. The gown was minimal yet exquisite, its daring thigh-high slit revealing glimpses of her toned leg. Instead of the flashy accessories her companions flaunted, she wore understated diamond studs and a delicate chain, as if she belonged in an exclusive gala, not a strip club.

Her stiletto heels glinted faintly, the red soles marking her as a woman accustomed to luxury.

Their contrasting styles created a striking tableau, each one standing out in her own way. Together, they were magnetic—a blend of urban grit, high-fashion bravado, and unshakable elegance that drew every pair of eyes in the room, including Monster's.

His eyes skimmed over them, lingering briefly before shifting away. A brunette with braids past her waist danced on the edge of the crowd, her movements slow and smooth, each sway of her body commanding more attention than the loudest shout. Her lips curled into a knowing smirk, her confidence as striking as her beauty. Darting his eyes back to the bar, he noticed that the woman in the Fendi hoodie leaned into her friend, whispering something that drew a quiet laugh, but it was the shift in her friend's eyes that caught Monster's attention more. Her gaze drifted toward him, lingering just long enough for him to register the silent message. What did she say? Who was she?

Though Monster didn't outwardly react, the slight flare of his nostrils and the soft drumming of his fingers against the table hinted at his awareness of it all. The women, the movement, the heat—it was a world alive with power and temptation, but it all seemed to orbit him, waiting for his signal, waiting for him to decide when, or if, to unleash the storm simmering beneath his surface.

Tre sat beside him, practically vibrating with anticipation, his eyes were glued to the stage. A tall, chocolate-skinned dancer moved with a level of grace and power that commanded the room. She twirled around the pole with acrobatic precision, each spin pulling the crowd in like moths to a flame. The way the lights caressed her skin, making her shimmer, had Tre feeling like he'd been hit with Cupid's arrow.

He leaned forward, his breath hitching as her routine neared its climax. Every move she made seemed designed to hypnotize—her body gliding down the pole until she sank into a slow, intentional split that sent the crowd into a frenzy. Waves of crumpled bills cascaded to the floor at her feet, and Tre's grin deepened, his thoughts slipping into overdrive. He imagined the allure of her scent, the pulse of her heartbeat against his lips as he sucked her titties, her body moving in perfect rhythm with his as she rode him—every moment an intoxicating blend of heat and sweetness.

Monster didn't move, except for the rise and fall of his chest. While the men crowding the stage were entranced by the dancer's allure, Monster's focus remained unwavering, locked on something far more pressing. His mind worked like a machine, analyzing and piecing together the details that mattered. Money Bag Mafia wasn't invincible. Every fortress had its cracks, every boss had weaknesses, and Monster was here to exploit them all. His eyes moved with precision, scanning the crowd to see who lingered too long, who came and went too fast, and who tried too hard to blend in.

Sitting there, eyeing the woman at the bar in his peripheral, Monster replayed TJ's admission from the night before, the words gnawing at the edges of his mind. TJ's conniving ass had come up short, failing to reveal the Godfather's residence or any of Money Bag Mafia's drug operation locations. Half-baked intel that was enough to make Monster's blood boil. But TJ had managed to save himself by throwing out a name he thought was expendable: 44, the Godfather's right-hand man. "He your key," TJ had said. And without hesitation, Monster planned to turn that key until the whole operation came crashing down.

Tre leaned in, breaking Monster's thoughts. "You sure this the spot? I mean, ain't no guarantee 44 even slide through like the n***a said. What if he already put that n***a up on game?"

Monster's eyes cut to Tre, cold and unyielding. "I don't move on guarantees, shawty. I move on strategy. Strategy say this the spot. That weak-ass n***a's a snake, no question, but he knows better than to cross me. If he ever does, it'll be the end of him and anyone tied to him."

Tre nodded, his eyes locked lustfully on the dancer strolling toward the DJ booth. He knew better than to keep pressing.

The club doors swung open, and Q-Ball walked in like he owned the place. Built like an offensive lineman, he moved with the smooth confidence of a trained predator. His black sweatsuit was crisp, gold chains draped across his chest, gleaming under the lights. Heads turned as he strode across the floor, staff and patrons alike giving him space.

Monster gave a subtle wave, and Q-Ball sauntered over, sliding into the booth with ease. A waitress appeared almost instantly, rocking fishnets and a red bikini, her sly smile slicing through the room's haze with effortless allure. Monster peeled off a stack of hundreds, instructing her to bring a bottle of brown liquor for the table and the rest in singles. She returned moments later, setting the bottle down with precision, while slipping the cash into his hand. After a quick tip, she vanished back into the thrumming crowd.

Q-Ball leaned back, his big frame filling the booth as he glanced between Monster and Tre. "So what's the move? You want me to snatch that pussy n***a outta here? If that's the case, you gon' need to fatten up the bag. How you even know he gonna show?"

Monster poured himself a drink, the liquor catching the dim light as he set the bottle down with meticulous care. "TJ said 44 comes here damn near every day to politic. But he got a weakness—he love spendin' money on these bitches. So it don't matter if he show today or not. This the groundwork, my boy. You don't catch no prey without settin' the trap first. Now, what I need is somebody who can get close to him."

Q-Ball nodded, his smirk fading as the weight of Monster's plan pressed down on him like a vice. The music thundered around them, the bass rattling the glasses on the table, but their corner of the club felt like a different world—heavy, suffocating, on the brink of snapping. Q-Ball's eyes shifted to Monster, who was completely absorbed in 44, oblivious to the disaster at the Tavern that was entirely his own doing. And Q-Ball sure as hell wasn't going to risk incriminating himself. Revenge had Monster too mentally tangled to connect the dots. Q-Ball was already pissed that he'd added another body to his count for nothing. He took his time pouring a drink, each movement deliberate, his face a mask of unreadable calm. "So, you need a bitch who's down for whatever?" he asked, his voice low and steady, the tension between them thick enough to cut—like a fuse ready to blow.

Monster sipped his drink, his gaze drifting to the two hustlers strolling through the entrance, their flashy outfits catching the club's erratic strobe lights. His tone carried quiet authority, cutting cleanly through the noise with undeniable command. "Exactly. She gotta be 'bout her paper and know how to play her part. Can't afford no slip-ups."

Q-Ball downed his drink in one gulp and leaned forward to pour another, his gold chains glinting under the flashing lights as he moved. "I got just the one. Sunset. She the baddest bitch in here and hungry as hell for that bread. She'll do anything if the money's right."

Monster's eyes narrowed, his intensity radiating through the fog of smoke and chaos. "Make it happen."

Q-Ball stood, scanning the room with the precision of a hawk in flight. The dancers were in full swing—some moving slow and sultry, while others threw it back like rent day was around the corner. The DJ switched the track, flooding the club with a high-energy anthem that sent the crowd into a frenzy. Men waved bills in the air, their cheers echoing through the room as the woman on stage gripped the pole with effortless confidence. Her body moved with graceful ease, every motion seamless and intentional as she pulled herself up, her toned muscles flexing under the neon glow. She hooked one leg around the pole, spinning in a slow, hypnotic circle, her long hair cascading like a silken curtain.

With a quick shift, she inverted herself, hanging upside down with perfect control, her rhinestone-covered bodysuit shimmering like a galaxy of stars. The crowd erupted as she released one hand, extending her arm gracefully while her body twisted in mid-air, defying gravity. As she slid down in a controlled descent, she arched her back, her movements were sensual yet commanding, captivating every pair of eyes in the room.

When her feet finally touched the stage, she didn't hesitate. She bent over, gripping the pole with one hand, her back curving into a flawless arch that emphasized each line of her figure. With slow, seductive movements, she began twerking, her body moving to the rhythm with a hypnotic precision that commanded attention. Her heels clicked against the floor in sync with the beat, while the air around her filled with the rustle of bills raining down like a cascade of leaves. Each motion exuded a magnetic power, her allure undeniable. The energy in the club surged, the crowd completely mesmerized by her performance.

Q-Ball's gaze landed on a petite Latina dancer weaving effortlessly through the tables, her hips swaying to the heavy bass that pulsed through the club. Her honey-toned skin glistened under the flashing lights, and her sleek ponytail swung with every step. With ease, Q-Ball intercepted her mid-stride, leaning in close to whisper in her ear. Her expression shifted subtly—just enough to signal she understood. She nodded, her dark eyes shifting toward the dressing room before she disappeared into the shadows, her figure swallowed by the thick curtain.

Moments later, the curtain swayed open, and she stepped out. Sunset was a showstopper. Her caramel skin gleamed under the neon glow, every movement fluid and commanding. Long honey-blonde hair cascaded down her back in soft waves, framing her striking cheekbones and bold features. Her sheer, sleek black bodysuit left little to the imagination, each curve accentuated by the lights that danced across her figure. She walked with a magnetic confidence that turned heads and silenced whispers, her heels clicking like a countdown as she approached Q-Ball. Without hesitation, she leaned in, wrapping him in a brief hug, her presence exuding warmth and poise despite the intensity in the air.

Monster took a slow sip of his drink, letting the burn settle as he leaned back, his gaze taking her in. Her flirty smile was captivating, but it was the confidence in her eyes that caught him. She was undoubtedly a woman who knew her worth and her game. He liked that. She wasn't just here to impress; she was here to handle business.

"So, you Sunset?" he asked, his tone cool and steady as Q-Ball guided her closer and slid into the booth beside him.

She cocked her head slightly, honey-blonde hair brushing her shoulder as she spoke, her voice smooth and laced with intrigue. "Who wanna know?"

"Somebody 'bout to drop a whole lotta dead presidents if you really 'bout it like Q says you are," Monster replied, sliding a thick stack of hundreds across the table. "That's a band upfront. Four more if you can finesse a n***a for me."

Her eyes flicked to the money, lingering just long enough to show she wasn't easy to impress, then locked back onto him. "Depends who the n***a is. All money don't spend the same when it come with drawbacks."

Monster leaned forward slightly, his voice low. "44. Tall, dark-skinned Rasta, flashy as hell. He come in here often. Your job? Get close to him. Make him take you back to his spot or a hotel. Once he does, you hit up Q-Ball. That's it. We handle the rest, and the rest of the money's yours."

Sunset reached for the cash, her manicured nails gleaming under the lights like polished gold. She flipped through it with practiced ease before sliding it into her garter belt. "Five racks to run game? Sounds like light work."

"Don't get it twisted," Monster said, his tone sharpening just enough to let her know he wasn't playing. "44 ain't average. He dangerous, and he smart. One wrong move, and it's a wrap. You sure you can handle this?"

Sunset's lips curved into a sly smile, her confidence radiating like heat. "Baby, I can handle anything as long as the money keep comin' correct."

As she spoke, her mind raced with thoughts she kept hidden behind her cool exterior. She knew exactly who 44 was. She'd seen him in the club plenty of times, always surrounded by a pack of flashy dudes and moving like he owned the place. She'd even danced for him a couple of times, earning big tips and noticing the way he always sized people up like he was calculating his next move.

But she wasn't intimidated. She'd read men like 44 before—charismatic, controlling, and convinced they were untouchable. He might've been dangerous, but Sunset knew how to navigate his type. The way he looked at her, the way he liked to show off his money? She could handle him, no question. Her confidence wasn't just for show. She'd played this game before, and as far as she was concerned, 44 was just another player who thought he was running things. Little did he know, she could flip the script with a smile and a sway of her hips.

She didn't let any of that slip, though. Instead, she kept her sly smirk and leaned back slightly, letting Monster believe she was just cool under pressure. "I'm good. Trust me, I got this. I know who he is."

Monster studied her for a moment longer before nodding, satisfied. He didn't know she'd already sized 44 up long before this deal was on the table. She wasn't just confident—she was ready. Monster leaned back, nodding once. "Bet. Then we locked in."

As Sunset slipped back into the crowd, her figure blending with the dancers and hustlers, the club's energy kicked up a notch. The bass hit harder, vibrating through the floors, while dancers climbed higher, their moves more seductive, more daring.

Tre was in his element, leaning back in his seat while a plus-size, chocolate-skinned dancer enthralled him, her movements slow and hypnotic, pulling his attention deeper with every sway. Q-Ball laughed beside him, tossing singles into the air with one hand, his other hand holding his drink like a trophy.

The DJ grabbed the mic, his voice booming through the speakers as the lights dimmed. "A'ight, y'all! Time to turn this bitch up! Show some love for Desirée!"

The crowd roared as a curvy, brown-skinned dancer strutted onto the stage, her body glistening under the spotlight like molten gold. Her confidence was palpable, every move precise as she commanded the room's attention. Monster smirked, watching the frenzy she ignited in the crowd. But his mind wasn't on the stage, it was locked on the mission. Sunset was the first move on the chessboard, and he was already calculating the endgame. When she played her role, 44 and the Godfather would fall like dominoes.

This wasn't just the start of a plan—it was the start of their downfall.

Chapter 49

"Reputation and Tease"

Damn, you're dazzling, Amani!" Cle blurted, unable to hold back the words as he stepped out of the Godfather's office to use the bathroom. His eyes followed her graceful movements down the hallway, mesmerized by the hypnotic sway of her hips. Amani carried herself with an elegance that demanded attention, her presence intoxicating. Selfish fantasies of bathing the smooth skin of her body with his tongue and sinking his teeth into her plump, melon-sweet lips as she rotated her hips beneath him flashed through his mind endlessly. She was a vision, an enigma he couldn't resist admiring. Yet, the fear of the Godfather kept those forbidden thoughts firmly in the realm of fantasy. To pursue Amani would be to court danger he wasn't prepared to face.

"Thank you, Cle. When did you get here?" Amani inquired, glancing over her shoulder. Her eyes caught the way his gaze lingered on her body, tracing her curves instead of meeting hers. Her voice was calm, yet laced with a subtle edge of awareness.

"I came in right after your homegirls left," Cle responded, his voice faltering slightly as he shifted awkwardly, his bladder reminding him of his urgent need. "They were stepping off the elevator as I was getting on."

Amani gave a small nod before turning her attention forward again, her composure unshaken despite Cle's obvious admiration.

"Damn, sis, you really out here trying to command all the attention, I see," Onyx teased as he walked into the hallway, a playful grin spreading across his face. His eyes scanned her with brotherly pride, appreciating how stunning she looked in her burgundy Very Demure set and matching open-toe stilettos. The shoes showcased her perfectly polished white nails, completing her look of understated power and elegance.

"Always," Amani shot back with a smirk, her confidence radiating as she adjusted the strap on her blazer.

The Godfather returned to the desk, zipped up a large travel bag, and handed it to Gunna for safekeeping. The Godfather observed the twins silently, his mind already running through the details of the day ahead. With only six kilos left in his stash, he needed the upcoming meeting to proceed without a hitch. Failure wasn't an option, especially if it meant turning to TJ for another lifeline. He gave T-Roc and Gunna precise instructions on how to handle the money before walking them—and Cle—toward the door.

As the Godfather turned around, after locking the door behind him, his eyes caught an unexpected sight: Stacy, squatting naked in the bedroom doorway, her body on full display as she teased herself. The brazen act stirred something primal within him—a desire he didn't want to acknowledge, let alone nurture. But his body had a mind of its own, and it had been far too long since he'd indulged in her affections. The mesmerizing sight of her juices dripping from her pussy, pooling into her hand before cascading onto his hardwood floor, ignited an unrelenting wave of desire that surged through his mind and body, leaving him completely entranced.

Shaking off his hesitation, he strolled into the kitchen and paused by Amani. Leaning in close, his lips brushing her ear as he whispered something that made her laugh softly, her shoulders shaking with amusement. Grabbing a banana from the counter, he straightened his posture and walked down the hallway as she prepared herself a smoothie.

Without a word, and to his disbelief, she continued squatting in the doorway, her fingers moving against her clitoris with an abandon that revealed her hunger for his attention. Each moan spilling from her lips dripped with seduction, igniting a deeper, more primal desire inside him, pulling him toward her like a force he couldn't resist.

The Godfather extended a hand to Stacy. Her eyes locked with his, a glimmer of mischief and desire sparkling within them. Slowly, she withdrew her hand from her pussy, lifting it to her mouth to taste, before gently placing it in his. The Godfather pulled her to her feet with an almost careless ease, his grip firm yet lacking tenderness. She leaned into him, her bare skin brushing against the fabric of his shirt, the heat of her body seeping into his own.

With their steps slow and purposeful, he guided her toward his bedroom. The air between them was filled with unspoken understanding, a shared knowledge that this wasn't about love or connection but rather a temporary escape from the pressures and chaos that weighed them both down. The bedroom door clicked shut behind them, sealing them in a private world where words were unnecessary, and the rules of the outside didn't apply.

Stacy's hands instantly began to roam over his chest, her touch needy and insistent, while his own hands moved with a calculated restraint, exploring her curves as though seeking solace rather than pleasure. For him, it was about quieting the restless storm inside, silencing the relentless demands of responsibility and control, if only for a moment.

Her lips trailed from his neck to his chest, down his stomach, and lowered to the tip of his dick after she unfastened his pants and lowered them to his knees. Planting fervent kisses on his growing erection, each touch slow and intentional, as if she were savoring every moment, Stacy slid her tongue along the side, teasing and tasting his skin before gently easing his dick into her mouth. Her nails lightly traced the muscles in his chest, leaving a trail of warmth as she took him deeper. Her movements were slow and deliberate as she swirled her tongue along the base, sucking with a steady intensity. Lifting her eyes to meet his with a look of deep affection, she pushed him all the way into her throat without gagging, then swayed her tongue along the bottom of it while sucking him intensely like a pacifier.

"Ummmmmmm…," the Godfather let out a soft groan, his fingers threading through her hair, urging himself deeper. Stacy responded eagerly, her movements becoming more confident, a teasing moan escaping her lips as her neck arched and swayed with a rhythmic grace.

But even in the heat of the moment, his mind still wandered. Thoughts of the six kilos left in his stash, the tension of the day's deal, and the looming specter of TJ refused to completely fade. He closed his eyes, forcing himself to focus on the present—the warmth of her touch, the softness of her lips, the fleeting distraction she provided. For now, it was enough. Enough to silence the weight of his responsibilities. Enough to remind himself that even in the midst of chaos, there were stolen moments of reprieve, however hollow they might feel once the night was over.

Amani's gaze drifted from the fish tank as her brother returned to the living room thirty minutes later, phone pressed to his ear and an air of confidence radiating from his posture. Onyx leaned casually in the doorway, sucking his teeth and striking a model-like pose that made her smirk. It was their thing—a playful bond they'd shared since childhood, and she couldn't help but mirror his stance, tilting her head slightly.

Disconnecting the call, Onyx gave her a nod. "You ready?"

"You got a little drip, but I'll always be the eye-candy of the family," she teased, brushing past him to grab her purse from the room.

"Eye-candy? More like the candy nobody eats, but whatever, just don't lose your footin' in those stilettos trying to prove it, 'cause this meeting is too important for me to sit at the hospital with you right now," Onyx smirked, adjusting his watch as she shot him a bird without looking over her shoulder. "I mean, somebody's gotta keep this family's reputation intact, and clearly, it's muthaf**kin' me."

"Let's do it," she added, her voice light but confident as she exited the room. The rhythmic click of her stilettos echoed through the space, a subtle soundtrack to their exit.

"Keep the family's reputation intact?" Amani retorted, rolling her eyes as she swung her purse over her shoulder and brushed past him exiting the front door. "Last I checked, you were the one who got us kicked out of Auntie Tamika's cookout before you went away, trying to steal her potato salad recipe."

Onyx chuckled, unfazed, as the memory flashed in his mind. "And I'd do that sh*t again. That recipe was gold—unlike the 'a'ight... and I do mean 'a'ight outfit you're wearing. But hey, at least you're trying."

Amani shot him a glare as she approached the elevator, barely suppressing a grin. "Boy-bye! Keep talking, Onyx. When white and green bumps start showing up all over your body from messing with Stacy, I'll see who's maintaining the reputation then," she joked, bursting into laughter as the elevator doors opened.

Onyx gave her a side-eye, shaking his head. "You're real bold for someone who still cries over *Grey's Anatomy* reruns," he shot back, stepping into the elevator. Amani followed, still laughing, the tension between them dissolving into their usual sibling banter. Stepping off the elevator onto the main floor, Onyx carried himself with effortless confidence, his polished demeanor drawing subtle admiration from the onlookers. Amani, walking just a step behind in her burgundy Very Demure set, matched his energy effortlessly, the sleek cut of her outfit hugging her figure with understated elegance. Together, they moved through the lobby like a storm gathering quiet momentum, each stride purposeful, each glance exchanged saying more than words ever could.

The sharp clack of Amani's stilettos echoed, matching the steady rhythm of their strides. Onyx's jacket caught the light, highlighting his muscular features, while Amani's ensemble exuded poise and power. The siblings had a magnetic presence, their energy commanding attention without a word. Heads turned as they passed, whispers following in their wake. Amani noticed a few curious stares lingering on her outfit and distinguished a quick, knowing smile. Onyx smirked, leaning in slightly as they stepped into the garage.

"Guess you're not completely embarrassing today," he teased, his voice carrying a lightness that balanced the weight of their destination.

Amani rolled her eyes, her grin full of venom. "Embarrassing? No, embarrassing is the way you were moaning on that video Stacy has of y'all," Amani lied, just to shut his mouth and plant something discomforting in his mind.

Chapter 50

"Under Pressure"

"I promise you, I'll pick Mama up and take her to your place so she can see all those nasty-ass sex toys in your drawer if you don't tell me the truth," Onyx said, his voice low, but there was a definite edge to it. The playful teasing in his words didn't mask the simmering frustration beneath. He was grasping at any thread to get to the truth, not liking the direction his mind was going. The thought of Stacy—someone he was no longer involved with—potentially recording their private moments and showing them off to others stirred something deep inside him, something possessive and protective. With every step they took toward the garage, the weight of the idea grew heavier in his chest, like a knot he couldn't untangle.

Amani's eyes lifted toward him, her lips curling into a smirk. But there was something about the way she carried herself—effortless yet strong—that made Onyx hesitate before pushing further. She was never one to back down, never one to let anyone get under her skin, especially not when it came to family. But there was an unspoken energy between them, a playful undercurrent in their banter as they ascended levels.

"I was just playing with your big head butt, boy," Amani retorted, her tone a mixture of amusement and defiance. Her eyes sparkled with a mischievous glint, but her next words made it clear where her loyalty lay. "You know damn well I would've hit her in her sh*t for disrespecting you like that." The confidence in her voice was unwavering as she paused at the entrance, shooting him a knowing look. She didn't have to explain further; her loyalty to him was clear, and the unspoken bond between them ran deep.

As they reached his personal section, their laughter faded into a comfortable silence, the conversation still lingering in their minds. Onyx was grateful for her support, even if it came in the form of teasing. He shot her a sideways glance, his lips twitching into a reluctant smile.

"A'ight, a'ight. But don't ever joke like that again," he muttered, though there was no real heat behind his words. He knew she was just trying to lighten the moment, but the idea of anyone disrespecting his family, especially over something as personal as his relationship with Stacy, was no joke.

Approaching his Stingray, Onyx reached into his pocket and pulled out a sleek BMW key fob. Amani, assuming they'd be taking his Stingray, veered toward the passenger side, ready to settle in. But his voice stopped her short. "Sis, I need you to drive," he said, his tone smooth, almost nonchalant.

Her eyes lit up instantly. Driving was her thing, especially when it came to fast cars. The thought of pressing the Corvette's accelerator to the floor again sent an electrifying thrill through her. She extended her hand, ready for the keys, her grin widening in anticipation. But the moment she saw the unfamiliar key fob, her excitement shifted to confusion. Her brows knit together as she glanced between him and the fob. "Hold up—this ain't for the 'Vette. When did you get a BMW? And where is it?" Her gaze scanned the lot, searching for anything that stood out. She cocked her head, giving him a playful smirk. "I can't believe you went corporate on me."

Onyx chuckled, shaking his head. "Sis, you know I don't even like those kinds of cars."

Before she could retort, her finger accidentally pressed the panic button by mistake, and the alarm blared, echoing through the garage. Amani's head snapped toward the sound, which came from a car hidden beneath a protective cover parked across from them.

"Turn it off before you scare the whole damn building!" He exclaimed, laughing as she walked toward the commotion.

Onyx shot her a knowing smile before sauntering toward the covered car. "Chill, I think you're gonna like this," he said, gripping the tarp and pulling it away with a flourish. Underneath was a gleaming white BMW i8 with a sleek black trim, its futuristic design and aggressive stance radiating luxury and performance. The car practically sparkled under the lights, its sharp curves catching every glint in the dimly lit garage.

Amani stopped in her tracks, her mouth parting slightly as she took it in. "Damn, O," she muttered, her tone caught between admiration and disbelief. Stepping closer, she let her hand hover over the hood, her eyes tracing every detail. "I'll give it to you—this is clean. I ain't even mad. This bitch nice."

Onyx leaned against the car, smirking. "I mean, if I'm gonna make a switch, I'm gonna do it right."

She raised a brow, crossing her arms as her lips curved into a sly grin. "You better buckle up, 'cause I'm about to see what this baby can really do."

"Just don't make me regret this, a'ight? I have a very important meeting to attend." He said, opening the door.

Sliding into the driver's seat after watching her brother secure the cover in the trunk, Amani's eyes sparked with wild anticipation as she adjusted the mirrors, her hand trailing sensuously over the wheel. "Don't worry, I'll get you there," she purred, the raw edge of her voice daring and inviting, "but you might want to call on the Lord before we leave this garage."

Onyx climbed into the passenger seat, buckling up as Amani brought the engine to life. Before she could take off, he reached over and gently placed his hand on hers, his voice calm, laced with quiet warmth. "Before you start driving this car like you stole it, just know—it's yours. My way of saying I love you and I'm sorry for what you had to deal with. I had Gunna pick it up for me before they came earlier."

Amani froze, her eyes widening as his words hit her. She turned to him, her expression a mix of disbelief and excitement. "Wait, this is mine? You serious?"

"It's all yours," Onyx affirmed with a nod. "I know I can't erase everything, but I can at least make sure you're riding right."

Without a word, Amani leaned across the console and pulled him into a hug. "I love you, O," she murmured, her voice steady, but rich with emotion. When she pulled back, her smile stretched wide, filled with something that felt lighter than her usual guarded demeanor. She adjusted the seat, gripping the wheel as the low, powerful hum of the engine settled into her ears. "Let's see how she moves. Pray bruh!"

The i8 eased out of the parking spot, smooth and precise, but once they hit the open road, Amani's foot pressed into the accelerator. The car leapt forward, the engine growling with a sleek boldness that matched her vigor.

Onyx braced himself, gripping the door handle as she weaved through traffic with daring precision. "I should've kept my $25,000 and bought your reckless ass a bus pass," he muttered, his expression caught somewhere between exasperation and amusement.

Amani glanced his way, mischief lighting her face. "Bus pass? Boy-bye. You know you're loving this ride."

Before he could argue, she leaned forward and turned up the radio, catching Lil Baby's latest single. She nodded to the beat, shoulders swaying as the rhythm took over. "This right here? My song," she said, her tone playful and full of life.

Onyx let out a reluctant laugh, shaking his head. "Yeah, okay. Just don't wreck my—I mean, your car while you're over there vibing."

Amani smirked, shooting him a quick look before refocusing on the road. "You should stop playing with your music, though. For real," she said, her voice shifting to something more serious. "You saw the love they gave you at the concert. Way more than the headliners."

Onyx stared out the window, her words hanging in the air like a challenge he didn't want to face. "Yeah, maybe," he murmured after a pause, his voice softer than usual. But his mind was already elsewhere, racing ahead to the meeting that awaited him.

In just a few moments, he'd be sitting across from a Colombian boss—a man who could open doors to a real distribution plug. This wasn't just a meeting; it was a chance to solidify his position, to step into a level of power and control he'd always known was his destiny. Music might've been a side hustle, a spark of something raw and real, but this? This was the real game.

Being a boss wasn't just what he did—it was who he was. And as she drove en route to their destination, every move he'd made, every risk he'd taken, felt like it had led to this moment. Nothing was more evident than where they were headed now.

"Not maybe, O," Amani countered, her tone firm but supportive. "You've got it. Don't let it go to waste." With that, she pressed the accelerator, the i8 gliding effortlessly through the intersection and weaving through lanes, as if it ruled the road. The hum of the engine intertwined with the music and the unspoken bond between them, carrying them forward with a momentum neither could deny.

Freestyling in his mind to the beat, Onyx bobbed his head in rhythm, letting her words fade into the background. His focus was locked on the side mirror, scanning for anything out of place. With Monster still alive and prying into Money Bag Mafia whereabouts, Onyx knew vigilance was non-negotiable. The last thing he wanted was for Amani to be caught in the crossfire again.

When a police cruiser merged into their lane and flicked on its lights, Onyx's body tensed. He sat up straight, his instincts kicked in. With calm precision, he slipped the Kimber Stainless Target II from his waistband and nudged it under the seat with his foot. His jaw clenched as he reached for his seatbelt and clicked it into place. Losing his freedom now, on the verge of securing his legacy, wasn't an option. The thought simmered in his mind, but outwardly, he remained composed.

Amani, unfazed, pulled the car over smoothly before picking up her phone and setting the camera to record mode on the console. With a steady hand, she pressed the button to lower her window and placed both hands visibly on the steering wheel. As one officer approached her side, his hand gripping the holster of his gun, the other began pounding on Onyx's window with his baton, his actions abrupt and excessive.

"License and registration," the officer demanded, his tone brisk and authoritative.

Amani didn't move a muscle. Her gaze remained steady as she addressed him. "What's the purpose of this stop?" she asked, her voice calm and precise, her hands firmly on the wheel.

The officer's hand tightened around his gun, his frustration boiling over as he barked, "I said license and registration, ma'am, and I mean now!" His aggressive tone filled the air, and when Amani didn't move fast enough, he assumed his instincts were correct—that the car was stolen or contained drugs. His temper flared as he yanked at the door latch, but it wouldn't budge—it was locked. His patience snapped, and he drew his weapon, pointing it directly at Amani's head.

"Lady, get your ass out of the damn car, now!" the officer barked, his voice low and threatening. "I'm not gonna repeat myself!"

Amani's pulse quickened as her eyes locked on the barrel of the officer's gun. For a moment, flashes of the incident she fought hard to bury surfaced—panic, helplessness, the cold, unrelenting fear of that day. Her breath caught, her mind threatening to spiral back into the darkness. But she clenched her jaw, steadying herself. She was no longer the same person who had been caught off guard before.

Her hands stayed firmly on the steering wheel, her grip unwavering despite the tremor that threatened to creep in. She forced herself to remain focus, channeling the strength she had built since that day. Her voice pierced through the mounting tension, clear and commanding. "I'm not moving from this seat until you request for your commanding officer and inform him that you've got a gun pointed at my face."

Her tone was calm, and each word carried the weight of someone who refused to be broken. Amani had faced the worst in her brother's absence and survived. She wouldn't allow fear to consume her now. Instead, she met the officer's gaze, her expression resolute, a silent declaration that she would not cower—no matter what.

In the passenger seat, Onyx's muscles tensed. He unbuckled his seatbelt and opened his door, complying with the officer's demands to defuse the situation. Amani, however, wasn't backing down. Her education in criminal justice had prepared her for moments like this, and she knew their rights. Despite the officer's demands and unrelated questions, Amani refused to comply.

"Sir," she continued, her voice steady, "I need you to know this interaction is being live-streamed. You should also know that I'm unarmed and you haven't told me why I was stopped in the first place. If you shoot me for not stepping out of the car, the world will see everything. And let me make something clear—press 3 on my phone, and you'll call the Governor's Secretary. Press 5, and you'll get the Attorney General. Press 9, and you'll reach the Mayor. You seem real interested in how I got this car rather than telling me why you pulled me over, so maybe one of them can explain who I am to you."

The officer's eyes darted to the phone on the console, its camera capturing every detail. The realization hit him hard—this wasn't just another stop, and any misstep could cost him his career, or worse. His confidence wavered, his gun lowering as the weight of Amani's words began to sink in. He glanced at his partner, who was pinning Onyx against the car, clearly rattled by the situation.

Amani's voice chimed in again, firmer this time. "I shouldn't have to repeat myself. Call your commanding officer now, Officer Palmer, and let him know Ms. Amani Thompson is requesting his presence."

The officer hesitated, glancing nervously between Amani and his partner. The acknowledgment of her claiming to know the Attorney General and Mayor, coupled with the presence of the camera and her calm but unyielding demeanor, left him unsure whether to push further or back down. Racial profiling to see if they could confiscate some money, drugs, or valuables given the car's status, had him now scared and confused about what to do.

Finally, he tapped the roof of the car to signal his partner attention. "Sorry, Ms. Thompson," he mumbled, his bravado fading. "You're free to go. We have to take this call, partner." He turned back toward the patrol car, pretending to press the button on his radio as though responding to a dispatch. His partner released Onyx, and the two officers retreated with their heads lowered as the weight of their misstep became clear. They realized they had crossed the wrong person at the wrong time, leaving them to silently question whether there would be consequences for their actions.

"Sis, you crazy as f**k," Onyx blurted once he was back in the car and she began to pull off. He couldn't believe what had just happened and literally thought the officer's aggression was going to explode when she refused to obey his orders. "Your lying ass know damn well that you've never met any of those people, and they're not on your f**kin' speed dial."

"Bruh, you know yourself that influential people will always intimidate the weak," Amani said with amusement, a playful smirk tugging at the corners of her lips. Giggling as she watched his hand shake while retrieving the gun from beneath the seat, she couldn't do anything but smile because she knew her actions saved them both. "Crazy is the last thing I'll ever be. I just know how to give these lame-ass officers a taste of their own medicine," she said, lifting her phone to show him that she was recording instead of live-streaming. Realizing her brother's street knowledge didn't grant him awareness of everything, she began to educate him on how to manipulate the subconscious mind of officers now that video exposes their depravity and immorality.

Sitting there, absorbing her wisdom, Onyx realized he had never truly known his sister—and admired her even more. She was no longer just a scammer in his eyes. She was a certified manipulator. Showing an unexpected sign of appreciation for her saving his freedom, he reached over, grabbed her hand, and lifted it to his mouth for a kiss as they cruised down the expressway ramp. She demanded that every horse under the hood stretch its legs.

Chapter 51

"Silent Moves, Loud Intentions"

Cle gripped the steering wheel with one hand, his other resting casually on his lap, fingers drumming against his thigh. The midday sun reflected off the windshields of passing cars, the cityscape of Atlanta stretched endlessly ahead as he sped down the expressway. The smell of fresh leather filled the car, faintly mingling with the sweet, fruity aroma of the mango vapor he exhaled. He was en route to deliver to his two regulars, the doctor and the flight attendant, who always went out of their way to be more discreet than the rest of his clients.

The Godfather's teachings echoed in his mind—a philosophy that changed how Cle approached the game. "Hustle smarter, not louder. Don't stand on corners: stand on principles. Serve people who have something to lose, who care about quality." Cle couldn't argue with the strategy—it kept him off police radars and insulated Money Bag Mafia from all petty drama. Moving weight this way was like playing a high-stakes game of chess in the shadows.

As he pulled up to his first drop-off, his phone buzzed in the cupholder. The name popped up—Calista. He smirked, shaking his head at her persistence. Picking up, he answered with a low, gravelly, "Yo."

Her voice came through with urgency. "Baby, yeen gon' believe this sh*t, but I'm at Velvet Dreams with my girls, and Monster sittin' at a booth in front of us with two n***as. I thought you'd wanna know."

Cle's smirk straightened. The mention of Monster immediately stirred something inside him, a mix of loyalty to the Godfather's empire and a deep, personal urge to defend Amani's honor. He played it cool, though.

"Good lookin' out. I'll owe you one," he said, his tone smooth but final.

"You owe me more than one. You can start by treating me to a little TLC and those new J's," she quipped before hanging up the phone.

The thought of Monster being so brazen boiled Cle's blood. That pussy n***a had no respect for boundaries or family. The memory of how he'd disrespected Amani and Stacy replayed in Cle's mind like a bad record, but it was the sight of those tears in Amani's eyes that hit the hardest. His grip tightened around the steering wheel.

Cle punched in Bishop's number. The phone barely rang once before Bishop's voice came through—loud and charged with adrenaline. 'What's the move, n***a?"

"Aye, word just came through—Monster's posted up at Velvet Dreams," Cle said, his tone was flat. "Slide through and meet me there."

The line clicked dead, no need for pleasantries when there was work to be done. Bishop felt a rush of adrenaline as he reached for his Glock 22, kissing it at the thought of Monster. That snake had been breathing borrowed air for too long, and it was undoubtedly time for him to be introduced to his Black Talons.

He didn't just want Monster dead—he needed it, craved it. The image of Monster and his crew laughing about what they had done to the Godfather's sister made his blood boil. This was the vengeance he had wanted the Godfather to grant him, and now that Monster was in plain sight, acting like he was untouchable, Bishop was definitely about to deliver the final verdict.

Cle's smirk lingered briefly before he tossed the phone back into the cupholder. The name "Monster" was like a hot coal burning in his mind, but he had a job to finish before he could deal with it. He navigated his Dodge Ram 5.7 Hemi off the expressway and onto Riverdale Road, the towering trees lining the street casting fleeting shadows over the sleek black paint of his vehicle.

As he rolled to a stop at the red light, his eyes darted to his phone, fingers moving with precision as he typed: "Be outside. I'm 'bout to pull up." The message was clipped and direct—this wasn't a time for pleasantries. His heart thudded in sync with the ticking traffic signal, rage simmering beneath his calm exterior.

The light turned green, and the cars ahead surged forward, shattering the brief stillness of the intersection. He slid the phone back into the cupholder with a controlled ease, his focus narrowing on the road stretching out before him. Anticipation coiled tightly in his chest, an edge of adrenaline sharpening his every movement. His trigger finger twitched, urgency simmering beneath his steady exterior. The clock was ticking, and he was right on time.

The townhouse complex came into view: identical units, neat lawns, and clean stoops. By the time he pulled into a discreet corner near her place, she was already stepping outside. She had a designer bag slung over her shoulder and sunglasses perched on her nose, the picture of casual wealth.

There was something different about her today, something in the way she carried herself. She'd gone the extra mile, her pale skin glowed under the winter sunlight, her fitted knit sweater clinging to her curves and paired with high-waisted leggings that emphasized every line of her silhouette. Over-the-knee boots completed the look, adding a bold edge, while the faint scent of sandalwood and vanilla followed her as she stepped to his car. But Cle barely noticed. His mind was elsewhere, consumed by the storm brewing over Monster's name.

"You on time today," she quipped, a coy smile on her lips.

Cle admired how clean she kept things, how she understood the value of discretion—a rare quality that made her one of his most reliable clients. He nodded, keeping his words brief. "Always."

She gave a small smile, almost hesitant, as if expecting more— waiting for him to comment on her effort, to give her even the smallest indication that he noticed. But Cle's focus was locked. He kept the exchange quick, seamless, refusing to deviate from the plan.

The flight attendant slid the cash into his hand, her fingers brushing his just a moment longer than necessary, hoping to catch his attention. But it was no use. Cle was miles away in his head, already plotting his next move. He handed over the tightly sealed package with mechanical efficiency, his gaze distant and unreadable.

Her smile faltered, disappointment spreading across her face. She had taken the time to look good, smell good, and even rehearsed what she would say if he lingered or gave her an opening. But there was no warmth in his demeanor, no crack in the armor that said he noticed her at all. Her hope of seducing him inside, of even sharing a moment with him, faded with every passing second.

Without a word, she turned on her heels and walked back toward her townhouse, her brisk steps masking the sting of rejection. The door closed behind her as though nothing had happened, but the charged silence lingered in the air, unspoken and unresolved.

Cle retrieved his phone and pressed his foot into the accelerator, the Dodge Hemi roaring forward. The screen illuminated with the name "The Godfather" after he dialed the number. He tapped the call button and brought the phone to his ear. It rang once. Twice. Three times. Then it went to voicemail.

A rare surge of unease gripped Cle's chest. The Godfather never missed a call, especially not from him. Was he caught up in something? Was something being orchestrated in the shadows as a result of the attack on Salvage, and they were keeping him out of the loop? Cle tapped the wheel, trying to steady himself, forcing the thoughts aside. The Godfather's silence gnawed at him, but there was no time to dwell on what he couldn't control. If this was a burden he had to carry alone, so be it. He was ready. The haunting image of Amani's tear-streaked face twisted his gut like a vise, each passing mile only steeling his resolve.

The memory hit him with an unexpected force, unbidden and relentless, crashing over him like a wave he hadn't braced for. Those goddamn tears Monster had put in her eyes—they haunted him. A burden he couldn't shake, a reminder that he'd failed her once before. But not this time. This wasn't about Money Bag Mafia anymore. Cle wasn't just going to kill Monster for the family. He was going to kill him for Amani. To prove that no one, not even a snake like Monster, could disrespect her and walk away breathing.

The Dodge tore through the city streets, weaving through traffic as his mind raced. He thought about Amani, about what this would mean to her. How would she react when she found out what he'd done? Would she finally see him for who he was—a man who would move mountains for her like her brother? The thought stirred something primal in him, igniting a fire that made his pulse quicken.

He couldn't stop the fantasies that followed, vivid and intoxicating. Would she grant him the ultimate reward—her body, her touch, her surrender? His mind lingered on the ways he'd fantasized about making her climax in ways no other man could. Amani didn't know the depths of what he felt for her, how far he would go to protect her, to claim her as his.

Taking Monster's life wouldn't be about earning points or chasing recognition—it never had been, and it never would be. This was about respect. About guarding what mattered most. But beneath the steel resolve and cold calculation, there was something deeper, something raw and unspoken: hope. Hope that maybe, just once, she'd see him differently. That she'd look at him the way she looked at those other n***as. That, even for a fleeting moment, she'd see the man he truly was—the man he wanted to be for her. And if she did? That single moment of recognition would be worth it all.

Ahead, the rumble of a '69 Pontiac GTO "The Judge" caught his attention as it roared past on the opposite side of the street. Its deep growl, like thunder rolling over the asphalt, momentarily snapped him back to the present. The bright Carousel Red paint and bold black stripes demanded attention—a street showstopper impossible to ignore. For a split second, he thought about the raw power it carried—the Ram Air III engine snarling under the hood—and how it mirrored the fire raging in his chest.

The thought lingered—unrelenting, heavy, raw—before his focus snapped back to his HEMI, to the road, to the task at hand. The sun cast a bright glow over the earth as Cle eased his vehicle into the parking lot, the club's tinted windows reflecting the daylight like dark, glossy mirrors. The low thump of bass seeped through his windows, vibrating in sync with the tension knotted in his chest. He killed the engine and stepped out, his dark hoodie draping his face in shadow as he moved with purpose across the pavement toward Bishop's blacked-out SUV.

Bishop lowered the tinted window, his nod brief but heavy with unspoken weight, the kind of acknowledgment that didn't need words. From the backseat, Shadow leaned forward, his tattooed hand clasping Cle's in their customary handshake—quick and firm, a language of loyalty and trust. Shadow's eyes, shadowed by the dim light of the parking lot, darted back to the scene outside, dissecting every detail with an intensity that suggested he saw more than anyone else dared to notice.

"What's the move?" Bishop asked, his voice a quiet rumble, steady and unspoken. It wasn't loud, but it carried the kind of calm that preceded chaos—the calm of someone ready for whatever lay ahead. His mind, however, was elsewhere. He couldn't shake the thought of Salvage—the fact that he'd sent someone to kill him weighed on him like a stone. The more he thought about it, the more it stirred something dark in him, fueling his growing hunger for vengeance. He wanted Monster gone. He needed it. Every thought, every impulse, was driving him closer to that final, inevitable moment.

As they weighed their next move, Cle's phone vibrated in his pocket, breaking the tense stillness. He snatched it out, expecting a message from the Godfather, but instead, it was from Calista: a confirmation that Monster was still inside, throwing cash around like he owned the place. Cle sucked his teeth, frustration simmering beneath the surface. Monster's reckless arrogance was a fuse waiting to be lit.

Shadow leaned forward, his response to Cle's acknowledgment direct and unwavering. Bishop's reaction was instant—his hand slid to his waistband and drew his gun with steady resolve. His tone was low, words clipped. "We can't hit him here, Cle. Cameras are everywhere. Heat'll rain down on the family, and we can't afford that."

Bishop exhaled through his nose, the weight of restraint evident in his steady silence. Shadow was right—one reckless move now could crumble everything.

"Just take me up the street," Shadow said, his voice steady but loaded with intent. "I'll grab a hotbox we can use. I just need a screwdriver."

Cle gave a short nod as Bishop mentioned he had one in the back. Without another word, Cle turned and stepped toward his vehicle while Bishop and Shadow pulled out of the lot, the vehicle blending into the light traffic under the harsh glare of the midday sun. Left alone, Cle settled into the driver's seat, the faint thrum of the club's bass barely audible over the distant hum of the city. The midday sun made every detail sharp—the pale winter light casting soft shadows on the cold asphalt, the faint glint bouncing off car hoods, and the club's doors alive with the blur of patrons coming and going.

His gaze stayed fixed on the entrance, tension coiling tighter with every second. In his mind, the scene played out clearly: Monster's body jerking violently as bullets ripped through him. The image gripped him with a dark satisfaction, a slow, almost imperceptible smile curling at the corner of his lips. The thought of retribution burned hot, fueling the fire steadily rising within him.

When Bishop and Shadow finally returned, they parked across the street instead of pulling back into the lot. Shadow texted Cle from the driver's seat, letting him know they were ready. The car they'd brought back was battered and untraceable—the kind made for dirty work. Bishop sat in the passenger seat, his posture relaxed but his eyes sharp, his calm demeanor exuding the patience of a sniper waiting for the perfect moment to strike.

Cle's phone buzzed just as he considered texting Calista for an update on Monster. He answered immediately, the Godfather's gravelly voice cutting through. "What's the status?"

Cle quickly relayed the situation, his words precise, each one carrying weight. The Godfather's response came swift, unyielding, and shocking in its calm authority. "Stand down. No action in public—too messy. Follow him. See where he goes and inform Gramz." It wasn't the explosive command he expected, but the cold calculation behind it hit harder, a reminder of why his word was law.

Disappointment curled in Cle's chest like smoke, the weight of the decision crushing any hope of taking matters into his own hands. He thought of Amani, of the triumph she'd never see from him, but the Godfather's word was final. "Got it," he said curtly, ending the call.

As he prepared to update Bishop, the club doors swung open. Monster emerged, his crew flanking him like soldiers, their laughter cutting through the sunlight, loud and grating against Cle's nerves. They moved with a reckless confidence, like kings with no fear of the crown being taken. Cle's heartbeat slammed against his ribs as his hand hovered over the door handle, instinct urging him to act, but the command had been given. His thumb hovered over the phone's dial pad, ready to call Bishop when—.

Blocka! Blocka! Blocka! Blocka! Blocka! Blocka!

The sharp ping of metal echoed as bullets tore into the car's body. Shards of glass rained down in brittle cascades, windows shattering under the relentless onslaught. Each impact rang out like a hammer striking sheet metal."

Cle froze, his chest tight as chaos consumed the lot. His breath came in shallow bursts, his fingers gripping his strap like a lifeline. He hadn't relayed the orders, and the Godfather would demand answers—answers Cle didn't have. How would this fall back on the family? The weight of uncertainty pressed down on him like a heavy shroud, leaving him paralyzed, torn between the instinct to act and the dread of what might come next.

Chapter 52

"Riding the Edge"

Driving with no regard for traffic laws, Amani couldn't help but laugh at her brother's reactions—the way he gripped the door handle, his face twisting with every sharp turn, and the way she dashed between cars. "I'm surprised you didn't snatch the damn door handle off with how tight you were gripping it," she teased, still grinning as she exited the expressway.

Onyx rubbed his hands across his face, his heart still racing from her reckless driving. "You gon' make me tell you something," he said, still trying to calm his nerves. "I'm driving back instead of letting your crazy ass. You're not about to kill me."

Amani continued giggling, her eyes glancing at the GPS as she drove through Woodstock. When they finally reached their destination, she backed the car into a parking spot and shifted it into park. "I really like the way this moves, bruh," she said, her tone full of admiration for the car's power.

Onyx's eyes scanned car after car, his gaze restless like waves searching for the shore. He didn't know what the Colombian looked like or what kind of vehicle he'd be arriving in—all he'd been told was to call once he was there. Pulling out his phone, he dialed T-Roc to ensure they were in position. Although he couldn't spot them, T-Roc's steady response gave him the confidence to proceed. Ending the call, Onyx immediately dialed Maximiliano.

"I'm here," he said evenly when the Colombian answered.

After a brief exchange, Onyx turned to Amani, updating her on the plan as they exited the car. He was so focused that he didn't realize a small smile had crept across his face until Amani's voice brought him back.

As they stepped out of the car, Amani's fingers glided over the sleek curves of her new BMW i8, a slow, appreciative touch that mirrored the satisfaction gleaming in her eyes. She strutted to the front of the vehicle, where her brother stood, her presence effortlessly commanding. Catching the look on his face, she raised a brow and smirked. "What you smilin' at, bruh?" she asked as they made their way toward the building.

"I'm smilin' because Mom blessed me with an incredible sister," Onyx said, his voice carrying warmth that belied the darker truth behind his grin. Beneath the surface, thoughts of Monster churned like a rising typhoon. He was putting on a show, projecting an air of invincibility, but deep down, the cracks in his armor were growing. The streets were watching, and Money Bag Mafia's name hung in the balance—a fragile reputation teetering on the edge of being dismissed as a joke.

Marko's reckless decision to seize the store by force had already thrown everything into turmoil. Now, Onyx had to figure out how to smooth things over with the owner without sparking a full-blown retaliation. But it didn't stop there—Monster's attempt to have Salvage killed had gone horribly wrong, ending with the death of his girl instead. That mistake was a ticking time bomb, one Onyx couldn't afford to ignore. To make matters worse, his trigger-happy soldiers were itching to take out Monster in broad daylight, a move that would only escalate the chaos, pushing it beyond anything he could control. The weight of it all pressed on him, each problem stacking higher, like bricks crushing his chest, daring him to crumble under the pressure.

Amani's lips curled into a sly smirk. "Oh, I thought you were cheesin' 'cause Stacy texted you the baby kicked!" she teased, bursting into laughter as Onyx's face contorted in pure disgust.

"Girl, stop damn playin' like that," Onyx muttered, giving her a playful shove. The annoyance in his tone was genuine. The thought of Stacy tying him down with a kid sent a chill through him. "Ain't nothin' funny about that joke. Quit clownin'."

Amani's laughter only grew louder as they neared the entrance of the upscale restaurant, her amusement echoing through the crisp air. Onyx, however, had already shifted his focus. His eyes caught the movement of two white Escalades pulling into the lot, one trailing the other with deliberate precision.

"Stay behind me," he said, his voice low and steady as his hand instinctively moved to his waistband, gripping the handle of his gun. Without breaking stride, he positioned himself slightly in front of Amani, his muscles coiled as the vehicles rolled to a smooth stop. Every muscle in his body braced for the unknown.

The Escalades idled for a moment before the faint thrum of music seeped through the first SUV's open door. Onyx loosened his grip on his weapon slightly but kept his guard up. The air between them was fraught with the weight of uncertainty. His phone vibrated in his pocket, pulling his focus. Retrieving it quickly, he answered, "Yeah." The calm voice on the other end gave clear instructions, and Onyx nodded. He gestured for Amani to follow as he approached the SUVs.

The echo of her heels against the concrete was deafening, each step amplifying their shared unease. Outside of prison, Onyx had never encountered someone with the level of power and mystique that Maximiliano possessed. Every step closer to the vehicles felt like he was sinking deeper into unknown territory. The driver of the first SUV emerged, his movements smooth and measured, exuding quiet authority. Onyx gave him a small nod in acknowledgment, though his muscles remained taut. The driver extended his hand, silently requesting their phones. Onyx hesitated for a fraction of a second before complying.

He watched as the man walked both devices to the second SUV driver window. Onyx's gaze darted to Amani, her expression calm but her eyes watchful. She didn't speak, but he could sense the questions swirling in her mind. When the driver returned and opened the door to the first SUV, Onyx leaned slightly, peering inside. The emptiness of the back seat unnerved him more than he expected. This wasn't a casual meeting—it was a carefully orchestrated move, one that made it clear he was dealing with someone who left nothing to chance.

Understanding the stakes, Onyx climbed into the SUV, then extended a hand to Amani, pulling her in beside him. The door clicked shut behind them with a sound that felt more final than it should have. Holding Amani's hand tightly, Onyx took a slow breath, bracing himself for whatever came next.

"Relax, my friend. The two of you are safe. My people will bring you both to me," Maximiliano's voice flowed through the Escalade speakers, his rich Colombian accent giving his English a distinct rhythm and weight, making it sound both inviting and commanding.

As the driver got in and shifted the SUV into gear, Onyx scanned the area. The unsettling silence made him feel watched, even with no visible cameras. He kept his gaze fixed on the driver, his mind running through possibilities. He didn't know if Maximiliano was watching, but he refused to show uncertainty. He kept his posture steady, his thoughts grounded in the present, determined not to project any fear.

"Bruh, where are we going?" Amani's voice broke the silence, her casual tone belying the unease she must've been feeling.

"I don't know," Onyx replied, shrugging as his mind swirled with unknowns. The anticipation of meeting Maximiliano had shifted from excitement to unease. What he had expected to be a straightforward dinner with the head of a powerful Colombian family now felt like a blind journey, with no control, no insight, and no way of knowing what was really in store for them.

After what felt like an eternity, the vehicle slowed, and the driver veered off onto a private road. They passed through an imposing gate, its heavy metal bars closing behind them with a soft thud. Onyx leaned forward, scanning his surroundings. The sound of the engine echoed through the emptiness as the driver turned into a well-lit area, finally coming to a stop.

"We're here," the driver said, his voice calm, almost rehearsed. Onyx's gaze shifted to the impressive sight ahead of them: a sleek twin-engine helicopter parked in front of a massive hangar. The aircraft lustrously reflected the sun, its presence commanding attention. The hangar loomed behind it, its shadow stretching across the landing area, a silent symbol of the power and wealth Maximiliano wielded. Onyx had no idea what was coming next, but one thing was clear—the world he thought he knew was about to shift drastically.

Amani noticed Onyx's quiet intensity as they stepped out of the SUV and followed the driver toward six imposing figures by the helicopter. The brilliant sunlight blanketed the scene, casting everything in clear relief. The hangar itself seemed to pulse with an air of authority, its open expanse framed by the hum of activity and the faint scent of jet fuel. Every step they took brought them closer to an unknown, yet unmistakably powerful, presence.

As they approached the helicopter, Onyx was met first by Maximiliano's security team. Their movements were precise and mechanical, their expressions unreadable. They searched him thoroughly, the sweep of a Non-Linear Junction Detector confirming there were no hidden devices on him. When they demanded his gun, Onyx handed it over without hesitation, though the weight of the moment settled heavily on his shoulders.

"Damn, who the f**k you got us meetin', bruh, to be goin' through all this?" Amani muttered, her voice laced with sarcasm as they searched her for wires and weapons before allowing her to climb into the helicopter. She glanced around at the plush interior, running her fingers over the leather seats with a mix of curiosity and irritation. "Flyin' us out in a chopper just to meet him? Shiddd… he might deserve the Stacy treatment."

Onyx shot her a look, the faintest smirk tugging at the corner of his lips. "Someone who's makin' it real clear I'm steppin' into deep waters—and I better know how to swim," he said, his voice steady but carrying an unshakable edge.

The pilot flipped switches, the blades' low whine building into a powerful roar. The vibrations rippled through the cabin as Onyx handed Amani a headset before adjusting his own. He tightened his seatbelt, his gaze briefly passing over her before turning to the window. The ground beneath them began to fall away as the helicopter lifted into the air. It was Onyx's first time flying, and the rush of adrenaline coursing through him was undeniable. The landscape below blurred into a tapestry of greens and grays, but his mind was locked on the unknown ahead.

Amani leaned back, her posture relaxed though her eyes betrayed her unease. Neither spoke as they ascended, both feeling the weight of the moment pressing down on them. Onyx stared at the sprawling horizon, his mind racing. This wasn't just a flight—it was a step into a world where every move mattered, and every decision carried consequences they could neither foresee nor control.

Chapter 53

"Beneath the Surface"

Glancing across the sky, Amani watched as the helicopter beat the air into submission, its blades slicing through the atmosphere with a relentless precision. The sun, now dipping lower on the horizon, bathed the world in a warm, golden glow, casting long shadows across the ocean. "This is so beautiful," she murmured, letting her eyes wander freely over the vast expanse of water and sky, captivated by the serene beauty surrounding them.

As the helicopter moved like a bird of mercy with the wind, gliding gracefully through the air, the two of them exchanged light banter, their laughter mingling with the rhythmic thrum of the blades. The minutes seemed to stretch on, the sound of their voices a comforting contrast to the vast silence of the world below. After nearly an hour and a half, the pilot began the descent, the massive yacht below coming into view.

When the helicopter finally touched down on the helipad, Amani couldn't help but feel a surge of excitement. She turned to Onyx, her voice tinged with disbelief. "How in the f**k you meet this n***a?" she asked, watching as a tall, muscular man with distinctly Colombian features approached the helicopter. As the man opened the door, Onyx and Amani stepped out, the cool air rushing around them. They followed the man toward an outdoor lounge area, the sound of their footsteps muted by the soft carpeted pathway along the deck. The lounge was luxurious, with a wrap-around sofa offering a stunning view of the ocean. The atmosphere was one of understated power, and Onyx could feel the weight of what was about to unfold.

"I am seriously in awe of this yacht's beauty," Amani exclaimed, strutting across the plush carpet, her feet sinking into its luxurious texture. She moved with ease toward a rich cherry-wood sofa, the warm tones of the wood complementing the golden glow of the sunset pouring through the windows. "Now this is luxuriously comfortable," she added, sinking into the cushions with a contented sigh. The pristine design of the yacht amazed her, every inch of it a testament to wealth and taste.

"Damn, this is like a real house on the water," Onyx murmured, his gaze sweeping over the expansive space. From the elegant chandeliers to the polished wood floors, everything about the yacht screamed luxury. He took it all in, studying the intricate details—the plush velvet curtains that swayed gently in the breeze, the sleek lines of the furniture, and the grand open space that seemed to stretch endlessly. "This is some next-level sh*t," he added, shaking his head in disbelief.

"My friend, you are right. That was the goal when I asked my designer to make it this way," the voice responded, smooth with a trace of a Colombian accent. A medium-sized, striking man descended a grand spiral staircase, his dark green eyes gleaming in the light. His posture was strong and confident, every movement measured. He had a rugged yet refined look, with defined cheekbones and an aquiline nose that added to his commanding presence. Despite the authority he exuded, there was a calmness in his demeanor, one that spoke of both power and grace. He looked effortlessly put together, dressed in a simple yet expensive outfit that spoke volumes without shouting. "So you're the gentleman who saved my son's life in Edgefield?"

Onyx rose from the sofa and extended his hand for a firm shake. "I just assisted someone I consider a friend, sir," he said humbly, but his voice carried the quiet confidence of a man who had seen his share of struggles and victories. Before he knew it, Maximiliano pulled him into a brief embrace, a gesture of respect, then turned to Amani.

"I always think angels are a myth," Maximiliano said, his eyes glinting with admiration as he turned to Amani. His hand reached out to take hers, lifting it to his lips with an old-world charm. "But clearly, I was wrong." His voice was smooth, like velvet, but there was heat behind it, showing more than just politeness. "Come, let me show you all of Belleza Imperfecta."

As Maximiliano led them through the yacht, Amani and Onyx couldn't help but be in awe. The onboard gym was state-of-the-art, with sleek machines and a panoramic view of the ocean stretching endlessly beyond the windows. The guest rooms were nothing short of spectacular—tall ceilings, marble floors, and vast open spaces that made the idea of sleeping on the water feel like a dream. They passed through an onboard professional-grade home cinema, the screen so large it seemed to swallow the room, and a jaw-dropping Jacuzzi room that was more like a spa, with gold fixtures and plush towels waiting on the side. On the upper deck, a grand circular bar gleamed, and the submerged viewing lounge offered a breathtaking view beneath the waterline—fish, coral, and the deep sea itself all visible through the glass.

"This is unreal," Amani whispered, her voice full of wonder as they passed from one extravagant space to the next. Everything about the yacht was designed to impress, and Maximiliano seemed pleased to share it all with them.

Later, as they sat down to a gourmet meal on the deck—Wagyu steak, roast goose, shrimp sashimi, rice, diced fruit, and apple Tatin with ice cream—Amani leaned back, savoring the flavors. The soft breeze from the ocean mingled with the rich aromas from the table, and she found herself smiling at the sheer luxury of it all. But the true highlight of the evening came unexpectedly when Maximiliano suggested a 3-point shooting contest. Amani, never one to back down from a challenge, stepped up to the edge of the deck, her basketball skills on full display. With each shot she made, Onyx and Maximiliano exchanged impressed glances. And when she sank the final shot, the celebration was nothing short of joyous. Amani danced in victory, her laughter ringing out like music in the cool evening air.

"I told you she was an angel, my friend," Maximiliano said energetically, his voice was warm and filled with admiration as Amani did a little victory shimmy, her energy infectious.

Onyx shook his head, grinning. "Yeah, yeah, you got me. She's definitely something else."

As the day stretched on, the yacht became a world of its own, a floating kingdom where time seemed to slip through their fingers, and the lines between luxury and reality blurred. Standing beside his sister against the deck railing, Onyx gazed out at the ocean, its dark waters shimmering under the glow of the yacht lights, the reflections dancing like liquid gold. The cool breeze rolled over him, carrying the scent of salt and possibility. In this moment, he felt certain—this was checkmate. He had made the right decision to pour more of his focus into the streets instead of waiting on music to pay off. Every second on this yacht was a testament to how far they had come, but also a stark reminder of how much further he had yet to go.

"I could live on this beautiful vessel," Amani's low tones broke through his thoughts, and he turned to see her, her eyes reflecting the vastness of the ocean. A light spray mist from the waves sprinkled over both of them, adding a refreshing chill to the warm, golden light settling over the deck. The calmness of the moment felt surreal, especially considering the volatile nature of the world they'd just stepped into.

Maximiliano's presence disrupted the tranquility. As he approached with his phone pressed to his ear, his tone was firm and commanding, his words sharp in Spanish. His voice was laced with authority, and his posture was impeccable. Despite the conversation on the phone, his eyes remained locked on Onyx and Amani, as if weighing their every move. The air thickened with unspoken intensity, like the stillness before a storm.

Onyx felt Amani's grip tighten around the railing; her usual carefree demeanor was replaced by unease. He couldn't blame her. The yacht had been their sanctuary for a while, but now it was beginning to feel more like a gilded cage. Maximiliano's power was undeniable, and Onyx knew they were in deep waters. He didn't know what game the Colombian was playing, but he sure as hell wasn't about to let his guard down.

Maximiliano ended his call, his eyes now fully on them. There was a heaviness in his gaze, a silent understanding that the moment they'd been waiting for was fast approaching. The calm of the sea and the luxury of the yacht were all just distractions. Onyx could feel the weight of the situation bearing down on him. He'd been in tight spots before, but this was different. The stakes were higher. Everything was on the line.

This was the checkmate—the silent acknowledgment that he was accepted into the fold. Onyx couldn't help but wonder what kind of shipment he'd be trusted with, what kind of risks he'd be expected to handle. The weight of the unspoken question hung in the air, but his mind was already racing with the possibilities. Would they test his loyalty or was this just the beginning of something darker?

"So, you've seen an aspect of my world," Maximiliano said, his voice smooth but carrying an unmistakable edge. He gave a slight nod to the ocean, as though acknowledging the vastness of it all. "But there's more beneath the surface. Much more."

Onyx nodded, weighing Maximiliano's words carefully before responding. 'I'm here to learn, but more importantly, to be an asset—never a liability,' he replied. His voice was steady, but inside, he was calculating his next move. He knew better than to show weakness—especially now, when everything was riding on the decisions he made.

Amani, sensing the change in the air, adjusted her posture, her gaze darting between Onyx and Maximiliano. She wasn't one to be intimidated easily, but even she couldn't shake the sense that they were walking a fine line.

"Onyx," Maximiliano started, his tone cold yet calculating, "What do you do to someone who blatantly disrespects you?"

Onyx's eyes met Maximiliano's without hesitation. The question lingered between them, and Onyx didn't flinch or back down. He'd been tested before, in ways far uglier than this—this was just another round in the game. He was no stranger to disrespect, especially from those who thought they could push him around. But he wasn't some rookie to be toyed with.

Without truly assessing the question or gaining a clear understanding of how the disrespect had been implied, he spoke instinctively, his response driven by a lifetime of being tested. He had been underestimated his whole life, but no more.

"I make an example of him so everyone knows not to f**k with me," Onyx said, his voice steady, unshaken. He didn't need to raise it—his presence alone carried the weight of every lesson carved into him by the streets, every betrayal that had hardened him. The scars, the losses, the blood and sweat—it all spoke for him. And if there was one thing he refused to be again, it was overlooked.

Maximiliano's eyes moved with a mixture of amusement and interest. He was sizing Onyx up, testing him. He had seen many men come and go, but this one... this one had something that could either make him a valuable ally or a dangerous enemy. He took a step closer, his gaze never leaving Onyx's. "I like that answer," Maximiliano said, the Colombian accent on his words thickening with the weight of his approval. "But remember, my friend, you step into my world, you play by my rules."

"Understandable," Onyx's voice was low, his tone rough with emotion as the words fell from his lips. The tension between them hung in the air, but Onyx wasn't about to let fear or hesitation show. His gaze never wavered from Maximiliano's, even as the man's icy words cut through the space between them.

Maximiliano's eyes bore into Onyx's with a venomous intensity. "If you understand, then who gave you the right to bring your sister here, huh?" His voice was cold, each word calculated and laced with disdain. "I extended you an olive branch, but you brought someone I don't know. You didn't even ask me. How do I know she's not the Feds? Or worse—an informant? Disrespect like this doesn't fly in my world." His anger simmered beneath the surface, controlled but unmistakably menacing.

With a swift motion of his hand, Maximiliano called his security onto the deck. The door slid open, and seven sharply dressed men stepped onto the deck, their eyes scanning the space, their presence overwhelming. Amani and Onyx exchanged uneasy glances, the weight of the situation settling in. Neither of them knew what to expect, and the sudden shift in atmosphere sent a chill down their spines.

Onyx opened his mouth to speak, but Maximiliano cut him off, his voice hard and final. Maximiliano's gaze darkened as he glared at Onyx, his voice rigid with quiet fury. "You think you can step into my world and make your own damn rules, huh? If I let this slide, others will think they can do the same, just like you said, Onyx. And that's something I'll never tolerate. So here's the deal: You decide which one of you gets to leave on the helicopter and which one meets the ocean. Or maybe neither of you will."

The words hit Onyx like his heart was being stabbed. His heart hammered in his ribs, each beat a painful reminder of the impossible choice he was about to make. The decision—his sister or himself—was unimaginable, yet it was hanging over them like a guillotine. For a split second, everything went silent, the weight of the choice suffocating him. He couldn't breathe. Amani's face flashed in his mind. Her eyes—full of trust, full of life. He couldn't let her go. Not like this. Not for a man like Maximiliano.

Desperation clawed at him as he fixed his gaze on Maximiliano's eyes, searching, pleading, hoping this was all a cruel joke meant to test his resolve. But all he found was sincerity, cold and unyielding. There was no trace of bluff or mercy, just the unrelenting reality of a man who wouldn't hesitate to follow through.

But leaving her behind? The thought was unbearable. His heart pounded against his chest, a drumbeat of anguish and rage. He had to make a choice, but how could he? How could he choose between the two of them? The seconds stretched, pulling him into a dark, suffocating void. His mind raced but couldn't settle. The pressure clawed at his insides, his throat tightening with every passing moment.

Then, instinct took over, and the words tore from his chest, raw and desperate. "I'll sacrifice myself," Onyx said, each word a heavy stone he couldn't take back. "I brought her here, so I'll take whatever comes. She stays." The words burned like fire. He had made his choice, but it felt like a dull knife twisting in his skull. He wasn't ready to die. He wasn't ready to leave everything behind. But it was his responsibility. He was her protector. He owed her this.

Amani's eyes widened in horror. She screamed his name, her voice cracking with disbelief. "No! Onyx, no!" Her hands stretched towards him, her body trembling with fear. "I can't lose you. Please, don't do this Mr. Maximiliano!"

But it was too late. Maximiliano's men moved quickly, grabbing Amani and forcing her aside with cold precision. Onyx's instincts kicked in as he lunged toward her, desperation fueling his every move. "Let her go!" he roared, his voice breaking through the tension. He managed to break free from one guard's grip, his hands reaching for Amani, but another man slammed a forearm into his chest, shoving him back with brutal force.

Amani screamed his name, her voice cracking with terror. "Onyx! Stop!" She fought against the iron grip of Maximiliano's men, tears streaming down her face.

Onyx staggered but didn't fall. His chest heaved as he glared at Maximiliano, his body taut and coiled like a spring, ready to snap. But the guards were too many, their precision too precise. They boxed him in, leaving him no room to maneuver. His fists clenched as frustration surged through him, but deep down, he knew—there was no escape. Saving her was all that mattered.

Maximiliano didn't flinch, his expression cold and unmoved by the chaos. "Enough," he said, his voice calm but commanding, silencing the struggle around them.

Breathing hard, Onyx's shoulders sagged slightly. His mind screamed for a way to fix this, to protect Amani, but there was no time. No options left. He had made his choice.

Maximiliano turned to one of his men, gesturing for the gun. The Ruger GP100 glinted in the light as it was handed over. Onyx's heart clenched, but he stood tall despite the guards' looming presence. He met Maximiliano's gaze, his eyes filled with defiance. He wouldn't look away. He wouldn't beg. Not now. Not ever. Maximiliano's gaze never left him as he gripped the gun. The air between them was heavy with the weight of the moment. Onyx wasn't afraid. Not anymore. He had made his choice.

Time froze as Onyx's life flashed before him in vivid, haunting fragments. The first car he stole—his hands trembling as he gripped the wheel. The first person he killed—blood staining his soul more than his hands. The endless nights of hustling, each deal dragging him deeper into the game. His mother's tear-streaked face as the judge sentenced him, her sobs drowning out the gavel's strike. The suffocating nights in prison, staring at the ceiling, the weight of his choices crushing him. He promised his mother that he'd be better, swore he'd leave the streets alone, pursue music, and make her proud. But now, that promise, shattered and meaningless, was destined to bring her even more pain and sorrow.

But was it all for nothing? Was his climb to the top destined to end here, on a yacht deck surrounded by men who didn't care about his life? Amani's laugh echoed faintly in his mind, a flash of sunlight in a storm of regrets. Her face—the one thing he couldn't lose, the one person he couldn't fail. He'd done it all to protect her, to give her something better than this. But now she was here, caught in the crossfire of his mistakes.

Onyx's breaths came in shallow gasps, his chest tightening under the crushing weight of it all. His sister's face lingered in his mind, vivid and unrelenting—her once-bright smile now dimmed, eclipsed by the growing shadow of his regrets. That shadow, dark and unforgiving, had finally consumed him, leaving nothing but the hollow ache of his failures.

Raising the gun, Maximiliano pressed the cold steel between Onyx's eyes. Onyx refused to blink, his stare locked onto Maximiliano's in a silent battle of wills. "To be a boss, you must always remember there are consequences to your actions," Maximiliano said, his voice dripping with cold finality. His words lingered, stark and overbearing—then, suddenly—BANG! BANG! The gunshots shattered the silence, deafening in their wake.

Onyx's scream pierced the air, raw and agonizing, cutting through the chaos. He fought against the men holding him back, his sobs echoing over the waves. "Amani! Amani!"

The world around her dimmed, the warmth draining from her body with every shallow, ragged breath. Amani gasped, her lungs fighting for air, but the pain and panic coiled tighter in her chest, squeezing the life from her. Her body was failing her, betraying her at the worst possible moment. Her pulse slowed. Her vision tunneled. The yacht's deck wavered beneath her, tilting as if the whole world had lost its balance. Then—her legs gave out.

She collapsed, her body hitting the cold floor of the yacht. The impact barely registered, lost beneath the suffocating weight pressing down on her. Her mind slipped further into the haze, everything fading into an eerie stillness as a vasovagal response dragged her under.

The taste of salt filled her mouth—was it seawater or her own blood? She couldn't tell. Her trembling fingers scraped against the deck, desperate for an anchor, but nothing could stop the downward spiral.

In her fading moments, her gaze found Onyx. His face blurred, streaked with tears, his voice calling her name a distant echo. Her lips trembled, forming silent words—I'm sorry. The agony in his eyes burned into her soul as the darkness finally consumed her. Amani's body crumpled, lifeless to those around her. Her pulse weakened, her unconscious mind slipping deeper, leaving Onyx's cries as the last sound etched into the quiet void.

"To Be Continued"

The Forged Path II

A Tale of Power, Betrayal, and Redemption